BARRY SQUIRES, FULL TILT

HEATHER SMITH

PENGUIN TEEN
an imprint of Tundra Book Group, a division of
Penguin Random House of Canada Limited

Published in hardcover by Penguin Teen, 2020
Published in this edition, 2022

1 2 3 4 5 6 7 8 9 10

Manufactured in Canada

Library and Archives Canada Cataloguing in Publication

Title: Barry Squires, full tilt / Heather Smith.
Names: Smith, Heather, 1968- author.
Description: Previously published: Toronto : Penguin Teen, 2020.
Identifiers: Canadiana 20200408062 | ISBN 9780735267480 (softcover)
Classification: LCC PS8637.M5623 B37 2022 | DDC jC813/.6—dc23

Library of Congress Control Number: 2019950471

www.penguinrandomhouse.ca

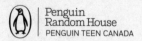
Penguin
Random House
PENGUIN TEEN CANADA

To the real Big Gord, who taught me to just get on with it.
And, always, to Rob.

PROLOGUE

If this were my memoir, it'd probably begin with *It all started at the bingo hall*. There'd be a picture of me on the cover, my heels clicked together in midair, and on the back there'd be a blurb from Pope John Paul II saying, "The best damn book I've read since the Bible." The title would be *All Tapped Out* and underneath, instead of *by Barry Squires*, it'd say *Written with passion by Finbar T. Squires*, in honor of Nanny Squires, because she was dramatic like that.

But this isn't a memoir. Memoirs are for people who've lived long, amazing lives and have inspirational stories to tell. All I did was follow my dream of becoming a Full Tilt Dancer. And that went tits up pretty quick.

CHAPTER ONE

I'd seen the Full Tilt Dancers perform a thousand times, but it wasn't until the opening of Frankie McCall's Bingo Hall that I wanted to be one of them. Maybe it was how their tartan uniforms glowed under the neon sign. Maybe it was how their shoes clacked on the large piece of plywood Frankie had put down on the pavement. More likely, though, it was because I'd spent the last year getting kicked out of every club and extracurricular activity I'd joined, and Nanny Squires said that if I didn't find an outlet for that temper of mine, I'd have a heart attack by the time I was twenty.

The parking lot in front of the hall had been cordoned off for the performance. Mom stood behind me with her hands on my shoulders while Dad, the good son that he was, brought Nan to the front to find a chair. I wished my baby brother, Gord, was there because he'd have loved the traditional Newfoundland music, but he was home with our older sister, Shelagh, who'd stayed behind to clear up after our big Sunday lunch. My other brother, Pius, wasn't impressed. "Stop being a saint, will ya?" he'd said. "You're making the rest of us look bad." Pius, or Sweet Sixteen, as Mom had been calling him since his birthday, had a big mouth and a comment for everything. When he'd heard that we were going to see the Full Tilt Dancers, he'd said, "Irish step dancing's for tools." As I stood in the crowded parking lot, mesmerized by the frenetic movements of the troupe, I felt like our Black and Decker 400-watt variable-speed jigsaw. Because if step dancing was for tools, I was the biggest one in the shed.

Frankie McCall stood under his bright neon sign tapping his foot and clapping his hands.

"Look at him," said Mom. "He's like the cat that ate the canary."

The Full Tilt Dancers had been scheduled to perform at the One Step Closer to God Nursing Home, but McCall had lured them away with the promise of five free bingo games per person. Father O'Flaherty's Full Tilt Dancers were the most sought-after act in the city—with the popular bagpiper Alfie Bragg and His Agony Bag being a close second.

The bingo fanatics of St. John's had been thrilled to learn that Frankie McCall was building a new bingo hall. The parish hall, where the game was normally played, had a rat problem. Nan blamed the infestation on the Hawkins Cheezies that were sold at the snack bar. "Finding one of those on the ground is like striking gold for a rat," she'd said. I agreed. I'd been known to eat a few off the floor myself.

Bingo attendance at the parish hall had diminished and when the town blabbermouth, Bernadette Ryan, called in to the VOCM *Open Line* radio show to say that her ninety-nine-year-old bingo-loving grandmother was showing signs of the plague—runny nose, fatigue, weakness—people refused to go altogether. Our old parish priest, Father Molloy, tried to reason with his parishioners, saying that the place had been fumigated, not once but twice, but Bernadette would not be silenced. She said that fumigation wasn't enough, that during the Great Plague of London contaminated bedding and clothes were burned to avoid contagion; therefore, the rat-infested parish hall should be burned to the ground. That's when Frankie McCall stepped in with the news that he'd be building a new bingo hall on behalf of the church. On the day of the announcement,

Father Molloy called McCall a "great philanthropist." Mom said, "Philanderer, more like." When I asked what that meant, she told me to go ask my Aunt Tilly. As far as I knew, I didn't have one.

After the dancers' opening performance, Frankie gestured to the double doors, which were blocked off by a piece of yellow police tape.

"That's what you get," said Frankie, "when you leave the village idiot in charge of the ribbon cutting."

The "village idiot" was ninety-four and Frankie's mother. I sidled up to her. "That son of yours is a hard ticket."

"Don't worry," she said. "He'll get his comeuppance."

Frankie made a cutting motion with his fingers. "Where are the scissors?"

The village idiot passed him a pair of pink plastic safety scissors. I laughed my arse off and said, "Nice one, missus."

Frankie broke a sweat as he hacked through the tape. On the final snip, the Full Tilt Dancers did a celebratory step dance. The dancing was good but "I'se da B'y" was too obvious. If it were up to me, we'd have sung "Bingo." *There was a Frankie had a hall, and BINGO was the game-o. B-I-N-G-O.* Clearly this troupe needed my out-of-the box ideas. When the applause faded I told my parents that my new life goal was to become a Full Tilt step dancer.

"Not a chance," said Dad. "We'll be drove nuts with the racket."

"But I have a feeling," I said. "It's stirring deep in my loins."

"For goodness sake, Barry," whispered Mom. "You should never talk about your loins in the shadow of the basilica."

"You just made that up," I said. "They talk about loins in the Bible all the time."

Dad ushered us toward the hall. "Come on. Bingo's starting."

"Bingo shmingo," I said. "We're talking about my dreams here."

"The answer is no," said Mom. "You'll only quit after a few weeks anyway."

"And the last thing we need is you clicking around the house like a moron," said Dad.

I picked up a rock and lobbed it at the neon sign. "Well, screw ye all!"

The rock landed two feet short of its target.

"You're lucky you missed," said Frankie McCall. "A move like that could get your whole family banned from the hall for life."

"So help me God," said Mom, "if you screw this up for me, I'll disown you."

She loved a good game of bingo.

As we filed into the hall, Dad pulled me back by the elbow. "What the hell is wrong with you, Barry? The first time your mother leaves the house since Gord's been born and you have to turn into the Antichrist."

I yanked my arm away. "If you must know," I said, "I'm Jesus's number one fan and that, sir, makes me pro-Christ. Very pro-Christ indeed."

"Don't 'sir' me, Barry," said Dad. "I'm your father, for Christ's sake."

"Taking the Lord's name in vain," I said. "*Now* who's the Antichrist?"

I caught up to Nanny Squires, who was waiting for me at the snack bar. Every week she bought me a treat— my reward for helping her keep track of the twenty cards she played at once. "Get whatever you want," she said. As I browsed, my stomach rumbling, she added, "Except Hawkins Cheezies. They started the plague, you know."

Frankie Hall had done an outstanding job stocking the new snack bar. I was spoiled for choice! "Look, Nan," I said, "they even have May Wests." But Nan didn't respond. She was too busy marveling at the shininess of the new counter. "I hope they use Comet on this," she said. "It'll help keep the sparkle."

I picked a bag of salt and vinegar chips and we joined my parents at a crowded table.

"What's up with these cards?" I said. They were different than the ones we usually played. They didn't even have the word *bingo* written across the top.

"Frankie wants to try ninety-ball bingo," said Nan.

"He played it when he was on holiday in the UK," said Mom.

"Concentrate now, Finbar," said Nan. "There'll be no letters called, just numbers."

"This is madness," said Dad. "Pure madness."

The four of us sat with our bingo dabbers hovering over the cards, waiting for the caller to shout the numbers. The sound system crackled to life.

"*Tickety-boo, sixty-two.*"

"What the hell?" said Dad.

Frankie McCall was standing nearby. "It's how the British do it," he said. "Doesn't it add another level of fun?"

"*Cup of tea, number three.*"

I recognized that voice. It was Uneven Steven, the colorful Englishman who was a fixture in the downtown core.

"*Dirty Gertie, number thirty.*"

"What a load of old foolishness," said Mom.

"*Dancing queen, seventeen.*"

Dad elbowed me in the ribs. "There you go, Barry. A new lucky number for ya."

The laughter at the table caused a growling deep in my belly.

"Control yourself, Fin-bear," said Mom.

My fist closed in on the bingo dabber till Nan's cards were swimming in ink.

"Look what you're after doing!" said Nan. "I was one away from four corners."

"These artistic types," said Dad. "They're so high-strung."

I punched my bag of chips.

"Chips on the floor, forty-four."

I ran outside and lobbed another rock at the sign.

"Hey, watch it!"

Billy Walsh, from ninth grade, was sitting on a concrete wall eating a feed of fish and chips. We'd hung around a bit last year, before he'd moved up to high school.

"You almost hit me," he said.

He was a year older but twice my size. I was about to say sorry when I was blinded by a light. It was warm and powerful and made me tingle all over. I squinted toward the source. It was the sun reflecting gloriously off the silver taps of his dancing shoes.

"Do you hear that?" I asked.

"Hear what?"

I smiled. The chorus of angels singing hallelujah was for my ears only. I, Barry Squires, was meant to tap for Jesus.

I hopped up onto the wall next to him. "Tell me. What do you have to do to become a Full Tilt Dancer?"

He popped a chip in his mouth. "Sell your soul to the devil."

"Fair enough," I said. "Anything else?"

He shrugged. "Sign yourself up for the auditions."

"When are the auditions?" I asked.

"September."

"That's six months away," I said. "I can't wait that long."

"Patience is a virtue, kid."

"What about the uniform?" I said. "How do I get one of those?"

"O'Flaherty sells them. A hundred and twenty-five bucks."

The uniforms were Newfoundland tartan, which was mostly green with red, yellow, and white stripes. Nan said they looked patriotic. Pius said they looked like snots.

"A hundred and twenty-five bucks?" I said. "What a rip-off."

Billy stroked his vest. "This here's quality merchandise," he said. "One hundred percent polyester."

"One hundred percent, you say?" I was impressed. My school uniform was only sixty. The rest was cotton.

Billy dipped his cod in a blob of ketchup.

"Just be warned," he said. "The life of a dancer is not all sunshine and roses and luxurious textiles. There's a lot of prejudice in this biz. Especially for us male dancers. We're totally misunderstood."

I reached over and took a chip. "Never let the bastards get you down, Walsh."

It was what Nan said to me when I was kicked out of Scouts. (Except she didn't call me Walsh.)

I hopped off the wall.

"Hey," he said as I walked away. "Were you the one who punched a hole through the confessional screen?"

"Father Molloy was way out of line. Ten Hail Marys for one little sin?"

"What was the sin?"

"Punching a hole through the classroom door."

I went down Church Hill making a clicking noise with my mouth every time my sneakers hit the pavement. When I walked in the house, Shelagh passed me the baby. "Your turn. Pius is at hockey and I'm going to MUN to study."

Ever since Shelagh got her acceptance letter to Memorial University, she'd been hanging out there as if she were a current student.

"You'd better watch out," I said. "They'll be so sick of your ugly mug, they might kick you out before you even start."

"I'll be graduating with honors in June," she said. "Trust me, this ugly mug is one they'll be happy to have."

I was due to graduate in June too. I wondered if the high school would be happy to have my ugly mug.

Gord grabbed a clump of my hair with his chubby little hand. I'd missed him at the opening of the bingo hall.

"Guess what, Gord?" I whispered. "I'm going to be a Full Tilt Dancer."

★

Sometimes, in Newfoundland, you can have four seasons in one day, so even though it was the end of March (and spring should have been on its way), I stuffed Gord in his snowsuit to keep him warm on our post-bingo afternoon jaunt. As usual, I started by naming the homeowners and house colors. "Merchant, red. Coady, white. Walling, black." It was a tradition I'd started to keep things interesting back when I wasn't allowed to take Gord off York Street. Now that we were allowed to go farther I kept it up because Gord screamed if I didn't. Sometimes I wished Gord was as flexible with his routines as he was with his body. I saw him kiss his own arse once.

"Hanrahan, green. O'Brien, blue."

"Ahhh-baaa, ahhh-daaaa, ahhh-paaa."

Only six months old and speaking in whole sentences. It was no wonder I took every opportunity to show him off. He was practically a child genius.

Part of our routine was going to Caines. If Boo wasn't busy selling smokes or dishing up his famous Jiggs Dinner, he'd sit us down and tell us a ghost story. He'd seen a headless dude on Signal Hill once. He'd come upon him on a dark and stormy night and they'd locked eyes. Locked eyes! I couldn't believe it. Sometimes Gord nodded off during Boo's stories, but as soon as we'd leave the store he'd perk right up. It was the air that did it—it was fresh and salty and went right up our noses. He'd perk up even more when I'd take him to the harbor. I'd tip his stroller over the dock and say, "Hope you can swim, Gord!" He loved that. An old woman yelled at me once. She said I was foolhardy. I said, "Take a chill pill, missus. He's got a seatbelt on."

Today, instead of going to Caines, we went back to the bingo hall. The plywood was still outside.

"Watch this, Gord!"

I copied the dance moves the Full Tilt Dancers had done earlier. The almighty racket was glorious. There was no music, so I sang.

The night that Paddy Murphy died
is a night I'll never forget.
Some of the boys got loaded drunk
and they ain't been sober yet.

I *da-da-da*-ed the bits I didn't know and when the words came back I belted them out.

14

Mrs. Murphy sat in the corner
pourin' out her grief,
when Kelly and his gang
came tearing down the street.
They went into an empty room
and a bottle of whiskey stole,
and kept that bottle with the corpse
to keep that whiskey cold.

"A corpse is a dead body, Gord," I explained. "The b'ys weren't really celebrating Pat Murphy's life. They just wanted an excuse to party. That's what I think anyway. I'm not one for lyrics, not really. It's the melody I like. What about you, Gord? Do you like the melody? What do you think of my dancing, Gord? Pretty good, huh? What's with your face, Gord? You're not poopin', are ya? If ya shits your pants, we'll have to go home."

Gord laughed his sweet baby belly laugh, the one that erupted for the first time two months ago when I stubbed my toe on his high chair. I'd hopped on one foot shouting "ouch, ouch, ouch!" and the *ha-ha-ha* that burst out of his body was hearty and deep. Tears had pricked my eyes— not from the pain that throbbed in my foot but from the happy pain that throbbed in my heart.

I checked Gord's bum. He hadn't pooped his pants, so we continued on to Bannerman Park. I tried stuffing him into a baby swing. "You're some fat, Gord. But don't worry, once you start walking you'll lose all that weight. Just don't go losing your cheeks, okay? That's what makes you cute. No one likes a baby with skinny cheeks."

I pushed him high. "Hold on, Gord. If you fall out and die, Mom will kill me."

The last thing I wanted to do was ruin Mom's day. After months of the baby blues, she was finally having a good one.

★

We'd been surprised to see her up before noon this morning. We were sitting around the table eating Nan's pancakes when Mom appeared. "Are you coming to church with us?" I asked.

She ruffled my hair. "I prefer to pray in the privacy of my own home, thank you very much." She stole a piece of bacon off Dad's plate.

"Hey!" he said. She bent over and gave him a kiss on the lips. He beamed. The sight of her—fully dressed and ready to take on the day—raised our spirits.

And when she'd walked out the back door with a basket of freshly laundered clothes, we couldn't help but smile. Mom lived for laundry. She measured our lives by it: "Look at the size of the underwear I had to get Barry this week—my little boy is becoming a man . . . Shelagh's certainly got a lovely figure. 36C was my size too when I was her age. They're shriveled up a bit now, mind . . . Gord's going to need to move up a size in these sleepers. I hope I can get another pair with monkeys on them, they're my favorite."

A blast of cold air had filled the house but no one said a word. Nan quietly pulled a blanket over her knees, Shelagh slipped on her dressing gown, and Dad pulled Gord's high chair out of the draft. Pius, on the other hand, strutted around in his NHL boxers. "Some Newfoundlanders you are."

We watched as Mom reached into the basket and carefully pinned our clothes to the line. She smiled at us through the open door. "It's some day on clothes."

It was a phrase meant for days when the sun was splitting the rocks, but Mom hung out clothes all year long. Sometimes they came in as stiff as a board but we didn't care. When Mom hung out clothes, she was happy. And that meant that we were happy too.

The line shrieked as Mom yanked it through the pulley.

"That line needs oiling," said Nan.

Dad gazed out the window. "It's music to my ears."

I rubbed my goose-pimply arms. "Mine too."

★

Gord and I left Bannerman Park and went back to the bingo hall, where I showed him off to a table of old biddies. Even with cigarettes hanging out of their mouths, they managed a "God love him." They were a talented bunch.

Mom frowned when she saw me. "When you're fourteen, you can take him farther. Until then I want you sticking close to home."

"I only wanted to show him the new hall," I said. "We usually only go as far as Caines."

It was a lie, of course. I took Gord everywhere. I took him to the Zellers mall once. We rode a horse for a quarter. It wasn't a real horse. Real horses neighed. This one played the *William Tell* overture.

When we got home we watched *Rugrats* until Mom came back and put Gord down for a nap. When Dad and Nan went to the kitchen for a cup of tea, I loaded the *Riverdance* video into our VCR. Dad had given it to Mom for Christmas because Mom had a thing for Michael Flatley, who was the lead dancer. He wore bolero jackets over his shirtless torso and thin headbands across his forehead. Pius said he looked like a tool. Mom said he was making a statement. "Yeah," said Pius. "'Look at me. I'm a tool.'"

In order to master the art of Irish step dancing, I

watched the video not once, but twice. I pinned my hands to my sides and did what I figured was a pretty good rendition. Every now and then I added a quick flick of a leg in the air. It seemed to be a *Riverdance* signature move. I made it my own by adding a wink. I danced in this fashion from one side of the room to the other. There was no way I could wait until September for the Full Tilt auditions. I was too good. And how could I deny the troupe what was clearly a God-given talent? It wouldn't be fair.

So that night, after one of Nan's Sunday pot roasts, I cleared the living room and gathered everyone around. I brought in an extra kitchen chair for when Mom and Dad invited Father O'Flaherty over for an encore. O'Flaherty was relatively new to town, having taken over for Father Molloy, who'd brought shame upon the Full Tilt Dancers by using money they'd earned at a competition to buy himself a rabbit fur fedora down at Chafe and Sons. Mom and Dad hadn't had the chance to have a one-on-one with Father O'Flaherty yet, so not only would I be fulfilling a dream by becoming one of his dancers, I'd be bringing people together.

When everyone was seated, I went to the back porch and taped pennies to my shoes.

"Hurry up," said Shelagh. "I've got a chemistry test tomorrow."

"And I've got a life to live," said Pius.

In a spur-of-the-moment decision, I took off my shirt and put on the faux-fur shrug that hung on the coat rack. I tied a shoelace around my forehead. With my inner Flatley successfully channeled, I clicked into the living room with my head held high.

"Jesus, Mary, and Joseph," said Mom.

Nanny beamed. "God love him."

Dad looked grief stricken.

"Look," said Pius. "It's Dorkel Fattly."

I sucked in my gut and struck a matador pose in the doorway.

The room fell quiet.

Too quiet.

Shit.

I'd forgotten the music.

Without breaking character, I shuffled toward the stereo and pressed Play with my toe.

Then I shuffled back again.

"That was smooth," said Pius.

A Celtic reel danced out of the speakers. I stayed perfectly still.

"Are you going to dance or what?" said Dad.

Didn't they know? Flatley never made an entrance till halfway through the song.

It was hard to hold my matador pose with Shelagh

huffing and Mom tutting and Pius swearing under his breath. *They'll be sorry*, I thought, *when their cold, dead hearts come to life at the sight of me soaring over the sofa.*

"Why's he just standing there?" said Shelagh.

"Because he's an idiot," said Pius.

I could feel a growling, deep inside my belly. I tried some deep breathing.

"An idiot with asthma, by the sounds of it," said Shelagh.

"Are you going to start or what?" asked Dad.

"It's not my turn," I said. "I don't come on till the other dancers leave the stage."

"What other dancers?" said Mom.

Nan looked around the room. "I see them," she said. "Their costumes are as green as the rolling hills of the Emerald Isle."

"Oh for God's sake," said Dad.

"Bah-gah!" yelled Gord.

I put my finger up to silence them. We'd reached my favorite part and I wanted to savor it. Drums rolled in like a musical snowball, the sound growing bigger and bigger as it filled the room.

In three . . .

In two . . .

In one . . .

The fiddles burst in with a frenzy and so did I.

With my hands on my hips, I leapt into the room. I spread my legs as wide as I could and thrust my chin in the air. *This'll show 'em. The bastards.*

The china cabinet shook when I landed.

"Lord dyin' Jesus," said Mom. "There goes my great-grandmother's tea set."

A clickity-click to the left.

A clackity-clack to the right.

A few spins here.

A couple of twirls there.

God, I'd picked a long song.

I put my hands on my knees and did some kind of crisscross motion with my arms.

Then I did the Charleston.

Focus, Squires, focus. What would Flatley do? I pictured him in all his shirtless glory. "You got this, Finbar," he said in my imagination. It was all that I needed. With my arms glued tight to my sides, I tapped the bejeezus out of the floor. I stared straight ahead at the soon-to-be-filled-with-Father-O'Flaherty-chair and hoped to God I had an encore in me.

I tried not to look cocky as I bowed.

Gord clapped his hands.

"Bravo, bravo!" yelled Nan.

The rest of them doubled over laughing.

"Someone call the doctor," said Shelagh. "Barry had a fit."

Pius pinged my makeshift headband as he left the room. "If I ever see you doing anything like that again, I swear to God I'll punch your face in."

I picked Gord up and slung him on my hip. The little snot-rag was the only one I could stand to be around. (Well, Nan too, but I could hardly storm off with her in my arms.)

I sat on my bedroom floor and peeled the pennies off my shoes. Gord tried to put them in his mouth. I grabbed them. "Dirty," I said. "Bah," he said back.

I stretched out on my bed with Gord on my chest. He tried to pick up my nipples.

"No, Gord. They're attached."

He reached out and touched the raised patch of purple that splashed across my cheek.

I pushed his hand away. "No!"

I felt bad. How was he supposed to know about birthmarks? I played pat-a-cake to make up for it. As I sang about the baker's man, I reflected on my performance. Maybe, instead of a live show, I should've videotaped myself, and added lots of cool edits and slo-mo in the post-production. It worked wonders in *Riverdance*. Who knows? It could've made all the difference.

*

There was something about Sunday nights that made my bedroom ceiling really interesting. Pius was in the bed next to me reading *Gretzky: An Autobiography* and I could hear *Fawlty Towers* reruns from downstairs and "Wonderwall" on repeat from Shelagh's room. I pictured Gord asleep in his cot and all around me was the smell of our Sunday supper, corned beef and cabbage, still strong in the air. Everything around me—what was in my ears and up my nose—was comforting, but Sunday nights meant Monday mornings. I stared at the bumpy texture of the ceiling. We'd had a leak the year before and the whole thing had to be redone. The painters recommended stucco because it hides imperfections, unlike the smooth surface we'd had before. They called it a popcorn ceiling but it didn't look like popcorn. It looked like crushed meringue. I thought about school the next day. Soon I'd feel like a frayed puzzle piece—no matter how hard I'd try to fit in, there'd always be bits sticking out.

I remembered that time in the dumpster. The older boys had said my face was dirty, so they chucked me in like a piece of trash. The parish hall curtains broke my fall. They were old and worn and smelled of smoke. The boys got suspended, but they were only trying to put me in my place. No one likes a puzzle with bits sticking out.

I looked up into the crushed-meringue sky and heard fading laughter, the dumpster boys' and then my parents'. *Fawlty Towers* came to an end and there were footsteps on the stairs. "Wonderwall" faded to black.

CHAPTER TWO

Getting to school on time was pure guesswork because there were no clocks in our house—Dad couldn't stand the ticking. As a clockmaker at Just a Matter of Time, he said his days were filled with a "bloody cacophony of ticks and tocks." He only owned one timepiece, a wrist-watch, which he kept in his bedside table and checked just once in the morning, so he could gauge when to leave for work. I left shortly thereafter and hoped for the best.

As always, Uneven Steven greeted me on the corner with a big "'Allo, Squire." I used to correct him by saying "It's Squires, with an *s*," until he told me that calling someone squire in England was the same as saying buddy or fella. It was just one of our many lost-in-translation moments.

We first met on the corner of Cochrane and Duckworth—I was walking past it, he was sprawled across it. I had no problem with the disadvantaged, I was always praying for them at mass, but did they need to take up the whole sidewalk? My foot got caught in his rucksack and I ended up doing a crazy hokeypokey until I was finally freed. I said "arsehole" as I stumbled away. He shouted, "Oi, who you callin' a merry old soul?" I knew nothing about Cockney rhyming slang back then—I just thought he was deaf. The next day as I passed, he gathered his things and said, "Good day, Your Highness. Is the sidewalk to your liking?" I said, "No. You forgot the red carpet." He laughed his head off. It was the beginning of a beautiful friendship.

Uneven Steven spent his mornings on the corner of Cochrane and Duckworth, having spent the night at the Harbour Light Centre. Visiting him required a bit of a detour but I figured school could wait—a top o' the morning to the disadvantaged was far more important.

I returned Steven's *'Allo, Squire* with a "What's the time, me ol' trout?"

Steven looked at his watch. "8:49."

School didn't start till nine. I dropped my schoolbag.

"Loads of time. Congrats on the job, by the way," I said.

"Oh, I don't work at the bingo hall anymore. Frankie McCall fired me after my first shift."

"How come?"

"The Sullivan sisters complained when I called *eighty-eight*."

"What's eighty-eight?"

"Two fat ladies."

"You didn't look at them when you said it, did you?"

"Couldn't help it, mate."

"This'll cheer you up," I said.

I took a homemade roll out of my pocket. "Have a squeeze of me grandmudder's buns."

He took it in his grubby paw and grinned. "Cheeky devil."

I liked giving the disadvantaged a laugh.

"Guess what?" I said. "I'm gonna be a Full Tilt Dancer."

"Irish step dancing?" he said. "If you want to be a dancer, mate, you need to be a bit more rock and roll. I can show you some moves, if you like."

Uneven Steven claimed he was a popular rock star in the sixties and seventies, known for his signature moves. No one believed him. Not when his left leg was three inches shorter than his right.

"I don't like rock and roll," I said. "I like Irish music."

"Ireland is the armpit of Great Britain," said Steven. "And why you'd want to look like a bloody leprechaun dancing around in a tartan vest is beyond me."

I was disgusted. Since when was leprechaun an insult?

"Step dancing," I said through gritted teeth, "is cool."

"Cool? You need your 'ead checked, mate. All that clickin' and clackin'. It's a bloody racket, that's what it is."

I whacked the bun out of his hand like an archer shooting an apple off somebody's head. "What would you know, you stupid limey? You don't know nothing about nothing."

He picked up the roll and flicked off the gravel. "Don't know nothing about nothing?" he said. "That's a double negative, Squire. Double negatives don't make no sense."

For someone who left school at fifteen, Uneven Steven was incredibly smart.

He patted his cardboard square. "'Ave a seat, you silly teapot lid."

Teapot lid. That was a new one.

"Tell me," he said. "Why do you *really* want to join Father O'Flaherty and his poncy dancers?"

I took the dirty roll from him and gave him a new one from my lunch bag. "The thing is," I said, "I need a thing."

"A thing?"

"Pius is a jock. Shelagh's the president of student council. And you," I added to humor him, "you got that whole rock star thing going. I just want to be part of something."

"And you really want this step dancing malarkey to be your thing?"

"Nanny Squires says I need to do something physical, to get all my angst out."

His blue-gray eyes sparkled through lashes that Shelagh would kill for. "Angst, eh?"

"And I really do think it looks cool. Their feet move so fast and the taps are so loud. It's almost . . . violent. It's like they're kicking the shit out of the floor. The problem is, they audition only once a year—in September."

Uneven Steven took a bite of my grandmother's roll and looked to the sky.

"'Ere's what you do," he said after a minute or two. "Get yourself down to the nursing home and offer to do a performance. Make sure it's a Thursday night, that's when Father O'Flaherty visits. If he sees potential, he might arrange an audition. Better yet, he might invite you to join on the spot."

"A performance?" I said. "In public? I'm good, but I'm no Michael Flatley."

"Don't worry, mate. They're gonna love you."

"My own family laughed their arses off. These old people, they might boo me right off the stage."

"They won't."

"How do you know?"

"There is no stage. According to Alfie Bragg, you stand on an *X* in the Last Chance Saloon."

"The what?"

"The Last Chance Saloon. It's what the residents call the special events lounge."

"Why?"

"Because, mate, it might be the last time they get to see great entertainers such as yourself. They're no spring chickens, you know."

I stood up and put my backpack on. "So no pressure, then."

He swallowed the last bite of bun and patted his stomach. "Ta for this, Squire. It really filled a hole in me old Auntie Nelly."

*

Michael Whelan rushed past me as I made my way toward school. "Better get going, Wine-bar. Bell's gonna go."

I sighed. Mr. McGraw had meant well by telling the class the scientific name for the birthmark across my cheek, but hearing the words "port-wine stain" only gave the bastards more inventive ways to insult me. Wine-bar, a play on my full name, Finbar, quickly caught on. So did Merlot and Cabernet, which were types of wine, not port, so not only were my classmates bastards, they were stupid bastards.

Nanny Squires told me to be confident about my birthmark. She said I was as good as the next person. Better, even. She said, "When you walk into that school you need to act like you own the place." It was good advice. Because when I walked around all cocky and bold, the names bounced off me. But on the bad days, when I woke up wishing I had a different face, I was suddenly an arsehole magnet. It wasn't just "Hey, Merlot," it was "Hey, Barry, you've got a little something on your face," or a chorus of "Freaks Come Out at Night." Damian Clarke and Thomas Budgell were the worst. When we'd moved to junior high, they'd spread the rumor that I was highly contagious and anyone within three feet would be afflicted. They called me Moses for a while after that because of the way I parted the crowd in the hallway like it was the Red Sea. Yep, on the bad days my face was as attention-getting as Frankie McCall's neon sign. It was a beacon for bastards.

I stood outside school for another ten minutes, then went straight to the principal's office.

"Mornin', Judy," I said, slinging my schoolbag around the wooden desk she kept in the corner. "Aren't you a vision of loveliness today? Green is really your color— reminds me of the rolling hills of the Emerald Isle."

"Who sent you here, Barry?" she said. "Whoever it was gave up way too early."

"Well, Judes—"

"That's Mrs. Muckle to you, Mr. Squires."

I smiled. "I think we know each other far too well for silly formaldehydes, don't you?"

"The word you are looking for is *formalities*."

I shrugged. "Ehh, close enough. Starts with an *f*, ends in an *s*."

It was tricky, this balancing act I did each day. The key was to be disruptive enough to be kept out of class, while not being too hard on poor old Judy—it wasn't her fault my face was a beacon for bastards.

"Well?" she said. "Who sent you here?"

"No one. I sent myself."

"Why would you do that?"

"I was extremely late this morning."

She looked at the clock. "For the love of God, Barry, it's not even 9:15. And don't you have English with Mr. McGraw first period? Of all the classes you shouldn't be missing."

I picked up the nameplate on her desk. It was shaped like a Toblerone. "The thing is, Judes, and I'm just being honest with you, I have a feeling if I go to class, I might punch someone in the face. So it's best I stay here."

"What do you mean you *have a feeling*?"

"It's, like, deep down in my bones. I'm feeling a punch coming on—like how Nanny Squires knows when it's going to rain."

"For goodness sake, Barry. Can't you just ignore it?"

"Nanny Squires says I should never deny my feelings. She says us Catholics are repressed enough as it is." I took off my jacket and sat down. "Don't worry. I'll just sit here at my desk and do my work."

"That is not *your* desk."

I wanted to say, *Well, my name's on it,* but thought better of pointing out the *FTS* I'd carved into the wood with the metal pointy thing from my math set.

"I'm practically the only one that uses it. In fact," I said, waving her nameplate through the air, "I could use one of these bad boys myself."

She came around from behind her desk.

"Hiding in here all day won't help," she said.

I stared at her shoes. They were high heels and red. Nan would call them "fantabulous." Mom would call them "slutty."

"You're letting them win, Barry. You deserve to be in the classroom just as much as anyone else. Don't let them drive you away." She looked at me and smiled. "Now get to class."

I looked up. "Judes?"

"Yes?"

"I hope you don't mind me saying, but I like your shoes. They're really fantabulous."

"Mr. Squires?"

"Yeah?"

"If I hear you calling me Judes again, you'll get detention for a week."

I shrugged. "Fair enough."

Thomas Budgell passed me on my way to class. He called me Pinot Noir in an exaggerated French accent. I could have just ignored him, but how could I deny that feeling deep in my bones? It was a short walk back to the principal's office. I said I didn't lay a finger on him but his bloody lip proved otherwise. Thomas was sent back to class but I stayed with Mrs. Muckle. She said, "What am I going to do with you, Barry?" I suggested a game of Go Fish. It was a joke but she took a pack of cards from her desk. "Crazy Eights," she said. "Go Fish drives me cracked."

★

Funny thing happened at gym class that day. Mr. Nolan had us doing the dreaded Canada Fitness Test. We took turns doing flexed-arm hangs, standing long jumps, and sit-ups while Nolan timed, measured, and counted. Only a few people did well at it and I wasn't one of them.

Suddenly, I wasn't Wine-bar. I was "Jesus, Barry, this is hell," and "Christ, Squires, Nolan's going to kill us." For forty minutes, we were all frayed, and I wished hell lasted forever.

★

After school I headed for the nursing home. I passed Uneven Steven on my way.

"How's Judes?" he asked. (He loved my tales from the principal's office.)

"She had a face on her like a smacked arse," I said. "That woman is as crooked as sin."

Steven laughed. "Maybe she'd lighten up if you weren't in so much Barney Rubble all the time."

I passed him what was left of my lunch. "Don't worry," I said. "She'll light up like a Christmas tree when she finds I'm going to perform for the oldies at the nursing home. I'm going there now to set it up."

He unzipped my lunch bag. "Make sure to tell 'em you're good friends with Alfie Bragg," he said, trying to open an Oreo with his sausage-sized fingers. "That way you'll be a shoo-in."

"But I barely know Alfie Bragg."

The Oreo crumbled to bits. "Tell 'em anyway. One little porky pie won't do no harm."

I twisted my last cookie in half and handed it to him. "You're right. Honesty is never the best policy. Remember when I told Judes she'd put on a few over Christmas?"

Steven's grin emerged through his thick beard like the sun coming through a black cloud.

"I tried to warn her," I continued. "I said, 'Judith, my duck, you'd better tell those students you'll only accept non-edible gifts.' But would she listen? No. She kept stuffing her face with Pot of Gold. I knew she'd come back the size of a house."

I waited for Steven to laugh his big, deep *ha-ha-ha*, and when he did, I felt like I'd just scored the winning goal in the biggest sporting event in the world. He slapped his knee and said, "You kill me, Squire, you really kill me." Inside, I was bursting—because laughter is the best medicine and Steven once said he was sick in the head.

"Well, I gotta go," I said. "Cheerio and ta-ta and all that other bullcrap you Brits get on with."

He was still chuckling as I walked away. Not only had I scored the winning goal, I was the MVP.

Heading off to the nursing home meant missing my favorite part of the day—getting Gord up from his nap. Nanny Squires liked him up by 3:30, so I always made sure to be home by 3:20. That way I could spend ten minutes on the floor next to his crib, watching him breathe. Breathing with Gord calmed the army men down. The army men marched through my brain all day long. I didn't know who or what they were fighting but they were angry. They ransacked my thoughts, tossing them aside and breaking them in two. It was hard to explain the army men to Mrs. Muckle or Mr. McGraw. It was easier to let them think I was too lazy to live up to my potential. I loved watching Gord sleep. His little pink lips and rosy-pink cheeks hypnotized me. The army men too. With each fall and rise of the breath, they marched to the barracks and climbed into their cots for a nap.

I'd miss Gord today. Breathing wasn't the same without him.

★

The One Step Closer to God Nursing Home was part hotel, part hospital. Its lobby was impressive, with fancy armchairs and a grand fireplace, but it smelled like Gord's room after a diaper change—strongly deodorized with an underlying scent of bodily functions. Some residents lounged in their Sunday best, others wore pajamas and slippers. One old fella wore a top hat and tails. They all had one thing in common, though: they were ancient. Still, I liked this ragtag group of wrinklies. I mean, who doesn't like old people? They spend their days giving out Werther's and wisdom by the bucketloads, all with a twinkle in their eye. Maybe, I thought, this wasn't about getting noticed by Father O'Flaherty. Maybe, just maybe, this was about giving back. I puffed out my chest and made a beeline for the reception desk. It was time to arrange the performance of a lifetime.

As I crossed the room, a sweet old lady in a bright yellow dress and a flowery sunhat caught my eye. I crouched before her, resting my hands on the armrests of her wheelchair.

"If I may be so bold as to say," I said, gazing into the deep crevices of her old-iferous face, "you are the epiphany of a blooming daffodil on a summer's day."

"It's *epitome*," said the old fella in the top hat and tails. "*Epiphany* is an entirely different animal."

The old lady's voice was a croak. "I wandered lonely as a cloud, that floats on high o'er vales and hills, when all at once I saw a crowd, a host, of golden daffodils."

Wandering? Not with those withered old legs. I wanted to compliment her poem but it wasn't very good, so I said, "I must say, you have the perfect voice for a cartoon witch."

Giving back felt amazing.

I continued on, tipping an imaginary hat to Mr. Top Hat and Tails, who swiftly stuck his cane in my path. I flew into the welcoming arms of an overly made-up woman. "Well, well. Aren't you a handsome young man?" Before I could react, she planted a rather slob-iferous kiss on my cheek. In the spirit of giving, I said, "You're not

BARRY SQUIRES, FULL TILT

too bad yourself," but to be honest, she had a face only a mother could love.

I continued on my journey to the reception desk. An old woman in a lavender pantsuit shuffled toward me. Her eyes twinkled like stars. She stopped in front of me. "Why, hello there, sonny."

She opened up a large purse and reached inside. She dug this way and that. Slippery little devils, those Werther's. When her eyes lit up, I put out my hand. A moment later, a crumpled old tissue fluttered toward it. I pulled my hand away in disgust. As I walked onward, I pictured the shiny taps on the bottom of Billy Walsh's shoes. It was the only thing that kept me going.

Finally, I'd arrived. The receptionist smiled. Her name-tag said Patsy, and even though she was old, her hair was dyed purple, like the punks down on Water Street. I was starting to give her the ins and outs of my perfor-mance when she said, "We're not fussy, my duck. I'm sure you'll be delightful."

"Shall we say 7 p.m., then?" I said. "Thursday eve-ning?"

"Sure," she said, penciling me in on her empty desk calendar. "Why not?"

I asked if I could see the Last Chance Saloon, and she frowned and said, "If you mean the special events room, it's down the hall and to the left."

There were doors down both sides of the hallway, and in the room behind each one was an old person. I made sure to give each and every one of them a nod and a wink because Nan always told me not to tar people with the same brush and just because three wrinklies tried to kill me—one with a cane, one with a kiss, and one with a germ-filled snot-rag—I shouldn't assume they were all a bunch of bastards. My open-mindedness paid off when a little old lady looked up from a book and winked back. I popped my head in her door. "How ya doin' today, missus?"

She said, "Not too bad, considering."

"Considering what?"

She threw her hands up in the air. I took that to mean everything.

"What's your name?" I asked.

"Edie."

"Don't let the bastards get you down, Edie."

She smiled. Good ol' Nan—her words of wisdom were quickly becoming the most useful phrase in my whole vocabulary.

"I'm Barry Squires," I said.

She cocked her head like a dog hearing the word *walk*.

"Aren't you the youngster who punched a hole through the confessional screen?"

"The one and only." I grinned.

She grinned back. I liked this Edie. Even if she was half drunk on the whiskey she was hiding behind her book.

"Whatcha reading?" I asked.

She peered over the book. The fact that it was upside down should have worked in her favor, but she seemed unable to focus on the title. "I, er—"

"Never mind, Edie," I said. "It's what's on the inside that counts."

I winked again and continued on to the Last Chance Saloon.

The *X* was there, just like Uneven Steven had said. I surveyed the area with my hands clasped behind my back. *Yes,* I murmured. *This will do very well. Very well indeed.* All I needed was to check out the clickability of the floor. Acoustics were very important in step dancing. Or so I supposed. I didn't have any pennies to tape to my shoes, so I looked around for something metal I could hit against the floor to mimic the clicks. There was a wheelchair in the corner but that would be too big. I went back to the lobby, where Mr. Top Hat and Tails was sitting. He was snoring now, the bastard. His cane was resting against the arm of the chair. He obviously didn't need it, so I took it.

The cane had a rubber stop on the bottom, but the top part was silver and in the shape of a lion's head. I felt quite grand walking back down the hallway with it. When I walked past Edie's room, I said, "Hello, m'lady."

"What are you doing with Buster's cane?" she asked.

"Buster?" I said. "Sounds like a dog."

"Looks like one too," she said. "A bulldog."

I wagged a finger at her and smiled. "You're a cheeky old devil, Eeds."

When I got back to the saloon, I turned the cane upside down and tapped the lion's head against the floor. Not as echo-y as pennies. But not bad. Satisfied with the click-ability of the venue, I decided to have a quick practice. I did the routine I'd performed for my family and then, in a moment of brilliance, decided to incorporate the cane. I leaned on it with both hands. I clicked my heels to the left, then to the right. Maybe, I thought, I could blend Irish step dancing with old-fashioned tap. I held the lion's head with one hand and walked rhythmically around it. If I combined the classiness of Fred Astaire with the cockiness of Michael Flatley, I could be the creator of a whole new genre of dance. I gave it a try. Instead of keeping my arms pinned to my sides, I added some visual interest by holding the cane in front of me—the lion head in my left hand, the rubber stop in my right. Moving the cane in a circular motion, I proceeded to kick the shit out of the floor while singing "Tea for Two" in an Irish accent.

"What the hell are you doing?"

Buster the bulldog tore across the room, his jowls flapping in the wind. When he made a grab for the cane, I swept it up into the air, then hid it behind my back.

"Whoa there, Buster," I said. "Looks to me like someone doesn't really need a cane at all. How's about I borrow it for a week?"

"Borrow it? Absolutely not! That is *my* cane and I need it to walk."

I put on my patient-but-firm Judy Muckle face. "Now, Buster," I said. "I think we both know that's not true."

His face turned as purple as Patsy's hair. "What the hell are you talking about? Of course it's true. I need that cane! I'm eighty-one years old, you know."

I smiled. "Don't you mean eighty-one years *young*?"

I hoped he could see the kindness I was forcing into my eyes.

"Isn't age but a number?" I said. "Don't you think this cane is holding you back from who you really want to be? Don't you think that maybe, just maybe, you're using this cane as a crutch—an *emotional* crutch?"

God, I was good.

He lurched forward and snatched the cane from behind my back. "I don't know who you are, kid, but you're a lunatic. I can see it in your eyes. A raving, psychotic lunatic."

"A lunatic?" I said. "I'm not the one dressed like Mr. bloody Peanut."

"If I was Mr. Peanut," he sputtered, "I'd be wearing a monocle."

I nodded in agreement. "You'd be wearing spats too."

His eyebrows moved halfway up his forehead. "*You* know what spats are?"

"My nan's favorite movie is *Puttin' On the Ritz*. She has a thing for Fred Astaire."

Buster looked off into the distance. "Don't we all?"

"I'll be dancing here Thursday night," I said. "Wanna come?"

His face filled with even more wrinkles. "Dancing?"

"Yeah," I said. "You know . . ." I stomped my feet a few times and finished off with jazz hands.

"Ha! You call that dancing?"

"*Semi-Irish-jazzy-step-tap-dancing*, to be exact. Will you come?"

"I wouldn't miss it," he said, turning to leave. "It's been a while since I've seen a good comedy routine."

Old people. They were always getting confused. I was going to call after him and say, "No, not comedy . . . dancing!" But I didn't want to embarrass him.

CHAPTER THREE

Gord was up from his nap, sitting in his high chair and sticking a Cheerio up his nose. His arms started flailing the minute he saw me. "Bah. Bah."

I bent down close. "Guess what, Gord? I'm dancing at the nursing home on Thursday."

He slapped me across the face.

"Jesus, Gord!"

Shelagh looked up from her homework. "It's your fault. You're always invading his personal space."

Nan filled the teapot and looked around. "Now where's that teapot lid?"

"Teapot lid—kid!" I shouted.

Shelagh jumped a mile. "What the hell, Barry?"

"I just figured out something Uneven Steven said."

"That man is a nutcase," she said. "He's always talking in riddles."

I pulled Gord out of the high chair. As soon as he was in my arms, he started biting my cheek.

"Ha!" said Pius as he walked into the room. "He thinks that thing on your face is a plum."

"Pius!" said Nan.

I didn't wait for the apology he'd be forced to give. I stormed off to my room and sat Gord on my bed.

"Repeat after me, Gord. Pius . . ."

"Ba."

"Is a . . ."

"Ah."

"Arsehole."

"O-ba-da-bah-gah!"

I was amazed. His language skills were really coming along.

We listened to Raffi's "Baby Beluga" over and over. On the ten-millionth play, we heard Mom calling from the hall.

"Now where's my little blunder?"

Dark humor. That's how Uneven Steven described Mom's nickname for Gord. But Gord was a surprise, not a mistake. I whispered in his ear. "Did you hear that? Mommy's looking for her little *wonder*."

Mom opened my door and looked at Gord like he was the best thing since sliced bread, which he was. Wonder bread.

"Look what I've got," she sang.

She pulled a pair of monkey sleepers out of a Zellers bag. They were the same ones she'd bought sized 0–3 months, then 3–6.

"They had them in six to twelve months too," she said.

"You went out?" I said.

"Just nipped out for some fresh air."

I didn't react but my insides jumped for joy.

"Guess what?" I said.

She scooped Gord up and breathed him in. "What?"

"I'm going to be giving a performance at the nursing home."

"Really?" she said. "Doing what?"

"Step dancing. I'm going to prove myself to Father O'Flaherty."

The surprise on her face turned to concern.

"Don't get your hopes up, okay, Barry?"

"I won't," I said. "But I'm pretty sure I'm gonna nail it."

She sat down with Gord on her lap and cleared her throat. "The thing is, Barry, being a Full Tilt Dancer . . . it costs money."

"I know," I said. "A hundred and twenty-five dollars."

Gord crawled away from her and into my arms.

"It's a total bargain," I said. "Think about it—you get the vest, the pants, and the tap shoes too."

She looked down at my bedspread, picked at a loose thread. "I could get an outfit like that down at the Sally Ann for a quarter of that."

"But the pants and vest wouldn't be Newfoundland tartan, now, would they?" I said. "And I think I heard somewhere that wearing secondhand tap shoes was unlucky."

She looked up. "I'm sorry, Barry. It's too much."

I could feel the growling stirring in my belly. "All the other parents pay it."

"Well, those parents have more money than sense."

I rolled my eyes. "Money *is* cents."

"Not *cents*," she said. "*Sense*. As in sensible?"

I passed Gord back. If I was going to have an effective freak-out, I was gonna need two hands.

"Tell me," I said. "Is it *sensible* for a parent to buy a child who will never amount to anything brand-new hockey equipment while denying the child with the most potential the very tools he needs to succeed in life?"

"That's different," she said. "Pius sticks things out. You, on the other hand, drop out of every extracurricular activity you join."

"I don't drop out!" I yelled. "I get kicked out!"

Mom shook her head. "That temper of yours will be the death of you."

"So you want me dead now," I said. "Is that what you're saying?"

"What I want," she said, "is for you to control your anger."

"And what *I* want," I said, "is a Newfoundland tartan outfit."

"It's too expensive."

"Maybe I could earn the money," I said.

"Earn it how?"

"By taking care of Gord."

"I'm not paying you for that, Barry. Taking care of each other is just part of being a family."

I was starting to wonder if I'd liked her better when she stayed in her room.

"But I go above and beyond with Gord," I said. "For instance, today I taught him a new word."

"You did?" she said. "What word?"

I scrambled to think of a word that wasn't arsehole.

"Arson."

"That's not funny, Barry."

I'd forgotten about the fire. Pius had claimed he was sober, but everyone knew he'd gotten into the communion wine before snuffing the candles after mass. Father Molloy smelled the burning from the sacristy and called the fire department. Pius had to give up his altar boy duties after that. And they say *I'm* the one that can't stick things out.

When Mom took Gord to his room for a diaper change, I went downstairs and sat in the front window. I found it comforting, pulling back the sheers and watching people return to their homes after a hard day's work. Especially in the cold, dark months when they'd turn on their lights and I could see right inside their houses. Mrs. Inkpen's dog, Labatt, greeted her every day by stealing one of her nursing shoes after she'd just slipped it off. Mr. O'Brien went straight to his bedroom and changed from his mechanic coveralls to his Snoopy pajama bottoms. They were his favorite. Mr. Power came home and went straight to his wife for a kiss. She'd be in the kitchen cooking and as he'd walk away, loosening his tie, she'd smack his bum. If things were the other way around and the neighbors were watching *my* house, they'd see me move away from the window when Dad pulled up. They'd see me pretend to read *The Herald* as he ruffled my hair, only looking up when he walked away. They'd catch my smile and they'd understand—it's not cool to greet your dad like you're five, not when you're twelve. Except when there's fish and chips involved.

One whiff and I ran to the door. Brown paper bags filled his arms. Grease stained the bottoms and steam rose from the tops. Inside was a feed of Ches's Fish and Chips. I couldn't wait to dig in.

"Grab the Pepsi, Barry."

We moved to the table. Everyone followed their noses and met us there.

"What are we celebrating?" said Pius. "We haven't had Ches's since my birthday six months ago."

"Your birthday was December," said Shelagh. "Try again."

He paused. "Okay, four months. So what? I was close."

She shook her head. "Poor, dumb Pius. It's March. Try using your fingers this time."

He raised his hand. "I'll be using my fingers to smack you across the face in a minute."

"Give it up," said Dad. "Both of ye."

He smiled at Mom. It was a reassuring smile and suddenly I got it. We *were* celebrating. The laundry on the line, the trip to Zellers.

"Excuse me," said Shelagh. "Did anyone hear what Pius just said? He said he was going to smack me. SMACK ME!"

"BAH-DAH!" yelled Gord.

"Oh, shut up, Shelagh," said Pius. "As slapable as your ugly mug is, you know I'd never lay a finger on you."

"Now, now," said Nan. "Let's all calm down and enjoy our Ches's."

"By the way," said Pius. "I hear you and Bob the Schnoz are doing more than running student council."

"Shut up, Pius," said Shelagh.

"Who's Bob the Schnoz?" I asked.

"Bob Myrick. Shelagh's vice president. His nose is the size of the basilica."

"Pius," said Nan. "That's not nice."

"Well, it's true," he said.

Mom rubbed her temples. "You know, I think I might go lie down."

"But I have a song," I blurted.

"A song?" said Dad.

I nodded. "To sing."

"Lovely," said Nan. "What's it called?"

I thought fast.

"'Baby Beluga.'"

"God help us," said Pius.

Mom stood up.

I belted it out.

"Baaa-by be-luuuuu-ga!"

Nan swooned. "God love him. He's got the voice of an angel."

Dad ruffled my hair as he went after Mom. "He sure does."

I sang to my battered cod.

"You can shut up now," said Pius.

But I didn't shut up. I sang until Nan and Gord were my only audience. When the song was over, they clapped.

"Bravo, bravo," said Nan.

"I think I'll go lie down," I said.

"You do that, love," said Nan.

As I left the room, I ruffled the wisps on the top of Gord's head.

*

The next morning I walked into Mr. McGraw's English class in the middle of a vocab test.

He pointed at the door. "I think it's time we had a little chat, don't you?"

"Absolutely," I said. (I'd been wondering why his sweaters had elbow pads and now would be the perfect opportunity to ask.)

Out in the hallway, Mr. McGraw clasped his hands behind his back and rocked back and forth on his feet. "I have two problems with you, Squires."

"Just two?" I said.

(Mrs. Muckle had a trillion.)

"Number one. You're always late—"

I held up my hand. "Whoa there, Trigger. It's a proven fact that people who run late are optometrists—and being full of optometry is a great personality trait."

"Optometry isn't a personality trait," said Mr. McGraw. "It's an occupation."

"You mean I could make an entire career out of posi-tive thinking?"

"The word you're looking for is *optimist*," he said. "Not *optometrist*."

I shrugged. "Ehh, close enough. Starts with an *o*, ends in a *t*. The point is, people who are late don't do it out of laziness or disrespect—they do it because they think they have way more time than they have. Because they're pos-itive thinkers."

Mr. McGraw rubbed his chin. "Interesting."

I waited for him to continue. "What is?"

He re-clasped his hands and resumed rocking. "You've been storming out of my English class for the last six months. Now, a positive thinker would stick each class out, believing that it could only get better, that education is of the utmost importance."

I nodded. "I take it this is problem number two."

"Indeed it is, Finbar."

I rubbed my chin. "Interesting."

"What is?" he asked.

"You seem to be suggesting that my escape-atory behavior is down to a lack of positivity but what's inter-esting is—"

He raised a hand to silence me. "*Escape-atory* is not a word, Finbar."

"Indeed it's not," I said. "But I think we can both agree it should be."

He rolled his eyes.

"Watch yourself," I said. "If the wind changes direction, your eyes will get stuck up in the back of your head forever."

"That's an old wives' tale, Finbar."

"Is it now?" I said. "Then explain to me how it happened to Thomas Budgell's father's sister's daughter."

"You mean Thomas Budgell's cousin."

As usual Mr. McGraw felt the need to complicate things with unnecessary details. I gave him a patient smile. "If you like."

I clasped my hands behind my back and rocked back and forth on my feet. "Now, if you'll allow me to finish. I think you'll be surprised to learn that the reason I storm out of your class is not because of *my* lack of positivity, but because of yours. Take, for example, your incredible disrespect for inter-student engagement. Your constant shushing while I am engaging in meaningful dialogue with my fellow classmates is extremely rude."

"Finbar—"

I raised a hand to silence him. "And this interrupting, sir—it's getting out of control. Not to mention this nasty habit you have of calling me Aleck. You can call me *smart* all you want, but if you don't start calling me by the name my mother lovingly gave me when I was expelled from her womb, you and me are going to have a problem."

He folded his arms. "Are you finished?"

"Not quite," I said. "If you wouldn't mind, I have a question."

He looked intrigued. "Go ahead."

"It's the elbow pads," I said. "I can see getting holes in the knees of your pants, especially if you pray a lot. But what in God's name causes holes in your elbows?"

He caressed the suede pads on his beige wool sweater. "You don't like them?" he said. "I thought they made me look professorial."

"If *professorial* is a fancy word for poor," I said, "you're nailing it."

He looked deflated. "This sweater cost me 39.99."

"I hope you don't mind me saying, sir, but you must have more money than sense."

He sighed.

"I like your shoes, though," I said, even though they were nothing special. "They're really fantabulous."

He smiled. "Thank you, Finbar. Now, the reason I called you out here is—"

"I know, I know," I said. "You have all kinds of problems with me because I'm a horrible person. Don't go thinking you're something special. You're not the only one who thinks so."

I looked to the ceiling. I thought I saw the face of God in a water stain. He was laughing at me.

"Just so you know," said Mr. McGraw, "I'm something of an optimist too."

I heard a rustling sound and cast my eyes downward. In his hand was a pastel blue candy wrapped in translucent paper, the kind they sold in the tourist shops downtown.

"I thought a little incentive might help," he said. "One piece of saltwater taffy every time you make it to the bell. Deal?"

My mouth watered. "Deal."

As we shook on it, I said, "Thank you, sir. I can't think of a better incentive than a colorful confection made from the very waters that surround us on this beautiful, ruggadacious island."

He looked at me thoughtfully. "I don't get it, Finbar. You obviously have a love of words—admittedly you make most of them up, but still. You could do really well in my English class. You just need to apply yourself and focus."

It was easier said than done. The inside of my brain was like one of those wind booths on game shows—the kind where paper money gets blown around and the contestant has to try to grab as many bills as possible. My thoughts were like the money. They were all over the place. I'd try to grab one, but then another would blow by, then another, and another. How could I possibly decide which thought was worth more than the other? It was easier just to let them all blow away.

"Mr. McGraw?"

"Yes?"

"I just want you to know—even if you did have holes in your sweaters and you had to sew on patches because you were too poor to buy new clothes, you'd still be a nice teacher."

"That's a really kind thing to say, Finbar."

The bell rang through the halls.

"Darn," I said. "I guess I'll have to apply myself next time."

Mr. McGraw sighed. "I guess so."

As I walked away, he said, "By the way, saltwater taffy is not actually made of saltwater."

"Perhaps not," I said. "But I think we can both agree that it should be."

★

Later, at recess, I was in the office taking the vocab test I'd missed earlier. It caused the army men in my head to have a war. They fought over what meant what. They used their bayonets to poke holes in my definitions. They shot through my confidence. They marched to the sides of my brain. They wanted out, to the playground, where the cold air made happy faces healthy and red.

"Concentrate, Finbar," said Mrs. Muckle.

I chewed my pencil. "You try concentrating in the middle of World War III."

I answered two more questions, then walked out because, as I said to Judes, recess was my God-given right.

✷

On the walk home from school, it suddenly dawned on me that the answer to *fluke* on the vocab quiz was "a parasitic flatworm" not "when you pass a vocab quiz you didn't study for."

It was the mist that made me realize my mistake. There was a layer on my face that perked me up and made everything clearer. The mist could switch on my brain in an instant—which was weird because water and electricity don't mix.

Maybe, I thought, I could sell the stuff. I'd start by collecting empty spray bottles from all the neighbors on York Street and label them: ST. JOHN'S MIST! CLEARS HEADS INSTANTLY! SATISFACTION GUARANTEED OR YOUR MONEY BACK! Once filled, I'd sell them to tourists for five dollars a bottle. I could become a bloody millionaire!

I made a pit stop at Duckworth and Cochrane to tell Uneven Steven all about it. "Squire," he said, "you won't be a millionaire. You'll be a *billion*aire. You'll be rolling in the bread and honey."

"Bread and honey, money," I said. "I'm practically bilingual now!"

I walked home with a spring in my step.

"Mudder!" I said as I burst through the door. "I need some spray bottles. Pronto."

Nan's face said it all. *Sorry, my duck. She's back in her room again.*

The mist evaporated into thin air.

"But it was some day on clothes."

Nan smiled. "Hormones are a funny thing."

"There's nothing funny about hormones," I said.

Except for that joke Pius told me during church last week:

How do you make a hormone?

Pinch her tit.

Hilarious.

Nan pushed herself up from her rocker. "Let's find you some spray bottles."

I headed upstairs. "Forget it."

Gord was asleep on his side. I sat on the floor and leaned against his cot rails. His chubby cheeks sagged forward and there was a patch of drool on his Humpty Dumpty crib sheet.

I didn't get it. Mom could find happiness on a clothesline but she couldn't find it in Gord's face?

I reached through the slats and put my hand on his arm.

"Wake up, Gord. It's time to get up to no good."

I lifted him out of his crib. The weight of him, it was everything.

I breathed him in. He was a flower I couldn't stop smelling. Even with a soaking wet diaper.

Nan freshened him up.

"Don't take him far."

"I won't."

"One hour."

"I know, I know."

I was well aware of the one-hour poop window. I didn't want to be caught out with a smelly baby just as much as Nan didn't want Gord sitting in a shitty diaper. As for Gord, I don't think he cared either way.

We named the homeowners and house colors on York, then headed downtown.

"Give us a cuddle," said Uneven Steven when we reached his corner.

I passed Gord over like he was one of Nan's buns.

"Here ya go," I said. "Give him a squeeze."

I noticed Steven's sleeping bag. "You sleep out here last night?"

He nodded. "There was a fight down at the shelter over some Persian rugs."

It took a few seconds to register. "Hugs?"

He shook his head. "I thought you were bilingual."

"I am," I said, "but I'm not fluent."

"Drugs," he said. "Anyway, I left when the old bottles and stoppers showed up."

"Coppers," I said. "See? I really get you, Steven."

His eyes welled up.

"Oh, come on," I said. "No need to get all emotional."

Then I realized.

"Gord! Let go of that beard!"

He didn't listen. Babies can't follow simple instructions until they're twelve to fifteen months old. I reached into the hairy unknown and untangled Gord's fingers.

Steven rubbed his chin. "Ta for that, Squire."

We continued on. When we reached Fred's Records, I parked Gord on the sidewalk and went inside. Standing in the front window, I put my lips to the glass and blew. When my cheeks puffed out, Gord laughed.

"Stop drooling on the goddamn glass."

It was the guy behind the counter.

"It's my brother," I said, pointing out the window. "He's only got a few months left to live. I was only trying to give him a few last laughs."

The guy came over with some Windex and a cloth. "You shouldn't joke about things like that."

"It wasn't a joke," I said. "It was a lie."

I pointed at the Windex. "When that bottle's empty can you save it for me?"

He shrugged. "Sure. Why?"

"I'm gonna bottle and sell me some St. John's Mist."

"You're going to sell it to yourself?" he said. "That's a terrible business plan."

"Don't be obtuse," I said.

He snorted. "Like you know what that means."

"Annoyingly insensitive or slow to understand," I said. "It's what my English teacher called me when I asked him how Shake's pear could have possibly written *Romeo and Juliet*. A piece of fruit can't write a book. It doesn't even have hands. When he called me obtuse, I thought he was calling me fat but that's *obese*. If it wasn't for the dictionary, I'd have probably got him fired."

Windex guy laughed. "You're funny, kid."

"I called my brother *fermented* once. What I actually meant was *de*-mented. *Fer*-mented means slowly turning into alcohol. Although he did smell like beer once. After a school dance. He threatened to punch my lights out if I told Mom and Dad. I like words. If only they weren't so easily confused."

The guy put down his cleaning supplies and stuck out his hand. "I'm Tony."

I ignored his hand and sang, "Tony Chestnut Knows I Love You." I pointed to all the right body parts at all the right times: toe, knee, chest, head, nose, eyes, and heart. I ended with a big double-point at Tony.

"You're weird, kid."

"I sing that one to Gord all the time."

I looked out the window.

"God almighty!"

I ran outside to find Gord rolling down Duckworth.

"Somebody catch that baby!"

I caught him just as he rolled onto Prescott.

I said, "Don't cry, Gord," but he wasn't crying—he was laughing his sweet baby belly laugh.

I laughed too. "You're cracked, Gord."

We continued on, passing a tourist shop full of T-shirts and souvenirs. I pictured St. John's Mist in the front window. It could be a bestseller.

Down at the harbor there was a cruise ship as tall as Atlantic Place. It had been in Ireland and Florida and New York. I hoped they weren't expecting spring weather. I could almost see my breath today. Gord and I smiled as the passengers filed off. "Go to Caines if you want a real Newfoundland experience," I told them. "Boo makes a mean Jiggs Dinner."

An older woman in a yellow leisure suit stopped. "What's a Jiggs Dinner?" she asked.

"Salt beef, cabbage, potatoes, turnip, and carrots," I said. "All boiled together into a delicious concoction of salty goodness."

She smiled at her husband. "These Newfies sure are friendly."

Nan hated the word Newfie. She said it was a slur. Mom, on the other hand, didn't mind it at all. I was about to tell the woman to be careful, that using the term could cause offense, when her husband passed me a five-dollar bill. "Here ya go, champ." I tucked the money into my pocket. Five dollars' worth of candy at Caines was worth way more than giving a lesson on social justice. I gave the husband a wink. "Thanks, skipper."

Next to the cruise ship was a navy ship offering tours. The sign said ALL CHILDREN MUST BE ACCOMPANIED BY AN ADULT, so Gord and I quickly slipped on behind a blue-eyed family of four. We were heading up the gangplank when another kid tagged along behind us. I gave his brown skin a once-over. "Take a hike. You're going to blow our cover."

"Frig off, b'y," he said. "I'll do what I likes, how I likes, whenever I likes it."

His Newfoundland accent was thicker than mine. "Sorry. I thought—"

"I knows what ya thought," he said. "It's called stereo-typing. Give me a cut of that money you fleeced off that tourist and we'll forget all about it."

I liked this kid. He was a sly one. A real sleveen. Like me.

"How about we go to Caines after the tour?" I said. "I'll buy you a bag of roast chicken chips."

"Throw in a bottle of birch beer and you've got a deal."

I gave him a wink. "Done."

The blond family was moving to the upper deck. "Come on," he said. "Mom and Dad will wonder where we're to."

I laughed. "Like anyone's gonna believe you belong to them."

"Whatever," he said. "If we gets kicked off, we gets kicked off. There's plenty of other no good to get up to today."

I grinned. "I'm Finbar. You can call me Barry."

"Saibal," he said. "Saibal Sharma."

"Sigh-bull," I repeated. "Bulls don't sigh."

"That's because they're too busy running around china shops," he said.

"Ha!" I said. "Good one."

I tried to pull Gord out of his stroller. "Come on, fatso." Saibal helped.

We sang the Village People's "In the Navy" as we climbed the stairs to the upper deck. We were met with disapproving frowns.

A navy man glared at us. "Could you keep it down? I'm *trying* to give a presentation here."

I gave him a jaunty salute. "Aye, aye, captain."

The presentation was boring. Saibal rolled his eyes. I pretended to yawn. The navy man asked if there were any questions. I raised my hand.

"What's long and hard and full of seamen?"

Except for Saibal's snort beside me, the deck fell silent.

"That's very inappropriate," said the navy man.

"Inappropriate how?" asked Saibal. "The answer's 'a submarine.'"

I spoke to Gord in a baby voice. "Some people have the dirtiest minds, don't they?"

The navy man growled. "Where are your parents?"

I looked at the family nearby. The father looked away. "Dad," I said. "How could you?"

The navy man moved toward us.

"Run!" said Saibal.

We took off down the stairs. Saibal snatched the stroller for a quick getaway. When we got out of sight, he set it back down.

"You, sir," I said, "are a scholar and a gentleman."

Saibal looked impressed.

We settled Gord into his seat and headed down Water Street.

At the war memorial, Saibal paused. "Hang on."

He approached a couple of tourists and spoke in a singsong-y accent. "Can you spare some change for a poor refugee? I am so verrry, verrry hungry."

He came back with a handful of coins.

"Geez, b'y," I said. "If you rolled your *r*'s any harder, you'd break your tongue."

"Nah," he said. "My mother tongue is so thick, you'd need a sledgehammer to break it."

At Caines, Boo thanked me for sending tourists his way and gave us 20 percent off. Saibal used his change to buy a bowl of turkey soup, and when we got outside he gave it to a woman begging on the corner.

We sat on the cold, brown grass near the war memorial. Saibal held Gord in his lap.

"You know," I said, opening my birch beer, "you were kind of stereotyping *yourself* with those tourists."

"Hey," he said, "if people are going to assume I'm a refugee, I might as well work it to my advantage."

"People around here wouldn't assume that," I said.

He gave Gord a lick of his chip. "*You* did."

"No, I didn't."

"Yes, you did. When you told me to take a hike, you

made a walking gesture with your fingers because you figured I didn't speak English."

"I did?"

He popped the Gord-licked chip into his mouth. "Yep."

"Oh. Sorry about that. But, for the most part, I think Newfoundlanders are pretty open to people of different races."

"Do me a favor, Finbar," he said. "Don't act like you know what it's like to be brown in this town, because you don't."

"Ha! Brown in this town. That rhymes."

Saibal grinned. "Yeah. I'm a poet and didn't even comprehend that that was the case."

I laughed. "You can call me Barry, by the way."

"I think I'll stick with Finbar," he said.

"Why?"

He drained the last of his birch beer. "Because only a Finbar would call me a scholar and a gentleman. A Barry could never be so distinguished."

"Righty-ho," I said, standing up and dusting myself off. "Finbar it is."

I put Gord back in his stroller and tipped an imaginary hat to Saibal. "Now I must bid you good day. See you tomorrow?"

He smiled. "I'll be here."

CHAPTER FOUR

Back at home, I watched *Riverdance* for ten minutes. I didn't feel the need to watch any more. After all, I had the technical side of Irish step dancing down pat. What I needed to work on was balance and light-footedness. Mom said if I broke one more of her grandmother's tea-cups, she'd nail my feet to the floor. I said, "You'd crucify me over a broken cup?" and she said, "Those cups are bone china, you know."

I decided that in order to dance with lightness and grace, I'd need to dress the part. I went to Nan's closet. It was full of possibilities. (And lacy garments I'd never unsee.) I tried on a white blouse with frilly sleeves. In a move that could only be described as bold, I left the bottom few buttons undone so that I could tie the ends together just above my belly button. A button fell off, but that was okay. Nan said being an artiste was about breaking boundaries and I was awesome at breaking things.

Michael Flatley would never wear polyester slacks from Kmart, so I moved from Nan's closet to my sister's, where I borrowed on a permanent basis a pair of her black leggings. For the first time in my life I was jealous of the female sex. They could keep their periods and maxi-pads and cramps and bras . . . but leggings? They were like a second skin. I knew without a doubt that these super-stretchy wonder pants were going to make my wildest dreams possible. I, Finbar T. Squires, was going to end my routine with the splittiest splits in the history of dance.

It was time to put the training program I'd dreamt up the night before into action. It was really quite good. Groundbreaking, even. Someday I'd make an instructional video for other dancers. I mean, why keep such a secret weapon to myself? But sharing my untested-but-sure-to-be-brilliant idea with the masses would have to wait—I had the performance of a lifetime to prepare for.

I went to the basement and put on the footwear that would revolutionize the dance world.

Hockey skates.

I walked around and around in circles.

The blades made a satisfying click on the concrete floor.

I was a bit wobbly at first but by the tenth lap I was feeling incredibly stable. It was as if I was wearing a pair of Nan's orthopedic shoes. I stood on one foot for forty-five seconds, then switched to the other. Incredibly, both my core and butt muscles were engaged.

This was SO going to work as a training program for dancers. I mean, everyone could get their hands on a pair of skates, and now I could claim proven results in only five minutes!

If only my training program had a name.

I walked around in circles and thought some more.

I needed something catchy. Something fierce.

Then it hit me.

The Balance and Stability Training Academy 4 Real Dancers.

BASTARD for short.

I decided it was time for a dress rehearsal. I mean, why hide my talent away in a basement?

I floated up the stairs with Shelagh's portable CD player in tow and went out to the road where there were no china cabinets to shake or teacups to break. I was feeling pretty positive. If I could Irish step dance in hockey skates, just imagine what I could do in the tap shoes I was planning to borrow on a permanent basis from Billy Walsh!

Little Len from next door came outside and watched as I set up in the middle of the road. I gave him a wink. "Enjoy the show."

I pressed Play, not really caring what came on (I could dance to anything), and got into my opening position (the matador one). When Michael Jackson's "Thriller" blasted through the speakers, I moon-skated from the Coadys' front door to the Merchants'. The blades screeched against the pavement like nails on a chalkboard. I told Little Len to turn up the music. Neighbors emerged from their front doors. I pinned my arms to my sides and broke out into a mighty fine step dance. As a nod to the King of Pop, I interspersed the Irishness of my performance with a few crotch grabs and pelvic thrusts. I grabbed the sky and when I brought it to my heart, I saw faces filling the second-floor windows, and by God those faces were smiling. Not only was I breaking barriers in the dance world, I was single-handedly bringing happiness to the people of York Street.

It was time for my big finish.

I waited for the music to end.

Then—

R-i-i-i-i-p.

The splittiest splits really were the splittiest.

A cold blast of air wafted through the arse of my wonder pants.

I quickly sat on my knees and smiled at God.

In the silence that followed, I heard a scream.

"Get my bloody skates off your bloody feet!"

I turned around. As Pius got closer, his anger turned to horror. "What the hell are you wearing?"

I rolled onto my arse and tried to bum-scootch away, but Pius pulled me along by the blades.

"Pius! Stop! I'm getting road burn!"

He dragged me to the sidewalk and roughly tugged off the skates.

"Good God, Barry. You're such an embarrassment."

I followed him, stocking-footed, toward the house. Nan and Gord were in the doorway. Nan started to clap. Good ol' Nan. One person clapping was always followed by another, then another . . . that's how it worked. I looked around. The neighbors just stood there like a bunch of bastards.

When Nan's applause trailed off, I bowed, because the number one rule in the entertainment biz is never let them see you sweat. On the outside I was as cool as a cucumber, but on the inside I felt a growling, deep inside my belly. I gave a final wink and a wave before stepping into the house, where I immediately swung for Pius. He caught my arm. "Calm down, Fin-bear."

"You ruined my performance," I growled.

"You dulled my blades," he said.

"I was *trying* to making my dream a reality."

He let go of my arm with a shove. "How is dressing like a pirate and dancing on hockey skates a dream?"

"I was practicing," I said. "Success doesn't come overnight, you know."

"You'll never be a dancer, Barry," he said. "You've got terrible rhythm and no pizzazz."

"How dare you?" I yelled.

"Baaaaa-daaaaa!" yelled Gord.

"Shhh," said Nan, bouncing Gord in her arms. "Your mother's resting."

Shelagh walked in with an armful of books. "Are those my leggings?"

I shook my head. "No."

She looked closer. "They are. I can't believe you're wearing my leggings."

"I don't know what you're talking about," I said.

She gestured to my crotch. "Ew. Gross. Your *thing* is stretching the material."

I looked down. My crotchticular region *was* looking rather pronounced. I smiled. "Thanks, Shelagh."

"You should see the back of them," said Pius. "He's torn the arse right out of them."

"Mom! Barry wrecked my leggings!"

"Shhh," said Nan.

"And he's wearing Nan's shirt!" Pius called.

"For the love of God," said Nan. "Keep it down."

But we didn't want to keep it down.

"Aaaaaaaaaaah!" I shouted.

We looked to the ceiling. A moment later, a bed squeak. We waited for a "Jesus, Mary, and Joseph, will ye give it a rest," but all we heard was silence.

Shelagh and Pius looked to the floor.

I cleared my throat and hooked my thumbs into my waistband.

Shelagh looked up. "What are you doing?"

"You wanted your pants back, didn't you?"

"Oh, for God's sake," said Nan.

I wiggled my hips from side to side. Shelagh covered her eyes. "Please don't."

I slid the leggings down to my ankles.

Pius grinned. "You're cracked, Barry."

I slipped one foot out, then the other.

"Here you go," I said, holding them out for Shelagh. "You wanted them. Take them."

When she uncovered her eyes, I swung them through the air like a lasso. I gyrated my hips with each spin.

"Ew, Barry," she screamed. "Stop that!"

"Oh my God," said Pius. "He's got a hole in his undies."

They were laughing but that was the point. If making them smile involved a sneak peek at my genitalia, then so be it.

I spun the leggings two, three, four more times and then let them go. They flew through the air and landed on Shelagh's head. We laughed loudly; Gord too. I wondered if Mom was listening upstairs. I hoped she was. I hoped she knew what she was missing.

★

Takeout meant Mom didn't feel like cooking, and when Mom didn't feel like cooking, Nan and Dad usually didn't bother either—they just threw their hands up in the air as if to say, "What's the point?" As for the rest of us, well, we wouldn't know how to cook if our lives depended on it—which they kind of did, really. I mean, if you didn't eat, you'd die. Maybe that was what Mom wanted. To die. After all, she barely ate. All she'd had for breakfast that morning was three single Cheerios. She'd picked them off Gord's chin when I brought him to her for a cuddle. I was thrilled when I saw how he made her smile but on reflection it was no big deal. I mean, you'd have to be the Wicked Witch of the West not to smile at Gord.

I sat in the front window watching neighbors coming and going. There was condensation on the glass. I drew a penis. There was a doily on a side table next to me. I put it on my head. Our car puttered up and pulled over. I let the window sheers drop and waited. A moment later

Dad came in. He had six cold plates from Caines. "What do you have on your head, you fool?" I pulled off the doily and he ruffled my hair. We sat at the table, all six of us. Mom's supper was in the fridge. When I was done eating, I brought it up to her. I sat at the foot of her bed and watched her nibble the turkey, pick at the potato salad, and lick a beet. She seemed interested in my description of Mrs. Muckle's fantabulous shoes, and when I told her the rumor about old Judes having an affair with Roger Graham from Graham's Groceries, her eyebrows went up. I hadn't seen Mom's eyebrows go up in a long time, so I told her that Mrs. Muckle and Roger Graham were caught having an intimate moment in the walk-in freezer at Graham's Groceries. It wasn't true but Mom smiled in disgust, so I kept going. "Mrs. Graham caught them," I said. "Mrs. Muckle claimed that Mr. Graham was just warming her up, but Mrs. Graham said she wasn't born yesterday and slammed the door on them. The next morning a cashier found them and called 911. It took them three days to thaw out." Mom's eyebrows went up again, this time in doubt. I'd gone too far. "How about these cold plates?" I said. "Pretty good, huh?"

"They're okay," she said, pushing aside the savory dressing.

"Boo makes that himself, you know," I said. "He calls it *stuffing*, for the Americans who come off the cruise ships. Even *they* think it's the best part of the cold plate."

"It's delicious," said Mom. "I'm just not that hungry right now."

"Guess what?" I said, thinking up another lie. "At school we went on a field trip to Mount Scio Farm, where savory is made."

"Is that right?" said Mom.

"Yep. The owner said savory has many health benefits. It helps with sore muscles, concentration, energy, and mood."

I raised my eyebrows when I said *mood*.

Mom stared at her dinner with wet eyes.

I reached for the plate. "I'll take this downstairs."

"Leave it," she said.

I looked at the flowers on her nightgown. They were forget-me-nots, the kind Dad wore on his lapel on Memorial Day. I chewed the skin around my thumbnail. Mom reached out, lowered my hand.

"Tell me more about Mrs. Muckle and Roger Graham," she said.

I let out the breath I didn't know I'd been holding.

"Well," I said, "apparently Mrs. Muckle had frostbite on her nipples."

Mom scooped up some dressing and smiled.

★

Later that evening, I sat on Gord's floor and sang him a bedtime song. I made a different one up each night. Tonight's was called "The Lovely Lass with the Gargantuan Ass." It was about a girl who let her siblings use her butt as a pillow. My favorite line was "The sea of children suddenly parted when the lovely lass unexpectedly farted."

Coincidentally, later in bed, Pius let one rip.

I said, "Remind me to never use your butt as a pillow."

He stuck his nose further into his book. "Shut up, weirdo."

I closed my eyes, then opened them again.

"Pius? Do you think Mom—"

"I said shut up."

He put his book down and turned off the light.

I closed my eyes once again and drifted off to dreamland, where Saibal and I shared a birch beer in India.

★

The next morning, I had a few minutes to spare, so I plunked down on Uneven Steven's piece of cardboard and told him every detail of my performance on York Street the day before.

"You wore a frilly top and your sister's leggings?" he said.

"Yep. But, to be honest, I'm not sure I'm cut out for this dancing malarkey. My brother says I have no pizzazz. Maybe I should just drop the whole thing."

"Don't be daft," said Steven. "Do you think I would have played with the Beatles in '64 if I had given up on my dream?"

I smiled. "You played with the Beatles? Wow. That's impressive."

"Don't listen to the naysayers, Squire. I believe in you."

I gathered my things and stood up. "So you'll come to the performance at the nursing home?"

Steven grinned. "I wouldn't miss it."

★

I went straight to the office and pointed at the clock.

"Look! It's 9:05."

Mrs. Muckle reached under her desk and pulled out a bag.

"For you."

I looked inside. "An alarm clock?"

She nodded. "Mr. McGraw got it down at the Sally Ann."

I was both touched and horrified.

I gestured to the chair across from her. "May I?"

She poured herself a cup of tea. "Two minutes."

I took a seat. "I have a new friend," I said. "He's a refugee. From India."

Mrs. Muckle looked intrigued. "Really?"

"I met him downtown. I bought him some birch beer because his lips were dry. I don't think he'd had a drop to drink in days."

She raised an eyebrow.

"Come to think of it," I said, smacking my lips together, "I'm feeling a tad parched myself."

She poured some tea into a second mug. "You're only getting half a cup."

I shook my head. "If we all had your attitude, Judes, refugees would be dying of thirst all over the place."

She set the pot down. "Don't call me Judes."

I took a slurp of my tea. "Guess what?"

"What?"

"If I fail eighth grade, we'll get to spend another year together."

"You're not going to fail eighth grade, Barry."

"I might."

"You won't. Your grades are just about good enough. Thanks be to Jesus."

"But if I did, it'd be okay, right? I mean, another year might do me good."

"Barry, I know going to a new school is scary—"

"I'm not scared."

I took another slurp of my tea.

"Guess what else?" I said, changing the subject.

Mrs. Muckle sighed. "What?"

"Gord can sit up for six seconds without falling on his face."

Her face lit up. "Is that right?"

I beamed with pride. "He's pretty advanced for his age."

"And how's your mother?" she asked.

Dad had been in to talk to Mrs. Muckle about "the situation" and now she was nosier than ever. Caring, almost.

"She's like a yo-yo," I said.

"Up and down?" said Mrs. Muckle.

I nodded. "She didn't even eat the dressing on her cold plate last night. I mean, where would we be if we all refused savory when we felt a little down? It's our duty as Newfoundlanders to eat it. I mean, if Mount Scio Farm goes out of business, we're doomed. We might as well kiss goodbye all that makes us stand out as a unique culture."

"Don't be so foolish," said Mrs. Muckle. "Mount Scio Farm will never go out of business. Savory is like crack around here."

"If it was like crack," I said, "Mom would have wolfed down her supper like there was no tomorrow. But maybe she doesn't care about tomorrows—maybe she just cares about herself, and that's why she stays in her room all day and leaves the rest of us wandering around wondering if she'll ever come out."

Mrs. Muckle reached for me. "Barry—"

I pulled my hand away. "Thanks a bunch, Judes. Your prying has made me late for class. And on the one day I show up early too."

She looked at the clock. "I suppose 9:05 *is* early by your standards."

I drained my tea and made a face. "Where did ya get your teabags? The bottom of St. John's Harbour? You'd think on a principal's salary you could get some bags made with quality leaves. What are ya? From the mainland or something? Geez."

She sighed. "That's enough, Barry."

"Is it?" I said. "I'm not so sure. I could go on about this for days. Because that tea tastes like crap. Like actual crap. Like a cup of warmed-up shit."

Mrs. Muckle stood up. "Get out, Barry."

"My pleasure," I said.

I wasn't lying. It *was* a pleasure. Things were back to normal. I was the annoyer and she was the annoyee. Anything more than that involved feelings, and the last thing I wanted to feel was feelings.

I stood in front of Mr. McGraw's door and took a deep breath. A moment later I waltzed in like I owned the place.

"Top o' the morning, Mr. McGraw. How's it hanging?"

"You're late, Finbar. You need to get a late slip from Mrs. Muckle."

"Mrs. Muckle?" I said. "That old windbag is the reason I'm late. She invited me for tea in her office and spent a good twenty minutes talking about the quality of her bags."

Mr. McGraw looked skeptical. I nodded to the phone on the wall. "Call her if you want."

He shook his head. "Just sit down and get to work."

I paused before heading to my desk. "Might I ask, sir, does our little 'incentive' deal still apply even though I'm a tad late?"

He looked at the clock and nodded. There was still forty minutes left and I was in the mood for saltwater taffy. If I made it to the end of class, I'd pick a blue one.

I took my seat. We'd been working on our persuasive essays. Mine was blank except for the stick man I'd drawn in the margins. His name was Twig.

I gave Twig a hat.

Everyone around me was writing furiously.

I wondered what I could write about.

I gave Twig a penis and laughed out loud. Mr. McGraw gave me a warning look.

I gave Twig a pair of tartan pants.

And a vest.

Good old Twig. He was an inspiration.

I wrote my title: *Why I Should Be Given One Hundred and Twenty-Five Dollars for a Tartan Outfit and Tap Shoes.*

I looked to the ceiling and thought about what being a Full Tilt Dancer would mean to me. I started with "Dancing is my life" and thought some more.

I stared at the back of Karen Crocker's head. Her braids were uneven. I tapped her on the shoulder. "Who did your hair this morning? Your one-eyed nan or your drunk mother?"

Her hand shot up in the air. "Sir, Barry thinks he's funny but he's not."

Mr. McGraw's warning look got warn-ier.

Damian Clarke was in the desk across from me. He leaned over. "Guess what? My essay is almost done. It's called 'Why Everyone in St. John's Should Chip In and Get Barry Squires Some Plastic Surgery for That Thing on His Face.'"

Normally I'd have punched him in the nose but there was the saltwater taffy to think of—not to mention Mr. McGraw's undying faith in me.

I raised my hand. "Sir? Would you happen to have a thesaurus? I'm writing my essay on 'Why I Hate Damian Clarke,' but I'm overusing the word *arsehole*."

Mr. McGraw frowned. "Mind your mouth, Finbar."

"I'm sorry," I said, "but I'm running out of descripatory words. I mean, I've used *dickhead* ten times already, and I've positively exhausted the word *fuckface*."

Mr. McGraw walked toward me in a rage.

I put my hands up. "Whoa there, Trigger—"

He grabbed me by the elbow. "Out."

"Geez," I said. "You really don't want me to have that saltwater taffy, do you?"

He pulled me out of the classroom and into the hallway. He put his face in mine and said, "Don't act like I'm the one breaking the deal here. You know exactly what you're doing."

Something inside me shook. It felt like my heart but it was probably my soul.

"Well?" he said. "What are you waiting for? You've got what you wanted. You're free to go. Have fun hiding in Mrs. Muckle's office all day."

I tried to think of something to say that would make his face go from red to its normal pasty white.

"Tomorrow will be different," I said. "I'm going to write the best, most heartfelt essay you've ever read. It'll be enough to bring a tear to a glass eye."

He rolled his eyes.

"Watch yourself," I said. "Remember what I said about Thomas Budgell's father's sister's daughter."

He didn't laugh.

"Just go, Barry," he said. "I've got a class full of students waiting to learn. I've spent enough time on you."

For some reason my feet wouldn't move.

McGraw waved me away. "Go."

"Sir, I . . ."

What I wanted to say was stuck in my throat. "Damian, he . . ." I put my hand to my cheek. It was such a small part of me—why was it the whole to everyone else?

"Finbar," said Mr. McGraw. "You can't control what other people say, but you can control how you react to them."

Billy Walsh appeared in the hallway. When he saw us, he step danced his way to the bathroom. Mr. McGraw applauded. It didn't surprise me. The Full Tilt Dancers were gods in this school.

"Maybe," I said, "step dancing could be the whole of me."

Mr. McGraw looked puzzled. "What?"

"Nothing."

I felt his eyes on me as I walked away.

As I turned the corner, I saw him fiddling with something in his pocket.

I wasn't too fond of saltwater taffy anyway.

★

Damian passed me in the hallway. "Look who it is! Chardonnay!"

I could've just told him that chardonnay was actually a white wine. That would've been enough to shut him up. But I punched him in the nose instead. The gym teacher heard the ruckus and dragged us to the office by the scruff of our necks.

Mrs. Muckle gave Damian a wad of tissues for his nose and sent him to the nurse.

She gave me a look of despair and told me to write an apology.

I settled into my desk. "I'll do my very best to make this genuine," I promised. "No matter how long it takes."

Then I began:

Dear Damian,
I'm sorry you are an arshole . . .

Mrs. Muckle looked over my shoulder. "Your *arsehole* is missing an *e*."

"An *e*?" I said. "That would make it *earshole*. Damian's full of shit, not wax."

She pointed to the door. "Out. You know how I feel about swearing."

"Actually," I said, "I *don't* know how you feel about swearing. I mean, how is *shit* worse than *arsehole*? And where does the f-word fit in? Maybe you could make me an easy-to-follow flowchart. I'd like to know where you stand on all this."

She walked to the door and opened it. "Go."

Poor woman, she was completely frazzled. I stood outside her office and gave her a moment to compose herself. When I returned thirty seconds later, she looked like a deer caught in the headlights.

"Oh, Judes," I said. "Don't you know you can't fill the emptiness inside you with food?"

She shouted "out!" again. A piece of Twix flew from her mouth. It landed by my foot. I wasn't sure what to do. Leaving it there seemed wrong. Especially when there were children starving in Africa. I picked it up and offered it to her. "Did you want this or . . ."

Her face turned the color of her fantabulous slut shoes.

I gave her a wide berth as I walked to the garbage bin under her desk. I paused behind her.

"I hope you don't mind me saying," I said, "but you seem a bit on edge. Perhaps you shouldn't be alone right now. I'll stay if you like. Just for one more period. Even though I'd hate to miss math."

"You can stay," she sighed. "But if I hear another word out of you . . ."

I dropped the Twix chunk in the garbage and backed away with my hands up. "You won't even know I'm here."

I sat down and rubbed my hands together over the apology letter. "Now," I said. "Time to return to the task I'd been working on so enthusiastically before you interrupted me with your nitpicky criticism."

She sucked in her breath.

I turned to her. "You know, you need to be more mindful of your breathing," I said. "Especially if you want to find inner peace." I stuck my fingers in my ears. "Watch and learn."

I inhaled through my nose, then exhaled through my mouth. *Bzzzzzzz.*

"Bumblebee breathing," I said. "I learned it at an anger management class my mother forced me to go to. It relieves stress, especially the angry kind. Apparently it takes a lot of practice. It hasn't worked for me yet. Which is not surprising. I'm not good at anything."

She threw me the other half of her Twix. "You're good at driving me nuts, I can tell ya that."

I wasn't sure that was the most appropriate thing for a school official to say to a student, but I gave her a wink and took a bite of the bar. "You're the bee's knees, Judes."

CHAPTER FIVE

After school I bundled Gord up and went to the war memorial. Saibal was already there with two birch beers and a giant sour key for Gord.

"He can't have that," I said. "He has no teeth."

Saibal put his pointer finger through the hole in the top and popped the long end in Gord's mouth.

"You don't need teeth to suck," he said. "And don't worry, I'll hold it so he doesn't choke."

Gord made a sour face on the first lick.

"He doesn't like it," I said.

A second later he was leaning forward with his tongue out, gagging for more.

"He loves it," said Saibal, popping it back in. "Just make sure you rinse his mouth out after so he doesn't get cavities."

"Even though he has no teeth?" I said, opening my can of pop. "Duly noted."

Saibal looked impressed. "You really have a way with words, Finbar."

"I have to admit," I said, "for the longest time I thought it was *Julie noted*. Then I saw it written down."

"Imagine if your name was Julie," he said. "Instead of saying okay, you could say 'Julie noted.'"

"Julie, dear, don't forget you have a dentist appointment at three," I said.

"Julie noted," said Saibal in a female voice.

I laughed and pointed to my face. "This is a port-wine stain, by the way."

Saibal wiped some drool off Gord's chin. "So?"

"I just thought you might be wondering."

"Why would I?"

I shrugged. "I dunno."

He crushed his empty can with his one hand. "So. What no good should we get up to today?"

"I want to buy a *Playboy* magazine."

"Ew," said Saibal.

"Not for me," I said. "For Billy Walsh. I need to borrow

his tap shoes. I figure a naked lady magazine would be a good trade."

"What makes you think he'd want a *Playboy* magazine?"

"He looks like a bit of a pervert."

Saibal shrugged. "Fair enough."

I puffed out my chest. "Guess what? I'm going to be a Full Tilt Dancer."

"Really?" said Saibal. "I tried out last year but Father Molloy said I wasn't a good fit."

He put finger quotes around the word *fit*.

"What are you suggesting?" I said.

"I'm suggesting I didn't have the right look."

He didn't put quotes around the word *look*, but I caught his drift.

"Father Molloy may be a fedora-wearing thieving jerk," I said, "but he's no racist."

Saibal frowned. "How do you know?"

"I just do."

"How?"

"Because Newfoundlanders aren't like that."

"Do tell," said Saibal, popping the sour key from Gord's mouth to his own.

"Way back in history," I said, "there was a Black man from the US who ended up on a beach in Newfoundland after a shipwreck. People saved him and nursed him back to good health and he was amazed because back at home, white people weren't nice to him. In Newfoundland, he was treated like all the other survivors."

Saibal threw the soggy sour key in the grass. "Nice story. Now tell me, how does that prove Father Molloy can't be racist?"

"It doesn't."

"Exactly."

"I'm just saying—"

"Don't be so naive, Finbar. Open your eyes and look around."

I did.

"Get a room!" I shouted to a couple making out under a tree.

Saibal laughed. "Come on," he said. "Time to buy some porn."

We headed toward Water Street.

The panhandlers knew Saibal by name.

"How come I've never seen you around here before?" I asked.

"I live in King William Estates," he said. "I wasn't allowed to get the bus until I turned twelve."

"King William Estates, huh? You must be loaded."

"My dad's a family doctor and my mom's a cardiologist."

"Does she use those big paddles like they do on TV?"

Saibal jumped in front of me and hit my chest with an imaginary defibrillator. "Clear!"

I jolted with an almighty shock.

"What do *your* parents do?" asked Saibal.

"Nothing as good as yours," I said. "Mom was a lunch lady before Gord was born and Dad fixes clocks."

"Interesting," said Saibal, even though it wasn't.

When we got to Atlantic Place, Saibal helped me carry the stroller up the steps.

The top shelf of the magazine shop had lots of choices.

"What do you think, Saibal?" I said. "They have *Penthouse* and *Hustler* too."

"Get the *Playboy*," he said. "Then, when you give it to Billy Walsh, you can say, 'A *Playboy* for a playboy.'"

I grinned. "I like the way you think, Saibal."

The lady behind the counter wouldn't sell us the magazine, so I gave it to Gord. When he ripped the cover in half, Saibal pointed to the YOU BREAK IT, YOU BUY IT sign. He slapped a five-dollar bill on the counter. "That should cover it."

We left before she could protest.

Back on Water Street, Saibal said, "When you think about it, my mom and your dad do the same thing. They both get things ticking again."

I liked that Saibal thought my dad and his mom were the same. I pictured my dad standing over a timepiece shouting, "Clear!"

"What are you smiling about?" said Saibal.

"Nothing," I said. "Come on. It's time to trade some porn for a dream."

★

The dancers practiced at the Benevolent Irish Society, or BIS as we called it. I caught Billy Walsh's eye from the window. A moment later, he was outside.

"What do you want, Squires?"

I gave him a devilish grin.

"A *Playboy*," I said, "for a playboy."

He looked confused. "What?"

Saibal elbowed me in the ribs. "Finbar. The magazine."

I looked around. "Gord! You dirty thing!"

His face was right in the centerfold.

I gave the magazine to Billy and proposed the deal. His eyes widened as he scanned the pages. He took his shoes off right then and there.

"I want them back in good condition."

I told him he could keep the magazine.

We went back to York Street to drop the shoes off.

When I got to the doorstep, Nan looked beyond me into the street.

"Who's that?" she said.

"That's Saibal," I said. "He's my—"

"Why is he on the curb?" she said. "Is he begging?"

"No, he—"

"He's begging, isn't he? Poor little thing. These refugees, they have a hard time when they first arrive, God love 'em."

"Nan. He's not—"

"Come over, my ducky," she yelled. "Come in and I gives ya some supper."

Saibal walked over and took Nan's hand in both of his. "Thank you so verrry, verrry much. I am so verrry, verrry hungry."

Nan was charmed. "God love his cotton socks."

I elbowed him in the side. "Drop the act, will ya? It's annoying."

He smiled. "I'm just filling the role that is expected of me," he whispered.

"Come in, come in," said Nan. "I'm just about to put supper on the table."

It was a home-cooked meal for once and I was glad. Mom's empty chair was a lot less depressing when we weren't eating off paper plates.

There was also a rack of freshly baked tea buns cooling in the kitchen. Saibal reached for one. "May I?"

I'd have had my hand smacked this close to supper but Nan smiled and said, "Yes, my duck. Take as many as you want."

Pius strutted in and nodded toward Saibal. "Who's that?"

"A refugee," whispered Nan. "Starved to death, the poor thing."

Pius passed him another bun.

When Dad and Shelagh came in, it was the same. One whisper from Nan and they were filled with compassion.

"I should call home," said Saibal, his accent thick. "Hopefully my mother can make it to the phone. Her legs, they do not work so well anymore. And my father, well, he is probably out begging."

I ignored the collective "awww" from my family and pulled Saibal roughly into the living room. "How long are you planning on keeping this up?"

He patted his stomach. "Until my tummy is verrry, verrry full."

His fake accent was getting on my last nerve.

He picked up the phone and called home. "What are ya at, Mudder? Me? I'm fine. Best kind. Listen, I got invited to a friend's house for supper. Yup . . . yup . . . yup. Okay, Mudder. Loves ya."

He hung up. "I have to get the seven-thirty bus back to King William," he said. "I hope I have time for dessert. If your nan's tea buns are anything to go by, dessert's gonna be tasty."

We turned toward the kitchen to find Pius standing at the door with his arms crossed. "I have to say," he said, "I'm verrry, verrry disappointed."

"Saibal's just filling the role that is expected of him," I said.

"Whatever," said Pius. "Ten bucks and I'll keep my mouth shut."

Saibal pulled a leather wallet out of his back pocket and gave Pius a ten-dollar bill.

At the supper table, Saibal asked if someone could pass the ketchup for his fried bologna.

"Your English is so good," yelled Dad.

"Bah-gah!" yelled Gord.

Nan put another slice of bologna on Saibal's plate. "Look at him. He's skin and bones."

He was anything but. Saibal had broad shoulders, a full, round face—he was the picture of health.

Pius passed Saibal the ketchup. "You know, Saibal," he said, "what you're eating there is pretty rare. It's not very often a hunter comes across the wild bologna. Fierce creatures, they are. They'd bite the hand right off ya."

Saibal laughed. "Go on wit' ya, b'y. We all knows this bologna was sliced off the Maple Leaf Big Stick."

There was a collective gasp.

"He's a bloody Newfoundlander!" said Shelagh.

"He took advantage of my good nature!" said Nan.

"He ate all the tea buns!" said Dad.

"Bah-gah!" yelled Gord.

Saibal just kept eating. That's how good fried bologna is.

"He was just filling the role that was expected of him," I said.

Mom walked in in her dressing gown. "Who's this?"

"Barry's new friend," said Dad. "He's a real little scoundrel."

Mom sat down. "So they're two peas in a pod, then."

Nan jabbed a bony finger in Saibal's direction. "I made trifle for dessert. And you, young man, are getting one scoop. Just like everyone else."

"Just like everyone else, eh?" said Saibal. "Sounds good to me."

★

I walked Saibal to the bus stop.

"Sorry about that. It's like they've never seen a brown person before."

"Well, there aren't a lot of visible minorities in this city."

I wrapped my arm around his shoulder. "I bet by the time we're twenty, St. John's will look like a rainbow."

"In case you haven't noticed," said Saibal, "brown isn't a color of the rainbow."

"Neither is white."

"I bet you turn red in the summer, though," he said.

"Fair point," I said

Saibal looked at his watch. "We have ten minutes before the bus comes. Want to go get up to no good?"

"Sure," I said. "Let's go throw rocks at my school's windows."

We threw assorted stones and pebbles, but nothing broke the glass.

"This is ridiculous," said Saibal. "What if there was a fire inside? You'd never break out."

"They don't care," I said. "This place is like a prison. I'm surprised there are no iron bars."

We stood back and took in the red brick building.

"I suppose if there was a fire, we would just *open* the window," I said.

"Yeah," said Saibal. "They're still a bunch of bastards, though."

We walked back to the bus stop.

"What's *your* school like, Saibal?"

He kicked a pebble with his shoe. "White."

I laughed. "Who paints a school white?"

"The school isn't white," said Saibal. "The people are."

I picked up the pebble and dropped it in a random mailbox. "All of them?"

He nodded. "Yup."

He started hopping over the cracks in the sidewalk. "Step on a crack, break your mother's back."

I joined in. "It's always the mothers," I said. "I feel bad for them."

"Good point," he said. "Let's change it to father."

"How about brothers?" I said. "*Older* brothers."

We stomped on every crack.

Saibal laughed. "Poor Pius."

We slowed down and caught our breath.

"Sometimes I make brown jokes," said Saibal.

I looked over at him. "You do?"

He nodded. "It's better if I make them first. Doesn't hurt as much."

It was an interesting strategy. *Maybe*, I thought, *I should try it with my face.*

"The kids think I'm cool and funny when I make fun

of myself. But there's this one kid, Freddie Fudge. I'll never win him over. He's been to the office six times for calling me a Paki. He doesn't say it out loud anymore. But I hear it, you know?"

"It's called telepathy," I said.

Damian Clarke was a master.

"Do you have a bully?" asked Saibal.

I pointed to my face. "Duh."

We kept walking.

"Maybe we could put an ad in the paper," I said. "Like they did in that movie *Desperately Seeking Susan*. You know, the one with Madonna? We could say, 'Desperately Seeking Brown Kids,' and maybe you'd find a friend."

Saibal smiled. "That's okay, Finbar. I already have a friend."

I hoped he meant me.

We sat on the curb under the Route 12 sign. Saibal flicked an ant off my jeans.

"My mom has the baby blues," I said. "That's why she was in her dressing gown."

"That's too bad," said Saibal.

"Yeah," I said.

The Metrobus rounded the corner.

"See ya tomorrow, buddy," I said.

"See ya, Finbar."

★

I popped into Gord's room before going to my own. He was asleep but I whispered to him anyway. "I won't see you after school tomorrow. I have a performance at the nursing home. It's important. This could be my big break. You understand, right?"

He let one rip. It was long and wet and bubbly. I took it as a yes.

★

Saibal and I walked against the wind to the One Step Closer to God Nursing Home. Our hoods were up and our hands were stuffed in our pockets.

"I'm froze to death," said Saibal.

"Me too," I said.

As we moved out of the downtown area, row houses became detached homes and the steepness of the roads leveled out. We made our way up Portugal Cove Road and when we reached Elizabeth Avenue, we stopped at Regatta Ford to warm up. In the corner of the showroom, there was a candy machine. Saibal put in a quarter and twisted the knob. I put my hand at the bottom of the chute and collected the colored sour candy. We ate them in a Ford Crown Victoria. Red food dye came off on my fingers, so I wiped them on the leather interior.

Saibal was in the driver's seat playing with the steering wheel.

"Oh, shit," I said, looking out the back window. "It's the cops!"

Saibal grabbed the wheel and put his foot on the gas. He made car noises while I held the Jesus bar and said, "Burn rubber! The pigs are gaining on us."

Saibal bounced around on his seat, his eyes straight ahead. "Why did you have to kill him, Finbar? He was your big brother."

"That blackmailer was no brother of mine," I said. "I promised I'd get that ten bucks back and I did."

"But did you have to rip out his insides and step dance on them?" Saibal said. "It was a bit cruel, even for you."

"He got what he deserved," I said.

"Oh no," said Saibal. "Up ahead! It's Deadman's Pond."

"Step on the brakes!" I yelled.

"They're not working," he cried.

We tumbled about in our seats as the car went over the cliff. Saibal died with his head on the horn. I died laughing.

"Ahem."

A car salesman was standing by Saibal's open window.

"His parents are doctors," I said. "They asked us to pick out a luxury sedan on their behalf."

The man opened the door. "Out."

We put up our hoods and went back out in the cold.

"Too bad Gord missed that," I said.

"Yeah," said Saibal. "He'd have pooped his pants."

"Literally," I said.

We continued up Portugal Cove past the Holiday Inn. The nursing home was in the distance.

"I hope O'Flaherty shows up," I said.

"I'm sure he will," said Saibal.

"I'm nervous," I said.

"You could always wait for the September auditions," said Saibal.

"I can't disappoint God," I said. "He gave me a sign, you know."

"I'm sure he'd understand," said Saibal.

"What about you, Saibal?" I said. "Do you believe in God?"

"I believe in a few," said Saibal. "My favorite is Shiva. He's the god of destruction."

"Maybe you can pray to him the next time we're throwing rocks at the school window," I said. "It'd be nice for the glass to break for once."

"He only destroys evil," said Saibal.

"School's evil," I said.

"True," said Saibal. "I'll see what I can do."

Patsy greeted us at the nursing home. "They're waiting for you."

I took Billy Walsh's tap shoes out of my backpack. They were two sizes too big.

"Here," said Patsy, crumpling up the *Evening Telegram*. Saibal shoved the balled-up newspaper into the toes.

"Perfect," I said, rocking back and forth.

The Last Chance Saloon was packed with old people sitting on plastic garden chairs. Uneven Steven waved from the front row. I clicked toward him, waving and winking to the oldies as I passed them by. Saibal followed behind.

"Hi, Steven," I said.

Steven looked beyond me.

"'Allo, Saibal."

"You two know each other?" I said.

"Saibal organized a sock drive for the Harbour Light Centre last year," said Steven. "I had warm plates of meat all winter."

"He means feet," said Saibal.

"I know what he means," I said. "I'm not a garden tool."

"Fool?" said Saibal.

"Bingo!" said Steven.

"Bingo?" said Edie from the second row. "I thought we were here for a show."

"And that you are, Eeds," I said.

I stretched my arms over my head and bent from left to right.

"Nice to see you warming up," said Uneven Steven. "I'd have never kept up with Jagger without a few pre-show stretches."

"You played with the Stones?" said Saibal.

"Keith Richards had the sniffles," said Steven. "I was his fill-in."

"Unbelievable," said Saibal, sneaking me a wink.

I smiled. It was nice of him to play along.

I was swinging my leg over the back of a garden chair when the elusive Father O'Flaherty walked in. I say *elusive* because Father O'Flaherty was a man who kept a low profile, and elusive means hard to find. It's what Mr. McGraw called me whenever my homework was due. Father O'Flaherty had been in town for almost six months now but none of the parishioners really knew him. Our old parish priest, Father Molloy, was out and about all the time—at Tim Hortons having a chat and a double-double, down on George Street having a pint of "medicinal" Guinness, in Bannerman Park sunbathing in his Speedo. Father O'Flaherty, on the other hand, only made himself available during official religious duties. He did spend a lot of time with the Full Tilt Dancers, though. Apparently, like me, he was quite taken with *Riverdance*. He even flew to Dublin to see one of their shows. According to Billy Walsh, it was O'Flaherty's goal to make the Full Tilt Dancers the best Irish step dance troupe in Canada. *If that's the case,* I thought, *he'll definitely need the likes of me.* I clicked over to him.

"Fancy meeting you here."

He looked me up and down. "Do I know you?"

"You will soon," I said.

"Who knit ya?" he asked.

"My conception had nothing to do with needles and wool," I said. "The tools of the trade were more, how shall I put it, biological. But to answer your question, my parents are Brendan and Margaret Squires. From York Street."

He scowled. "So you're the infamous Finbar Squires."

I put out my hand. "The one and only."

He didn't shake it.

"Father Molloy told me about you. You're the youngster who punched a hole though the confessional screen."

"In one blow," I said. "But my talents don't stop there."

I nodded toward my tap shoes, then raised my eyebrows.

"You're a dancer?"

I smiled. "Some might call me the best-kept secret in the dance world."

He looked intrigued. "Really?"

I put a finger to the side of my nose and walked away.

Uneven Steven gave me a thumbs-up. "Good luck with the ol' Jack Palance."

"That means dance," said Saibal.

"Just so you know," I said, "Cockney is my second language. So I don't need *you* acting like you're some kind of goddamn translator."

Saibal elbowed Steven in the arm. "Someone's getting themselves into a real cream puff."

"That means huff," said Steven.

"I knew what he meant," I said, even though I hadn't.

I stood on the *X* and looked around. "Music, please."

"Performers usually bring their own equipment," called Patsy.

"But this is the Last Chance—I mean, the special events room," I said. "How in God's name does it not have a sound system?"

"You think this place has money for a sound system?" she said.

I closed my eyes. *Focus, Squires, focus. What would Flatley do?*

A raspy and somewhat muffled voice rose from the crowd.

"Are you just going to stand there or what?"

I opened my eyes to see an old woman sneering at me through her oxygen mask.

"Take a chill pill, Darth."

Patsy wagged her finger at me. "You, young fella, are a disgrace."

So much for "We're not fussy, my duck. I'm sure you'll be delightful."

"I'm going back to my room," said a man in the front row. "*Land and Sea* is on."

"Me too," said another. "Tonight's episode is 'The Trouble with Beavers.'"

"Ooooooh, beavers," everyone murmured.

"Wait," I said. "Don't go."

I looked to Buster and Edie for help. Buster gave me a wink and started *da-da-da*-ing the *Land and Sea* theme tune. Edie joined in. Soon the whole room was filled with song.

Uneven Steven caught my eye. "What are ya waiting for?" he growled. "Dance."

I pinned my arms to my sides and danced to the delightful ditty that filled Newfoundland homes on a weekly basis. It was a bit slow, but beggars can't be choosers. When they were done, I said, "Thanks, b'ys. I really appreciate it. How's about we do something faster this time?"

Edie started them off.

Beer, beer, beer, tiddly beer, beer, beer!

An Irish drinking song. Perfect.

A long time ago, way back in history,

When all there was to drink was nothin' but cups of tea,

Along came a man by the name of Charlie Mopps,

And he invented a wonderful drink and he made it out of hops.

Everyone joined in. They swung their arms in unison. I channeled my inner Flatley and kicked my legs high in the air. The singing was so loud you couldn't even hear the thuds as I landed. It was brilliant.

He must have been an admiral, a sultan, or a king,

And to his praises we shall always sing.

Look what he has done for us, he's filled us up with cheer!

Lord bless Charlie Mopps, the man who invented beer, beer, beer,

Tiddly beer, beer, beer . . .

Buster caught my eye and threw me his cane. I caught it with one hand and broke into the Charleston. Then I twirled it like a baton and did my signature moonwalk.

It was time for my big finish. I landed the splits without the pain showing on my face. The room erupted in cheers.

Uneven Steven wiped a tear from his eye.

Saibal started a standing ovation. It took a full six minutes for everyone to get to their feet, but still.

I clicked my way over to Father O'Flaherty. "Well?"

"Well what?"

"How's about you invite me to join that troupe of yours?"

He laughed. "I don't think so. There's no room for temperamental divas in the Full Tilt Dancers."

My grip tightened around Buster's cane. "I'm going to tell my nan."

Father O'Flaherty looked amused. "And what's *she* going to do?"

I snorted. "What's she *not* going to do, more like."

"What's that supposed to mean?"

"My nan's almost a hundred," I said. "She'll be dead soon. Apparently she's willed it all to the church, but one word from me . . ."

O'Flaherty's brow furrowed. I moved my mouth toward his ear. "Mark my words. I *will* be in your dance troupe."

I turned on my heel and stormed out of the room. Out in the lobby, I swung Buster's cane like a baseball bat, knocking three table lamps to the floor. They smashed into a billion pieces.

Uneven Steven came barreling behind me.

"Bloomin' heck, Squire! Have you gone Patrick Swayze?"

In the distance, we heard a mass shuffling.

Steven grabbed the cane. "Make yourself scarce, Squire."

I ran like the wind to York Street.
Every click was a stab to the heart.

*

I sat on the floor and put my hand through the slats. I put my hand on Gord's arm and matched my breathing to his. I'd missed our bedtime song, so I wiped my eyes and sang:

Beer, beer, beer, tiddly beer, beer, beer . . .

CHAPTER SIX

I thrust the tap shoes into Billy Walsh's chest. "Here."

"How did it go?" he said.

"Swell."

He looked at his crotch. "Wish I could say the same."

"Were you thinking about God?" I said. "He likes to invade impure thoughts."

"It wasn't God," he said. "It was me mudder invading my underwear drawer. She found the *Playboy* and dragged me to confession."

"Jesus Murphy," I said. "What did Father O'Flaherty say?"

"He said he'd have to confiscate it but Mom had already burned it. He seemed disappointed."

"Better luck next time," I said.

When I walked into Mr. McGraw's class, he told me Mrs. Muckle wanted to see me. I walked into her office like I owned the place.

"Can't get enough of me, can you, Judes?"

She pointed at the chair across from her. "Sit."

She said she'd heard about the incident at the nursing home.

"I'm sorry it didn't go as planned, Barry, but you must control that temper of yours. Apparently you were so upset, you ran out of the home and accidentally knocked over three lamps."

"Who told you that?" I asked.

"Steven Morris."

"Steven who?"

"Steven Morris. You know, the homeless man?"

"Oh. Uneven Steven."

"Don't call him that," she said. "It's cruel."

"Cruel is having one leg longer than the other," I said. "Or a port-wine stain across your face."

"Oh, Barry," she said.

Her voice had gone soft and I wanted it hard again.

"It wasn't an accident," I said. "I whacked the lamps with a cane."

She sighed. "In any case, Steven has offered to replace them."

I clasped my hands behind my head and relaxed back. "Well, there you go," I said. "Problem solved."

"No," she said. "Problem *not* solved. That man doesn't have two pennies to rub together. You should be the one taking consequences for your actions. Not him."

"You know," I said, putting my feet up on her desk, "this incident is not a school issue, and quite frankly this conversation is starting to feel a little bit inappropriate."

She pushed my feet to the floor. "Father O'Flaherty felt it was his duty to inform me of your behavior. It takes a village, you know, Finbar."

"Oh, please. What does Father O'Flaherty know? He certainly doesn't know a good dancer when he sees one."

"Actually," she said, "it was your attitude that bothered him. He said your dancing has potential."

I sat up. "He did?"

She studied my face. "Why do you want this so bad, Barry?"

"Everyone wants to be known for something," I said.

She opened her mouth and closed it again.

"Go on," I said. "Tell me. What am I known for?"

The answer was written all over my face.

"Your humor. Your smarts. Your way with words."

I sighed. "In adult circles, perhaps. But with the other students?"

Again, she had no answer.

I stood up and leaned forward.

"You know exactly what I'm known for, Judes." I pointed to my cheek. "You're looking at it."

"Barry," she said. "Sit."

I sat back in my seat.

"Not there," she said. "At your desk."

I smiled. "*My* desk?"

"Your name's on it, isn't it?"

I sat down at the desk in the corner and ran my fingers along the *FTS* I'd scraped into the wood. Mrs. Muckle passed me a piece of paper.

"Father O'Flaherty's a reasonable man. Write him a letter. Plead your case."

I nodded. "Thank you, Judes."

I began.

My dearest Father O'Flaherty,
Some of the greatest artists in the world are the temper and mental type. Ozzy Osbourne bit the head off a bat live onstage. Van Gogh cut his own ear off. It kind of puts things in perspective, doesn't it? When you think about it, my behavior was nothing more than a little tantrum, and let's face it, it was kind of justified. I mean, how can you have a musical performance without music? But I—

"Judes? What's the word you use when you want to change the subject? Begins with *d*? Sounds like *digest*?"

"Digress," she said.

But I digress. This dancing malarkey is about more than being temper and mental. It's about being chosen. You see, Father O, I received a message from God himself. He told me to dance. There was an almighty glow and everything. So you see, you don't really have a choice in all of this. I was meant to be a Full Tilt Dancer. God said so.

Sincerely and with the utmost of respect and gratitude,

Finbar T. Squires

Mrs. Muckle read it over.

"It's *temperamental*, not temper and mental," she said. "And don't call him Father O. It's the height of rudeness."

"Other than that," I said, "is it good?"

She sighed. "Well. It's passionate."

"It's like they say," I said. "Go big or go home. And speaking of going home—I'm feeling a bit emotionally drained. I think I might call it a day."

She passed me my schoolbag. "Go to class, Barry."

*

Mr. McGraw kicked me out of class. It wasn't my fault everyone jumped on their chairs. I was sure I saw two rats scurrying across the floor with foam around their mouths. Turns out I'd just imagined them. I blamed McGraw. His talk about compound adjectives was mind-numbing. As for my peers, why should I be blamed for their over-reaction? They could have just stayed seated with their legs up, like me. I left on a high note, though, passing in a copy of my letter to Father O'Flaherty as my persuasive essay. I said I'd be happy with a B-plus if he couldn't find it within his cold, dead heart to give me an A. It's amazing how many shades of purple and red the human face can turn. It's really quite mind-blowing.

I managed to sit through my other classes without causing a disruption. Mostly because I'd mastered the art of dreaming with my eyes open. In science, I was Father O'Flaherty's lead dancer and by the end of last period, I was on stage with Michael Flatley. All in all it was a successful day, even without a saltwater taffy reward.

On my way home, I went to the corner of Cochrane and Duckworth because Uneven Steven hadn't been there before school.

"Did you sleep in this morning?" I asked.

He nodded. "I was up late last night replacing the broken lamps."

"Where did you buy them?" I asked.

"I said replacing, not buying."

"So you robbed them?"

"I may be a lot of things," said Steven, "but I'm no tea leaf."

"So you borrowed them?"

"I went to the dump," he said. "They're ugly and cracked but they work."

"Thanks, Steven. You're a pal."

I went home and got Gord. Saibal was at the war memorial with two birch beers and a Pixy Stix for Gord.

"He can't have that," I said.

"It's just a bit of sugar," said Saibal.

He ripped the paper straw with his teeth. "Open up, Gord."

Gord tipped his head back and opened wide.

"Oh my God!" I said. "A tooth!"

"It looks like a Chiclet," said Saibal.

I ran my finger along the pearly-white eruption.

"He's growing up," I said.

"His first tooth," said Saibal. "Let's take him to Bannerman Park to celebrate."

We arrived at the park to find the swings wound over the top bar.

"Some people have too much time on their hands," I said.

"Now what are we going to do?" said Saibal.

"We could go throw rocks at my school again," I said.

"Why don't we complain to the city," said Saibal. "These swings are their responsibility."

"Better yet," I said, "let's take it up with the lieutenant governor."

"Good idea," said Saibal.

Government House was just across the street. We crossed Bannerman Road and headed toward the grand brick building.

"My parents got invited to the garden party last year," said Saibal. "Someone thought my dad was a server and handed him an empty glass."

"That's the height of rudeness," I said.

"It was a good party, though," said Saibal. "There was a band and everything."

"My nan has always wanted to go," I said, "but I think you gotta be someone to get an invite."

"Your nan's someone," said Saibal.

"It's okay," I said. "She doesn't have a big hat anyway."

Saibal stayed with Gord while I climbed the stairs and rapped on the door. A maid in black-and-white uniform answered.

"I'd like to speak to the lieutenant governor," I said.

"Do you have an appointment?" she asked.

"I most certainly do."

"Your name?"

"Finbar T. Squires. The *T* is for Turlough. I'm telling you this because a highfalutin middle name such as mine is an indication of the grand family from which I was born into. We really are quite the bunch of someones."

She stared at me blankly.

Gord rat-tat-tat-tatted like a machine gun.

"Babies are so uncouth," I said.

She turned back into the building.

"Don't forget," I said. "Turlough. Spelled with an *o-u-g-h* but pronounced like 'lock.' It means 'dry lake,' which is an oxymoron."

The door slammed in my face.

"That went well," said Saibal.

A few moments later, the door opened again. A man in a gray suit stood in the doorway.

"Finbar Turlough Squires?"

I was amazed. Namedropping really worked. Even if it was your own.

I put out my hand. "The one and only. And you, sir, must be the lieutenant governor of this very fine province I'm proud to call home."

The man took my hand. "I'm his private secretary. You can call me Gord."

My eyes lit up. "He's Gord too," I said, pointing at the stroller.

"A fine Scottish name," said the man.

"My mother felt it was important to acknowledge the long line of Scottish royalty on her father's side," I said.

In reality, Gord was named after Gordon Lightfoot. Apparently Dad agreed because her second favorite singer was Elvis.

Big Gord looked at Saibal. "And what's your name?"

"Saibal," said Saibal. "It's Indian."

"An Irishman, a Scotsman, and an Indian," said Big Gord. "You three should walk into a bar."

"The past, present, and the future walked into a bar," I said.

"Let me guess," said Big Gord. "It was tense."

We all laughed. Except Gord. He knew nothing about grammar.

"So," I said. "Where's the big man himself? We kind of have a bone to pick with him."

"He's in a meeting," said Big Gord. "Is there anything I can help you with?"

I pointed across to Bannerman Park. "Some yahoo has swung the swings around the top pole and we can't reach them."

He went inside and grabbed a cap. It was navy with a braid above the peak.

"You're going to help us?" I said.

"Why wouldn't I?" asked Big Gord.

"Because you're an important someone," I said.

He smiled. "I hear you're quite the someone too."

Big Gord stretched his arms in front of us as cars whizzed by.

"Okay," he said. "It's safe to go."

We parked Gord near the swings. A seagull landed on the canopy of the stroller.

"Yah!" yelled Big Gord.

"Bah!" yelled Little Gord.

The seagull flew away.

Big Gord stood in his suit whacking the swings with a stick. I told him how my nan had always wanted to go to the garden party and about Saibal's dad being mistaken for a server.

"Not that there's anything wrong with being a server," said Saibal. "It's just that people make assumptions."

"Do you think if the whole world was blind, there'd be no prejudice?" I asked.

Big Gord unraveled one swing and moved to the next.

"To quote Thomas Hardy," he said, "'There is a condition worse than blindness, and that is, seeing something that isn't there.'"

"What does that mean?" asked Saibal.

"It means that sometimes people see what they want to see," said Big Gord. "Like differences."

"Why would people want to see differences?" I said.

Big Gord unraveled the last swing. "Maybe it helps them feel superior."

He put down the stick and put a hand on Saibal's shoulder. "What they don't realize," he said, "is that they may *feel* superior but they *look* like pompous twits."

He gave a little bow. "Good day, boys."

We watched him walk away.

"He's a nice man," said Saibal.

"Bah-gah!" yelled Gord.

★

At suppertime, Mom came to the table fully dressed and ready to eat. She doled fish and brewis onto everyone's plate.

"I have some news," she said.

"Good God," said Pius. "You're not pregnant, are ya?"

Mom gave a little laugh. "No."

Dad put his arm around her.

She cleared her throat. "A few weeks back I went to the doctor. He gave me some antidepressants. I'm starting to feel better. I'm sorry for being so absent."

It sounded rehearsed. I wondered if she'd been practicing all morning.

"I have some news too," said Nan.

"Good God," said Pius. "You're not pregnant, are ya?"

Nan laughed. "Go 'way with ya, Pius. You're as foolish as an odd sock."

She looked at me and smiled. "Father O'Flaherty called. He said you can join the troupe on a trial basis."

I grinned. "I knew he'd see things my way."

"I have news too," said Shelagh.

"What is it?" asked Mom.

Shelagh looked to the table. "I want Pius to ask."

Pius looked up from his fish and brewis. "What?"

"I want you to ask about my news. The same way you asked everyone else."

As soon as he asked it, we understood.

Mom's voice was a growl. "You silly girl."

"What about Bob?" said Shelagh. "Is he silly too?"

Dad put his head in his hands. "Just what we need. Another mouth to feed."

The concern about money surprised me. The last time I checked, sex before marriage was against our religion. Then again, so was taking the Lord's name in vain and Lord Jumpin' Jesus, we did enough of that.

When Shelagh started crying, I took Gord upstairs. "Well, one good thing's come out of it," I whispered. "Mom can't call you her little blunder anymore."

★

HEATHER SMITH

Shelagh cried for three days. "There goes my studies at Memorial."

"And whose fault is that?" said Mom.

Dad, who was still in shock, could only nod in agreement.

Nan, on the other hand, moved on. "Shelagh's not the first pregnant teen," she said, "and she won't be the last."

I overheard Pius ask Shelagh if Bob was a good guy and when she said yes, he said, "Good."

I didn't care either way. I just hoped Mom's happy pills were extra strength.

*

A few nights later, just as things were settling down, all hell broke loose. Pius and his hockey friends were in the basement kicking the crap out of each other in a makeshift boxing ring while the rest of us were upstairs watching *The Price Is Right*. An overexcited contestant in a Hawaiian shirt was losing his shit over a game of Plinko when there was a knock on the door. I peeked out the window. "It's a guy with a big schnoz." Shelagh's face turned red, then white, then green.

"It's okay, love," said Mom. "Invite him in. We'll have to meet him sometime." My poor mother. If she had a white flag, she'd have probably waved it.

Shelagh went to the door but never came back.

"Don't worry," I said. "I got this."

Just as I was positioning myself behind the slightly open front door, Pius and his friends came upstairs. Pius said, "When is a door not a door?"

The answer was "when it's ajar," but I didn't respond. I had work to do. "Shush," I said. "I'm eavesdropping."

I reported back to the living room in a loud whisper.

"He says he hasn't told his parents yet."

"She told him he has to."

"He says he's scared."

"She said tough shit."

"He said maybe she should make this go away."

"She said it's her body and she'll damn well decide what to do with it."

"He says of course it's her decision. He's sorry."

"She says she doesn't want to fight."

"He says he doesn't either but he can't tell his parents."

"She says he has to."

"He says he's sorry but he can't do it. His parents will kill him."

Pius pushed me out of the way. "Not if I kill him first."

With the door now wide open, I was able to give a full play-by-play.

"Pius just punched Bob in the face. I think Bob just called Pius a rubberducker. Shelagh's saying the Hail Mary."

Dad, Mom, and Nan ran to the door. I grabbed Gord from Nan's arms. "This is gonna be good, Gord," I said. "Real good."

I gave the gathering neighbors a little wave as I settled onto the front steps with Gord. Pius and Bob were squaring off again. The adults were saying, "Stop this right now!" At least I think they were—it was hard to hear them over the chants of "Kill him!" coming from Pius's friends. Pius was scuffing his foot like a bull about to charge when Shelagh blocked him from Bob, saying, "Please don't kill the father of my child." The neighbors gasped. Mom, suddenly aware that the neighbors were watching, started applauding. "Aren't they marvelous?" she said. "The best youth acting troupe in town."

Nan herded everyone back into the house, where Shelagh wiped the blood off Bob's face with his own shirt—I don't think she loved him enough to use her own. Nan put the kettle on and sliced up one of her boiled raisin cakes. Dad snorted. "The best youth acting troupe in town." We all laughed. Even Mom. The hockey boys said Nan's cake was the best they'd had. Nan beamed. When the teapot was drained, Pius invited Bob downstairs to check out the makeshift boxing ring. He said he figured Bob could use some pointers. Bob said he'd like that. He also said he'd tell his parents that night. It's

BARRY SQUIRES, FULL TILT

amazing what a punch in the face, a cup of tea, and a slice of boiled raisin cake can do.

★

I probably shouldn't have broadcast it, but when I saw the petition, I had no choice. It was posted on the lunchroom wall and as I approached it, a kid in fifth grade said, "Sorry, but I had to sign it. Herpes is very contagious. Especially when it's on your face."

I looked around. Damian Clarke and Thomas Budgell were doubled over. With all eyes on me, I said, "This practical joke has come at a very difficult time. My teenaged sister is pregnant. My family is in crisis. I'd appreciate prayers, not stares."

A hush fell over the room. After all, premarital sex was against our religion. For the rest of the day, I was left alone. I had successfully managed to get the focus off my face and onto the shame of my family. All in all, it was a good day.

★

After school Saibal and I pushed Gord up Signal Hill.

"When's the baby coming?" he asked.

"September. Shelagh's three months already."

Saibal pinched Gord's cheeks. "You're gonna be second fiddle soon, buddy boy."

"No one will ever replace Gord," I said.

At the top of the hill, we sat on a wall overlooking the harbor. Saibal held Gord tightly in his lap and the wind whipped at our faces. The basilica stood out in the distance, surrounded by the old buildings and colorful houses of downtown. A coast guard boat made its way out through the Narrows.

"We're lucky to live here, aren't we, Saibal?"

"We sure are," he said.

I wondered what time it was.

"My first dance lesson is soon," I said.

"But you don't have a uniform," said Saibal.

"Whenever I bring it up, Dad tells me to hold my tongue," I said. "I brought pennies to tape to my shoes, though."

"You can't do that," said Saibal. "It's very unprofessional."

"What else am I supposed to do?" I asked.

"How 'bout this," he said. "You go to practice and promise O'Flaherty the money will be there by the end of class. In the meantime, I'll drop Gord off, get the bus home, grab my bank card, get the bus back, go to the Royal Bank, get you some money, and meet you at the BIS for the end of class."

"Really?" I said.

I was stunned. A bank card at age twelve?

He put an arm around my shoulder. "What are friends for?"

We headed back down the winding, steep Signal Hill Road.

Gord, who rarely got fussy, got fussy.

When we got to a relatively straight bit of sidewalk, I said, "I have an idea."

I gave Saibal the stroller and ran ahead.

"Okay," I said, turning around and bracing myself. "Let him go."

Saibal laughed. "What? I can't do that."

"Yes, you can," I said. "I'll catch him. Don't worry."

Saibal shrugged and let go. Gord shrieked as the stroller sped down the incline.

"I gotcha, Gord!" I said. "I gotcha!"

The stroller raced toward me. When it got close, I reached out and grabbed Gord by the waist.

"Bah!" he yelled.

Saibal caught up to us.

"He wants to go again," I said.

At the next straight stretch of sidewalk, we switched. I trusted Saibal to catch him and he did.

At the bottom of the hill, I said, "Nan made raisin squares this morning. She'll probably only give you one, seeing as you're not a refugee anymore."

Saibal tightened Gord's seatbelt. "Oh, don't you worry," he said. "I'll get at least three squares off your nan."

"How do you plan on doing that?" I asked.

"I'm gonna charm the pants right off her."

"Please don't," I said. "She'll catch her death."

Saibal took Gord home and I went to the BIS. Father O'Flaherty said that as a man of the cloth, he had no choice but to have faith in my promise of money, so he gave me the uniform. I put on the Newfoundland tartan pants, a crisp white shirt, and the tartan vest. I thought I'd feel like a dancer, but the only thing I felt like was a leprechaun, not that's there's anything wrong with that.

Then I put on the shoes.

They were brand-new, not like Billy's, which were faded and worn. These were shiny and black and the silver taps clicked like no penny could.

I strutted out of the bathroom and down the hall.

Click.

Click.

Clickity-click.

I entered the practice room with my chest puffed out and took my place amongst the evenly spaced rows of dancers. Father O'Flaherty cleared his throat. When I looked up, he pointed to the door. "The beginners are down the hall, second door on the right."

I smiled. "Give me a couple of weeks. I'll be back."

As I walked down the hall, I chuckled at the thought of me being a beginner. Ha! A beginner doesn't watch *Riverdance* two times in a row. Especially when the running time is seventy-one minutes. I mean, that's dedication.

I walked into the second door on the right. Some of the dancers were barely up to my knees. The tallest barely reached my shoulders.

The teacher introduced himself. "I'm Brian."

"I know who you are," I said. He was in the grade below me at school.

We practiced pointing our toes by dipping them in the Atlantic Ocean.

"Brrrr," said Brian.

The little fellas were having a grand time.

But I wasn't *brrrr*-ing. I was *grrrr*-ing.

We skipped across the room to the Pacific.

"Ahhhh, much warmer," said Brian.

"No offense, Brian," I said. "But these infantile shenanigans are beneath me."

A moment later I was peering through the window on O'Flaherty's door. They were dancing to "Mari-Mac." With my hands on my hips, I leapt into the room. I spread my legs as wide as I could and thrust my chin in the air. *This'll show 'em. The bastards.* I landed with a thud and continued dancing, tapping in and out through the rows of stunned-yet-amazed boys. Always considerate and thinking of others, I timed my kicks so as not to cause testicular injury. At the end of the third row, Father O'Flaherty blocked my way, but not even his physical presence could stop me. With my arms pinned tight to my sides, I step danced in place.

"Are you done?" he said.

My voice was breathless. "Does it look like it?"

His jaw hardened. "You have two choices," he said. "Go back to the beginners' room or go home."

"You've put me in a difficult position," I panted.

"I'll make it easy for you," he said. "Go home."

I was kind of relieved. My plates of meat were killing me. Things would be better next week when I'd be feeling more refreshed.

I clicked my way to the door.

"Finbar?" he said.

I paused. Maybe this was where he'd tell me I showed potential, where my hard work would pay off.

"Don't come back," he said.

My face fell. "What?"

"You can leave the uniform in the cloakroom."

My jaw hardened. "You, sir, are a dream killer. A hope dasher. A spirit squasher."

"Perhaps, Squires," he said, "you'd be better suited to

the local acting troupe. You seem to have a flair for the dramatic."

I didn't disagree. I probably *would* excel in theater. But that was beside the point. I refused to be fooled by his flattery.

"Yes, Father," I said. "I do have a flair for the dramatic. So allow me to leave you with some parting words."

I cleared my throat.

"Dimes are silver, pennies are brass, why does your face look like your ass?"

The boys roared with laughter. O'Flaherty sputtered. Fearing that he might need CPR, I left. It wasn't very Christian, refusing to give the kiss of life to a man of God, but neither was crushing the hopes and dreams of a twelve-year-old boy.

I left the uniform in a pile on the cloakroom floor and went outside to wait for Saibal. He'd probably be on his way back by now. I felt bad about the wasted journey. I'd suggest blowing the money at Caines to make up for it.

★

"Don't listen to the likes of Father O'Fart-ity," said Saibal. "He wouldn't know talent if it hit him in the face."

"I know," I said. "It still hurts, though."

"Let's drown our sorrows with a couple of birch beers."

"And some chips and a Caramel Log?"

"Why not?" said Saibal.

We took our stash to the bandstand in Bannerman Park to shelter from the rain, drizzle, and fog. We sat on our knees to keep from freezing our arses off and pulled our hoods up over our heads.

"I like this weather," said Saibal.

"Me too," I said. "It makes me feel alive."

"Warm days are boring," said Saibal. "It's the same outside as it is in. But on damp days, the cold on your cheeks lasts for ages and when your mudder touches them with the back of her hand, she makes you a cup of tea with bucketloads of sugar."

"Sometimes," I said, "when the fog is as thick as pea soup, I go downtown and walk in the alleys and imagine getting murdered by a serial killer with a machete. It's never happened, though."

"I'll come with you next time," he said. "We can get killed together."

"That'd be nice," I said.

A seagull landed on the bandstand steps. Saibal threw it a chip.

I closed one eye and stared into the opening of my birch beer. I had no reason to do this. I already knew it was pink.

"How about we go to the nursing home?" said Saibal.

BARRY SQUIRES, FULL TILT

It was the perfect suggestion. A dance with the oldies was just what I needed.

"You, sir," I said, "are like a blast of Newfoundland weather."

Saibal grinned. "I make you feel alive?"

"No," I said. "You're as thick as pea soup."

Saibal threw a chip at me. It bounced off my nose.

"Come on," I said. "Let's go have ourselves a good old knees-up."

★

We sat in the Last Chance Saloon with Buster, Edie, and a handful of others. They'd been in the lobby when I'd arrived but as soon as I said, "Let's dance," they got to their feet and followed me down the hall like I was the Pied Piper of Hamelin, except they weren't rats and I didn't have a flute.

Buster tapped his cane against the floor. "Are we going to have a song and dance or what?"

"Absolutely," I said. "But first—"

Saibal and I pooled our change together and set about taping coins to the soles of everyone's shoes, including our own. Once we got everyone to their feet, we moved to the middle of the room, where we had a good old-fashioned Newfoundland kitchen party. Our shoes sounded way better than the ones I'd been wearing earlier. It must have been the acoustics of the room.

We sang "Lukey's Boat" and "Rattlin' Bog." We tapped, shuffled, boogied, and waltzed. Edie's hands were like two chunks of ice, but I held them anyway as we stepped side to side, clicking in unison. More people came and joined in. Saibal was spinning someone around in a wheelchair and a little old lady in orthopedic shoes was doing a slow but impressive Charleston. They formed a circle around me, and Buster said, "Take it away, Barry!" I did the fastest step dance in the history of man and my face wore the world's smuggest look, and I thought, "If O'Flaherty could see me now."

CHAPTER SEVEN

There was a freak snowstorm in April that lasted three days. It came over Easter, and on Good Friday I suggested we bond as a family by painting eggs but everyone had an excuse. Shelagh said she couldn't even look at an egg without throwing up, Pius said decorating eggs was for morons, and the adults were watching *Jesus Christ Superstar*. The only person mildly interested in painting eggs was Gord, but he had no fine motor skills. I asked Mom if she'd managed to buy any Easter chocolate before the storm. She said no but all was not lost because at least she had a turkey.

"All is not lost?" I screamed. "If I don't get a Mr. Solid, there'll be hell to pay."

The Easter Bunny had been bringing me a Mr. Solid ever since I had teeth.

Mary Magdalene was on the TV singing "Everything's Alright" to Jesus. Mom joined in and sang it to me.

"Everything is *not* all right!" I screamed.

"Bah!" yelled Gord from Dad's lap.

I stormed into the kitchen and looked in the fridge. There were four eggs left. One for each kid. I found a magic marker and wrote our names on them: Pius, Preggo, Finbar, and Gord. I went outside and threw them at the window. That'll teach 'em.

The snow was deep but I had on my big snow boots, so I trudged all the way from York to Springdale. I threw snowballs at the Harbour Light Centre till somebody answered the door.

"Uneven Steven, please," I said.

"Whom shall I say is calling?" asked the man in the doorway.

"The one he calls Squire," I said, to add an air of mystery.

A moment later Steven appeared.

"Come in, Squire," he said. "We're about to have a cup of Rosy Lee."

I followed him to a big kitchen and joined a group of men at an oversized table. A man with a tattooed face put a Mr. Solid in front of me. "Here ya go, fella."

"You, sir," I said, "are a scholar and a gentleman."

I took off the wrapping and bit the ears off. Turns out, the center had received a box of donated Easter chocolate.

"Listen, fellas," I said. "The Easter Bunny's been a bit distracted this year 'cause her teenage daughter is preggers. How's about I shovel the driveway in exchange for seven Cadbury cream eggs?"

"Deal," said the man with the tattooed face. "But I'll help. It's a big job."

We went outside and as we shoveled side by side he told me he'd just been released from the pen.

"Six years for armed robbery," he said. "Whatever you do, kid, don't do drugs."

When we got inside, a man with a long, yellowed face filled a Sobeys bag with way more than seven cream eggs.

"Thanks, buddy," I said.

Uneven Steven made me hot chocolate to warm up and spoke to the group about the hardships of being a performer

"I hear ya," I said. "I think I've got a blister developing on my big toe."

Then he told us about the time a photo of him ended up in *Rolling Stone* magazine.

"It was '79," he said. "My buddy Joe Strummer pulled me up onstage during one of their gigs. Let's just say my dance moves stole the show."

He got up and limped to the kitchen sink. The tattooed man gave me a wink. I felt bad for Steven, with his made-up stories. I'm sure he did wonderful things in his life. Why didn't he share *them* instead?

I followed Steven to the sink and whispered, "Why would someone tattoo their face? I'd do anything to get rid of this mess on mine."

"Where would I be if I got my leg fixed?" he said. "It was what I was known for. Like Jagger's lips. In my opinion, you should stick with what you're born with. Imagine if Freddie Mercury got his teeth fixed. It could have changed the whole structure of his mouth and affected the way he sang."

I stuck out my front teeth and sang "Another One Bites the Dust." It sounded terrible.

"Give us a dance then, Barry," said one of the men.

The man with the tattooed face lifted me onto the table. Another played the fiddle. It felt good to entertain down-and-outs. I hoped I'd added a little something to their humdrum lives.

*

On the way home, I stopped at the Hanrahans. Mrs. Hanrahan's husband killed himself because he'd grown up in the Mount Cashel Orphanage. The news had come out years earlier that the Christian Brothers had been abusing the boys. It was enough to make Mom stop going to church. Dad still went, though. He took us with him while Mom stayed home and cooked the Sunday dinner. I felt bad for Mrs. Hanrahan. Her kids were the kind you'd see out in their pajamas at the crack of dawn, pulling up the neighbors' potted plants.

When she answered the door, I said, "You get out to the stores this week?" And when she said no, I gave her the contents of the Sobeys bag, minus the seven Cadbury eggs. "Happy Easter."

"Thank you, Finbar," she said. "Between you and Mrs. O'Brien, I'm all set. She brought a turkey over this morning."

I said, "This storm's screwing everybody over," but truth be told, she'd have struggled regardless.

When I got home, Dad was cleaning the window. I could barely see him through the snow, which had begun to fall quite heavily again.

"I don't need this, Barry," he said. "I've got enough problems."

"What do you mean, problems?" I said. "Mom's on happy pills and so what, Shelagh's pregnant. It's not like she's been diagnosed with cancer or anything."

I had hoped that would put things in perspective for him. Instead, his face turned purple.

"Barry. Do you ever think about things before you say them?"

"Well, duh. You have to think in order to form words, otherwise you'd say nothing at all."

I continued toward the house.

"By the way," I said, holding up the Sobeys bag, "I saved Easter."

★

The power went out on Saturday, but it turned out to be the best day ever. We sat around the fire and when we got hungry, we put a skillet in the flames and fried bologna, and when we played Scrabble, they even scored my made-up words, and during Trivial Pursuit, when Dad asked the Arts and Literature question "Who painted *The Birth of Venus*?", Shelagh placed a hand on her tummy and Mom reached over and said, "Any kicks yet?" and Shelagh smiled and her eyes went teary.

When the power came back on, my eyes went teary too.

★

The adults slept in on Easter morning because it was too snowy for church. Not that Mom would have gone, but

Dad and Nan would have dragged us there. I took Gord downstairs and placed a cream egg in each of our spots on the table. I put one on the tray of Gord's high chair. "This is symbolic because you've only got one tooth," I said. "But don't worry, I'll give you a lick of the center."

At ten o'clock they were still asleep, so I shouted, "Jesus rose from the dead today. The least you bastards can do is get out of bed!"

A few moments later, they appeared.

"Look," I said. "The Easter Bunny came."

Nan tightened the belt on her dressing gown. "Oh, Barry. How lovely."

"A single egg," said Pius, biting his in half. "How delightful."

A splodge of yolk dropped onto his chest.

Shelagh held her stomach. "I think I'm going to be sick."

Mom nodded at Dad. "Go get the Zellers bag from upstairs."

"I thought you didn't get out to the stores," I said.

"I was only teasing," she said. "Has the Easter Bunny ever let you down?"

Dad came back and Mom passed us each a Mr. Solid and a chocolate egg. Each of the eggs came in their own cardboard box, and through the plastic window we could see our names written in white icing. I opened it up and cracked off the *F*. Mom ruffled my hair. "Sorry the Easter Bunny slept in," she said. "The pills make her sleepy."

That night we sat around the table, all seven of us, stuffing ourselves with turkey. I was grateful that God was being good to us. I hoped he was being good to the Hanrahans too.

★

It stopped snowing overnight and the next day the city got dug out. The plows were loud but the sound I liked the most was the screech of the clothesline. It was cold but sunny, and Mom was in her element.

"It's some day on clothes," she called to Mrs. O'Brien, who was shoveling her back step.

Mrs. O'Brien laughed. "Indeed it is."

Nan spooned some oatmeal into Gord's mouth.

"Did you see his tooth?" I said. "It looks like a Chiclet."

"He's some boy," she said.

Mom came in looking satisfied. "When the roads are clear, I think I'll go get some sleepers for the new baby."

Just then Shelagh came downstairs. Her hand was on her stomach and she was crying. We jumped up, all three of us.

"What's wrong?" said Mom.

Shelagh's voice was a whisper. "Bob broke up with me."

★

Pius said he was going to punch Bob's schnoz in again.

Dad told him he was going to do no such thing.

"His family thinks I'm a slut," said Shelagh. "They want to know how they can be sure the baby is Bob's."

"Well, it'll be pretty obvious if it comes out with a giant nose," I said.

"Finbar!" said Nan. "You of all people should know it's never nice to make fun of people's appearance."

"How dare you bring up my cheek at a time like this," I said.

Mom put her arms around Shelagh. "Things will settle down," she said. "They'll come around."

"And what if they don't?"

"You have us," said Mom. "And we'll always be here for you."

"Hair, hair," I said, wondering if it was *here, here.*

Dad waved a VHS tape in the air. "I think we could all use a laugh."

We gathered around the TV and when *Fawlty Towers* came on, we chuckled because the sign outside the hotel said FARTY TOWELS.

★

Going back to school after a long weekend was always hard, but I managed to arrive at Mr. McGraw's class on time and hungry for taffy.

"Good morning, sir," I said. "I do hope you have a pastel blue on hand."

Mr. McGraw smiled. "I'm sure I do."

Halfway through the class, Damian Clarke passed me a picture of Mikhail Gorbachev. There was an arrow pointing to the port-wine stain on his bald head. Written across the top were the words "Finbar Squires's long-lost dad."

I smiled. "That's funny," I said. "Real funny."

Then I tipped Damian's desk over with him in it.

The upside was Mrs. Muckle had a package of Purity Ginger Snaps on her desk, so even though I had to write "I will control my temper" one hundred times, I had some cookies for energy.

★

After school, Saibal and I took Gord to Fred's Records. We asked Tony to put on The Wiggles' "Big Red Car" and to our surprise, he did. We pushed Gord around the store and Tony sang along. Gord shrieked to the *toot-toot*s and the *chugga-chugga*s, and customers looked at him like he was the cutest thing on earth, which he was. Afterwards we walked to Lar's Fruit Store—but we

BARRY SQUIRES, FULL TILT

didn't buy fruit, we bought custard cones, and when Gord tried to hold his, I said, "Look, Saibal. He has dimples where his knuckles should be," and Saibal said, "He's some cute."

On the way back to York Street, we found a pay phone and looked up Bob the Schnoz's number. It wasn't under Schnoz, though. It was under Myrick, which was his last name.

"It's ringing," I said.

"Hello?"

The voice sounded motherly.

"Do you have Robin Hood by the bag?"

"Um . . . yes, I do."

"God almighty, woman! You'd better let him go!"

I hung up.

It was Saibal's turn.

"Hello?"

"Do you have Aunt Jemima by the box?"

The motherly voice turned not-so-motherly.

"Don't call back here again, you little shaggers!"

We doubled over laughing. Gord too.

"That'll teach 'em," I said, though I wasn't sure what.

Saibal opened the phone book. "What's your bully's name, Finbar?"

I grinned. "Damian Clarke. Why?"

He smiled. "You'll see."

He flipped to the Cs. I scanned the listings and pointed. "That one."

He dialed the number and held the receiver to both our ears.

"Hello?"

It was Damian.

"Oh, hello," said Saibal. "Can I speak to Mrs. Wall, please?"

"Sorry, wrong number."

"How about Mr. Wall?"

"I said wrong number."

"What about Harry Wall? Is he there?"

"No."

"Sally Wall?"

"How many times? You've got the wrong number!"

"I don't understand," said Saibal. "There are no Walls in your house at all?"

"None!"

"That's weird," he said. "What's holding up your roof?"

He slammed the phone down and we burst out laughing.

"Thanks, Saibal," I said. "That made my day."

He clapped me on the shoulder. "Anytime."

We were just leaving the pay phone when a man with a bottle in a brown paper bag staggered toward us. He stopped in front of me and said, "With a face like that, I'd walk backwards."

"Piss off," said Saibal.

"Shut up, wog," said the man.

For once I was speechless.

Saibal grabbed the stroller and almost mowed the man down. "Come on, Finbar."

When we got home, he told Nan what had happened. "You poor little things," she said. She sliced off two huge slabs of her homemade bread and slathered them in partridgeberry jam. Saibal dug right in but I just stared at mine. It was funny how you could know something and not know it at the same time. Like the word *wog*. I hadn't heard it before, but I knew what it meant by the way it was said.

"Saibal?" I said.

"I'm okay," he said. "Eat your bread."

I took a bite.

"I'm okay too," I said, in case he was wondering.

"I know you are, Finbar," he said. "You're hard as nails."

He invited me to his house for supper. Pius pulled me aside before we left. He said I should bring a banana, because banana was good for cooling down hot and spicy curry. Turns out they served Jiggs Dinner. Mr. and Mrs. Sharma were really nice. Out of the blue, because they were doctors, I said, "How much would it be to get this taken off my face?"

Mr. Sharma said he was no expert but he did a dermatology residency once. He said laser surgery was a possibility but he wasn't sure if it was covered by the government. Mrs. Sharma said I was a beautiful boy and I should leave my face alone.

Later, at home, I sat next to Gord's crib. He was already asleep. I watched his breath go in and out, in and out. I hoped he'd never hear the word *wog*. I reached through the slats and stroked his cheek. He'd be beautiful no matter what.

★

It was blowing a gale and the whole house shook. I had trouble falling asleep but eventually I did, and when I woke it was dark and my life had changed.

I couldn't see Pius but I could sense him. He slid one hand behind my lower back and the other onto my shoulder blade. As he pulled me toward him, I knew something bad had happened. I could feel it in the tremble of his hands. In the tremble of his breath. In the tremble in the air around us.

He moved a hand up to the back of my head and pulled me into his cold, bare chest. He'd have spoken if he could but how could he speak the unspeakable?

The wind rattled the window. I imagined myself outside.

When I looked to the heavens, they opened up. Hail pelted my face. I said, "It's okay, God. I'm hard as nails." I stayed in that moment until Pius started rocking. Back and forth. Back and forth. He said, "Oh God, oh God, oh God," and I said, "Nan?" and he made a sound that was a gulp and a sob, and when he said, "No, not Nan," I knew. I wrapped my arms around his waist and said, "But he's just a baby."

★

Pius pulled a blanket around us. "The wind woke Mom, so she decided to check on him. She knew he was gone right away."

I didn't ask how. I didn't want to know.

The paramedics and police were still in the house when Pius took me downstairs. Dad's nose and eyes were red. He was thanking the paramedics. I didn't know what for.

When Dad saw me, his bottom lip shook. "They said it might be cot death."

I said, "Cots don't kill babies."

It was almost May but it felt like December. I shivered in my pajamas. Dad turned up the heat and reached into a laundry basket. He grabbed a shirt that was folded on top, a green plaid flannel, one of his. He helped me into it.

Pius said, "I'm going back up."

"I don't want to go," I said.

Dad sat with me on the couch. He had a hand on my leg. We stared at the coffee table.

After many minutes Dad took my hand. I didn't want to follow him but I did.

Mom was sitting in a rocker by the window. The Humpty Dumpty blanket was in her arms. I assumed Gord was in it.

Nan stood above her. Her eyes were puffy and swollen.

Shelagh was in the corner, rubbing her swollen belly like it was a crystal ball. That's when I started to hate her.

Mom looked up. Her face looked different. It was longer. Like her muscles had stopped working.

"Come here, love," she said.

I felt a growling, deep in my belly. "No."

"Barry," said Dad.

Shelagh reached for me. She had a nerve, the traitor. Having a baby when Gord was gone.

"You," I growled. "You stay away from me."

I felt Pius's hands on my shoulders. "This might be your last chance."

I twisted away, almost knocking him over.

"Barry," he said. "Stop."

"Let him go," said Dad.

A paramedic blocked my way at the front door. "Son—"

BARRY SQUIRES, FULL TILT

My hands formed fists, so I started to punch him. He grabbed my wrists. I wanted to fall into his chest and cry but that would mean someone died, so I kneed him in the groin.

I ran to Bannerman Park and sat on a swing. It was dark and cold and the wind howled. I hoped Gord wasn't scared of the rattling at his window. I sat till the sun came up. Dad's shirt was a hug. My stomach growled. Gord would be up soon. I'd make him his oatmeal, just like usual. I sat some more. I wondered why Pius had been hugging me while I was trying to sleep. Must have been a dream. Kids passed in the distance, schoolbags on their backs. Shit. Gord's oatmeal. Never mind. Nan would have made it by now. She'd have sprinkled it with cinnamon. He'd have liked that.

After a while, I walked to school. Everyone stared.

"Barry," said Thomas Budgell. "What are you wearing?"

I looked down. My pants had Spiderman on them. Like they were pajamas or something.

I went to Mr. McGraw's class. I remembered some kind of deal. A reward if I was good. I took my seat. When Mr. McGraw saw me, he said, "Barry, can I talk to you outside?" It was a familiar feeling, being pulled out of class. I said, "Did I do something bad?" And he said, "Barry, I'm so sorry." My hands formed fists, so I started to punch him. He grabbed my wrists and I fell into his

chest. He put his arms around me but I don't know for
how long because the world wasn't spinning properly, not
since I'd had that bad dream about Gord dying.

★

Dad took me home. He said, "Gord's at the funeral home."

They cried all day long. The bastards. They didn't *have*
to believe it. No one was forcing them.

I went to the war memorial. When Saibal saw me, he
put his head in his hands.

I stroked his hair. "Don't cry. It didn't really happen."

He looked up. "It didn't?"

I pulled my hand up my sleeve and wiped his tears.

"Of course it didn't."

He wanted to believe me, so I said, "Come on. I'll
show you."

The house was busy with visitors.

"That's weird," I said. "There must be some kind of
celebration."

I snuck inside. A moment later I was pushing the
stroller toward Saibal.

"Gord is *so* glad to be out of there," I said. "Houseguests
make such a fuss over him."

Saibal looked at the stroller.

Then he looked at me.

"Jesus, Finbar. You left his coat wide open."

My eyes filled with tears.

He bent down and zipped up the imaginary zipper.

"Let's take him up Signal Hill," he said.

Passersby stared as we made our way up.

"Your turn, Saibal," I said. "He's getting heavy."

Saibal took over. "You're some fat, Gord. You're like a tub of lard."

At the top of the hill, Saibal tightened Gord's seatbelt. "You ready, Gord?"

I ran ahead and braced myself. "Okay, Saibal. Let him go!"

The stroller raced toward me.

I could see him.

Plain as day.

Gummy smile.

Wisps of hair blowing in the wind.

Big blue eyes staring at me.

I caught him around the waist.

"I gotcha, Gord. I gotcha."

I fell on my knees and draped my arms over the empty stroller.

Saibal draped his arms over mine.

"What are we going to do, Saibal?"

"I don't know, Finbar."

★

We sat cross-legged on the sidewalk.

"I don't want Shelagh's baby to have the stroller."

Saibal looked around. "We could throw it in Dead-man's Pond."

We pushed it through the bushes and to the water's edge. Saibal took one end and I took the other.

"One, two, three."

One big splash and it was gone.

We walked back home. All around us the world ticked along. People went about their business and I thought, "Don't they know? A baby died today."

Saibal hugged everyone in my family, even Shelagh. Mom hugged him the longest. She said, "Gord loved you. Did you know that?" and all he could do was nod. The kitchen was full of food brought by neighbors. I wasn't hungry but Nan said I had to eat. Saibal and I sat in the kitchen eating beef stew. When Shelagh came in, I dropped my spoon. Saibal followed me to my room.

"I hate her," I said.

He nodded. "I know."

We played Go Fish until it was time for him to leave.

Before he left I asked him to keep going to the war memorial.

BARRY SQUIRES, FULL TILT

"I don't want things to change," I said, even though everything had.

"I'll be there every day," he said. "Promise."

★

I went to sleep.

When I woke it was still dark.

I went to Gord's room.

I sat on the floor and put my hand between the slats.

I moved my hand around the empty space.

Then I went to my parents' room and climbed between them. They wrapped their arms around me. I prayed in my head. *Please, God, tell them to tell me it'll be okay.* They didn't pass on his message. Maybe they didn't believe it. Or maybe God never told them in the first place. Maybe he'd failed me again.

★

Nan was a machine. Cooking, cleaning, making and taking calls. I walked past the bathroom. She was on her hands and knees. Shelagh passed by too. She said, "Scrubbing that toilet won't bring him back," and I said, "Shut up, Shelagh," not because I disagreed but because I hated her.

*

For the next few days, blood and breath ran through our bodies but we were barely alive. We were half dead. Maybe three-quarters. A big fat chunk of us was missing. A ginormous tub of lard.

I saw Dad sitting on his bed, his wristwatch in his hand. He said, "I wonder what time he died."

It was a weird thing to wonder. What did it matter?

"What time was he born?" I asked.

My father was as surprised by my question as I'd been by his.

"2:33 a.m.," he said. "He was a chubby little thing. Thighs like a speed skater." Dad smiled just a bit. He strapped his watch around his wrist. "I miss him, Barry."

"I know," I said. "Me too."

*

Saibal was at the war memorial with two birch beers.

"What do you want to do today?" he asked.

"I want to kick the shit out of the floor."

We went to the nursing home. They all knew. It was in the paper. They didn't say much. I got a few sorrys, and

a hug from Buster and Edie, and that was it. I appreciated that. I wasn't there to talk.

We went to the Last Chance Saloon. We were so
loud, we drew a crowd. The songs were lively—"Squid
Jiggin' Ground," "Aunt Martha's Sheep," "Feller from
Fortune" . . . When I pictured the Humpty Dumpty
blanket, I danced harder. When I pictured Gord dead,
I sang louder.

Before I left, Buster asked when the funeral was. I
said, "Don't know. Don't care." He opened his mouth to
say something, then closed it. As I walked out the door
he told me to take care and I said, "Will do."

CHAPTER EIGHT

There was a visitation at the funeral home. I went to the Harbour Light Centre instead. Uneven Steven told me that when he was little, his sister died. She was born with a disease and died when she was two.

"Did you see her after she died?" I asked.

"Yes," he said. "I held her."

"I didn't hold Gord. If he's an angel, he's probably mad."

"Gord? Mad?" he said.

I smiled. Gord was the happiest baby on earth.

We spent the rest of the day playing cards around the big kitchen table. The men talked about their lives. They were tough and broken and soft and hard, and they said they wouldn't be defined by their pasts, and I hoped I'd always be defined by Gord because if I wasn't, he might get forgotten.

✳

"I'm not going."

I said it ten million times.

Nan threw her hands up in the air. "We can't force him. What are we going to do? Tie him to the car?"

"Don't be an arsehole, Barry," said Pius.

Mom and Dad were too tired to argue.

Shelagh rubbed her belly. "Come on, Barry. You have to go."

I picked up a vase of flowers and threw them against the wall.

"Fuck you."

I wanted Mom to call me Fin-bear, but she stared at the flowers. "Those were from the O'Briens."

"Clean that up, Barry," said Dad.

Then they left.

I sat in the front window and stared out at York Street. A car pulled up. Saibal got out. He was wearing a suit. He waved to me. "You coming?" I shook my head. He stared at me. I stared at him. He got back in his car and drove away.

BARRY SQUIRES, FULL TILT

I went to Caines. Boo said, "How are you doing, Barry?"

"I'd like a sour key, please."

"Here ya go," he said. "On the house."

I wandered around downtown sucking on it.

I was at the intersection of Duckworth and Prescott when I heard the *beep-beep-beep* of a car horn. I turned around. The One Step Closer to God minibus was careening toward me.

"God almighty!" I yelled.

The bus jumped the curb and came to a stop near my foot. The door opened.

"Quick," yelled Buster. "Get in!"

I hopped on board and took a seat next to Edie.

"I didn't know you could drive a bus," I said.

He laughed. "I can't."

"Where are we going?" I asked.

"Where do you think?" said Edie.

I stood up. "I'm not going."

Buster put his foot on the gas. "Oh yes, you are."

I fell back into my seat.

"The church is full," said Edie. "But it feels empty without you."

I said out loud what I'd been thinking all day. "I don't want to see the coffin."

Buster and Edie exchanged a look through the rear-view mirror.

Edie took my hand. "There's a big picture of Gord on a table at the front of the church," she said. "He's wearing a pair of sleepers with monkeys on them."

"He's smiling at the camera," said Buster. "His tongue is stuck out and there's drool dribbling down his chin."

"You focus on that, Barry," said Edie. "Think of it as a celebration of his life."

I didn't feel like celebrating but I did feel like remembering.

"Okay," I said.

Edie took my hand and I relaxed as much as I could in a speeding bus.

*

Heads turned as I walked in. Mom and Dad moved apart so I could sit between them. They each took a hand and gave it a squeeze. I was the baby now but I didn't want to be.

Father O'Flaherty shot me a dirty look, which I thought was pretty outrageous considering the circumstances. I immediately tuned him out. I focused on the photo of Gord in his monkey pajamas. I pictured how happy Gord was when I pretended to dump him in the harbor. Then I heard Pius's voice. He was up at the altar. He talked about how smart Gord was. And how funny and cute. I heard the rustle of paper and when I looked up, he smiled and said, "I asked friends and neighbors to share their memories." Boo from Caines said Gord was his favorite customer. Tony from Fred's said Gord lit up the whole store. Mrs. O'Brien said she loved the sound of Gord's laugh ringing from our open window to hers.

I looked back at the photo.

My heart was full but it felt empty without him.

★

Father O'Flaherty shook our hands. When it was my turn, I said, "Your oral presentation skills need work."

He said, "This anger will pass, my son."

Pius came over and pulled me outside. He spread his arms apart and said, "Punch me."

I took a swing. He'd tensed but I managed to knock some wind out of him.

He caught his breath. "Better?"

I nodded.

He spread his arms apart again. I walked into them.

He said, "We'll get through this," and I almost believed him.

★

Back at the house Nan told Mrs. O'Brien that they think Gord died of SIDS.

"Sid's what?" I asked.

Nan added three sugars to my tea. "Sudden Infant Death Syndrome."

I poured my tea down the sink.

Saibal and his parents came to give their condolences. They were two of the many people who came to visit. It felt like a party but it was far from it. Saibal came to my room and we played Operation. I kept hitting the sides but Saibal had a steady hand.

"You have the hands of a surgeon," I said.

Saibal extracted the broken heart. "Runs in the family," he said.

I tried for the funny bone. *BZZZZZZ.*

"You, on the other hand," said Saibal, "have the hands of a sturgeon."

I laughed because sturgeons don't have hands.

"Saibal?" I said. "Can you get your mom and dad?"

A moment later they were at the end of my bed. I addressed my first question to his mother.

"Tell me," I said. "How in God's name can a baby's heart stop for no reason?"

She opened her mouth but nothing came out.

"You don't know?" I said. "Some heart doctor you are."

"And what about this SIDS business?" I said to his father. "Sounds like a load of old poppycock to me."

Saibal's mom spoke softly. "Being angry is normal—"

"I'm not fucking angry," I said.

Saibal's dad stood up. "We'll give you a few minutes to calm down."

When they left, I kicked the Operation game to the floor. "Some help they were."

Saibal took another game off my shelf. "Battleship?"

"Okay."

After I sunk his battleship, I said, "Can you go get your parents again?"

A few moments later they were back.

Saibal's dad spoke first. "Your parents are happy for us to answer any questions you might have."

"I only have one," I said.

He nodded. "Go on."

My voice broke when I said it.

"Why?"

★

Sometimes bad things happen to good people. That's what they said. It wasn't a very satisfying answer but then they explained SIDS. They said it's the sudden, unexplained death of a child under the age of one. It's unpredictable and unpreventable. Researchers are working to understand it. I listened real hard. The army men in my head stood at attention. I understood everything but it was hard to take. I didn't want it to be true. When they were done, I said sorry for earlier. They said I was going to have lots of ups and downs, and that grieving is complicated. They invited me for supper the following evening and I said, "Let me know if you're making curry so I can bring a banana." It felt weird to laugh but I figured it was just one little up in a million downs.

★

We sat around the table, just the six of us. Dad wanted to check in, see how we were doing. The visitors were gone and the house was so quiet I could hear the refrigerator hum. Nan opened a tin of shortbread cookies from Mrs. Hanrahan. Shelagh took one and spoke to her belly. "Hope you like butter, little one," she said. "Shortbread's my favorite."

"No one cares about your stupid baby," I said.

"Finbar," said Nan. "That's not fair."

"You know what else isn't fair?" I said.

Shelagh stood up. "I'm going to bed."

"Please stay," said Mom.

Pius took a pile of sympathy cards off the kitchen counter.

"Come on," he said. "Let's have a look through these. Together."

Mom smiled at him. "My sweet sixteen."

She hadn't used the nickname in months. Pius blushed at the sound of it.

Shelagh sat back down.

Dad opened the first one. "This one is from"—he squinted at the signature—"the Fizzards? Who in God's name are they?"

Nan laughed. "No idea."

"Wait now," said Mom. "The Fizzards live out on Barnes Road. Dennis Fizzard is Aunt Jacinta's brother-in-law."

"Oh yes," said Nan. "Now aren't they the ones that always had a cow tied up in their front yard?"

"A cow?" said Pius. "No way."

"Yes way," said Dad. "And on Christmas Eve in '82— or was it '83?—the cow escaped and ran over the crowds coming out of midnight mass."

"Are you serious?" said Shelagh.

"Oh yes," said Mom. "Father Molloy sprained his ankle that night."

"Too bad he didn't end up in a full body cast," I said.

Mom patted my hand. "Now, now, Fin-bear."

The next card made everyone cry. It was from a Mrs. Down in Harbour Grace.

"Who's Mrs. Down?" asked Dad.

Mom looked up from the card. "She lost a baby to SIDS. Emily Louise. She was eleven weeks old."

So it was a real thing. Cots *did* kill babies.

Dad picked up the envelope. He traced the curly writing with his finger like it was from a long lost friend.

Some of the cards were Hallmark but even the flimsy and cheap ones meant something.

That night I heard Mom wailing from her bedroom.

At two in the morning I went to the bathroom and heard a noise outside. I looked out the window and saw Nan sweeping the sidewalk outside our house.

Grief was complicated.

*

A week later Dad went back to work. He wore his watch around his wrist. It seemed to weigh him down on one side. He put clocks in every room. All day long, it was a bloody cacophony of ticks and tocks. "Every moment counts," he said. Mom went back in her room. I rarely saw her. Every now and then I'd knock on her door and sometimes she'd say, "Come in." I'd open the window and say, "It's some day on clothes," but she'd just put her arms out and I'd climb into them. We'd lie there staring at the popcorn ceiling, neither of us saying a word. When I'd leave, she'd say, "Shut the window, Barry."

★

I dropped a pencil in class once. Damian Clarke picked it up and said, "Here ya go, buddy," so I stabbed him with it.

Mrs. Muckle said, "What are we going to do with you, Barry?"

I said I didn't know.

★

Sometimes, at supper, Nan pulled Gord's high chair to the table but it slid across the floor too quickly.

The weight of him, it was everything.

★

I dreamt of Mom by the window, a blanket in her lap. I'd walk toward her but then I'd wake. One night I stayed dreaming. I peeled the blanket back. It was a Cabbage Patch Kid. My head was sweaty and my throat hurt from the scream. Pius said, "You okay, Barry?" I said, "Ever wish it would all go away?" and he said, "Every day."

*

Shelagh got fatter and fatter. If I had a magic wand, I'd make it stop.

*

The days and weeks melted into each other. Someone set fire to them and watched them burn. I don't know who. Maybe it was God. May became June. The weather was warming up and school was coming to an end. People asked me how I was but I had no idea. I should have recorded myself so I could watch it back. Did I go to school every day? I must have. Would I pass eighth grade and move on to high school? Who knew? The only thing I knew was that Gord was still dead and time was moving further away from his ever existing.

*

Saibal sat at the war memorial in a T-shirt and jeans. "Some warm out, isn't it?"

I supposed it was for Newfoundland. There was a chill in the air, but at least the sun was out.

"Practically tropical," I said.

"Gord would have liked summer," he said.

I stretched out on the grass.

"Sometimes I watch the time change on my alarm clock. The second hand is lucky. It gets to *tick-tick-tick*, but the minute hand has to just sit there, watching time pass and waiting to move forward."

Saibal sat next to me. He put a blade of grass between his thumbs and blew. It made a whistling sound. I sat up.

"How did you do that?"

He picked me a blade and showed me how. It worked on my first blow.

We experimented with the way we held the grass to make different notes. We tried to play "Three Blind Mice." It sounded decent.

"Saibal?" I said.

"Yeah?"

"Sometimes . . . I think I need to see your mom. As a patient. Because my heart pains all the time."

"Maybe I could borrow her paddle thingies," he said, "and shock your heart back to its old self."

"Nah," I said. "You might accidentally kill me. Then where would we be?"

"True. Your parents can't go through that again."

We went to Caines and listened to Boo tell ghost stories. Some were really spooky. Gruesome even. But I wasn't scared. The scariest thing in the world had already happened.

Afterwards, Saibal and I walked out to the Battery. We sat overlooking the Narrows and watched a tour boat putter toward open water.

I said, "You went all the way out to King William Estates to get your bank card and I didn't even say thanks."

"That's okay."

"You prank-called Damian Clarke too. On my behalf. I should have prank-called Freddie Fudge but I didn't."

"It's okay, Finbar."

"No, it's not," I said. "I took you for granted."

I pulled a clump of grass out of the earth. "I took Gord for granted too."

Saibal made his hand into a fist. For a second I thought he was going to punch me, but he ran his fingers along his knuckles. "Remember Gord's dimples?" he said. "Ten little dents where his knuckles should be. You always seemed to notice the little things."

My eyes filled with tears.

"My heart's hurting again, Saibal."

He pushed me over and straddled my waist. "Clear!"

He hit my chest with an imaginary defibrillator and

I jolted with the almighty shock. I stared into the sky and said, "Look, Saibal. A pair of boobs." He lay beside me. "An elephant too." The clouds moved by slowly just for us. We watched them while my heart recovered.

*

I sat in the front window. Mrs. Inkpen's dog, Labatt, greeted her by stealing one of her nursing shoes. Mr. O'Brien went straight to his bedroom and changed from his mechanic coveralls to his Snoopy pajama bottoms. Mr. Power came home and went straight to his wife for a kiss. Funny thing was, Gord was still dead. Our car puttered up and pulled over. I ran to the door. Dad put his arms around me and ruffled my hair. He said I was a grand boy and we should go out for a plate of chips, so that's just what we did.

*

Usually a whiff of June would stir up the excitement of summer, but not even a custard cone from Lar's could revive the butterflies that lay dead in my belly. The ice cream was sweet and cool and velvety smooth, but there was no little tongue leaning in for a lick, so I was left with a bad taste in my mouth.

June in Newfoundland meant going out in shorts and T-shirts and hoping the weather got the point. I wore Pius's old soccer shorts and AC/DC shirt almost every day because it made me feel like he was near, though why I wanted that I didn't know.

Saibal and I were glued at the hip. One day we got the bus to the Avalon Mall. We tried to sneak into a movie but got kicked out. The security guard called us Crockett and Tubbs. I said, "I'm not fat." The security guard said I needed to brush up on *Miami Vice*.

On the bus home, Saibal said, "Tubbs is Black. Crockett's the white one. He wears shoes with no socks."

"That's a blister waiting to happen," I said.

We stopped in to Mary Brown's on the way home for a two-piece and taters. I held up my drumstick and said, "Mary Brown's—she's got the best legs in town."

Saibal smiled. "Open twenty-four hours a day!"

We took a handful of straws and blew the wrappers off. One landed on a high chair.

That was what June was like. Even the ups felt like downs.

★

On the last day of school I was the first to arrive at Mr. McGraw's class.

He took off his blazer and hung it on the back of his chair. "Well, well," he said. "I don't believe it."

"I went to Bannerman Park at six," I said. "I sat on a swing till my arse hurt."

He sat at his desk.

"Whenever I wake up now I can't get back to sleep," I said. "Because Gord is the first thing that pops into my mind. I mean, I can't just close my eyes and forget about him, can I? That wouldn't be very nice."

"Finbar," said Mr. McGraw. "Have you thought about talking to someone?"

I frowned. "I'm talking to you, aren't I?"

He smiled. "I suppose you are."

I scraped my nail on the wooden desk. "I like you, Mr. McGraw. Ditching your class wasn't about you. It was about me. It was about me being a puzzle piece with the ends all bashed up. I'll always stick out this way and that. First it was my face and now it's Gord. I feel like everyone's always looking at me. I hate it. It makes me feel really unconscious."

"I think you mean *self*-conscious," he said.

I smiled. "If you like."

I scraped a splinter out of the wood. I held it between my thumb and forefinger. It was thick on one end and pointy at the other, like a miniature sword. It'd be perfect for poking the likes of Damian Clarke and Thomas Budgell. It might even draw blood.

"I like it in the principal's office," I said. "I have my own desk there and the only person to bother me is Mrs. Muckle."

Mr. McGraw followed my eyes to the clock on the wall. Four minutes to the bell.

"Come here, Barry," he said.

I went to the front of the room. Mr. McGraw pulled open his desk drawer.

"Help yourself."

I chose a pastel blue.

"Tell Mrs. Muckle I sent you," he said. "You can make up the reason why."

I passed him my miniature sword. "I'll miss you, sir."

He took the sword and smiled. "I'll miss you too."

★

I waited for two minutes past the bell before waltzing into her office.

"Oh, for goodness sake, Barry," said Mrs. Muckle. "What now?"

"It wasn't my fault," I said, laying my schoolbag next

to my desk. "Thomas Budgell was being an arsehole, so I stabbed him with a miniature sword."

Her eyes widened. "With a what?"

I sat down. "Don't worry. It only drew two drops of blood. Three, tops."

She leaned back in her chair. "What are we going to do with you, Barry?"

"Nothing," I said. "It's the last day of school. I'll be out of your hair soon and you can forget all about me."

"Impossible," she said. "How do you forget the unforgettable?"

"You don't," I said. "Especially when the unforgettable is bad like me. Good things, though, you get scared of losing. Like what if they fade and you forget them forever?"

She came out from around her desk and crouched before me.

"It's the bad things that fade over time, Barry. I promise. You'll never forget Gord, and I'll never forget you."

I focused on her fantabulous slut shoes to keep my heart from aching.

"When I think of him," I said, "I think of that night. It ruins my memories."

"It won't always be that way," she said. "You just need to give it time."

She gave me a sheet of lined paper and a pen.

"I want three memories," she said. "The very best of all."

I wrote them quickly and with a smile on my face.

1. Watching him sleep.
2. Pretending to dump him in the harbor.
3. That time Saibal and me let him roll down Signal Hill Road.

"Interesting," said Mrs. Muckle. "Why these?"

"The first one was when I was the happiest, the second one was when Gord was happiest, and the third one includes Saibal."

Mrs. Muckle laughed. "Gord was happiest when he thought he was being dumped in the harbor?"

I smiled to think of it. "He shrieked his friggin' head off."

*

When I got home, Nan gave me a lassy bun and a cup of tea.

I looked to the ceiling. "What was that?"

"What was what?" she said.

"That noise," I said. "Sounds like someone's moving furniture."

Nan's voice went up an octave. "I didn't hear any-thing."

She was a terrible liar.

I pictured the layout of the house and ran upstairs.

"Get your grubby hands off Gord's stuff or by da Jesus, I'll knock you into next week."

Shelagh took a step back. "We just thought if we rear-ranged it, it would—"

"It would what?" I said. "Make us forget all about Gord so we can concentrate on your stupid kid?"

Shelagh started to cry. "You think this is easy for me?"

Nan appeared in the doorway. "Finbar, calm down."

"This is Gord's room!" I yelled.

Mom pulled the Humpty Dumpty blanket off the crib rail and moved to the chair by the window. Suddenly the wind, it was blowing a gale. The house was dark and our whole life changed. It was never going to go away, that feeling. That feeling of being robbed. We stood there, all four of us, wondering how we'd get through.

Mom reached her hand out to me. I went to her and took it. I imagined myself outside. Hail pelted my face. I said, "Help me, God. It hurts."

Mom gave my hand a squeeze. I squeezed back.

"Maybe," I said, "the chair would be better by the door. And the crib, we could put that against the wall near the window."

A moment later we set about moving the furniture.
I opened the window, let the bad memories out.

Afterwards, Shelagh touched my arm. "Thanks, Barry."
I pulled away. "I didn't do it for you. I did it for Mom."
I did it for Gord too.
The wind had no business in his room.

CHAPTER NINE

One morning in mid-July, I sat on Uneven Steven's cardboard and said, "If Shelagh's baby doesn't come out dead, I might kill it myself."

"Is that so?" he said.

I passed him one of Nan's partridgeberry muffins.

"I hope it's born with a port-wine stain all over its body."

He broke the muffin in two and offered me the top half.

"Have you ever noticed how ugly Shelagh is?" I said. "I don't know why anyone would want to have sex with her."

I smashed the muffin in my fist.

"She thinks her baby is the second coming of Jesus. She rubs her big, fat belly like it's something special. Mom and Dad do too. When they talk about the baby, they look happy, even though they're supposed to be sad. Wait till they see the hideous little gremlin that claws its way out of Shelagh's hoo-ha. That'll wipe the smile off their faces, the bastards."

I killed a few ants with the heel of my sneaker.

Steven licked a crumb off his bottom lip. "Anything else you'd like to get off your ol' George Best?"

I stood up. "No," I said. "I think that's it."

"Have a nice day, Squire."

"You too, Steven."

★

I walked toward the war memorial, wishing the sunshine was mist. I wanted to feel alive in a good way, not from the anger that pulsed through my veins.

"Saibal," I said. "I need your help."

He didn't ask with what, he just followed me back to the house. When no one was looking, we took the high chair.

"Deadman's Pond," I said.

Saibal nodded. "Understood."

We lugged it up Signal Hill Road. When we got to the pond, we collapsed from exhaustion.

"Jesus, Mary, and Joseph," said Saibal.

"And all the saints in heaven," I added.

The high chair was on its side. On the underside of the tray there was some dried oatmeal. I scraped it with my fingernail. It didn't budge.

"I wish your parents were here," I said. "I want to ask them a question."

"Ask me," said Saibal. "I'm smart."

I pointed to the tray. "Is Gord's DNA on this?"

Saibal squinted at the crusty oatmeal. "I would say so."

I examined the bottom of the tray. There was Gord crud everywhere.

"We don't have to throw it in Deadman's Pond," said Saibal.

"We don't?"

He shook his head. "Want to take it back home?"

"You don't mind?"

Saibal stood up and swept some loose grass off his shorts. "Let's go."

On the way back down the hill, I paused. "Wait. What if, before Shelagh's little monster arrives, they clean the high chair from top to bottom? What if they wash Gord away?"

Saibal had a look underneath. "From those crevices? Not even your nan could clean them out."

When we got home, Nan caught us with the high chair but turned a blind eye.

"Now," she said. "Who wants a nice cup of tea?"

She put the kettle on and showed us an invitation she'd received in the mail.

"I couldn't believe my eyes," she said. "The return address said Government House!"

Saibal and I smiled at each other.

"I'm impressed," said Saibal. "You've really got to be someone to get an invitation to the garden party."

"And you're something else," I said.

Nan smiled. "I suppose I am."

She topped up our tea from the pot.

"Nan?" I said. "Do you think I can come too?"

"I don't see why not," she said.

"You'll get to meet the lieutenant governor," said Saibal.

But I didn't care about that. I wanted to see Big Gord again.

★

Dad came home from work just before lunchtime.

"I took the afternoon off," he said. "Let's head out to Topsail Beach."

"The beach?" said Mom.

Dad pointed at his watch. "It's eleven forty-five. If we leave in fifteen, we'll be there by twelve thirty."

He turned to Nan. "Do you think you can throw a picnic together for us?"

"I certainly can," said Nan.

"What do you mean *for us*?" I asked. "Isn't Nan coming too?"

"Of course not. Where would she sit?" said Pius. "On the roof?"

"Maybe Shelagh can stay home," I suggested. "And Nan can come instead."

"Now, Barry," said Nan.

Mom looked around the kitchen. "I was going to wash the floors today."

Pius pulled a cooler out of the cupboard on the back porch. "You can wash the floors tomorrow."

"Don't worry," said Nan. "I'll take care of the floors."

"Can we stop for ice cream?" asked Shelagh.

"Shut up, you fat pig," I said.

"Barry," said Dad. "Enough."

He went to Mom, took her hand. "It'll be a grand day, I promise."

Nan waved from the window as we piled into the car. I refused to sit near Shelagh. Dad pulled me aside and told me to give it a rest. Pius overheard and said he didn't mind, he'd sit in the middle. He'd been pretty nice since Gord died, but I'd rather he was mean.

We headed out on Portugal Cove Road. We drove for a long time. Every now and then we'd round a bend and see the ocean. Then it would disappear again.

"I feel sick," said Shelagh.

We stopped at a convenience store with a big ice-cream cone outside. Shelagh ordered a double scoop.

"I thought you were sick," I said.

"Shut up, Barry."

She looked like the side of a house. I hoped she stuffed her face till she blew up.

I had a single scoop. Neapolitan. I wanted to give Gord a lick.

We ate our ice cream at a picnic table outside the store.

Pius had his hand on Shelagh's stomach.

"Holy shit," he said between licks. "It's kicking up a storm."

Well, whoop-dee-bloody-do.

Mom didn't have an ice cream but took licks off Dad's orange-pineapple.

"You should have got your own," he said.

She laughed. "I wasn't in the mood but I am now."

He leaned over and kissed her cheek. "This fresh air has done you good."

He went inside and got her a cone of her own.

We drove a while longer and turned down Topsail Beach Road.

"Isn't it grand?" said Mom.

The beach was dotted with people enjoying the sun. We unloaded the car and joined them. Dad told me to hold Shelagh's hand as she navigated the uneven terrain but I pretended not to hear. Pius helped her instead.

Mom and Dad spread two blankets out over the big beach rocks. I waited for Shelagh to settle her fat arse on one so I could choose the other. She sprawled across both. I sat blanket-less a few feet away.

Pius went for a walk. I watched him get smaller in the distance. Beachgoers waded into the ocean, waist high. It was too rough to venture out farther. The waves had all the power of Gord, whooshing in a way that made me breathe slower. In, out, in, out. I imagined his little chest rising and falling. I imagined him in my arms. It would have been his first time at the beach. The breeze would have lifted up his little wisps of hair, like a gentle wind through a field of grass.

My heart pained.

It would always hurt to do something new without Gord.

The problem was, it would always hurt to do something old too.

Like hanging stockings at Christmas.

Gord's was red with a toy soldier on it.

Grief was more than just complicated.

It was a trap.

"I'm going for a walk," I said.

"Be careful," said Mom.

She didn't want me to get swept out to sea. That happens sometimes.

On the shoreline I saw a condom. I'd tell Saibal about it later.

I walked till Mom and Dad were dots. Shelagh would look like a beached whale no matter how far I roamed.

Pius was up ahead skipping stones.

There were tears streaming down his face. Trillions of them.

I picked up a stone. It was flat and shiny and smooth.

"I bet I can skip this six times," I said.

"Bet you can't," he said.

I placed the stone along my pointer finger and secured it with my thumb. I pulled my arm back, cocked my wrist, and released. The stone landed in the water with a plunk.

Pius passed me another one. "Try again, dumbass."

★

We sat around the cooler eating bologna sandwiches.

"Nan must have caught one last night," I said.

"Fierce creatures," said Pius. "They'd bite the hand right off ya."

Our laughter rang from Topsail Beach to Signal Hill. It went into the sky and under the waves. Seabirds celebrated and marine life rejoiced. It danced on the wind in a tumbling whirl. It bounced off the cliffs and zoomed through the universe and then it came back to us, an echo lined with a sweet baby belly laugh.

★

The day came to an end. Ten to five by Dad's watch.

Pius sat in the middle on the way home. Shelagh was still a fat pig, boomerang laughter or not.

★

That night, there was a ruckus.

I sat up in bed. "What's happening?"

Pius was pulling a hoodie over his bare chest. "It's Shelagh. They're taking her to the hospital."

"Oh," I said. "Is that all?"

"Don't be an arsehole, Barry. It's too early. She's only seven months pregnant."

I put my head down and nestled back under my covers. So the baby would be premature. So what? At least it'd be alive.

The minute hand moved slowly on my alarm clock. The second hand mocked it with its *tick-tick-tick*. "Hang in there, buddy," I said. Being patient was hard.

Pius came back forty minutes later. "Dad just called. It was a false alarm. The baby's not coming just yet."

I didn't answer because I was pretending to be asleep.

When I heard Pius snoring, I reached over and pulled the batteries out of my alarm clock. "It's okay, buddy," I whispered. "You can rest now."

★

The next morning I went to Gord's room. His newborn clothes had been freshly laundered. I reached into his dresser and took the monkey sleepers sized 0–3 months. I hid them in the rafters in the basement.

★

I told everyone at the nursing home about the false alarm. Edie said one of her labors lasted seventy-two hours. She called the kid Trouble. I wondered what Shelagh would

name her kid. Probably Shitty McShithead or Ugly
McUggface.

Buster said I seemed tense, so we danced extra hard
and extra long. Saibal taught us a style of Indian dance
called bhangra. We bounced our shoulders a lot and
raised our hands to the sky. He admitted he didn't know
what he was doing, so he sang "The Night Pat Murphy
Died" in his Indian accent to add some authenticity.

Afterwards Buster said, "Guess what?" and when I
said, "What?" he took out his teeth.

I laughed till I cried.

Edie gave me a medal of Saint Elizabeth. She told me
to give it to my mother. I wondered if Saint Elizabeth was
the patron saint of dead babies. I looked at the embossed
woman on the silver medal and whispered, "Fuck you,
Liz." I put it in my pocket and wondered if I'd go to hell.

*

A week later it was the day of the garden party. Nan was
all done up like a stick of gum. She had rouge on her
cheeks and a hat on her head. Mom made me wear a shirt
with buttons and slacks, not jeans. As we walked out the
door, she said, "Behave yourself, Fin-bear."

We walked up Cochrane Street. When we reached
the top, we could see it: Government House. Nan linked

her arm through mine. "Look at all the people," she said. The grounds were full and from where we stood, we could hear the murmur of conversation and the faint sound of the CLB Band.

We crossed Military Road and made our way to the entrance. The gravel path crunched beneath our feet. Nan looked nervous as we joined the party of finely dressed guests.

"Can I go explore?" I said.

Nan nodded. "Be good."

"Good's my middle name," I said.

"I thought it was Turlough," said a voice.

I turned around. Big Gord looked smart in a pinstriped suit. He introduced Nan to the lieutenant governor. Nan curtsied. We ate triangle sandwiches. The CLB Band was playing "Fight the Good Fight." Nan chatted with an army man in a wheelchair. It was hot and I was getting bored. Big Gord nodded to two plastic chairs under a tree. "Let's take a load off." A server came by and offered us lemonade. Big Gord clinked his glass against mine. "Here's to looking up your kilt."

"Up yours too," I said.

He took a long sip. "Ahhh."

I could tell by his face the lemonade was sour.

I took a sip. "Ahhh."

A newspaper man took our picture.

"We might make it into the *Telegram*," said Big Gord.

"My name was in the paper once," I said. "Right after 'leaving to mourn.'"

Big Gord nodded. "I saw that."

"I have a Gord-sized hole now," I said.

He took another sip of his drink.

I did too.

He pointed to a man with medals on his blazer.

"Ralph Fardy," he said. "One hundred and one."

"He's lucky he got to get old," I said.

"Indeed," said Big Gord.

"I've got a medal too," I said.

I took Saint Elizabeth out of my pocket. "I was supposed to give this to my mother."

"Little things can bring great comfort," said Big Gord.

The band played "The St. John's Waltz." Big Gord tapped his foot.

I tapped my foot too.

"This is the kind of song that fills you up," he said.

I didn't ask with what. I knew what it was and it didn't have a name. It was a mixture of feelings that could make you laugh and cry.

I saw Nan near the band. She was swaying to the music in her big hat. I hoped she lived to one hundred and one.

I pictured Dad's wristwatch marking time with its *click-click-click*s. A steady rhythm no matter how time flies.

The song was coming to an end. Big Gord sang about a world of romance and not missing a chance to be dancin' the St. John's Waltz. And his voice, it filled up a spot in my Gord-sized hole.

★

Father O'Flaherty made an appearance before the end of the garden party. He stood in front of the CLB Band and said he had an announcement. There was to be a talent contest on the night of the St. John's Regatta. He said the winner would be picked by audience vote and the prize was six hundred dollars.

"I hope the Full Tilt Dancers can count on your support," he said. "The prize money will go toward new flooring, of which we're in desperate need."

The audience nodded and clapped.

I asked Nan if she could make her way home alone. When she said yes, I ran like the dickens to the nursing home.

★

"Six hundred dollars?" said Buster. "Where do we sign up?"

"We could get a new sound system!" said Edie.

"We could buy tap shoes for all!" said Buster.

I cleared my throat.

"I have a different idea."

It was weird to see their faces light up at the mention of SIDS. But six hundred dollars toward research was something to smile about.

I called Saibal when I got home. "You'd better make up some more bhangra moves," I said. "We've got a dance to choreograph."

When I hung up the phone, I went to find Mom. She was in Gord's room. I reached into my pocket and pulled out the medal.

"Saint Liz," I said.

Mom's eyes crinkled when she laughed. "Oh, Barry."

Big Gord was right. Little things did bring comfort.

★

We only had a week, so we practiced every day. Uneven Steven came because he said he had a lot of expertise in the area. He even brought two fellas from the Harbour Light Centre—one played guitar and one played accordion. We decided on Great Big Sea's "Goin' Up" because it was super lively but not too fast. Our choreography was very unique. Wheelchairs, walkers, canes, and a piece of plywood all played a part. (The plywood was for my solo.) Saibal made up some more bhangra moves, which added an element of the exotic.

On the day before the regatta, Uneven Steven brought in a VHS tape. He wanted to inspire us with a montage of his moves from back in the day. I was curious as to what kind of video proof he could have for what was surely a fictitious life. We sat around a small TV and watched as he popped in the tape and pressed Play. Our jaws dropped as a string of musical clips came to life on the screen. We watched as Steven performed onstage with Jagger, Bowie, Mercury, and McCartney.

Afterwards he said, "I know you didn't Adam and Eve me but it was all true." He gave his shorter leg a hearty slap. "This old girl has never let me down."

"Your leg's a girl?" I said.

"Eileen," he said. "Get it?"

It took me a second. "Ha! Good one!"

He stood up to leave.

"Hey," I said. "Want to join our troupe?"

He grinned. "I thought you'd never ask."

CHAPTER TEN

The Royal St. John's Regatta was held on the first Wednesday of August, weather permitting. The night before, Mom and Dad played what the locals called Regatta Roulette—partying all night down on George Street hoping to God the next day would be a holiday. Mom wasn't sure she'd be up for it but Nan said it would do her and Dad good. They must have had a decent time because they stayed out real late. I know this because they made a racket coming home, laughing and knocking things over. Turns out, their gamble paid off. The next morning the sun was shining and the probability of precipitation was low. Mom and Dad went back to bed but

I headed down to Quidi Vidi Lake with a pocketful of coins and a boatload of excitement.

★

Saibal and I joined the crowds around the lake. The fixed-seat rowing races had already begun but we cared more about the games of chance. We went from stall to stall, throwing darts at balloons, gambling on the money wheels, and placing bets on Crown and Anchor. Our change was going fast but we were having a blast. With my last quarter, I bought a single ticket at the Knights of Columbus booth. It spun around and around, fast then slow. When it stopped, the man called the winner's number. "Five-zero-three!"

I looked at my ticket. Five-zero-three.

Saibal raised my hand into the air. "Over here! Over here!"

There were lots of stuffed toys to choose from. I picked a stuffed monkey.

"You okay?" said Saibal.

"Yes," I said. "I'm okay."

The food smells made our stomachs growl.

"I could eat the arse off a low-flying duck," said Saibal.

"Me too," I said.

We bumped into Pius. He bought us a plate of fish and chips with dressing and gravy.

"Ugh," said Saibal. "Freddie Fudge is here."

I looked around. "Where?"

Saibal pointed to a kid with spiky hair.

"He looks like a broom," I said.

"Who's Freddie Fudge?" asked Pius.

"Saibal's bully," I said.

"Finbar has a bully too," said Saibal.

"Don't worry, b'ys," said Pius. "Bullies always get their comeuppance."

Pius left us to eat our food by the bandstand. The CLB Band played "Up the Pond" and it filled me up.

"Look," I said. "It's that guy from *This Hour Has 22 Minutes*. The one who's always rantin' and ravin' at the camera."

"Rick Mercer," said Saibal. "Dad thinks he's a tool but Mudder thinks he's gorgeous."

"We could get his autograph for her," I said.

"Okay," said Saibal. "He can sign this empty container."

As we approached him I was struck with an amazing idea. "Instead of an autograph," I said, "we should ask him to lick the gravy. That way your mom will have his DNA."

"Brilliant," said Saibal.

Rick Mercer was in the middle of a conversation, but celebrities were used to getting interrupted, so I said, "Excuse me there, buddy. You wouldn't mind giving this gravy a lick, would ya?"

He looked at the congealed globs on the cardboard.

"My mom's a fan," said Saibal. "We'd like to give her some of your DNA."

"Oh, well in that case," said Rick Mercer.

He stuck out his tongue and dipped it in the gravy.

"Anything else?" he said. "You need a kidney or anything?"

"I have a question," I said. "Why are you always screamin' and bawlin' on TV?"

"A good rant is cathartic," he said.

"I'd love to get paid for shouting my opinions," said Saibal. "But I'm too brown for TV."

"You never know," he said. "Give it a few years and someone like you might be the star of *22 Minutes*."

"You really think so?" said Saibal.

Rick Mercer nodded. "I really do."

And with that, he walked away.

"Wow," I said. "Giving away DNA just like that. That man's a national treasure."

"He's a scholar and gentleman," said Saibal. "That's for sure."

We weaved our way through the crowds, watching kids on bouncy castles and riding ponies.

"We're too old for that stuff, aren't we, Finbar?" said Saibal.

"Indeed we are," I said.

We continued down the lakeside.

"Look," I said. "Coming out of the beer tent. It's the lead singer of Great Big Sea."

"Jesus," said Saibal. "Who are we gonna see next? Joey Smallwood?"

"Not unless he's rose from the dead," I said.

I cupped my hands around my mouth and yelled in the direction of the beer tent.

"Alan Doyle!"

When he looked over, I said, "Stay where you're to till we comes where you're at!"

A moment later, we were face to face.

"We'll be singing 'Goin' Up' at the talent show tonight," said Saibal.

Alan Doyle let out a laugh. "Will ye now?"

"We'll be dancing too," I said. "You should come watch."

"All right, b'ys," he said. "I'll see what I can do."

I held up the chip container. "Listen, me ol' trout. We're collecting celebrity DNA. Rick Mercer gave it a lick. We'd be honored if you did too."

Alan Doyle shoved his face in the container and dragged his tongue from one side of the cardboard to the other.

"Mmmm," he said. "Fee and chee with D and G. You can't beat it."

I wondered if he was drunk but rumor had it Alan Doyle was the happiest fella in Newfoundland.

As we walked away I said, "He could tell what we ate by the gravy."

"The man's a genius," said Saibal.

"Let's see who else we can find," I said.

"If we see Gordon Pinsent, I'll shit me pants," said Saibal.

"Nan would kill for some of his DNA," I said.

We spent another two hours at the regatta but saw no one else famous. We did find a five-dollar bill, though. We spent it on bouncy castles and pony rides.

★

We hid the chip container and the stuffed monkey in some bushes and went to the nursing home for a quick practice. Soon after, we were piling into the One Step Closer to God minibus. There were twenty-three of us all together, including Uneven Steven, the two musician fellas from the Harbour Light Centre, and an actual licensed minibus driver. Quidi Vidi Lake was a different place than it had been earlier. The stalls and stands were broken down and litter covered the ground. A stage had been erected downhill from the bandstand and a good-sized crowd sat on the hill facing it. At 6 p.m., the emcee took the stage. There were twelve acts in total, including Alfie Bragg and His Agony Bag and a dog named Upright who could walk on two legs. Both acts were big hits. Alfie's droning version of "Danny Boy" was power-ful enough to bring a tear to a glass eye, and the two legs Upright could walk on were his front ones—no one saw that coming. As usual, the Full Tilt Dancers were standing-ovation amazing.

When the emcee announced our name—the Oldies but Goodies—a cheer erupted from the crowd. I followed the sound till I saw them. There they were, all five of them, sitting on the grass. Across Mom's lap was the Humpty Dumpty blanket. I swallowed a lump in my throat.

When the two fellas from the Harbour Light Centre started playing "Goin' Up," the crowd sang along. Every-one in Newfoundland knew Great Big Sea.

Our choreography was going as planned until Edie started a striptease. Thankfully she was having trouble with her buttons. Buster tried to distract the audience by twirling his cane. Old people, they've got no grip strength. Uneven Steven got it in the head. As he lay bleeding on the stage, Saibal executed his bhangra moves with extra oomph. The audience didn't know where to look. When Uneven Steven was taken off the stage, Alan Doyle hopped on. He strummed the hell out of his guitar. He didn't sing, he belted. We were lockin' the world outside, which was fine by me because who needs the world when you're havin' a time down at Quidi Vidi Lake.

Steven made it back onstage for the last few moments. He had a bandage on his forehead and blood dribbled down his cheek. When it came time for my solo, Alan Doyle said, "Take it away, me ol' trout." My pennies echoed all the way to Signal Hill. When the song ended, we didn't need a standing ovation because everyone was already on their feet.

Mom hugged me tight. Nan said I was a grand boy. Dad said it didn't matter if we won and I said, "But what about the money for SIDS?" Pius said, "It's the thought that counts." Shelagh placed her hands on her belly. There was a pain in my heart. It was sudden and strange and the ache was for her.

The audience was given ballots. Alan Doyle entertained the crowd by playing a few tunes with the Harbour Light fellas while the votes were being counted. Between songs Pius went up onstage and made an announcement. "Could Freddie Fudge please make his way to the stage? His prescription genital wart cream was found by the seniors' tent."

I looked over at Saibal, who was sitting on the hill with his parents. We laughed our arses off telepathically.

Alan Doyle played a few more tunes while we waited for the contest results. It was a good half hour before the emcee was back on the stage. The Oldies but Goodies gathered to hear the results.

"And the winner is . . ."

"I'm gonna piss myself," said Saibal.

"The Full Tilt Dancers."

I forced my hands together until they made a noise that sounded like clapping.

"I demand a recount," yelled Edie. "This election's been rigged."

I was starting to think her earlier visit to the porta-potty had been a trip to the beer tent instead.

Father O'Flaherty was presented with a giant check. He thanked the audience and said that the money had been intended for a new floor.

"Boo! Hiss!" yelled Edie.

He cleared his throat. "But it's come to my attention that there is a better, more deserving cause."

"Get off the stage, you old fool!"

"Edie. Shush!" I said.

"Finbar Squires, would you make your way to the stage?"

Saibal pushed me forward because I was frozen.

"Had the Oldies but Goodies won, this money would have been donated to SIDS research," said Father O'Flaherty. "The Full Tilt Dancers think this is a worthy cause and would like to present this check to the Squires family."

Father O'Flaherty shook my hand. I could barely look him in the eye.

"The anger," I whispered. "It's passing."

He passed me the check. "God bless you, Finbar."

I turned to the audience and held the check in triumph.

"One question," I said. "How am I going to fit this in the deposit envelope?"

The crowd laughed.

I jumped off the stage and grabbed Saibal. I picked him up and swung him around.

"This is the best day ever!"

Then I stopped.

Saibal hung in midair.

"You're allowed to be happy," he said.

I set him down. "Thanks, Saibal."

After a group hug with the Oldies but Goodies, Saibal ran to the bushes and got the chip container and the monkey. We brought the container to Steven.

"Will you give this a lick?" I said. "We're collecting celebrity spit."

"And seeing as you performed with the likes of Jagger," said Saibal.

Steven puffed out his chest. "I'd be honored."

He licked up a glob of gravy and grimaced.

"How's the ol' loaf of bread?" I asked.

He adjusted the bandage across his forehead. "I've got a bangin' headache, Squire. But I'll be all right."

Mom and Dad waved to us from the hill. Saibal and I joined them on the Humpty Dumpty blanket.

I sat next to Shelagh.

"Six hundred dollars," said Mom. "Wow."

The sun was going down over Quidi Vidi Lake. Ducks squabbled in the distance. A lone rower paddled toward the boathouse.

Dad looked at his watch. "We've been here two hours already."

Mom put her hand over the clock face. "Time slips away, love. Whether you count it or not."

"That it does," said Nan.

I put the stuffed monkey in Shelagh's lap.

"Here you go, Shelagh."

Pius laid a hand on my back.

"Gord would have liked the regatta," she said.

"Yes," I said. "He would have."

★

That night, only a few weeks after the first ruckus, there was another. Pius jumped out of bed. This time I followed.

Shelagh was standing in the hall, a puddle underneath her on the floor.

"God almighty," I said. "She's leaking!"

Mom shooed us away. "Go wake your father. Tell him to start the car."

Shelagh was as white as a ghost.

"Don't be scared," said Nan. "We've all been through it."

"I haven't," said Pius.

"I told you to go get your father!" said Mom.

"Barry," said Nan. "Grab some towels and wipe this up while we help Shelagh change."

"I'm not touching that," I said. "It came out of her hoo-ha."

"He needs another month," said Shelagh as she shuffled to her room. "He'll be too small."

"He?" I said.

Dad helped me clean up the puddle.

"Amniotic fluid," he said. "Isn't it wonderful?"

A pained shriek came from Shelagh's bedroom.

"Breathe," said Mom. "Breathe."

They bustled her down the stairs and out to the car.

"I can't do this," she cried.

Pius and I stood in the doorway.

"Good luck, Shelagh," I said.

Shelagh looked back. "Thanks, Barry."

★

We drank tea and ate a whole tin of shortbread.

"What time is it?" I asked every ten minutes.

Pius put on *Fawlty Towers* to pass the time. The sign outside the hotel said FLOWERY TWATS.

"What time is it?" I asked.

It was 6:23 a.m. when the phone rang. Pius answered.

"Wow," he said into the phone.

He hung up.

"It's a girl."

★

Dad drove us to the Health Sciences Centre. All around us, the world ticked along. People went about their business and I thought, "Don't they know? A baby was born today."

Everyone took turns holding her. I sat in a chair and waited. No one wanted to give her up.

When Pius placed her in my arms, he said, "She doesn't have a big schnoz at all."

Ten little fingers. Ten little toes. Cute little dimples where the knuckles should be.

I said, "You should call her Regatta."

They spoke at once, all five of them together.

"Shut up, Barry."

★

She was a month early but healthy as an ox.

A week later she was home.

I missed Gord.

I missed everything about him.

Saibal came. We stared at her while she slept.

She had spit bubbles on her lips.

He said, "It's not her fault."

I said, "I know."

★

I woke up. I'm not sure why. I went down the hall. Shelagh was sitting next to the crib, her hand in the slats.

"What if it happens again?" she said.

I sat beside her. "It won't."

She lay her head against the crib rails.

"Go back to bed, Shelagh," I said.

"I can't."

"I'll stay."

"You will?"

I nodded.

When she was gone, I put my hand through the rails.

"Hi, Molly."

I placed my finger on her palm. She closed her hand around it.

"Someday, when you're bigger, I'll take you out," I said. "Saibal will come with us. You'll like him and he'll like you. That's how it works. I'll take you to Caines and up Signal Hill. Someday I'll take you to the harbor and pretend to dump you in. Don't worry, you'll love it. Gord did."

★

I stayed with her till she cried to be nursed. Then I went to the basement. I pulled Gord's monkey sleepers down from the rafters. I added them to the dirty laundry and dumped the basket into the washing machine. I'd never done laundry before but it was pretty straightforward. I threw in some detergent, turned the dial to normal load, and hit Start. I put on Pius's hockey skates and worked on my Balance and Stability Training Academy 4 Real Dancers program, or BASTARD for short. When the laundry was done, I took off the skates and pulled the clean clothes into a basket.

Upstairs, I slipped on my shoes and went out on the back porch. The clothesline screeched through the pulley. I reached into the basket and pinned the items to the line: Dad's flannel shirt; my underwear with the hole in the arse; Mom's forget-me-not nightgown; Pius's hockey jersey; Nan's frilly shirt; Shelagh's wonder pants. I bent down and picked up Molly's sleepers. Out of the corner of my eye, I saw a shadow. I don't know how long she'd been watching. The sky darkened and the wind picked up. I looked to my mother and smiled.

"It's some day on clothes."

ACKNOWLEDGMENTS

Special thanks to Saibal Chakraburtty for helping me bring little Saibal into the world. I hope you are proud of your literary child. You should be. He's a whole lot like you.

To the Newfoundland actors, writers, comedians, and musicians who I have admired over the years: thank you for inspiring me with your humor, humility, warmth, and wit. Your skillful storytelling astounds me.

To the two celebrities who make cameo appearances in this book: you, sirs, are scholars and gentlemen. Thank you for (unwittingly) being a part of Barry's story.

To my editor, Lynne Missen: thank you for digging deep. Not only do you show me the holes in the story, you help smooth them over once they're filled in. You are a master.

To Peter Phillips, Sam Devotta, Vikki VanSickle, and all the fine people at Penguin Random House: thanks, me ol' trouts. Your enthusiasm and support is much appreciated.

To my agent, Amy Tompkins: it's nice to have someone rooting for you. Thanks for always being in my corner.

Finally, a shout-out to my family back in St. John's, whose hilarious shenanigans inspired the fictional Squires of York Street. Thanks for being half cracked.

In memory of Emily Louise Down.
October 5, 1987–December 20, 1987

HEATHER SMITH is originally from Newfoundland, and now lives in Waterloo, Ontario, with her husband and three children. Her east coast roots inspire much of her writing. Her novel, *The Agony of Bun O'Keefe*, won the Ontario Library Association's White Pine Award and the Ruth & Sylvia Schwartz Award, and was shortlisted for the Amy Mathers Teen Book Award and the Geoffrey Bilson Award for Historical Fiction. *Barry Squires, Full Tilt* was longlisted for the 2020 BMO Winterset Award, which celebrates excellence in Newfoundland and Labrador writing regardless of age group or genre, an award Smith won for her middle-grade novel, *Ebb and Flow*.

G 286 .M2 P542 1995

Pigafetta, Antonio, ca.
1480/91-ca. 1534.

The first voyage around the
world (1519-1522)

DATE DUE

JAN 0 5 2015			

DEMCO 38-297

MARSI

Luigi Ball

SO-AIE-541

Magellan's Discovery of the Strait and First Voyage Around the World. An engraving from Theodor de Bry's *Historia Americae* (1594) [Courtesy of The Newberry Library].

THE FIRST VOYAGE
AROUND THE WORLD

(1519–1522)

An Account of Magellan's Expedition

by

ANTONIO PIGAFETTA

Edited by

Theodore J. Cachey Jr.

MARSILIO PUBLISHERS
NEW YORK

Original Italian title:
Viaggio intorno al mondo (1522)

Translation copyright © 1995
by T.J. Cachey, Jr.

Introduction copyright © 1995
by T.J. Cachey, Jr.

Of this edition copyright © 1995
by Marsilio Publishers
853 Broadway
New York, NY 10003

ISBN HC 1-56886-004-8
ISBN PB 1-56886-005-6

Distributed by
Consortium Book Sales and Distribution
1045 Westgate Drive
Saint Paul, MN 55114

All illustrations by permission
of the Ambrosiana Microfilm and Photographic Collection
of the University of Notre Dame

For James

CONTENTS

INTRODUCTION

1. *". . . to gain some renown with posterity"*

The Colombian novelist Gabriel Garcia Márquez provided a most memorable recent introduction to Antonio Pigafetta's *First Voyage Around the World* (*Viaggio attorno al mondo*) when he evoked, at the beginning of his 1982 Nobel Lecture, the Renaissance traveler "who went with Magellan on the first voyage around the world," and wrote "a strictly accurate account that nonetheless resembles a venture into fantasy." In the words of the Colombian novelist, the Italian witnessed:

> . . . hogs with navels on their haunches, clawless birds whose hens laid eggs on the backs of their mates, and others still, resembling tongueless pelicans, with beaks like spoons. He wrote of having seen a misbegotten creature with the head and ears of a mule, a camel's body, the legs of a deer and the whinny of a horse. He described how the first native encountered in Patagonia was confronted with a mirror, whereupon that impassioned giant lost his senses to the terror of his own image.[1]

From here, Garcia Márquez went on to claim that Pigafetta's ". . . short and fascinating book . . . even then contained the seeds of our present-day novels," recognizing in Pigafetta a genealogical source for the "marvelous" realism

[1] "The Solitude of America," *New York Times*, Section IV, February 6, 1983, p. 17.

(more familiar perhaps as "magical realism") one has come to associate with the novelist's own work and that of other prominent Latin American authors. The political implications of these Renaissance origins were not lost on the Latin American Nobel Laureate. Indeed, the rhetorical category of the "marvelous" which characterized Renaissance literature of discovery and exploration had often veiled an act of power, and glossed over real conflict by evoking "a sense of the marvelous that in effect fills up the emptiness at the center of the maimed rite of possession."[2] Towards the end of his address, the Colombian novelist pointedly isolated the literary category of the "marvelous," synonymous with so much European "americanist" writing, and turned it back against the Old World. For Garcia Márquez it was the novelist's report of Latin America's incredible contemporary reality—the incessant upheavals, the military coups and massacres, the continent's surreal political melodrama— which was "strictly accurate" but nonetheless resembled "a venture into fantasy." Exploiting another trope of European americanist writing, the commonplace of the New World's immense proportions, Garcia Márquez observed that the number of *desaparecidos*, at that time 120,000, was as if all the inhabitants of Upsala were unaccounted for. He noted that the death toll from civil strife in Central America of 100,000 dead in four years was proportionally equivalent to 1,600,000 violent deaths in the United States. Europe's "marvelous" dream had become Latin America's incredible nightmare of war and massacre, of exile and forced emigration.

Garcia Márquez's citation of Antonio Pigafetta's *First Voyage Around the World* is perhaps the most recent, certainly the most resonant, in a long line of prestigious literary responses to this Italian travel narrative. If Pigafetta undertook his voyage, as he says, "so that I might be able to gain some renown with posterity" (¶2), he can be said to have succeeded brilliantly. The author's desire

---

[2] Stephen Greenblatt, *Marvelous Possessions: The Wonder of the New World*, Chicago: University of Chicago Press, 1991, p. 80.

for fame, for the extension of the self in space and time, is indeed a prominent motive in the *First Voyage*. Pigafetta's account of the circumnavigation expresses that same desire for the circumvention of death that is at the heart of travel literature itself, which has always sought to "fix and perpetuate something as transient and impermanent as human action and mobility."[3]

William Shakespeare's use of Pigafetta's *libreto* (or "little book," as the author terms it) in *The Tempest* is perhaps the best known manifestation of Pigafetta's literary fame during the Renaissance:

> CALIBAN: [*Aside*]: I must obey—his art is of such power,
>   It would control my dam's god, Setebos,
>   And make a vassal of him. (I, ii)

And later,

> CALIBAN: Oh Setebos, these be brave spirits indeed!
>   How fine my master is! I am afraid
>   He will chastise me. (V, i)

Shakespeare's "Setebos" derived from his reading of Richard Eden's 1555 Tudor English translation of Pigafetta's narrative. Pigafetta had first introduced the Teuhuelche name into European circulation when he described a pair of Patagonian giants who, upon realizing Magellan had had them placed in irons through subterfuge, "raged like bulls, calling loudly for Setebos to aid them" (¶29); later, in one of his native word lists Pigafetta defined "Setebos" as "their big devil" (¶39).[4] García Márquez, for his part, borrows from Pigafetta

---

[3] E.J. Leed, *The Mind of the Traveler: From Gilgamesh to Global Tourism*, Basic Books, 1991, p. 28.

[4] The extent to which Shakespeare's reading of Pigafetta's Patagonian encounters informs the Americanist thematics of *The Tempest* and the creation of Caliban remains an open question. At least one recent commentator has observed that Shakespeare ". . . read Pigafetta more carefully than is usually noticed . . ." (Bruce Chatwin, *In Patagonia*, New York: Summit Books, 1977, p. 91).

another moment from the same "marvelous" anthropological encounter with the Patagonians that had inspired Shakespeare. The giant described by García Márquez, who confronts a mirror and is rendered senseless in terror at his own image, has a distinctively Shakespearean or Calibanic resonance. That Shakespeare was a possible mediator of García Márquez's perspective on Pigafetta is suggested by an allusion to Shakespeare made in an earlier meditation on the difference between New and Old World language and poetics, where the Colombian author first expressed his appreciation for Pigafetta's *First Voyage* (calling it there *"uno de mis libros favoritos de siempre"*). Intriguingly, to illustrate the untranslatability of the Latin American experience, García Márquez used the example of the word *tempestad*: "When we write the word *tempestad*, the Europeans think of thunder and lightning, but it is not easy for them to conceive of the same phenomenon which we are seeking to represent."[5]

Shakespeare was not the earliest Renaissance poet to find inspiration in Pigafetta's *First voyage*. A preliminary draft of canto XV of Torquato Tasso's *Gerusalemme liberata* was largely based upon the American portion of Pigafetta's narrative. While most of the episode was suppressed in the poem's final version, it nevertheless represents an important moment both for the history of the elaboration of Tasso's poem and for the history of Italian Renaissance "Americanism" in general.[6] According to Tasso's original plan, the extra-

---

[5] "Fantasía y creacíon artística en América Latina y el Caribe," *Texto crítico*, 14, 1979, p. 6. On Shakespeare's *The Tempest* and the semantics of storms, which present points of differentiation between Old and New Worlds, see P. Hulme, *Colonial Encounters*, London: Metheun, 1986. For more on the contemporary Latin American literary reception of Pigafetta's narrative see H.E. Robles, "The First Voyage Around the World: From Pigafetta to García Márquez," *History of European Ideas*, vol. 6, no. 4, 1985, pp. 385-404.

[6] See T.J. Cachey Jr., "Tasso's *Navigazione del mondo nuovo* and the Origins of the Columbus Encomium (*GL*, XV, 31-32)," *Italica*, 69, 3, 1992, pp. 326-44; and "Dal Nuovo Mondo alle isole Fortunate," in *Le isole Fortunate: Appunti di storia letteraria italiana*, Roma: L'"Erma" di Bretschneider, 1995, pp. 203-62.

Mediterranean portion of Carlo and Ubaldo's marvelous voyage to Armida's island followed a radically different itinerary from the one familiar to readers of the *Gerusalemme liberata*. Rather than pass directly to the Fortunate Islands, the "barca avventurosa" set out upon the Ocean Sea bound for the New World. Tasso's heroes coasted a lengthy tract of South American *terra ferma* identified as the land of the "inospitali Antropofagi," and sighted along the shore the incredible "Patagon giganti" made famous by Antonio Pigafetta's narrative. The literary quality of Pigafetta's book strongly stimulated the imagination of the Italian epic poet, especially its "marvelous" treatment of the voyage. Tasso created a gallery of poetic marvels in a series of octaves based directly upon Pigafetta's prose account. Pigafetta's literary reception therefore, stretching from Torquato Tasso to Gabriel García Márquez, suggests intriguing lines of continuity, especially as regards the literary category of the marvelous, from the High Renaissance travel narrative, to late-Renaissance poetics of the marvelous (practiced and expounded upon at length by Tasso and other late-Renaissance literary theorists), to contemporary Latin American "magical realism."[7]

2. *The Book of a Courtier*

The prestigious literary circulation enjoyed by Pigafetta's book is due only in part to the heroic dimensions of its incredible historical subject—the Magellan-Elcano circumnavigation of the globe between 1519-1522. In fact, if the return of the *Victoria* and its few surviving crew represented the greatest and culminating feat of the Renaissance Age of Discoveries, so too Pigafetta's

[7] For the beginnings of research in this sense, see S. Greenblatt's discussion of the Renaissance poetics of the marvelous and travel writing in *Marvelous Possessions*, cit., pp. 77-82 and notes 69-80 on pp. 175-77.

account of that achievement, first published in manuscript between February and June 1525, represented the literary epitome, within its genre, of the High Renaissance Age of Discovery and Exploration.[8] One of the Renaissance *capolavori* produced by Italian courtier culture of the High Renaissance, Pigafetta's *First Voyage* belongs to the same generation, albeit in a minor generic key, as other more familiar Italian literary classics published in the first decades of the 16th century like Sannazaro's *Arcadia*, Machiavelli's *Prince*, Ariosto's *Orlando Furioso*, and Baldassare Castiglione's *The Book of the Courtier*. Like these works, Pigafetta's *First Voyage* emerges from a period of deep political and cultural crisis in Italy which began with the initial French invasion of the peninsula in 1494 and reached its height in the Sack of Rome in 1527. The breakdown of the Italian court system under the pressures of French and Spanish incursions, the religious revolution set in motion by the Reform, and the great Oceanic discoveries, all contributed to Italy's increasing marginalization within the context of early modern western European history. From a literary, and generally cultural point of view, the Italian High Renaissance therefore represents a kind of swan-song, a brilliant culminating flourish. Like the better known literary classics and art works of the period, Pigafetta's *libreto* achieves a kind of fulfillment or realization in its genre within an Italian context. And in its own way, like other Italian cultural products of the period, Pigafetta's *First Voyage* went abroad and achieved an international reputation, beginning with at least three French illuminated manuscripts and the Simon de Colines' *princeps* published in Paris (c. 1525).[9] Pigafetta's *First Voyage* illustrates in its own way, even at the reputedly unexalted level of the travel narrative, both the mobility of the

[8] B. Penrose in her classic study *Travel and Discovery in the Renaissance* observed that "as the first-hand narration of one of history's three greatest voyages, Pigafetta's book rivals Columbus's *Journal* and da Gama's *Roteiro*" (p. 375).

[9] This early translation and immediate reception beyond the Alps raised the famous red-herring about the original language in which Pigafetta composed the relation, now generally accepted to have been Italian. See the bio-bibliographic note.

cosmopolitan courtier and the exportability of Italian courtier culture of the High Renaissance. At the same time that Italian culture enters a period of deep crisis and growing marginalization, the Italian courtier traveler goes out into the world with pen in hand,[10] to assert a compensatory literary authority, in relation to European political hegemony established over the newly discovered lands by some of the same emerging European powers that were in the process of carving up the Italian peninsula.

The original Italian courtly derivation of the work merits further consideration, given that Pigafetta's *First Voyage* represents a particularly mature expression of courtly Italian Renaissance travel writing. Indeed, to speak of an Italian courtier genealogy for the work is to locate it within the "*lingua e letteratura cortigiana*" (courtly language and literature) which flourished on the peninsula briefly, between the end of the fifteenth and the first decades of the sixteenth century, and produced the Italian High Renaissance. Perspective on the literary and linguistic sensibility of our author is gained by considering his position in relation to the Italian "*Questione della lingua*," that is, as expressive of an Italian cosmopolitan court culture in contrast to vernacular humanist and municipal Florentine outlooks on the Italian scene. As we will see, Pigafetta stands in suggestive counterpoint to the classicizing vernacular humanism canonized by Pietro Bembo's *Prose della volgar lingua* (first published, like Pigafetta's narrative, in 1525) which resurrected the fourteenth century language and style of Petrarch (for poetry) and Boccaccio (for prose) as the standard paradigm for subsequent Italian literary history.[11]

---

[10] The technology of writing as symbol of European culture and as employed by Pigafetta constitutes an interesting theme in its own right, both implicitly and explicitly within the narrative (see for example ❡40 and ❡60).

[11] Pigafetta's language has been analyzed from a linguistic perspective (see the studies by Sanvisenti, Busnelli, and Beccaria cited in the textual notes), but his importance (and that of contemporary Italian travel writing in general) in relation to literary historiography regarding the contemporary "*Questione della lingua*" has not been particularly emphasized or developed.

But more particularly, it is important to appreciate how Pigafetta's book represents the culmination and at the same time the confluence of two particularly important sub-genres of Italian Renaissance travel writing. In the first place, Pigafetta appears at the end of a distinguished line of Italian Americanist *auctores* (an Atlantic tradition, if you will, which goes back to Boccaccio's *De canaria* in the fourteenth century and Cadamosto's letters in the fifteenth). If Pigafetta's is indeed a first-hand account of the circumnavigation, he nevertheless shows himself time and again to be extremely self-conscious about writing in the literary tradition of Renaissance travel. In the dedicatory letter to his book, for example, Pigafetta mentions that he had been prepared for his participation in the voyage by "having learned many things from many books that I had read" (¶2). And it is easy to imagine our author as a youth (he was born around 1492)[12] devouring one of the earliest collections of discovery voyages, published in his home town of Vicenza in 1507 by Enrico da ca' Zeno: Fracanzio da Montalboddo's *I paesi novamente ritrovati et Novo Mondo da Americo Vespucio Florentino intitolato*, a volume which included the narratives of the voyages of Cadamosto, Columbus, and Cabral, besides Vespucci. The Vicentine appears to be especially indebted to that universally read (as More tells us)[13] Amerigo Vespucci; but he also displays affinities to other Italian americanists, including, for example, Niccolò Scillacio (*De insulis*, 1494), and Michele Da Cuneo, whose letter to Hieronymo Annari (1495) represents a significant example of Italian courtly travel writing in its own right. Pigafetta's book, more or less contemporary with Verrazzano's 1524 letter to Francis I regarding his explorations of the North American coast, represents the culmination of the Italian *americanista* tradition, and recapitulates many of the salient characteristics of that tradition, such as an heroic ideological perspective, a relative detachment

[12] See the bio-bibliographic note.
[13] Raphael Nonsenso is said to have "joined up with Amerigo Vespucci. You know those *Four Voyages* of his that everyone's reading about?" (*Utopia*, Translated with an introduction by Paul Turner, Harmondsworth, Penguin, 1965, pp. 38-39).

from national political and commercial interests, as well as a paradoxically legitimating utilization of the "marvelous." Girolamo Benzoni's *Historia del nuovo mondo* (1565), the last major Italian contribution to the tradition of americanist travel writing, is, by comparison, only a highly interesting epigone of that tradition, and the *Historia* a masterpiece of Americanist plagiarism.

Pigafetta's book also represents the point of arrival for an important "Orientalist" sub-genre of Italian Renaissance travel writing. The *isolario*, or "Book of Islands" genre, might plausibly be termed 'Orientalist' since the earliest fifteenth century examples limited their coverage to the culturally exotic, and politically and commercially contested archipelagos of the eastern Mediterranean.[14] The fifteenth century *capostipite* of the "Book of Islands" genre, Crisotoforo Buondelmonti's *Liber insularum archipelagi*, circulated widely during the fifteenth and sixteenth centuries, and as a member of the Order of the "Sea Knights" of Rhodes, Antonio Pigafetta would surely have been familiar with this work.[15] To recognize the *First Voyage*'s affinity to the *isolario* tradition generally, and to Buondelmonti in particular, is to recover an important aspect of the work's original courtier Renaissance character which has been lost upon post-Enlightenment readers of the work.

[14] The "Book of Islands" genre and Pigafetta's *First Voyage* are early modern precursors of that discourse Edward Said has termed Orientalist: "dealing with the Orient—dealing with it by making statements about it, authorizing views of it, describing it, by teaching it . . . as a Western style for dominating, restructuring, and having authority over the Orient" (*Orientalism*, New York: Pantheon, 1978, p. 3).

[15] Pigafetta was most likely already a Knight in the Order of St. John of Jerusalem before his departure on the voyage in 1519 departure. See the bio-bibliographical note.

3. *Reading for Scholars and Princes*

The book's courtly americanist, and Orientalist origins are conveniently signaled in the dedicatory letter: by the presence of Pigafetta's fellow Vicentine and patron, the powerful ecclesiastic and diplomat Francesco Chiericati, who first took Pigafetta with him to Spain; and by the dedication of the work to the Grand Master of the Knights of Rhodes, the French noble, Philippe Villiers de l'Isle-Adam. Francesco Chiericati, with whom Pigafetta "discussed the great and marvelous things of the Ocean Sea (¶2)" possessed impeccable americanist credentials. He appears for example in the introduction to one of Matteo Bandello's *Novelle* (I, 34), at the court of Pandino upon his return from Portugal, recounting the marvels of the New World, and displaying: ". . . golden objects, pearls, precious stones and other beautiful things brought back from those countries. He exhibited also certain idols marvelously fashioned in mosaic, that those people, who have by now for the most part become Christians, used to adore. . . ."[16] Bandello has Chiericati go on to tell about the custom among some men in those new countries who vied to have their wives pass the night with foreign visitors, concluding that "jealousy has no place among those simple and primitive people, nor does it cause them to take up arms. . . ." An observation that leads, without fail, to a *novella* illustrating the negative effects of Old World jealousy. Beyond this literary representation, Chiericati's own travel writings, usually addressed to Isabella d'Este (to whom he recommended Pigafetta immediately following the return of the *Victoria*), include a fascinating account of a trip to Ireland,[17] and oscillate between the same poles of critical investigation and ingenuous enthusiasm for the marvelous which characterize Pigafetta's narrative.

[16] *Novelle di Matteo Bandello*, ed. G.G. Ferrero, Turin: UTET, 1974, pp. 287-88.
[17] For Chiericati see the textual note 3 at p. 125. His narrative describing a trip to Ireland in 1515 while he was Papal Nuncio at the Court of Henry VIII was published by J.P. Mahaffy, "Two Early Tours in Ireland," in *Hermathena*, XL (1914), pp. 1-16.

As a member of the Order of the "Sea Knights" of Rhodes, Pigafetta dedicates his *First Voyage* to the Grand Master Villiers l'Isle-Adam at a crucial historical moment. The Order of the Hospital of St. John of Jerusalem had since the fourteenth century represented "the bulwark of Christendom" in the Levant. The surrender of Rhodes and flight to Italy, which led to the Order's temporary settlement in Viterbo and later establishment in Malta, sent shock waves through Christian Europe. Clearly, no more dramatic period of crisis for the order, or of Christian power in the eastern Mediterranean, could be conjured up as a background for Magellan's circumnavigation. As we shall see in the next section, recognition of this "Rhodian" context for Pigafetta's *First Voyage* suggests a strong connection between Pigafetta's book and the "Book of Islands." For the moment, however, one can observe how Chiericati and the Grand Master provide a literary and ideological framework for a reading of the work.

The dedicatory letter also establishes the heroes of the narrative, for there are indeed two heroes of this epic: Magellan and Pigafetta, just as there are two heroic activities to be celebrated: exploration and narration. Pigafetta's recent Italian editor has persuasively illuminated the care with which Pigafetta structured the text so as to celebrate the heroic figure of Magellan *"bon pastore"* (good shepherd) and *"bon cavaliero"* (good knight). Magellan's death occurs in fact almost exactly at the midpoint of the narrative (¶100), and he emerges as an heroic figure worthy of the extraordinary geographical feat of the circumnavigation that he was tragically denied seeing through to its end.[18] But Pigafetta's treatment of Magellan should not obscure the extent to which the author stages himself as the hero of his own text, albeit in a quite subtle way. Pigafetta is careful to place his two heroes on the same social plane in the dedicatory letter, where they are described as members of prestigious religious-

[18] M. Masoero, "Magellano, 'bon pastore' e 'bon cavaliero'," in *La letteratura di viaggio dal Medioevo al Rinascimento: Generi e problemi*, Alessandria: Edizioni dell'Orso, 1989, pp. 51-62.

military orders setting out to discover spicery: Pigafetta styles himself:
"patrician of Vicenza and Knight of Rhodes" and Magellan: "a Portuguese
gentleman, comendador of the Order of Santiago de le Spada (¶3)." While
Magellan's death, following his preaching and thaumaturgic display (¶89)
among the Filipinos, which leads to many conversions, is described by
Pigafetta in the terms of a religious martyrdom, Pigafetta's own near-death
experience is no less resonant, from a literary perspective. Early on in the navigation among the islands of the Philippine archipelago, on the Feast Day of
the Annunciation:

> I went to the side of the ship to fish, and putting my feet upon a yard lead-
> ing down into the storeroom, they slipped for it was rainy, and consequently
> I fell into the sea, and no one saw me. When I was all but under, my left
> hand happened to catch hold of the clew-garnet of the mainsail, which was
> dangling in the water. I held on tightly, and began to cry out so lustily that I
> was rescued by the small boat. I was aided, not, I believe, indeed, through
> my merits, but through the mercy of that font of charity [the Virgin] (¶55).

Here the emphasis on Pigafetta's own travel as a heroic test, as a loss that brings
about a gain of stature and certainty of self is underlined. Pigafetta survives
this near-death experience, just as he had survived the crossing of the Pacific
("Nineteen men died. . . . Thirty-five or thirty men fell sick. . . . However, I, by the
grace of God, suffered no sickness"; ¶41). He survives the circumnavigation
itself, acquiring in the process an increased stature among mortals, emerging as
a worthy witness to Magellan's martyrdom and the achievement of the circumnavigation. The narrative presents the account of a kind of fictional death and
resurrection of Pigafetta, "fictional rather than real because death is used as a
context for the assertion of an essential and irreducible self; implicitly denied
is the reality of death as a dissolution of form and a solvent of identity."[19] Just

[19] E. J. Leed, *The Mind of the Traveler*, cit., p. 9.

as the circumnavigation is figured by Pigafetta as an escape from death, Pigafetta's book expresses at yet another level an heroic desire to circumvent death and to "gain some renown with posterity."

Without question, Pigafetta's experience and its writing are in their own ways celebrated as glorious and heroic. Besides "the great and wonderful things" to report from "my long and dangerous voyage," Pigafetta's "vigils, hardships, and wanderings (¶4)" recall the heroic *vigilie*, or sleepless nights of Amerigo Vespucci, canonized in the famous Stradanus engraving that portrays the Florentine sighting the stars during the middle of the night, while sailors lie slumped around him sleeping in a kind of New World Gethsemani. Like Vespucci, Pigafetta is careful to cite all the highly placed personages who legitimate his endeavor in one way or another—and what more appropriate patrons for a circumnavigation of the globe than the emperor and the pope. Pigafetta sailed in fact "by the good favor of his Caesarean Majesty" (¶1), and upon his return was summoned by the pope to recount his adventures. The author's reference to his "going to see his Holiness, Pope Clement" alludes to just one key moment in the remarkable history of Pigafetta's peregrinations after his return (these are detailed in the bio-bibliographical treatment which follows this introduction). At one point, there was actually the promise of Pope Clement VII's sponsorship for the printing of Pigafetta's book.

From a rhetorical perspective, the legitimating strategy of evoking highly placed patrons for one's explorations was of course commonplace. It had already been masterfully practiced by Vespucci: "two [voyages] were by command of the exalted King of Castile Don Fernando VI, to go west over the depths of the Ocean Sea, and the other two were by the command of the mighty King Don Manuel of Portugal, to go south. . . ."[20] Pigafetta adopts a similar strategy in both the dedicatory letter and in the work's concluding

[20] *Letters from a New World: Amerigo Vespucci's Discovery of America*, Edited by L. Formisano, Translated by D. Jacobson, New York: Marsilio, 1992, pp. 57-58.

paragraph, which is more explicit in this regard, and which represents a kind of *envoi* to the work (a quintessentially courtly form). The narrative, in fact, circles around like the voyage itself, and returns to the courtly context from which it had departed, with details concerning the courtly reception that awaited the author:

> Leaving Seville, I went to Valladolid, where I presented to his sacred Majesty, Don Carlo, neither gold nor silver, but things very highly esteemed by such a sovereign. Among other things I gave him a book, written by my hand, concerning all the matters that had occurred from day to day during our voyage. I left there as best I could and went to Portugal where I spoke with King Dom João of what I had seen. Passing through Spain, I went to France where I made a gift of certain things from the other hemisphere to the mother of the most Christian king Don Francis, Madame the Regent. Then I came to Italy, where I devoted myself forever and these my poor labors to the famous and most illustrious lord Philippe de Villiers l'Isle-Adam, the most worthy Grand Master of Rhodes.

While Amerigo Vespucci reports in his letters that he had explored and discovered at the command of the Kings of Spain and Portugal, Pigafetta records in a similar vein his post-circumnavigation tour, during which he was repeatedly called upon to recount his experiences at court. There had been an evident shift in emphasis since 1492, from the Genoese Columbus's claim to glory as "inventor" of a New World (as an explorer first and as a writer second), to Antonio Pigafetta whose claim on "some renown with posterity" is based principally upon his having composed a book about the circumnavigation. Vespucci occupies a middle position in this series. While the Florentine's contributions in the literary "invention" of America through the publication of the *Mundus Novus* and "Letter to Soderini" surpass and overshadow his contributions to geographical and navigational knowledge, the latter were nonetheless based upon some genuine expertise, given that Vespucci was appointed "Pilot Major" by the King of Spain in 1508. Italy's role however as historical protagonist in the discoveries and explorations, exemplified by the Genoese Columbus and other Italians, came to an end after one generation. Pigafetta's role as simple witness some thirty years following the discovery of America reflects the general decentering of Italy as the geographical, religious, and commercial center located at the heart of the Mediterranean Old World, and its increasing marginalization as the New World of Atlantic colonial nation-states emerged.[21] Moreover, the Italian Pigafetta's enduring fame as witness and scribe of an historical achievement effected by an Iberian power encapsulates the fundamentally humanistic and literary character of Renaissance Italy's response to foreign political domination and to its estrangement from "modern" European history.[22] In other words, Italian Renaissance culture's commitment to writing and its belief in the enduring status of the written word are powerfully illustrated even by an ostensibly non-humanistic text like Pigafetta's *First Voyage*. On this point, Italian vernacular court culture was evidently no less imbued with the same ideal which inspired the vernacular humanists and contemporary Florentines in their literary endeavors.

Pigafetta's request in the dedicatory letter that the Grand Master deign to take up "this little book . . . when you will take some rest from your continual

[21] Significantly, eighteenth-century Italian literary historiography already appears sensitive to this shift. Girolamo Tiraboschi, in that part of his *Storia della letteratura italiana* dedicated to the Renaissance period of discovery and exploration, excludes Pigafetta and the circumnavigation from his treatment since ". . . [Pigafetta] was no more than a simple passenger, and the idea and the success of that great exploit are owed to Magellan and his companions, among whom however we do find that there were two Genoese" (Firenze: Molini, Landi, 1809, Tomo VII, Parte I, p. 260).

[22] C. Dionisotti thus describes the Italian literary tradition that would emerge from the Renaissance: "It was, as the history of historiography teaches, a humanistic tradition, nourished by linguistic and literary successes, founded upon the persuasion that Italians indeed suffer the violence of historical events, but that they alone are capable, by choice and by education, to oppose that ephemeral and blind violence with the perennial, lucid validity of discourse, of writing" (*Geografia e storia della letteratura italiana*, Torino: Einaudi, 1967, p. 27).

Rhodian cares," speaks specifically to the travel narrative's function within the courtly literary system. There is a direct parallel in Vespucci's "Letter to Soderini" where the Florentine addressed the Gonfaloniere:

> . . . continually occupied as Your Magnificence must be with public concerns, still you must reserve some hours for recreation, and spend a little time in trifling or delightful things; and just as fennel is customarily placed on top of delicious foods to improve them for digestion, so you will be able to escape from your many occupations, to have this letter of mine read, so that you may take refuge somewhat from the continual care and assiduous consideration of public matters. . . .[23]

The precise echo of Vespucci's desire to assuage Soderini's "assiduous consideration of public matters" in Pigafetta's offer to relieve the Grand Master's "assiduous Rhodian cares" (¶4) underscores the analogous conceptions these authors had of the literary category in which they were writing. Travel is taken here as a recreative category of literature combining useful (particularly ethnographic and geographical) information, with delightful, "marvelous" matters. Moreover, it makes ideal reading for princes and scholars for it serves "to relaxe a little the intention of their thoughts, that they may be more apt and able to endure a continued course of study," as Lucian put it in the preamble of the *True History*.[24]

This courtly literary context for Pigafetta's *First Voyage* explains in large measure the role of the "marvelous" in Pigafetta's narrative, as well as much of the work's undeniable literary appeal. The narrative of the voyage more or less

---

[23] *Letters from a New World*, cit., p. 57.

[24] A passage which has been recently termed "perhaps the highest invitation to consider travel literature that which from the Odyssey forward it always has been: a literature of entertainment. . . ." M. Guglielminetti, "Il Messico a Venezia nel 1528: Benedetto Bordon e Hernán Cortés," in *L'impatto della scoperta dell'America nella cultura veneziana*, ed. A.C. Aricò, Roma: Bulzoni, pp. 108-9.

begins with a description of the miraculous tree of the waterless island of Hierro in the Canaries (on the threshold between the Old and New Worlds): "the leaves and branches of which distil a quantity of water . . . the people living there, and the animals, both domestic and wild, fully satisfy themselves with this water and no other." The first in a series of marvels which constitute Pigafetta's account of the outward passage, the marvelous tree of Hierro had, since Columbus, represented one of those classic Atlantic marvels which served rhetorically to mark the passage from Old World to New. The tree's status as a literary commonplace seems paramount here, especially in light of the fact that the expedition did not stop at Hierro. The marvelous serves Pigafetta to establish the authority of his account with the contemporary courtly audience which had come to expect such wonders from their travel narratives. Other marvels of crossing include tremendous storms and the repeated appearance of St. Elmo's fire, sharks with terrible teeth, and those birds mentioned by García Márquez, which "make no nest . . . because they have no feet, and the hen lays her eggs on the back of the cock, and hatches them." The marvelous "caccia de' pesci," with which our author highlights the passage through the strait of Magellan (later poeticized by Tasso), represents yet another marvelous "passage," which serves on the one hand to establish the alterity of the new worlds encountered and, paradoxically, to legitimize the veracity of Pigafetta's account. Another related strategy employed by Pigafetta, is exemplified by the stereotypical account of his first encounter with the natives of Brazil (¶16-¶21), based upon the authoritative descriptions of Columbus and Vespucci. In this regard Pigafetta continues in the line of Vespucci who had imitated Columbus in a similar fashion. The "inventor" Columbus not only discovered a continent but inaugurated a new americanist subgenre within the context of travel narrative, and thus became a model for imitation. After satisfying the readers' initial expectations, Pigafetta goes on to describe the famous encounters with the Patagonian giants, which can be seen as brilliant literary elaborations on a theme of American giants inaugurated by Amerigo Vespucci both in his first familiar letter and in the "Letter to Soderini."

This kind of appreciation for the Italian courtly literary context for the *First Voyage* also casts light on the notorious problem presented by the fact that in this, the most important by far of the first-hand sources regarding Magellan's voyage, there is so little information (and this is garbled and oblique) about the dramatic episodes of mutiny and desertion which plagued the expedition from the start. Indeed, the expedition's internal politics, which have always fascinated historians of the voyage, are generally elided in favor of the "marvels" of travel, the heroic stature of the captain-general, and the achievement of the circumnavigation. An initial incident in fact took place during the Atlantic crossing when Juan de Cartagena's insubordination led to his deposition as commander of the *San Antonio* and his being placed in the stocks. As we have just seen, Pigafetta, during this part of the voyage, instead treats us to a gallery of transatlantic "marvels." Generally speaking, the marvelous seems to expand and fill the narrative space in precisely those moments when trouble is afoot.

The mutiny which Pigafetta could not ignore took place at Port St. Julian by Gaspar Quesada, Juan de Cartagena, and Juan Sebastian del Cano on April 1-2, 1519. The story is perhaps best told by Magellan's excellent biographer Guillemard, who based himself upon a collation of all the sources.[25] While Pigafetta is generally considered the most important source for the expedition's history, on these episodes he was no help at all. Indeed, according to Guillemard, his account is "remarkable for its extraordinary inaccuracy" (p. 174); it seemed "incredible that an eyewitness—which [Pigafetta] undoubtedly was—should have failed to remember circumstances such as these, and the fact somewhat lessens the value of his book as a credible narrative . . ." (p. 174). For fuller and more accurate accounts of the mutiny, Guillemard must turn instead to the official historiographers such as the Spaniard Herrera and the

[25] F.H.H. Guillemard, *The Life of Ferdinand Magellan*, London: G. Philip, 1890, pp. 164-74.

Portuguese Barros, who had competing national interests to safeguard in their respective histories. At this crucial point in his narrative, Pigafetta is more concerned with the description of the encounter with the Patagonian giants which includes several well developed episodes (¶25-¶30). He squeezes his account of the mutiny (¶31) between the encounter with the Patagonians (the one that made an impression on Shakespeare) and the discovery of the strait (¶32-¶38). Certainly, from a literary perspective, Pigafetta's "marvelous" encounter with the Patagonian giants more than compensates for his lack of information about the mutiny. In any case, Pigafetta's intention to celebrate his hero Magellan did not require that he descend into the domestic details of who did what to whom, beyond the fact that Magellan won the day.

Pigafetta's remarkable detachment from the local political aspects of the voyage goes together with his emphasis on the marvelous and the heroic celebration of Magellan. Pigafetta seeks to create a sense of the marvelous in order to "fill up the emptiness at the center of the maimed rite of possession" to use Stephen Greenblatt's formula for Columbus's writing.[26] Columbus's claims of possession declared on the beach at San Salvador are no more plausible or legitimate than those made by European powers seeking to establish their hegemony over the Spice Islands. This was by means of a long tradition of legalistic fictions going back to the Papal Bull *Inter caetera* (1493) and the Treaty of Tordesillas (1494) in which the entire globe was divided into Spanish and Portuguese spheres of influence. The competing colonial claims of these emerging powers upon the whole world and the commercially motivated extension of European power are masked to some extent by Pigafetta's literary program. Magellan is heroically and unproblematically figured as a Christian Knight gone out to convert the heathen and subdue the infidel according to a broader supra-nationalist crusader ideal. Given the "international" courtly audience for whom Pigafetta's narrative was intended, political

---

[26] *Marvelous Possessions: The Wonder of the New World*, cit., p. 80.

disputes between European powers are naturally muted in favor of a general picture of Christian unity vis-à-vis the Gentile or Moorish peoples of the antipodes. Indeed it is remarkable that, besides making occasional reference to the "line of demarcation," Pigafetta never explicitly discusses the political issue which the historians tell us constituted the motivating force behind the circumnavigation in the first place: to determine the true position of the Spice Islands (or Moluccas), and to establish that they were on the Spanish side of the line.

Pigafetta also exhibits a relatively neutral perspective on the commercial aspects of the expedition, which is what one would expect given both his courtier social background and his epic-heroic literary intentions. Vespucci had already belittled the achievement of the Portuguese Vasco da Gama for sailing for primarily commercial reasons, a motivation which detracted from the heroic virtue of discovery as an end in itself.[27] The voyage of discovery, in order to the be the heroic object of epic celebration must find a way around the commercial bourgeois motive for travel more appropriate to the literary category of romance.[28] Like Vespucci before him, Pigafetta apparently had little direct economic or political stake in the voyage. Instead, he is *"Antonio Lombardo"* (Antonio of Lombardy) *"sobresaliente"* (a supernumerary), as he is called in the expedition's roster. The detached perspective of the courtly observer is drawn to the "marvelous" natural and anthropological world encountered, and celebrates both the heroic virtues of the captain-general (whose attributes of "bon pastore" and "bon cavaliero" are exalted beyond the

[27] ". . . such a voyage as that I do not call discovery, but merely a going to discovered lands. . . . It is true that the navigation has been most profitable, which these days is what counts most, and especially in this kingdom, where inordinate greed reigns out of all order. . . ." (*Letters From a New World*, cit., p. 17)

[28] See David Quint, "The Boat of Romance and Renaissance Epic," in *Generic Transformation from Chrétien de Troyes to Cervantes*, ed. K. and M. Brownlee, Hanover and London, 1985, pp. 178-202.

realm of immediate political contingency), and the epic geographical achievement of the circumnavigation.

4. A Unity of Narrative and Cartography

But it would be misleading to leave the impression that Pigafetta's narrative is
a marvel-filled evasionary travel narrative and hagiographic text, although it
presents elements of both. Indeed, *The First Voyage* is much more: its remarkably
accurate ethnographic and geographical account of the circumnavigation has
guaranteed its elevated status among modern historiographers and students of
the discoveries and earliest contacts between Europeans and the East Indies.
Recall that García Márquez emphasized in his Nobel address the accuracy of
Pigafetta's account "that nonetheless resembles a venture into fantasy." While
we have just seen how, with respect to the political implications of the marvelous, Pigafetta's procedure may constitute a diversion (which García
Márquez took pains to rectify), the ethnographic and geographic truth value
of Pigafetta's account is not finally undermined. Indeed, although it might
seem something of a paradox, there is clearly a sense in which the marvelous
aspects of the narrative serve rhetorically to authorize or enhance the truth
value of the ethnographic and geographic evidence. The post-Enlightenment
view of geography and ethnography as sciences distinct from the literary leads
us to see them as exclusive of literary "marvels," when for Pigafetta and his
Renaissance readers the "marvelous" and the true could still be not only co-
present but actually mutually reinforcing. In fact, structurally speaking,
Pigafetta's "marvelous" can be said to enclose the central experiences in the
book regarding the expedition's encounters in the Philippines and Moluccas.
The prominent place given to the marvelous natural and anthropological
encounters in the New World, based as they are on recognizable literary

CACHEY

stereotypes, and the Marco Polian encounters (second-hand reports) of India and China, which Pigafetta recounts before embarking on the return trip (¶196-¶200), serve as an authorizing frame for what's most new and most true in Pigafetta's narrative. Indeed, it is the extremely lucid and precise account of the time spent navigating the East Indian archipelagos of the Philippines and the Moluccas, including the repeated courtly negotiations with various indigenous groups, which constitutes, beyond the celebration of Magellan, one of the book's major interests.[29]

Two aspects of Pigafetta's account are particularly worthy of note in this regard. The first is Pigafetta's attention to the language of the peoples encountered, which results in wordlists or vocabularies, including extensive lists for the Philippine (160 words of what he calls "the language of the heathen" to distinguish it from the Malay Muslims) and Malay languages respectively (this last made up of some 450 words). The second is Pigafetta's contribution to the cartography of the East Indies, which takes the form of twenty-three painted maps, featured in the earliest manuscripts of the book. Both aspects were already present in the previous tradition: in Columbus and Peter Martyr's embryonic wordlists of the Taino language, and in the close linking of narrative account to cartographic record by Columbus and Vespucci. Pigafetta, however, raises both the treatment of indigenous languages and cartography to a new level in his *First Voyage*, and, on both counts, again appears informed by the peculiarly Italian courtier context for his writing.

The Vicentine's remarkably acute linguistic sensibility is evidenced throughout the narrative, and his extreme attention and remarkable ear for languages seems to reflect his formation as an Italian courtier. The linguistic character of

[29] For example J. Crawfurd in his *Descriptive Dictionary of the Indian Islands & Adjacent Countries* (London: Oxford University Press, 1971, reprint of 1856) cites Pigafetta's description of the court of Brunei, ". . . as giving the only authentic account we possess of a Malay court when first seen by Europeans, and before their policy, or impolicy, had affected Malayan society" (p. 71).

Pigafetta's text itself is an eclectic, yet highly efficacious mix of literary Tuscan, Venetisms and Iberianisms. The cosmopolitan linguistic *identikit* of our author is informed by his experience in an Italian court society which was open to diverse linguistic and cultural influences from abroad. From the beginning of the narrative he gives numerous Spanish and Portuguese technical terms, often, unlike Vespucci, glossing them for his Italian reader. Pigafetta's accounts of diplomatic negotiations (in which he participated on occasion as European ambassador) are particularly compelling. At one point Pigafetta translates what has since been identified as a common Malay idiom, when he reports that the Malay King "told us that he was like a child at the breast who knew his dear mother, who departing, was leaving him alone" (¶171). He even goes so far as to note that in the local language of Java, the name of the island is pronounced *Jaoa*, and not Java (¶192). The accuracy of his transcriptions of place-names is striking. The vast majority of Pigafetta's East Indian toponyms are easily matched to their modern equivalents. It is not surprising then if Pigafetta's record of indigenous toponyms, like his list of 450 words of Malay have been described by competent scholars as extremely accurate. The Malay vocabulary is one of the oldest written specimens of the Malay language, the earliest surviving manuscripts being dated from around 1500–1550. And Pigafetta's Philippine and Malay word lists cumulatively constitute a kind of implicit anthropological portrait of the East Indian societies encountered.[30] Clearly, Pigafetta's linguistic attitude presents a stark contrast to Pietro Bembo's classicizing vernacular humanism which was establishing itself at the same time in Italy with the *Prose della volgar lingua* (1525). The Vicentine occupies the most avant-garde position within the courtly linguistic perspective on the Italian *Questione della lingua*. Indeed, there appears a highly suggestive, even proportional

---

[30] For detailed commentary on these lists, on the manner of their compilation and the relevant scholarship, see A. Bausani. *L'Indonesia nella relazione di viaggio di A. Pigafetta*. Roma: Centro di cultura italiana Djakarta, 1972.

inverse relation between the Italian vernacular humanist Bembo's turning inward and back in time to erect Boccaccio and Petrarch as literary and linguistic *auctores* for Italian eloquence, and, simultaneously, the Italian courtier Pigafetta's linguistic opening to other worlds, at the farthest reaches of the globe.

Pigafetta similarly redirects an Italian cartographic tradition and sensibility in his twenty-three charts depicting the East Indian archipelagos. Although his book must first be restored, as in the present edition, to its earliest form as a synthesis of narrative and cartography in order for its contribution to that tradition to be adequately appreciated. This unity, which characterized the work from its first appearance in the earliest manuscripts, was lost as soon as the book began to be printed; neither the humble setting of the Colines *princeps* (c. 1525) nor the nondescript 1536 Italian imprint anonymously published by Giambattista Ramusio include the 23 charts which were an integral part of Pigafetta's original conception of the book (and neither did Ramusio later include them in his *Navigazioni e viaggi*). The separation of the maps from the narrative effected at the beginning of the editorial history has been continued by most editions, including, symptomatically, the most recent and otherwise authoritative edition of the Italian Ambrosiana manuscript upon which the present edition is based.[31] The interpretive result of this dismemberment of the book has been the loss of a sense of Pigafetta's original conception of the book as a unity of narrative and cartography, and its generic relationship to the tradition of Renaissance *isolari;* and especially the most important *isolario* of the fifteenth century and the genre's *capostipite*, Cristoforo Buondelmonti's *Liber Insularum Archipelagi* (The Book of the Islands of the Archipelago).[32]

[31] *Viaggio attorno al mondo*, ed. Mariarosa Masoero, Rovereto: Longo, 1986

[32] For discussion and bibliography regarding this text, for which unfortunately no modern critical edition exists (but see the edition prepared by L. De Sinner, Lipsiae et Berolini, 1824): see R. Almagià, *Monumenta Cartografica Vaticana*, I (1944). pp. 105-17; A. Campana "Da codici del Buondelmonti," in *Silloge bizantina, in onore di Silvio Mercati*, Associazione nazionale per gli studi bizantini, 1957, pp. 28-52; R. Weiss "Un umanista antiquario: Cristoforo

ILLUSTRATIONS

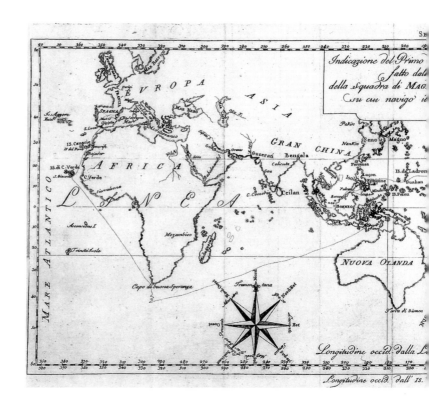

"Track of the first voyage around the world accomplished by the *Victoria* of Magellan's expedition between the years 1519-1522 upon which the Knight Antonio Pigafetta sailed." From C. Amoretti's edition (Milan, 1800).

The Strait of Magellan. From F.H.H. Guillemard's *The Life of Magellan* (New York, 1890).

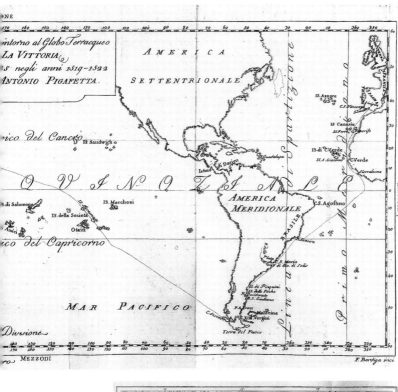

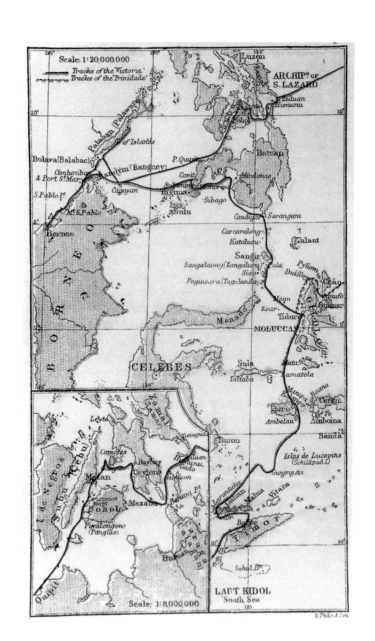

Scale: 1:20,000,000

Tracks of the 'Victoria'
Tracks of the 'Trinidade'

ARCHIP° OF
S. LAZARO

Luzon

Zuluan

Bohol

Batan

P. Quipit

Mindanao

Cavit

Palaoan (Palawan)

of Islands

Bolava (Balabac)

Cimbonbon
& Port St. Mary

Nauidym (Banguey)

Subanim
in sma

Monoripa

S. Pablo I.

Cagayan

Sibago

M. S. Pablo

Sulu

Candigar   Sarangani

Borneo

Carcaralong

Katalusu

Talaut

Sangir

Sangalaong (Zangalura)

Paia

Pyliom

Siao

DuiDor

Chao

Poginsara (Tagulanda)

Onufro
Chilmar

B   O   R   N   E   O

Megu
Zoar

Menado

Tidor

MOLUCCAS

CELEBES

Sula

Mata

Tabtabo

Lamatola

Mamya   Boana

Cerâm

Buro

Amboina

Buron

Ambelau

Banda

Islas de Lucopins
(Schildpad I.)

Leyte

Camotes

Minugua

Trangong Api

Baybay

Ceylon

Huan
Munu
Gado
Gilisson

Negros

Cebu

Mazaba

Baona Pt

Malna

Vitara

Matan

Surabuton

Laranatulor

Tenarafa

Bohol

Paralongon
(Panglao)

Mor   Balbo

TIMOR

Quipit

Bukamu

Sahul Br

Scale: 1:8,000,000

LAUT KIDOL
South Sea

G. Philip & Son

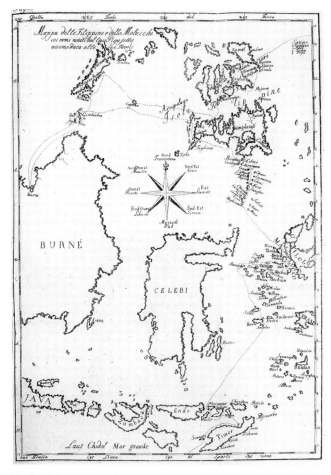

Tracks of the *Victoria* and *Trinidad* in the East Indies. From F.H.H.
Guillemard's *The Life of Magellan* (New York, 1890).

"Map of the Philippines and of the Moluccas with the names given by
Pigafetta adapted to his charts." Compiled by C. Amoretti for his edition
(Milan, 1800).

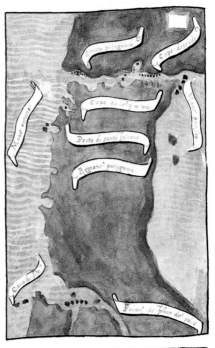

I. Chart of the "Patagonian Region" including Cape Santa Maria, the River of Juan de Solis, Port St. Julian, the Cape of the Eleven Thousand Virgins, the Patagonian Strait, Cape Deseado, the Ocean Sea (Atlantic) and Pacific Ocean.

II. Chart of the "Unfortunate Islands."

III. Chart of the "Island of Thieves."

IV. Chart of Zzamal (Samar), Zuluam (Suluan), Cenalo (Dinagat?), Ybuston (Hibuson), Hyunangan (Hinundayan), Humunu (Homonhon, with the scroll: "The Watering Place of Good Signs"), and Abarien (Cabalian?).

ysole'. Infortunate'.

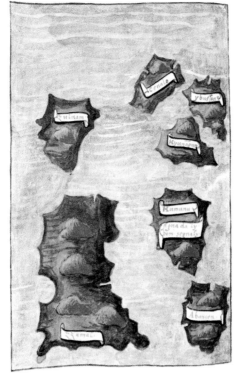

v. Chart of Mazzana (Mazzaua: Limasawa), Bohol, Ceilon (Leyte or Panaon), Baibai (Baybay), Canighan (Apit or Himuguetan), Ticobon (Pacijan), and Pozzon (Ponson).

vi. Chart of Zzubu (Cebu), Mattam (Mactan, with the scroll: "Here the captain-general died"), and Bohol.

vii. Chart of Panilonghon (Panglao).

viii. Chart of Caghaiam (Cagayan).

ix. Chart of Pulaoam (Palawan), Tegozzano porto, and Sundan.

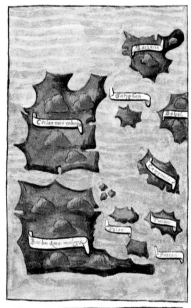

V

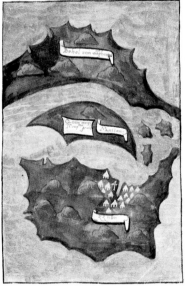

VI

VII

VIII

IX

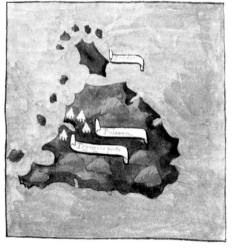

x. Chart of Burne and (Borneo) Laot, with the scroll: "Where the living leaves are."

xi. Chart of Mamgdanao (Mindanao), with Benaiam, Calagam, Butuan, and Cippit.

xii. Chart of Zzolo (Jolo), Subanin, Tagima (Basilan), Cavit (Cavite), and the scroll: "Where the pearls are born."

xiii. Chart of the islands of Ciboco (Sibago), Birahan batolach (Batukali?); Sarangani, Candigar (Balut?).

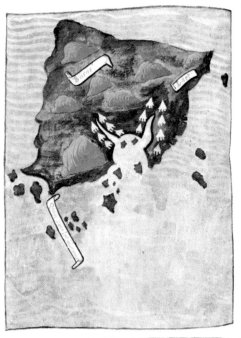

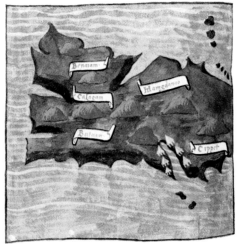

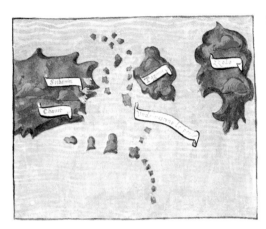

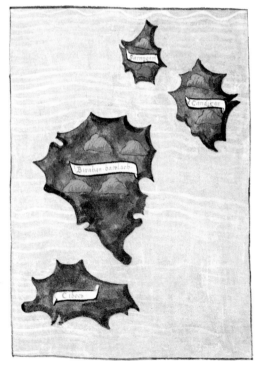

xiv. Chart of the islands of Sanghir
(Sanghihe), Nuza (?), Lipan
(Lipang), Cheai (?), Cabulazgo
(Kawalusu), Camanuca (?), Cabiao
(Kawio?), Cheva (?), Caviao (?).

xv. Chart of the archipelago of
Paghinzara including Paghinzara,
Ciau (Siau), Zangalura
(Sanggeluhang), Para, Carachita
(Karakitang), Cheama (Kima),
Meau, Zoar (Tifore).

xvi. Chart of the island of Tarenate
(Ternate), Giailonlo (Gilolo:
Halmahera), Maitara (Mutir) with
the scrool: "All the islands
represented in this book are in the
other hemisphere of the world at
the antipodes."

xvii. Chart of the islands of
Molucca including Pulongha,
Tadore (Tidore), Mare, Mutir
(Motir) and Machiam (Makiam)
with the scroll: "Cavi gomode, that
is, the Clove tree."

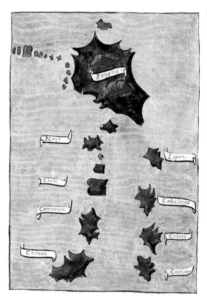

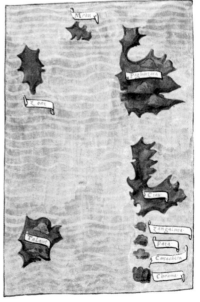

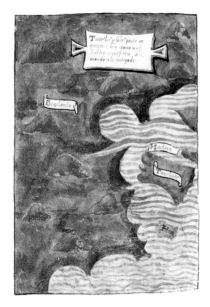

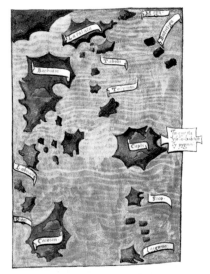

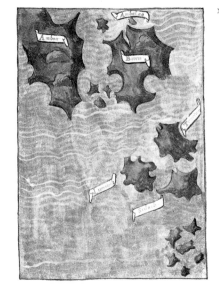

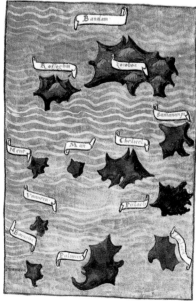

XV

XVIII. Chart of Maga, Batutiga, Caphi (Gafi), Sico, Laigoma, Caioian (Kajoa), Giogi (Goraitji?), Labuac (Labuha), Bachiam (Batjan), Tolyman (Tolimao), Tabobi, Latalata, and the scroll next to Caphi: "In this island live the Pygmies"

XIX. Chart of the islands of Ambalao (Ambelou), Buru, Tenetum (Tenado), Lumatola (Lifamafola), Sulach (Sula Besi), and Ambon (Amboina).

XX. Chart of Bandan including the islands Bandam, Zoroboa, Sanianapi, Chelicel, Pulach (Ai), Lailaca, Puluran (Run), Manuca (Manuk?), Baracha, Unuveru, Meut, Man, Rosoghin (Roseghain).

XXI. Chart of the islands Zolot (Solor), Batuombor, Mallua (Alor), Galiau (Lomblen?), Nocemamor (Nobokamor).

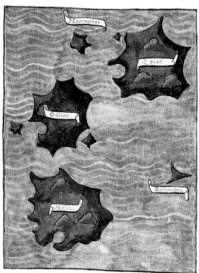

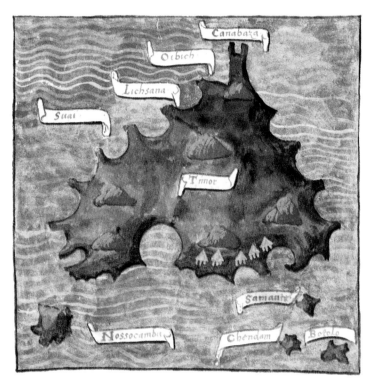

xxii. Chart of the island of Timor, Botolo, Chendam, Samante, Nossocambu, and capes on Timor including Suai, Lichsana (Líquicá?), Oibich, Canabaza.

xxiii. Chart depicting "Laut chidol, that is, the Great sea."

Buondelmonti (born around 1380) is primarily known for the *Liber Insularum* and the *Descriptio Cretae* (the Description of Crete), works authored during his travels in the Aegean, taking Rhodes as his base of operations, between 1415 and his death around 1431. A Florentine prelate and contemporary of Poggio Bracciolini, with contacts to the humanist circle of Niccolò Niccoli, Buondelmonti was one of the most significant figures of the fifteenth-century Aegean world that played host to a cosmopolitan and socially mixed culture with strong ties, through a dense network of diplomatic, ecclesiastic and commercial relations, to the world of Italian humanism. As a travel writer, Buondelmonti's most significant innovation was to fuse the humanistic genre of geographical encyclopedic compendia (like Boccaccio's *De montibus*, Bandini's *Fons Memorabilium Universi* and Da Silvestri's *De insulis et earum proprietatibus*) with that of contemporary sailing journals, charts and portolans. Both the *Liber insularum* and the *Descriptio Cretae* represent first-hand accounts of Buodelmonti's travels laced with antiquary commentary and accompanied by charts of the islands visited.

The original version of the work was dedicated to the humanist bibliophile Cardinal Giordano Orsini and forwarded to him in Rome in 1420. Surviving in at least four redactions made during the Quattrocento, it was subsequently enlarged, altered, emended, and improved throughout the 15th century. It is known in 64 manuscripts, only thirteen fewer than Marco Polo's travels, and evidently had an immense success during the Renaissance not only throughout Italy and in the Aegean, but also in other Western European countries. Not less than three vernacular translations of the *Liber* were done in Italy during the quattrocento. In addition, there was a translation in modern Greek in the fifteenth century, as well as one in English during the sixteenth century. The work's character as an historical and practical guide should be emphasized, as

Buondelmonti," in *Lettere italiane*, XVI (1964), pp. 105-16; and H. Turner "Christopher Buondelmonti and the *Isolario*," in *Terrae Incognitae*, 19, 1987, pp. 11-28.

this explains its wide diffusion among those who had the occasion to travel or
live in the Aegean. It should also be stressed that this diffusion was not limited
to Italian humanists or other erudite Orientalists. In fact, its popular character
is suggested by the several versions in various Italian vernaculars, as well as the
one in modern Greek. It is natural and reasonable to suppose that the work
enjoyed a particularly wide diffusion among members of the Order of St. John
of Jerusalem based on Rhodes.

Compelling analogies between Pigafetta's and Buondelmonti's books include
their island subject matter, their mode of literary treatment alternating between
narrative and expository modes, their first-person authorial perspective, and
last but not least the complement of island charts. The charts serve especially
to establish a generic link between Pigafetta's *First Voyage* and Buondelmonti's
Liber Insularum, the first and most important of Renaissance *isolari*. Both works
share the same unique manuscript typology characterized by colored maps of
islands embedded within the narrative, displayed at the appropriate moment,
usually following the relevant narrative regarding the island depicted, as illustrated below in sample manuscript pages from the two works.

From Pigafetta's *First Voyage*: the island Caghaiam (Cagayan Sulu). Ambrosiana Library,
Milan, L 103 Sup., fol. 40r.

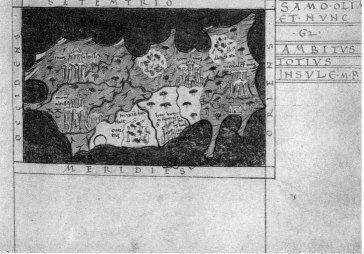

From the *Liber Insularum Archipelagi* (L'isolario "Buondelmonti-Martello" c. 1490): the island Sámos. Florence Biblioteca Medicea Laurenziana, XXIX 25 c. 35r.

The analogies in textual content, treatment, and manuscript typology suggest strongly that, when Antonio Pigafetta conceived of his *First Voyage*, he did so with the "Book of Islands" tradition—which would have been very familiar to his Rhodian brethren—very much in mind. The *isolario* format evidently would have presented itself to Pigafetta and his readers, beginning with the Grand Master of the Order, as an ideal means of representing the archipelagos of the East Indies.[33]

Each of the twenty-three charts is closely linked to a particular passage or passages from the narrative; from the first depicting the Patagonian strait at the end of a peninsular-shaped (perhaps suggesting an island form) South American continent to the last representing two unidentified islets in the midst of "Laut chidol, that is, the great sea." A few charts include charming iconographic features like the one which represents a lateen sailed catamaran and two bearded natives from "the island of thieves" (the Mariana islands). All charts include scrolls identifying island names, and sometimes topographical detail including hills and in some cases clusters of native houses standing on poles indicating villages, as well as other scrolls including allusions to noteworthy events related in the text, such as the one which identifies Mactan: "Here the Captain-General died." The relationship between narrative and cartography is intriguingly interactive, and it would well repay further investigation. The cartographic achievement of the twenty-three charts of Pigafetta's East Indian *isolario* is not as insignificant nor naive as it may at first appear. They in fact present an impressive cartographic record of the voyage, experienced from the perspective of the traveler, according to the

[33] The maps which complement his narrative have always been attributed to Pigafetta without controversy. In fact, a first-hand witness to Pigafetta's reception at Rome upon his return, the historian Paolo Giovio in his *Historiarum sui temporis* reports that "In tanto subternavigati orbis miraculo fidelibus testimoniis comprobato, multa nostris admiranda, observandaque posteris *pictura et scripti* adnotata deposuit" (*Historiarum sui temporis* XXXIV, Lutetia Parisiorum, 1553, p. 72).

structure of passage.[34] Carlo Amoretti, the discoverer of the Ambrosiana manuscript, was even able to recompose them as a plausible synthetic portrait of the East Indian archipelagos in his edition of 1800 (see map 4).

While an essential correlation between the "Book of Islands" genre and Pigafetta's *First Voyage* has not been previously made, it nevertheless appears that Pigafetta has significant claim on the legacy of Buondelmonti's *Liber insularum*—at least as important as the better known *isolari* published during the fifteenth and sixteenth century by Bartolomeo dalli Sonetti, Benedetto Bordon, and Tommaso Porcacchi.[35] It is not irrelevant to the history of the "Book of Islands" genre, that Pigafetta's manuscript book first appeared in the same years which marked the beginning of the sixteenth-century editorial establishment of the genre, in the "coffee-table book" form with which Renaissance scholars are most familiar.

It has recently observed how, from a narrative perspective, the literary vitality had gone out of these printed *isolari* of the Cinquecento, a decline attributed to the commercialization of the genre in the age of print. The sixteenth-century *isolario* is no longer connected with a first-hand travel narrative and becomes the mere compilation of already published materials (a process which was already underway in the fifteenth century in the incunable Bartolomeo dalli Sonetti's *Isolario* which recapitulated in part material from Buondelmonti). By

[34] Eric J. Leed, *The Mind of the Traveler*, cit: "The order imposed upon experience by the condition of mobility is an order of sequence, an order of 'one-thing-after-the-another,' a 'progress.' Motion resolves all orders of space—topographies, positions, scenes, containments, places—into an experiential order of continuously evolving appearances . . . " (p. 73).

[35] Bartolomeo dalli Sonetti was a Venetian shipmaster who printed an *isolario* around 1485 which included forty-nine maps of the Aegean and a series of sonnets derived in large measure from Buondelmonti's prose. Bordone, a Paduan illuminator, published in 1528 his *Libro de tutte l'isole del mondo* (see R.A. Skelton's facsimile edition, *Theatrum Orbis Terrarum*, Amsterdam, 1966). This work was reprinted three times, for the last time just a few years before Tommaso Porcacchi brought out his *Le isole più famose del mondo* (The most famous islands in the world) published in Venice in 1572.

the time one arrives at Tommaso Porcacchi's *L'isole più famose*, the genre is explicitly intended only for those interested in the maps, that is, for those who "dello studio della geografia si dilettano" (delight in geographical studies). The commercial success of Bordone and of Porcacchi "alienated from the *isolario* the readers of Ariosto and Tasso," for geography and travel narrative had in that genre been divorced.[36]

Thus the appearance of Pigafetta's *First Voyage* in manuscript, the most vital achievement after Buondelmonti in both the literary and cartographic aspects which originally distinguished the "Book of Islands," is contemporary with the literary decline of the genre in the age of print, which was reduced to a mere compilation of maps and inert, for the most part borrowed, textual material. Indeed, the progressive decline in literary vigor of the Cinquecento *isolario* appears irreversible, and is accompanied by an increasingly narrow geographical orientation. Bordone's book, for example, has been termed "*veneziocentrico*"[37] with its focus on the Mediterranean with Venice at its center. Porcacchi's 1572 edition opens with a treatment of Venice and the islands of the archipelago as if to reinforce their centrality to the author's and his prospective readers' world view. Pigafetta's mapping of the East Indies on the other hand had represented geographically the farthest point of arrival for the "Book of Islands."

It is no doubt symptomatic that it was in the transition from manuscript to print that the original conception of Pigafetta's book, its characteristic integration of narrative and maps, of literature and cartography, was first lost. The effects of printing which led to the commercialization and literary decline of the "Book of Islands" genre were certainly significant. Perhaps most telling however was the substitution of the geographer's for the traveler's viewpoint. The literary life goes out of the "Book of Islands" as soon as the first-hand

---

[36] M. Guglielminetti, "Per un sottogenere della letteratura di viaggio: Gl'isolari fra Quattro e Cinquecento," in *La letteratura di viaggio dal Medioevo al Rinascimento: generi e problemi*, Alessandria: Edizioni dell'orso, 1989, pp. 107-17.

[37] M. Guglielminetti, cit., p. 116.

narrative foundation is subtracted, as soon as the motion and change filtered through a traveler's subjectivity, which gives the narrative of travel its life, is lost. In any case, the heroic high Renaissance period of discovery and exploration, as far as Italy was concerned, came to an end with Pigafetta. His *First Voyage* represents the culminating achievement in the "Book of Islands" tradition, no less than it epitomizes the Italian Americanist tradition of De Cuneo, Vespucci and Verrazzano. Both Benedetto Bordone's 1528 *Libro de tutte le isole* and Girolamo Benzoni's *Historia del Nuovo Mondo* (1565) stand as epigones with respect to the Vicentine Knight of Rhodes, within their respective generic traditions, and within the context of a general history of Italian Renaissance travel writing which has yet to be written.

Finally, however, the proper collocation of Pigafetta's *First Voyage* within the limited context of Italian literary history may well appear too narrow a preoccupation for one confronted with what must be considered a still vital classic of Western travel literature. Indeed, the heroic early modern function of travel finds one of its most mature expressions in Pigafetta's narrative. Through the dangers and *vigilie* of the journey, the self of the traveler is reduced to its essentials, allowing one to see what those essentials are. Pigafetta's *First Voyage* is ultimately motivated and overshadowed by the presentiment of finality, of the terminability of human life. The monument which he erects to Magellan, to the achievement of the circumnavigation, but most of all to himself, who survived and lived to tell of "this long and dangerous navigation," still endures as a testimony to the power of that desire to circumvent death which is at the root of all travel literature, which seeks to fix and conserve through writing the instability and flux of human movement through space and time.

BIO-BIBLIOGRAPHICAL NOTE

Little is known of Antonio Pigafetta's life before the circumnavigation (1519–1522) beyond what he tells us himself in the dedicatory letter about his association with the papal ambassador and fellow Vicentine, Francesco Chiericati, which led to his participation in Magellan's expedition. More survives regarding his activities between 1522 and 1525, namely, during the period in which he composed *The First Voyage Around the World* and sought patronage for its publication. The last archival trace to survive records the conferral of the *commenda*, or benefice, of Norcia, Todi and Arquata upon Antonio Pigafetta by the Order of St. John of Jerusalem (or Knights of Rhodes) on October 3, 1524. This honor is directly related to the dedication of his book to the Grand Master of the Knights of Rhodes, which concluded his two-year search for courtly patronage. Nothing more is heard of Pigafetta after this date, a situation which has encouraged biographers to posit a variety of hypotheses: these range from an heroic end aboard the galleys of the Knights of Rhodes in battle with the Turks to a return "in patria" to the family's ancestral home in Vicenza.

Pigafetta belonged to a prominent noble Vicentine family which had arrived from Tuscany during the eleventh century and had quickly achieved prestige and wealth. Numerous members of the family attained distinction in political, economic and academic spheres. Indeed, the historian Paolo Giovio, in his account of Pigafetta's meeting with Pope Clement VII, confuses

Antonio with his relative, the Dominican friar Girolamo, who was noted at the time for his oratory and poetic production.[38] Giovio's error concerning the identity of our author is typical of the historiographic confusion surrounding the origins of the explorer that has reigned until relatively recently. Pigafetta's birth has been variously assigned to anywhere between 1480 and the late 1490s; and there have been numerous proposals as to who his parents were, from among the various branches of the Pigafetta family.

An initial breakthrough was achieved by C. Manfroni in the preface to his 1928 edition of Pigafetta's narrative:[39] A crew list for the expedition found in the Archives of the Indies, and probably intended to indicate the heirs in case of death, included the names of the explorer's parents: "*Antonio Lombardo hijo de Juan e Anzola su mujer.*" While archival research at the time did not succeed in identifying a corresponding couple, more recent work by G. Mantese has led to a resolution of the problem of Pigafetta's origins and also suggested his probable date of death. Through wills and other documents Mantese demonstrated the existence of Angela Zoga, wife of Giovanni Pigafetta, names corresponding to those on the crew list.[40] Later, on the basis of still other documents,[41] Mantese determined that Angela Zoga was Giovanni Pigafetta's second wife (hence the unusual expression: "*hijo de Juan e Anzola su mujer*"). A marriage contract written by the notary Gregorio da Malo informs us that, in March of 1492, Giovanni had married a noblewoman named Lucia, daughter of Marco Muzan, who thus would have been the mother of Antonio. The

---

[38] P. Giovio, *Historiarum sui temporis* XXXIV, Lutetia Parisiorum 1553, p. 172. The family produced two later geographical writers of note: Marcantontio Pigafetta, author of *Itinerario da Vienna a Constantinopoli* (London, 1585) and Filippo Pigafetta (1553–1604) who published an Italian version of Ortelius's *Theatrum* (1608), and the *Relatione del reame del Congo* (1591) which was translated into English (1597), Latin, French, Dutch and German.

[39] Manfroni, pp. 10-11.

[40] "I genitori di Antonio Pigafetta," in *Archivio veneto*, LXVII (1960), pp. 26-37.

[41] G. Mantese, *Memorie storiche della Chiesa vicentina*, vol. III, P. II, Vicenza, 1964, pp. 847-54.

birth of Antonio Pigafetta must have been therefore after 1492, and he would have been not older than 27 when he embarked with Magellan. This corrects the tradition dating back to the 18th-century historiographers which placed his birth during the 1480s. Furthermore, in a will which Giovanni Pigafetta drew up in 1532, two other children are mentioned, Valentino and Serafina, while Antonio Pigafetta is not. From this, Mantese inferred that Antonio Pigafetta was already dead in 1532. If Pigafetta was already dead in 1532, then, he would not have reached forty years of age; and it would thus have been impossible for him to have fought against the Turks with the Knights of Rhodes in the war of 1536, as some biographers have speculated.[42] That Pigafetta may have followed the Order to Malta when it transferred to the island in 1530 is perhaps suggested by one of the expressions he uses in his final paragraph of dedication: "Then I came to Italy, where I *devoted myself forever*, and these my poor labors to the famous and most illustrious lord Philippe Villiers de l'Isle-Adam, the most worthy Grand Master of Rhodes." But the truth is that absolutely nothing is known about the last years of Pigafetta's life after 1525.

The archival silence concerning Pigafetta's life before the circumnavigation and following the presentation of his *First Voyage* to the Grand Master is in some measure redressed by the engaging and relatively well-documented history of his peregrinations after his return from the voyage. Having disembarked with the eighteen survivors of the expedition on September 8, 1522, Pigafetta

---

[42] Mantese discovered yet another interesting document which sheds light on both the paternity and the death of Antonio Pigafetta. In a will dated June 25, 1524, Giovanni, apparently in an attempt to lure back home his globe-trotting son, left to Antonio, together with his other son Valentino, the income of his estate, but with a condition *"se vorrà abitare nella sua patria"* (if he will live in his homeland). But Antonio appears never to have returned home to settle in Vicenza. Other studies of Mantese touching on Pigafetta include "Vicenza ai tempi della guerra di Cambrai, *Archivio veneto*, CIX, V serie, n. 146 (1978), p. 199; and "Il secolo XV; inizio della dominazione veneziana e guerra di Cambrai," in *Malo e il suo Monte*, published by the Amministrazione Comunale di Malo, 1979, pp. 89-90 and 481-82.

traveled to the imperial court at Valladolid, and presented to Charles V, as he writes in his *envoi* (¶208), things to be prized above gold and silver, among which ". . . a book, written by my hand, concerning all the matters that had occurred from day to day during our voyage." Pigafetta had come to court apparently of his own initiative and independently of the commander of the *Victoria*, Juan Sebastián de Elcano, who was summoned by the Emperor on September 13, and appeared in October, together with the pilot Francisco Albo and the barber Hernando de Bustamante, before a court of inquiry into the voyage. Pigafetta seems to allude to a poor reception at the imperial court when he writes "I left there as best I could and went to Portugal." Perhaps anti-Magellan sentiments had something to do with Pigafetta's lack of success at court. That Pigafetta's celebration of the heroic Portuguese commander as it has come down to us in his *First Voyage* might not have met with favor there is suggested by the more or less official version of the circumnavigation given by Peter Martyr in his *De Orbe Novo* (Decade V, Bk. VII).[43] There, the court historiographer is clearly caught between a desire to magnify the undertaking but at the same time to undermine the reputation of Magellan, who is described as a traitor to his king and accused, among other things, of abusing the Spaniards.[44]

Already on October 21, 1522, the Mantuan ambassador Antonio Bagarotto reported from Valladolid to Isabella d'Este that the survivors of the expedition had brought back "a very beautiful book"; and on November 12, the same

[43] According to Ramusio, Martyr had written an earlier account of the voyage and sent it to Pope Hadrian VI in Rome. There it would have been lost during the famous sack of 1527 ("Discourse," translated in Stanley, p. 181).
[44] Antonello Gerbi wondered if Pigafetta might have been aware of the animosity that the chronicler of Spain bore Magellan, since he apparently did not provide Martyr with any information (their accounts are at odds on several points); Martyr in fact states that the eighteen survivors were completely illiterate (*Nature in the New World*, p. 101). Pigafetta's desire to protect his literary capital is evident in his coming to court independently; that he would have guarded it from the competing pen of Peter Martyr is highly plausible.

ambassador sent to Mantua extracts or a summary of that book, which may well have been Pigafetta's.[45] These letters represent first reports back to the court of Mantua which eventually led to Pigafetta's initial commitment to write the book for Federico II Gonzaga, Marquis of Mantua. Francesco Chiericati, Pigafetta's original patron at the imperial court, wrote from Nuremberg to Isabella d'Este, Federico's famous mother, on December 26, 1522, concerning "my Vicentine servant whom I sent from Spain to India who has returned very rich with the greatest and most marvelous things in the world, and a journal which he kept from the day he left Spain until the day he returned which is a divine thing; and your illustrious signoria will have complete knowledge of it shortly . . ." (Berchet, p. 175).

According to Pigafetta's own account in his *envoi*, he proceeded to Lisbon where he gave King João III an oral report, and then to France where he gave the Queen Mother, Louise of Savoy, mother of Francis I, "the gift of certain things from the other hemisphere." Most scholars pass over this stage quickly, as there does not appear to be any documentary support for these visits besides Pigafetta's own testimony. According to Ramusio, Louise of Savoy received a copy of Pigafetta's account and gave this text to J. Fabre (Jacques Lefèvre d'Etaples) so that it could be translated into French. This would have corresponded to the Paris imprint by Simon de Colines (the *princeps* of 1524–1525: see below). Ramusio had the Colines text translated back into Italian for his own editions of the text in 1536 (Venice: Zoppini), and later as part of the *Navigazione e viaggi* (1550, vol. I). While Ramusio's editions are derived from the Colines imprint, his account of the transmission of the text from Pigafetta to Louise of Savoy to Simon de Colines is without documentary support. In fact, Pigafetta himself makes no mention of giving a copy of his relation to Louise of Savoy, but simply "the gift of certain things from the other hemisphere."

---

[45] The relevant letters were published by G. Berchet in the *Raccolta Colombiana*, pt. III, vol. I: *Fonti italiane per la scoperta del nuovo mondo* (Rome, 1892), pp. 172-84.

Meanwhile, Francesco Chiericati wrote again from Nuremberg on January 10, 1523 to Isabella d'Este at Mantua announcing Pigafetta's arrival and expressing to her his hope that "in a few days, your excellency will have great delight and recreation in listening to that servant of mine, who has recently returned from the circumnavigation of the world, recount all the great and marvelous things that he saw and recorded during that voyage . . ." (Berchet, p. 176). Upon his arrival in Mantua in January of 1523, Pigafetta would have begun the composition of the definitive version of his *First Voyage*, and it was at this time that he presumably received a commission for the work from Federico II Gonzaga. Pigafetta was to continue work on the relation at Mantua, Vicenza and Rome (where he appears to have completed a version by April 1524). It was during the initial period at court in Mantua that he would have encountered the philosopher Pietro Pomponazzi, a Mantuan, who, lecturing on Aristotle at the University of Bologna soon after, on March 23, 1523, gave suggestive testimony regarding the implications of the voyage:

> I have received a letter sent to me by a friend of mine of the Veneto who accompanied the papal ambassador to the King of Spain and who, finding himself there, went along with an expedition sent by that king in the southern hemisphere; and he navigated there 25 degrees, after having passed the Torrid Zone. Now he writes to me that, leaving behind the Pillars of Hercules, they navigated in the southern hemisphere for three months and encountered more that three hundred islands separated one from the other, and that not only were they habitable but they were inhabited. What do you think of the reasoning of Aristotle and Averroes to demonstrate the opposite. Perhaps some of you will think that that merchant is telling me a sack of lies and that he is a big liar. No, dear sirs, it is not possible, he wasn't the only one on that voyage. . . .[46]

---

[46] Bruno Nardi first noted the passage and we cite from his *Studi su Pietro Pomponazzi*, Firenze, 1965, pp. 42-43.

Nothing else is known of the relations between Pomponazzi and Pigafetta except for this passage in which the philosopher refers to his "amico veneto"; nevertheless it suggests Pigafetta's celebrity in Italy at this time. In fact, following a period of time spent with his family in Vicenza, Pigafetta was received by the Venetian doge Andrea Gritti in November of 1523. The Venetian diarist Marin Sanudo described the great interest elicited by Pigafetta's oral presentation before the entire Venetian College at the Ducal Palace:

> There appeared before the College a Vicentine named the Knight errant, friar of Rhodes, who had been exploring three years in India, and he recounted orally about those things, such that the College listened to him with great attention, and he told half the voyage; and after dinner he was again with the doge and he related those things at length, such that his Serenity and all those who heard him were stupefied by those things which are in India. . . . [47]

This performance seemed to have had a resonance beyond the Hall of the Great Council since no sooner had Pigafetta returned from Venice to Vicenza, than he was called in December to Rome by Pope Clement VII. On the way to Rome, as Pigafetta himself tells us in the dedicatory letter, he encountered the Grand Master of the Knights of Rhodes, Philippe Villiers de l'Isle-Adam, to whom Pigafetta related his voyage and from whom Pigafetta received yet more encouragement and, apparently, promises of support.

Pigafetta worked on the book in Rome under the patronage of Pope Clement VII, a relationship which appears to have begun well enough. Pigafetta's writes with some embarrassment on February 2, 1524 to the Marquis of Mantua explaining that a higher power and promise of publication had pre-empted the Marquis' original commission: "I believe his Holiness desires it to be printed in his name; and to satisfy my promised debt to you, I will send the first to be

---

[47] M. Sanudo, *Diarii*, XXXV, col. 173.

printed to your illustrious signoria, or else I will write another one in my own hand . . ." (Berchet, p. 178).[48] But the Pope's promise to publish the book was not kept for reasons which are unknown. Apparently frustrated with the turn of events, Pigafetta sought to return to the service of the Marquis of Mantua in a letter of April 16, 1524 to the Marquis (Berchet, p. 179). He obtained a letter of recommendation from the Mantuan ambassador at the papal court at the time, Baldassare Castiglione, who wrote a revealing letter to the Marquis regarding Pigafetta a day earlier than the explorer's own missive:

> That nobleman Pigafetta who went to the Antipodes, recommends himself strongly to your excellency; and although he has had I don't know how little here from the pope together with many promises, if some benefice of St. John's (The Order of the Knights of Rhodes) were to become available (accascando qualche beneficio de san Giohanni), he nevertheless desires very much to serve your excellency; but I do not know if he would be contented with only a little . . . (Berchet, p. 182).

The letter is significant for the light it sheds on the patronage network within which Pigafetta was operating; it also provides a glimpse of the Vicentine's ambitious and jealous character, already suggested by his behavior immediately following his return to Europe on the occasion of his presentation to Charles V. Pigafetta was not going to sell himself short, and if that meant boldly pursuing his aim of publication and worthy compensation for his work, so be it. Castiglione's letter offers a glimpse of the state of play from Pigafetta's perspective during the spring and summer of 1524: on the one side Clement VII and the Knights of Rhodes, on the other Mantua and the Venetian presses. In fact, Pigafetta obtained the assistance of the Marquis of Mantua in obtaining a license to publish his work in Venice. Federico Gonzaga instructs his minister, Battista Malatesta, in a letter of July 19, 1524 to present a letter of Federico's

---

[48] An offer graciously accepted by Gonzaga in a letter of February 26, 1524 (Berchet, p. 180).

to the doge Antonio Gritti in support of Pigafetta's request for a license to print, and to support Pigafetta in any way possible. In addition, Malatesta put Pigafetta together with a printer, and made the arrangement that the work should be printed and that "the Knight should now pay fifteen ducats to cover half of the expenses and that the profit will be divided" (August 3, 1524; Berchet, p. 183).[49] The fact that Pigafetta did not pay the sum and that the printing of the book was never accomplished has been thought to reflect Pigafetta's impoverished state upon his return to Europe "certainly not loaded with gold, pearls and spices as many believed" (Masoero, p. 22). On the other hand, Malatesta, in his letter to the Marquis of Mantua, after explaining the arrangements he had made, could not conceal a hint of exasperation when he wrote: "however, as far as I can judge, he would like your excellency to give him that amount of money, and he has asked me faithfully to refer to you as much . . ." (Berchet, p. 183). Given what Castiglione has already suggested about Pigafetta's pretensions ("I do not know if he would be contented with little"), one might just as easily suppose the Venetian printing never came off because Pigafetta was looking for an arrangement more favorable to his own interests. In any case, in the final account of his patrons and peregrinations in the *First Voyage*, and especially in the concluding *envoi*, the court of Mantua (and any reference to Venice) is conspicuously absent.

A better arrangement did in fact present itself only a few months later when on October 3, 1524, the Knights of Rhodes' vacant *commenda* of Norcia, Todi, and Arquata was conferred upon Pigafetta, and this act, as noted earlier, represents the last secure biographical datum regarding the Vicentine to survive. Significantly, the formal request for a benefice from the Order had been made on July 25, 1524, that is, more or less at the same time that Pigafetta was pursuing most intensely Mantuan-Venetian press patronage. In other words,

---

[49] Pigafetta's formal request to the doge is dated August 5 (Berchet, p. 183, note 3). Marin Sanudo records the granting of the privilege, *Diarii*, XXXVI, col. 293b.

there seem to have been parallel and competing paths in Pigafetta's pursuit of publication and adequate compensation. In the end, the patronage of Knights of Rhodes must have represented the more attractive opportunity. The relationship between the date of the conferral of the benefice and the date of the completion of the manuscript and its presentation to the Grand Master remains an open question, as does the more general question of whether Pigafetta entered the Order of the Knights of Rhodes before or after the circumnavigation.

For the period between January 25, 1524 and June 25, 1525, the Grand Master was in Italy, where according to *The First Voyage*, Pigafetta presented him with the manuscript. R.A. Skelton has observed that the presentation of the text might have been made to the Grand Master sometime between the time when Pigafetta applied for the benefice (July 25, 1524) and when he received it (October 3, 1524): "if the presentation of his manuscript were designed to support his petition or to express his gratitude" (p. 16). But perhaps more telling is the other fact, also remarked on by Skelton, that Pigafetta's reference in the final paragraph to Louise of Savoy as "Regent" can only refer to the period between February, 1525 (battle of Pavia) and January, 1526 (Treaty of Madrid). Since the Grand Master was not in Italy after June 25, 1525, this passage and the presentation of the work would appear to date sometime between February and June 25, 1525. In other words, the benefice, requested and received between the summer and fall of 1524, would have represented the premise for Pigafetta's final preparation of the book for presentation to the Grand Master during the first months of 1525.

Pending future archival discoveries, the question of when Pigafetta first became a member of the Knights of Rhodes remains an open one. The tradition that Knighthood had been conferred upon him in recognition of the achievement of the circumnavigation begins with Ramusio.[50] The view that

[50] ". . . [Pigafetta], having gone on the voyage and returned in the ship *Victoria*, was made a Knight of Rhodes . . ." ("Discourse," p. 182).

CACHEY

he was already a member of the order before beginning his travels is based
upon the argument that the time between his return (September 8, 1522) and
Sanudo's account of his presentation to the doge and reference to him as a
"friar of Rhodes" (November 7, 1523) would have been insufficient to complete the inquiries into the nobility of his family, the novitiate, and other
rituals involved in entering the order.[51] Da Mosto, on the other hand, pointed
out that, in a time of military crisis for the Order, formalities were reduced to
the minimum, and that it is more probable that Pigafetta was admitted by
special procedure.[52] One should not neglect, however, the evidence presented
by Pigafetta's narrative itself as possibly bearing on the question. The general
ideological perspective of the document might be said to be entirely consistent
with what one might expect from a member of the Order of St. John of
Jerusalem: from the portrayal of Magellan as a crusading hero (a member of
the Military Order of St. James; ⟨3; and ⟨88) to more local observations like
the famous passage "When we cast them into the sea, the Christians went to
the bottom face upward while the Indians always went down face downward"
(⟨203). The thesis that Pigafetta was a Knight of Rhodes before his departure
is also supported by telling thematic features like the recurring topos of St.
Elmo's fire, as well as certain analogies and allusions which indicate, as Skelton
has observed, that Pigafetta was familiar with both the eastern and western
Mediterranean.[53] Finally, the work's generic affiliation with the *isolario* tradition, pointed out earlier, also suggests a fundamentally "Rhodian" formation
for our author, and leads us to believe that Pigafetta may well have been a
member of the Order of St. John of Jerusalem before departing with Magellan.

*   *   *

[51] Manfroni, pp. 11-13.
[52] Da Mosto, p. 29.
[53] Skelton, pp. 6-7.

xlviii

The text of Pigafetta's *First Voyage* survives in four manuscripts: one Italian (Milan, Bibl. Ambrosiana, L 103 Sup.), upon which this edition is based, and three French (Paris, Bibliothèque Nationale, Ms. fr. 5650; Ms. fr. 24.224; and Yale University, Beinecke Rare Book and Manuscript Library, Phillipps ms. 16405). All of the manuscripts include twenty-three colored maps of the islands visited and date from the first half of the sixteenth century.

The publication of the Ambrosiana codex in 1800 by Carlo Amoretti (Milano: G. Galeazzi) made it possible to resolve the doubts about the language used by Pigafetta.[54] It is now considered certain that the Vicentine wrote his account in Italian. The original did not survive and we possess in Italian only the Ambrosiana codex, which belonged to the "chevalier de Forrete": either Philibert de la Forest or Jean de Foret, both knights of Rhodes and contemporaries of Philippe Villiers de l'Isle-Adam. The title, by a later hand, reads *Notizie del Mondo Nuovo con le figure de' paesi scoperti, descritte da Antonio Pigafeta vicentino cavaglier di Rodi* (News of the New World with Figures of the Discovered Countries, described by Antonio Pigafetta, Vicentine Knight of Rhodes). The manuscript, which contains the so-called *Regole sull'arte del navigare o trattato della sfera* (Treatise on the Art of Navigation),[55] is generally considered apograph, that is, a direct copy of the original, and represents "the only remaining representative of the textual tradition deriving from Pigafetta's original draft."[56]

Two of the French manuscripts are in the Bibliothèque Nationale, Paris. The older, designated Ms. fr. 5650, is titled *Navigation et descouvrement de la Indie superieure faicte par moy Anthoyne Pigaphete vincentin chevallier de Rhodes* (Navigation

---

[54] For a detailed discussion of this problem and the relations between the manuscripts, as well as bibliography, see Skelton, pp. 16-27.

[55] This work has never been much appreciated. Todorash says, "To the historian it is, for the most part, an incomprehensible piece of curiosa" (p. 326). Stanley provides an English translation of Amoretti's abridged version on pp. 164-74.

[56] Skelton, p. 17.

and Discovery of India Major by me, Antonio Pigafetta, Vicentine Knight of Rhodes); it contains the dedication, twenty-three colored geographical maps and the *Description de la spere*. The other manuscript, Ms. fr. 24.224, is a copy of the preceding one, "more finely written and illuminated on vellum" (Skelton, p. 17) with miniature capitals and beautiful geographical maps but also "heavily bowdlerized by the elimination of any matter likely to offend modesty, and . . . severely pruned of details of navigation and geographical and ethnographical information" (Skelton, p. 24). The third and last French manuscript, the Beinecke-Yale, is entitled *Navigation et descouvrement de la Inde superieure et isles de Malucque ou naissent les cloux de Girofle, faicte par Anthoine Pigaphete vincentin Chevallier de Rhodes* (Navigation and Discovery of India Major and Islands of Molucca where Cloves Grow by A. P., Vicentine Knight of Rhodes). This manuscript, which does not contain the *Trattato della sfera*, is "the most magnificent of the four manuscripts in respect of its writing, its illuminations and its maps" (Skelton, p. 17). All three French manuscripts derive from a common source in a (lost) French translation from an Italian manuscript other than the Ambrosiana. Thus the French manuscripts are in many cases useful for an understanding of the text. Comparison of the two best French manuscripts (5650 and Beinecke-Yale) leaves little doubt as to the textual superiority of the Beinecke-Yale codex, and we have signalled significant variants in our notes.

The extremely rare first edition of the work mentioned earlier was printed in Paris by Simon de Colines, without date but probably in 1525. It is divided into one hundred and four chapters and is entitled *Le voyage et navigation faict par les Espaignolz es isles de Mollucques, des Isles quilz ont trouve audict voyage, de roys dicelles, de leur gouvernement et maniere de vivre, avec plusiers autres choses* (Voyage and Navigation of the Spaniards among the Moluccas, the Islands that they found during said voyage, the kings of these islands, their governments and manner of living, together with many other things). According to the colophon, the work was translated from Italian into French. It is generally attributed, based on Ramusio's statement cited earlier, to the French editor Jacques Lefèvre d'Etaples, at the request of Louise of Savoy. A facsimile edition and translation of this edition by P.S. Paige was published in 1969 (*The Voyage of Magellan*, Englewood, N.J.: Prentice-Hall).

The first Italian edition was prepared by Ramusio and published by Zoppini in Venice in 1536. It was essentially an Italian translation based on the Colines *princeps*, with the title *Il viaggio fatto da gli Spagniuoli atorno al mondo* (The Voyage of the Spaniards Around the World). The text was divided into 114 chapters and preceded by an anonymous *Avviso al lettore* as well as by the letter of Maximilian Transylvanus recounting the voyage (see below).

In 1550 Ramusio included Pigafetta's *First Voyage* in the first volume of the first edition of his *Navigazioni et viaggi* (Venezia, Eredi di Luc'Antonio Giunti) in a form which is very similar to that of the 1536 edition: *Viaggio attorno il mondo scritto per M. Antonio Pigafetta . . . tradotto di lingua francese nella italiana* (Voyage Around the World Written by Messer Antonio Pigafetta . . . translated from French into Italian). This edition includes a somewhat revised version of the *Avviso* of 1536, this time attributed to Ramusio, beneath the title *"Discorso sopra il viaggio fatto dagli Spagnuoli intorno al mondo"* (translated in Stanley, pp. 181-82 and Nowell, pp. 271-74) and is preceded by Maximilian Transylvanus's letter. The 1554 second edition of Ramusio's first volume appends a *"Narrazione di un portoghese compagno di Odoardo Barbosa sopra la nave Vittoria"* (see below). The third edition of Ramusio's *Navigazioni* (1563) introduced the division of the work into chapters.

The text of Ramusio's first edition was translated in abbreviated form into English by Richard Eden in his *The Decades of the newe worlde or west India . . . written by Peter Martyr* (London, G. Powell, 1555; 1577). This is the text from which Shakespeare derived Caliban's American demon "Setebos" (cf. ¶29 and note). A complete translation of the text was given for the first time in Samuel Purchas's *Hakluytus Posthumus or his Pilgrimes* (London, 1625; 1905 ed. vol. II, pp. 84-118).

The work was included in the celebrated eighteenth-century *Histoire générale des voyages* of Antoine-Francois Prévost,[57] but did not otherwise appear in any new editions before Carlo Amoretti's discovery and publication of the Ambrosiana manuscript in 1800 (Milano: G. Galeazzi). Amoretti published Italian, French (Paris: H.J. Jansen, 1801) and German (Gotha: Bey J. Perthes, 1801) editions of the text. The value of Amoretti's find was severely undermined however, by the fact that the text he published represented a rewriting or translation of Pigafetta's 16th-century Italian. The editor also bowdlerized the text in an effort to "exposit with the necessary decency the account of some strange customs written by him [Pigafetta] in frank terms which would offend the delicacy and modesty of the reader of good taste." Unfortunately, the numerous translations in a variety of languages led to the dissemination of this corrupted text, including the English language editions prepared by J. Pinkerton (*A General Collection of the Best and Most Interesting Voyages*, vol. XI, London, Longman, 1812, pp. 288-420) and by Lord Stanley of Alderly, and published in 1874 by the Hakluyt Society (*The First Voyage Round the World*).

On the occasion of the fourth centenary of the discovery of America, Andrea da Mosto prepared for the *Raccolta Colombiana* (p. V, vol. III, 1894) a diplomatic edition of the work which still remains important.[58] J.A. Robertson reproduced it in its entirety and added an English translation (*Magellan's Voyage Round the World*, Cleveland: A.C. Clark Company, 1906). This work included over 650 notes but unfortunately appeared in a limited edition of only three hundred and fifty copies. C.E. Nowell reprinted Robertson's 1906 translation without Robertson's notes in *Magellan's Voyage Around the World* (Evanston, Northwestern UP, 1962).

[57] Cited by Tiraboschi, cit., p. 260, as occuring in vol. XXXVII of the eighty-vol. Paris edition, Didot, 1748–89.
[58] Camillo Manfroni published in 1928 an edition based on Da Mosto in modernized Italian which is not without omissions and errors (*Relazione del primo viaggio*, Milano, Alpes; reprinted in 1983 by the Cassa di Risparmio di Verona).

On the occasion of the fourth centenary of the return of the *Victoria*, J. Denucé published an edition of the French ms. 5650 with variants from the Ambrosiana and the other French manuscripts. (*Relation du premier voyage autor du monde*, Anvers-Paris, G. Jaussens-E. Leroux, 1923). Another French edition based upon ms. 5650, transcribed in modern French, was published by Léonce Peillard and published in Paris in 1956. The Yale-Beinecke manuscript was translated and edited by R.A. Skelton (*Magellan's Voyage: A Narrative Account of the First Circumnavigation*, 2 vols., New Haven, Yale UP, 1969).

Two new editions of Pigafetta's narrative have recently appeared in Italy, both based upon the Ambrosiana manuscript. The first of these edited by M. Masoero is the text upon which the present edition is based: *Viaggio attorno al mondo di Antonio Pigafetta*, Rovereto: Longo Editore, 1987 (see Textual Note below). The other edited by L. Giovannini presents a more or less diplomatic transcription of the text (*La mia longa et pericolosa navigatione*, Milano, Edizioni Paoline, 1989). An abbreviated edition of the text, based upon the Ambrosiana manuscript and edited by M. Pozzi has appeared in *Scopritori e viaggiatori del Cinquecento e Seicento*, Milano-Napoli: Ricciardi, 1991, Tomo I, pp. 509-71.

Of great importance for an adequate appreciation of Pigafetta's narrative are contemporary accounts by other participants in the expedition, as well as those by second-hand historiographic sources. Most of the first-hand sources were collected and published by M. Fernández De Navarrete in vol. IV of his *Colección de los viajes y descubrimientos que hicieron por mar los Espanoles desde fines del siglo XV*, Madrid, Imprenta Real, 1825-37; several of these are translated into English in Lord Adderly Stanley, *The First Voyage Round the World*, London, Hakluyt Society, 1874. An essential bibliographical essay treating these sources and the circumnavigation generally is M. Todorash's "Magellan Historiography," in *Hispanic American Historical Review*, LI (1971), pp. 313-35.

Neither Magellan's own journals nor those of any of the other captains survived. The closest thing to an official report is the letter Juan Sebastián de Elcano (originally master of the *Concepción*, and commander of the *Victoria* after August 1521) wrote to Charles V (dated September 6, 1522) and the account of Elcano's oral testimony given 18 October 1522 at Valladolid. These documents are printed by M. Mitchell in *Elcano, the First Circumnavigator* (London, 1958, pp. 178-82). They are mainly concerned with the conduct of the fleet and the relations between its senior officers, about which Pigafetta says very little. Also significant is the fact that Gonzalo Fernández de Oviedo y Valdés refers to information given him verbally by Elcano more than once in his *Historia general y natural de las Indias* (prólogo de J. Natalicio Gonzalez; notas de José Amador de Los Rios, 14 vols., Editorial Guarania: Asunción del Paraguay, 1944, tomo IV, Bk. XIX, Part II, chps. 1-24).

The only surviving nautical documents written on the voyage or from memory are a handful of pilots' logs including most importantly the *Diario ó derrotero* of the pilot Francisco Albo, who began the voyage as boatswain in the *Trinidad* and ended it as pilot of the *Victoria*, the only ship to complete the first circumnavigation (in Navarrete. pp. 209-47; English translation in Stanley, pp. 211-36). Albo is more precise in the reporting of latitudes and longitudes than Pigafetta but his account begins only two months into the voyage with the departure from Cape St. Augustine in Brasil (November 29, 1519).

A *Roteiro* by a "nameless" Genoese pilot, to be identified perhaps as Leone Pancaldo of Savona or Juan Bautista de Punzorol (or de Poncerva), both of whom were taken prisoner in the *Trinidad* at Ternate is an account of the voyage from Spain to the Moluccas (edited in the *Raccolta di documenti e studi colombiani*, ed. Berchet, p. III, vol. II, Rome, 1893, pp. 272-87; English translation in Stanley, pp. 1-29). According to Todorash "nothing can be gained from a reading of this rather boring account," but it formed the basis for the report made by Antonio de Brito, the Portuguese governor who captured the crew of the *Trinidad* which had been forced to return to Ternate in November, 1522. Brito addressed a letter to King João III of Portugal dated 6 May 1523 which was printed by Navarrete, pp. 305-11.

Four other first-hand accounts survive including one by a seaman Ginés de Mafra, who returned with Pancaldo on the *Trinidad* to Spain, one of only five survivors of the fifty-three men left with Juan Carvalho at Tidore (published by Antonio Blázquez y Delgado Aguileras *"Descubrimiento del Estrecho de Magallanes,"* in *Tres Relaciones*, Madrid, 1920). The other three include: 1) the brief diary of an anonymous Portuguese companion of Duarte Barbosa (perhaps Vasco Gomes Gallego, who sailed as a common seaman on the *Trinidad*, or more likely Basco Gallego who sailed as pilot of the *Victoria*), first published in Ramusio's second edition of Volume I of his *Navigazioni* (1554) at fols. 408v.-409r; Stanley provides a translation at pp. 30-32; 2) the narrative of a seaman identified as Martín López de Ayamonte who deserted at Timor and was later taken by the Portuguese, published by Antonio Baião under the title *"A Viágem de F.M. por una Testemunha Presencial,"* in *Arquivo Histórico de Portugal* (Lisbon, 1933, vol. I, pts. 5 and 6, pp. 276-81); and 3) a *derrotero* by another unnamed seaman discovered in a manuscript in the University of Leiden library and published in 1937 by M. de Jong: *Um Roteiro inédito* (Coimbra, 1937).

Among the second-hand sources, the earliest printed narrative was by Maximilian Transylvanus, Peter Martyr's student and secretary to Charles V (the text is dated 22 October 1522): *De Moluccis Insulis* (English translations in Stanley, pp. 179-210; Henry Stevens, *Johann Schöner*, London, 1888, pp. 101-46; and Nowell, pp. 269-309). It was printed in Rome in 1523 and at Cologne in January 1524, and in later travel collections beginning with Ramusio's (1536, and in vol. I of the *Navigazioni e viaggi*, 1550). Like Peter Martyr and others, Maximilian obtained his information from Elcano and Francisco Albo and Hernando Bustamante at court in Valladolid. He was married to the niece of Cristóbal de Haro, the principal backer of Magellan's adventure, and thus may have had stronger than scholarly curiosity about the voyage. Skelton notes that Maximilian ". . . made a serious attempt to display the circumnavigation against the background of politics and diplomacy in the Far East" (p. 5). As noted earlier, Peter Martyr, "the first historian of America," includes an account of Magellan's circumnavigation in his *De Orbe Novo* (Decade V, Book VII). Antonio de Herrera y Tordesillas gives an account of the circumnavigation in his *Historia general de los hechos de los Castellanos en las islas y tierre firme del Mar Océano* (prólogo de J. Natalicio Gonzalez, Editorial Guarania: Asuncion del Paraguay, 1944, tomo III, Decada Segunda, libro quarto; and tomo IV, Decada Tercera, Libro septimo). Herrera was the official historiographer of the Indies from 1596 and had access to sources many of which have since been lost.

The Portuguese historians Gaspar Correa (*Lendas da India*, composed before 1563, Lisbon, 1858–66) and João de Barros (*Asia*, Lisbon, 1552–1615) represent other important sources. Todorash observes with regard to Barros that "this Portuguese royal chronicler not only used a great deal of first-hand material, but also had access to the correspondence between Magellan and Francisco Serrão and may even have used the lost account of the voyage written by Magellan himself" (p. 138). Both Barros and Correa utilized Antonio de Brito's letter as well as information and documents captured from the Spanish at Ternate. The sections on Magellan from Correa's *Lendas da India* have been translated, and are available in Stanley, pp. 244-56, and in Nowell, pp. 312-28.

NOTE ON THE TEXT

This edition is based on the most recent reliable Italian edition of the Ambrosiana manuscript prepared by Mariarosa Masoero (Rovereto, 1987). The paragraphing and the spacing between the paragraphs reflect those of the manuscript. The numbering of the paragraphs represents an innovation of Masoero's in the presentation of the text which we follow. The twenty-three maps are included in this edition as an insert, with references to their position, as they appear in the Ambrosiana manuscript. All bracketed material in the text are interpolations of the editor.

The classic Robertson translation (Cleveland, 1906) has been thoroughly revised for this edition. Besides the general updating which has been effected by revising the translation against the most currently authoritative text of the original, numerous and in some cases crucial errors of the Robertson translation have been corrected. For example, quite inexplicably, Robertson had translated Pigafetta's nationality as "Venetian" instead of "of Vicenza" at the works very outset (¶1). Another example is the expression in the work's final paragraph where according to Robertson's rendering Pigafetta reports his return to Italy "where I established my permanent abode" (¶208). This was an unfortunate and misleading interpolation based upon the translator's misunderstanding of the original (*Poi me ne venni ne la Italia, ove donnai per sempre me medesimo e queste mie poche fatiche a lo inclito e illustrissimo signor Filipo de Villers Lisleadam, gran maestro de Rodi dignissimo*). The translation has been revised for both style, content, and occasionally for interpretation, as when in Pigafetta's eulogy to Magellan, the word *fortuna* meaning "tempest" or "fortune" is taken in its more literal sense by the present editor. Contrary to Robertson's practice, place-names, including the many toponyms for the Philippines and Moluccas, as well as proper names, when clearly identifiable, have been rendered with their modern equivalents. Finally, however, the Robertson translation's principal virtue has been maintained, that is, its accurate portrayal of Pigafetta's prose style, achieved primarily through a highly literal rendering.

28 March 1518: Charles V issues a *capitulación* providing a fleet of five ships and some 250 officers and men for the expedition.

8 May 1519: A royal *cedula* is issued including seventy-four paragraphs of minute instructions for the voyage.

May 1519: Antonio Pigafetta arrives in Seville in time to join the expedition and participate in final preparations.

10 August 1519: The fleet departs Seville, anchoring at Sanlúcar de Barrameda, the outport of Seville for more than a month, in order to add to the provisions.

20 September 1519: The fleet weighs anchor from Sanlúcar and shapes its course southwest. Three years would pass before the *Victoria* returned.

26 September 1519: The fleet reaches Tenerife in the Canaries (¶9).

3 October 1519: The fleet departs Tenerife and follows a southwest course down to latitude 27° N, then changing course to south by west.

18 October 1519: The fleet experiences a series of storms off Sierra Leone (¶11).

29 November 1519: The fleet reaches Cabo Santo Agostinho at latitude 8° 21′ S, now Cabo Bianco, to the north of Recife (¶15).

13 December 1519: The fleet reaches Rio de Janeiro at latitude 22° 54´ S.

26 December 1519: The fleet departs Rio de Janeiro.

11-12 January 1520: The fleet reaches the Rio de la Plata (¶23), which Magellan called Rio de Solis after the explorer killed by natives there in 1516.

2 February 1520: The fleet departs its anchorage near Montevideo.

13 February 1520: The fleet experiences storms off Bahia Blanca.

27 February 1520: The fleet anchored off a broad bay; they called it *Bahia de los Patos* for the immense number of penguins.

31 March 1520: The fleet enters *Puerto San Julián* (in 49° 30´ S) where it remained for five months, until 24 August. Here the encounters with the Patagonian giants and the mutiny took place (¶25- ¶33).

3 May 1520: The *Santiago* is lost while searching for the strait (¶32).

14 September 1520: The fleet reaches Rio Santa Cruz at latitude 50° S, where it remained until 18 October.

21 October 1520: The fleet reaches Cabo Vírgenes on the feast of St. Ursula and the Eleven Thousand Virgins at latitude 52° 20´ S, longitude 68° 21´ W (¶34).

1 November 1520: Magellan discovers and names the strait *Todos los Santos* in honor of All Saints' Day (¶34-¶38).

November 1520: Esteban Gomez succeeds in the one successful mutiny of the voyage and together with the pilot Hierónimo Guerra takes command of the *San Antonio* and returns to Spain, arriving at the end of March 1521 (¶36).

28 November 1520: The fleet, consisting of *Trinidad*, *Concepción*, and *Victoria* passed Cabo Pilar (which Magellan named *Deseado*) on Desolation Island,

and entered the Pacific Ocean: "Wednesday, November 28, 1520, we debouched from that Strait, engulfing ourselves in the Pacific Sea" (¶41).

1 December 1520: After steering north along the coast of present-day Chile, the fleet sights Cabo Tres Montes in latitude 47° S.

24 January 1521: The fleet sights the uninhabited *Islas Infortunatas* identified by most authorities as Puka Puka in the Tuamoto archipelago in 14° 50′ S (¶42).

4 February 1521: The fleet sights the *Isla de los Tiberones*, probably Caroline in 10° 00′ S.

6 March 1521: The fleet sights the *Islas de Ladrones* or *Las Islas de Velas Latinas*, identified as Guam and Rota of the Marianas (¶46).

9 March 1521: The fleet departs from the Marianas on a course west by south.

6 March 1521: The fleet sights the mountains of Samar in the Philippines and anchors at the island of Suluan at latitude 11° N: "At dawn on Saturday, March 16, 1521, we came upon a high land at a distance of three hundred leagues from the islands of thieves" (¶50).

18 March 1521: Europeans make their first contact with Filipinos on Homonhon island.

25 March 1521: Pigafetta falls overboard and is nearly drowned: "I was aided not, I believe, indeed, through my merits, but through the mercy of that font of charity [the Virgin]" (¶55).

28 March 1521: The fleet anchors off Limasawa (Mazaua) at the southern entrance to Suriago Strait; Magellan and his men are well received there by the natives and good relations are established with Rajah Colambu (¶58-¶68).

7 April 1521: The fleet entered the port of Cebu where, following negotiations, merchandise was exchanged for provisions, and good relations were established (¶70).

14 April 1521: The Sultan Humabon is baptized (and renamed Don Carlos) by the flagship's chaplain with all pomp and circumstance. Rajah Colambu is also baptized and named Don Juan after the Infante (¶84). Magellan cures a sick elder, which leads to the burning of native idols (¶89).

27 April 1521: Magellan and sixty of his men in three longboats attack Rajah Lapu Lapu and his forces on Mactan. They are driven back to the ships and Magellan is killed (¶100).

1 May 1521: Massacre of Europeans in the island Cebu including Duarte Barbosa and twenty-five shipmates (¶103). At this time, the *Concepción* is abandoned (¶106). Only about 110 men still survived. João Carvalho was elected Captain-General.

21 June 1521: *Victoria* and *Trinidad* depart Palawan. They arrived at Brunei on the northeastern coast of Borneo July 9 (¶113).

29 July 1521: The Europeans attack a group of junks off Brunei, capturing four and killing several others (¶121).

15 August 1521: *Victoria* and *Trinidad* call at Cimbonbon (Banguey) on the south side of Balabac Strait, where they remain forty-two days repairing the ships and gathering provisions (¶128).

September 1521: Carvalho is degraded to his former rank of flag pilot; Gómez de Espinosa is elected Captain-General and Captain of the *Trinidad*; Juan Sebastián de Elcano is elected Captain of *Victoria* (¶128).

26 October 1521: The two ships experience storms in the Celebes Sea (¶133).

6 November 1521: *Victoria* and *Trinidad* arrive at the Maluccas: "Therefore we thanked God and as an expression of our joy discharged all our artillery" (¶136).

8 November 1521: *Trinidad* and *Victoria* enter the harbor of Tidore, most important of the five principal Maluccas (¶137).

9 November 1521: The Europeans are received at Tidore by the Sultan Manzor who declares that he and all his people wish to become vassals of the Emperor Charles V.

21 December 1521: *Victoria*, under the command of Elcano set sail for a nine month return voyage via the Cape of Good Hope, with forty-seven of the original crew and thirteen natives on board (eighteen Christian and three natives survived). Gómez de Espinosa stayed behind with fifty-three men to repair the *Trinidad* before attempting to return across the Pacific to New Spain where the cargo was to be carried across the Isthmus of Panama and shipped to Spain (¶179-¶180).

6 April 1522: *Trinidad* set sail from Tidore and struggled as far as latitude 43° N, before it was decided to return to Tidore. The ship and crew were eventually captured by the Portuguese Captain António de Brito. Only four of the *Trinidad*'s crew eventually returned to the Iberian Peninsula. Espinosa spent four and a half years in captivity in the east before returning to Spain.

10 January 1522: *Victoria* reaches Alor (Pigafetta's Malua) in 8° 20′ S latitude (¶187).

25 January 1522: *Victoria* departs Alor and arrived the next day at the island of Timor along which the ship coasted for three weeks while trading for provisions (¶190).

10-11 February 1522: *Victoria* sailed from Timor into the Indian Ocean, called *Laut Chidol* (¶ 201).

6 May 1522: *Victoria* doubled the Cape of Good Hope (¶202).

8 June 1522: *Victoria* crossed the equator for the fourth time since leaving Spain

9 July 1522: *Victoria* anchored in the port of Ribeira Grande on the Cape Verde island of Santiago. Between Timor and Cape Verde fifteen Christians and ten Indonesians died aboard the *Victoria*.

15 July 1522: *Victoria* departs hastily from Cape Verde islands. Thirteen members of the crew were detained by the Portuguese authorities.

28 July 1522: Tenerife of the Canary Islands was sighted.

7 August 1522: The volcanic summit of Pico in the Azores was sighted.

21 August 1522: *Victoria* headed for Cape St. Vincent and arrived there September 4.

6 September 1522: *Victoria* entered the harbor of Sanlúcar de Barrameda, and anchored off a quay at Seville on September 8. Only eighteen Christians and three Indonesians survived.

Antonio Pigafetta

THE FIRST VOYAGE
AROUND THE WORLD

The First Voyage Around the World

[1] Antonio Pigafetta, patrician of Vicenza and Knight of Rhodes, to the most illustrious and excellent Lord, Philippe Villiers de l'Isle-Adam, renowned grand master of Rhodes, his most honored lord.[1]

[2] Inasmuch as, most illustrious and excellent Lord, there are many curious persons who not only take pleasure in knowing and hearing the great and wonderful things which God has permitted me to see and suffer during my long and dangerous voyage, herein described, but who also wish to know the means and manners and paths that I have taken in making that voyage; and who do not lend that entire faith to the end unless they have a perfect assurance of the beginning: therefore, your most illustrious Lordship must know that, finding myself, in the year of the nativity of Our Savior 1519 in Spain, in the court of the most serene King of the Romans,[2] with the reverend Monsignor, Francesco Chiericati,[3] then apostolic protonotary and ambassador of Pope Leo X of holy memory (and who has since become bishop of Aprutino and prince of Teramo),[4] and having obtained much information from many

3

books that I had read, as well as from various persons, who discussed the great and marvelous things of the Ocean Sea with his Lordship, I determined, by the good favor of his Caesarean Majesty, and of his Lordship abovesaid, to experience and to go to see those things for myself, so that I might be able thereby to satisfy myself somewhat, and so that I might be able to gain some renown with posterity.

[3] Having heard that a fleet composed of five vessels had been fitted out in the city of Seville[5] for the purpose of going to discover the spicery in the islands of Malucca, under command of Captain-general Ferdinand Magellan, a Portuguese gentleman, comendador of the Order of Santiago de la Spada,[6] [who] had many times travelled the Ocean Sea in various directions, for which he had acquired great praise, I set out from the city of Barcelona, where his Majesty was then residing, bearing many letters in my favor. I went by ship as far as Malaga. From there I went by land to Seville.[7] After having been there about three full months, waiting for the fleet to be set in order for the departure, finally, as your most excellent Lordship will learn below, we commenced our voyage under most happy auspices.

[4] And inasmuch as when I was in Italy and going to see his Holiness, Pope Clement,[8] you by your grace showed yourself very kind and good to me at Monterosi,[9] and told me that you would be greatly pleased if I would write down for you all those things which I had seen and suffered during my voyage; and although I have had little opportunity, yet I have tried to satisfy your desire according to my poor ability; therefore, I offer you, in this little book of mine, all my vigils, hardships, and wanderings, begging you, when you will take some rest from your continual Rhodian cares, to deign to skim through it, by which I shall be enabled to receive a not slight remuneration from your most illustrious Lordship, to whose good favor I consign and commend myself.

THE FIRST VOYAGE

[5] The captain-general having resolved to make so long a voyage
through the Ocean Sea, where furious winds and great storms are
always reigning, but not desiring to make known to any of his men the
voyage that he was about to make, fearing they might be cast down at
the thought of doing so great and extraordinary a deed, as he did
accomplish with the aid of God (the captains who accompanied him,
hated him exceedingly, I know not why, unless because he was a
Portuguese, and they Spaniards);[10] desiring therefore to accomplish that
which he promised under oath to the emperor, Don Carlo, king of
Spain, and so that the ships might not become separated from one
another during the storms and night, he prescribed the following orders
and gave them to all the pilots and masters of his ships.[11] These were [to
the effect] that he should always precede the other ships at night, and
they were to follow his ship which would have a large torch of wood,
which they call *farol*.[12] He always carried that *farol* set at the poop of his
ship as a signal so that they might always follow him. Another light was
made by means of a lantern or by means of a piece of rush wicking
called *strengue*,[13] made of esparto which is well beaten in the water, and
then dried in the sun or in the smoke—a most excellent material for
such use. They were to answer him so that he might know by that signal
whether all of the ships were coming together. If he showed two lights
besides that of the *farol*, they were to veer or take another tack, [doing
this] when the wind was not favorable or suitable for us to continue on
our way, or when he wished to sail slowly. If he showed three lights,
they were to lower away the *bonneta* (bonnet-sail), which is a part of the
sail that is fastened below the mainsail, when the weather is suitable for
making better time. It is lowered so that it may be easier to furl the
mainsail when it is struck hastily during a sudden squall. If he showed
four lights, they were to strike all the sails; after which he showed a
signal by one light, [which meant] that he was standing still. If he

showed a greater number of lights, or fired a mortar, it was a signal of land or of shoals. Then he showed four lights when he wished to have the sails set full, so that they might always sail in his wake by the torch on the poop. When he desired to set the bonnet-sail, he showed three lights. When he desired to alter his course, he showed two; and then if he wished to ascertain whether all the ships were following and whether they were coming together, he showed one light, so that each one of the ships might do the same and reply to him.

[6] Three watches were set nightly: the first at the beginning of the night; the second which they call *modora*[14] in the middle, and the third at the end [of the night]. All of the men in the ships were divided into three *colonelli*:[15] the first was the division of the captain or boatswain, those two alternating nightly; the second, of either the pilot or boatswain's mate; and the third, of the master. Thus did the captain-general order that all the ships observe the above signals and watches, so that their voyage might be more secure.[16]

[7] On Monday morning, August 10, St. Lawrence's day, in the year abovesaid, the fleet, having been supplied with all the things necessary for the sea and men of every sort[17] (our number was two hundred and thirty-seven), we made ready to leave from the Mole of Seville.[18] Discharging many pieces of artillery, the ships set their foresails to the wind, and descended the river Betis, at present called Guadalquivir,[19] passing by a village called San Juan de Aznalfarache, once a large Moorish settlement. In the midst of it was once a bridge that crossed that river, and led to Seville. Two columns of that bridge have remained even to this day at the bottom of the water, and when ships sail by there, they need men who know well the location of the columns, so that the ships may not strike against them. They must also be passed when the river is highest with the tide; as with many other places along

the river, which have insufficient depth for ships that are laden and which are too large to pass. Then the ships reached another village called Coria,[20] and passed by many other villages along the river, until they came to a castle of the duke of Medina-Sidonia, called Sanlúcar, which is a port by which to enter the Ocean Sea. It is in an east and west direction with the cape of San Vincente, which lies in 37 degrees of latitude, and 10 leagues from that port.[21] From Seville to this point [Sanlúcar], it is seventeen or twenty leagues by river.

[8] Some days after, the captain-general, with his other captains, descended the river in the small boats belonging to their ships. We remained there for a considerable number of days in order to finish [providing] the fleet with some things that it needed. Every day we went ashore to hear mass in a village called Our Lady of Barrameda, near Sanlúcar. Before the departure, the captain-general wished all the men to confess, and would not allow any woman to sail in the fleet for the sake of better order.

[9] We left that village, by name Sanlúcar, on Tuesday, September 20 of the same year, and took a southwest course. On the 26th of that month, we reached an island of the Grand Canary islands,[22] called Tenerife, which lies in a latitude of 28 degrees, [landing there] in order to get meat, water, and wood. We stayed there for three and one-half days in order to furnish the fleet with those supplies. Then we went to a port of the same island called Monte Rosso[23] to get pitch, staying [there] two days

[10] Your most illustrious Lordship must know that there is a particular one of the Grand Canary islands, where one cannot find a single drop of water which gushes up [from a spring]; but that at midday a cloud descends from the sky and encircles a large tree which grows in that island, the leaves and branches of which distil a quantity of water.

At the foot of the tree runs a basin which resembles a fountain's, where all the water falls, and from which the people living there, and the animals, both domestic and wild, fully satisfy themselves with this water and no other.[24]

[11] At midnight of Monday, the 3rd of October, the sails were trimmed toward the south, and we took to the open Ocean Sea, passing between Cape Verde and its islands in 14 ½ degrees. Thus for many days did we sail along the coast of Ghinea, or Ethiopia; here there is a mountain called Sierra Leone (which lies in 8 degrees of latitude), with contrary winds, calms, and rains without wind, until we reached the equinoctial line, where we had sixty days of continual rain, contrary to the opinion of the ancients.[25] Before we reached the line, at 14 degrees, many furious squalls of wind, and currents of water struck us head on. Since we were unable to advance, and so as to avoid being wrecked, all the sails were struck; and in this manner did we wander here and there on the sea, waiting for the tempest to cease, for it was very furious. When it rained there was no wind. When the sun shone, it was calm.[26]

[12] Certain large fishes called *tiburoni*[27] came to the side of the ships; they have terrible teeth, and whenever they find men in the sea they devour them. We caught many of them with iron hooks, although they are not good to eat unless they are small, and even then they are not very good.

[13] During those storms the holy body, that is to say St. Elmo,[28] appeared to us many times, in the form of light. Once he appeared on an exceedingly dark night, with the brightness of a blazing torch, on the maintop, where he stayed for about two hours or more, to our consolation, for we were weeping. When that blessed light was about to leave us, so dazzling was the brightness that it cast into our eyes, that we all remained for more than an eighth of an hour blinded and calling for mercy, for truly we thought that we were dead men. The sea suddenly grew calm.[29]

[14] I saw many kinds of birds, among them one that had no anus; and another, [which] when the female wishes to lay its eggs, it does so on the back of the male and there they are hatched. The latter bird has no feet, and always lives in the sea.[30] [There is] another kind which live on the ordure of the other birds, and in no other manner; for I often saw this bird, which is called *cagassela*, fly behind the other birds, until they are constrained to drop their ordure, which the *cagassela* seizes immediately and lets the bird go.[31] I also saw many flying fish, and many others collected together, so that they resembled an island.[32]

[15] After we had passed the equinoctial line going south, we lost the north star, and from there we sailed south south-west until [we reached] a land called "the land of Verzin"[33] which lies in 23 ½ degrees of the Antarctic Pole [south latitude].[34] It is the land extending from the Cape of Santo Agostinho, which lies in 8 degrees of the same pole.[35] There, we got a plentiful refreshment of fowls, potatoes, many sweet pine-cones, in truth the most delicious fruit that can be found[36]—the flesh of the *anta*,[37] which resembles beef, sugarcane, and innumerable other things, which I shall not mention in order not to be prolix.[38] For one fishhook or one knife, those people gave five or six chickens; for one comb, a pair of geese; for one mirror or one pair of scissors, as many fish as would be sufficient for ten men; for a bell or a lace, one basketful of potatoes. These potatoes resemble chestnuts in taste, and are as long as turnips. For a king of diamonds which is a playing card,[39] they gave me six fowls and thought that they had even cheated me.[40] We entered that port on St. Lucy's day,[41] and on that day had the sun on the zenith; and we were subjected to greater heat on that day and on the other days when we had the sun on the zenith, than when we were under the equinoctial line.

[16] That land of Verzin is very bounteous and larger than Spain, France, and Italy put together, and belongs to the king of Portugal.[43] The people of that land are not Christians, and have no manner of worship. They live according to the dictates of nature, and reach an age of one hundred twenty-five and one hundred forty years.[44] They go naked, both men and women. They live in certain long houses which they call *boij*,[45] and sleep in cotton hammocks called *amache*,[46] which are fastened in those houses by each end to large beams. A fire is built on the ground under those hammocks. In each one of those boii, there are one hundred men with their wives and children, and they make a great racket. They have boats called *canoe*[47] made of one single but flattened[48] tree, hollowed out by the use of stone.[49] Those people employ stones as we do iron, as they have no iron. Thirty or forty men occupy one of those boats. They paddle with blades like a baker's peel,[50] and thus, black, naked, and shaven, they resemble, when paddling, the inhabitants of the Stygian marsh.[51]

[17] The men and women are proportioned as we. They eat the human flesh of their enemies, not because it is good, but because it is a certain established custom. That custom, which is mutual, was begun by an old woman, who had but one son who was killed by his enemies. In return some days later, that old woman's friends captured one of the company who had killed her son, and brought him to the place of her abode. She seeing him, and remembering her son, she ran upon him like an infuriated bitch, and bit him on the shoulder. Shortly afterward he escaped to his own people, whom he told that they had tried to eat him, showing them [in proof] the marks on his shoulder. Whomever the latter captured afterward at any time from the former they ate, and the former did the same to the latter, so that such a custom has sprung

up in this way.[52] They do not eat the bodies all at once, but every one cuts off a piece, and carries it to his house, where he smokes it. Then every eight days, he cuts off a small bit, which he eats thus smoked with his other food to remind him of his enemies.[53] The above was told me by the pilot, João Carvalho, who was with us, and who had lived in that land for four years.[54]

[18] Those people paint the whole body and the face in a wonderful manner with fire in various fashions, as do the women also. The men are smooth shaven and have no beard, for they pull it out. They clothe themselves in a dress made of parrot feathers, with large round arrangements at their buttocks made from the largest feathers, and it is a ridiculous sight. Almost all the people, except the women and children, have three holes pierced in the lower lip, where they carry round stones, one finger or thereabouts in length and hanging down outside. Those people are not entirely black, but olive-skinned. They keep the privies uncovered, and the body is without hair, while both men and women always go naked. Their king is called *cacich*.[55] They have an infinite number of parrots, and gave us eight or ten for one mirror; and little monkeys[56] that look like lions, only [they are] yellow, and very beautiful. They make round white [loaves of] bread from the marrowy substance of trees, which is not very good, and is found between the wood and the bark and resembles ricotta.[57] They have swine which have their navels on their backs,[58] and large birds with beaks like spoons and no tongues.[59]

[19] The men gave us one or two of their young daughters as slaves for one hatchet or one large knife, but they would not give us their wives in exchange for anything at all.[60] The women will not shame their husbands under any considerations whatever, and according to what was told us, refuse to consent to their husbands by day, but only by night.

The women cultivate the fields, and carry all their food from the mountains in panniers or baskets on the head or fastened to the head. But they are always accompanied by their husbands, who are armed only with a bow of brazil-wood or of black palm-wood, and a bundle of cane arrows, doing this because they are jealous [of their wives].[61] The women carry their children hanging [in] a cotton net from their necks.

[20] I omit other particulars, in order not to be tedious. Mass was said twice on shore, during which those people remained on their knees with so great contrition and raising clasped hands aloft, that it was an exceeding great pleasure to behold them.[62] They built us a house as they thought that we were going to stay with them for some time, and at our departure they cut a great quantity of brazilwood to give us. It had been about two months since it had rained in that land, and when we reached that port, it happened to rain, whereupon they said that we came from the sky and that we had brought the rain with us. Those people could be converted easily to the faith of Jesus Christ.[63]

[21] At first those people thought that the small boats were the children of the ships, and that the latter gave birth to them when they were lowered into the sea from the ships, and when they were lying so alongside the ships (as is the custom), they believed that the ships were nursing them.[64] One day a beautiful young woman came to the flagship, where I was, for no other purpose than to seek what chance might offer.[65] While there and waiting, she cast her eyes upon the master's room, and saw a nail longer than one's finger. Picking it up most gracefully and gallantly, she trust it through the lips of her vagina, and bending down low immediately departed; the captain-general and I witnessed that action.[66]

[22] Some words of those people of Verzin:[67]

For millet *maiz*
For flour *hui*
For fishhook *pinda*
For knife *tacse*
For comb *chigap*
For scissors *pirame*
For bell *itanmaraca*
Good, better   *tum, maragathum*

[23] We remained in that land for thirteen days.[68] Then proceeding
on our way, we went as far as 34 and ⅓ degrees toward the Antarctic
Pole, where we found people at a freshwater river,[69] called Cannibals,
who eat human flesh.[70] One of them, in stature almost a giant, came to
the flagship in order to assure [the safety of] the others his friends. He
had a voice like a bull. While he was in the ship, the others carried away
their possessions from the place where they were living into the interior,
for fear of us. Seeing that, we landed one hundred men in order to find
an interpreter and converse with them, or to capture one of them by
force. They fled, and in fleeing they took such large strides that we,
although running, could not gain on them.[71] There are seven islands in
that river, in the largest of which precious gems are found. That place is
called the "Cape Santa Maria." It was formerly thought that one passed
from there to the sea of *Sur*, that is to say the South Sea,[72] but it was
never further explored. Now the name is not [given to] a cape, but [to]
a river, with a mouth seventeen leagues in width.[73] A Spanish captain,
named Juan de Solis, was eaten by these Cannibals because he trusted
them too much, together with sixty men who were going to discover
lands like us.[74]

[24] Then proceeding on the same course toward the Antarctic Pole, coasting along the land, we came to anchor at two islands full of geese and seawolves.[75] Truly, the great number of those geese cannot be told; in one hour we loaded the five ships [with them]. Those geese are black and have all their feathers alike both on body and wings. They do not fly, and live on fish. They were so fat that it was necessary to skin them rather than to pluck them. Their beak is like that of a crow. The seawolves are of various colors, and as large as a calf, with a head like that of a calf, ears small and round, and large teeth. They have no legs but only feet with small nails attached to the body, which resemble our hands, and between their fingers the same kind of skin as the geese. They would be very fierce if they could run. They swim, and live on fish. At that place the ships endured a very great storm, during which the three holy bodies appeared to us many times, that is to say, St. Elmo, St. Nicholas, and St. Clare; whereupon the storm quickly ceased.[76]

[25] Leaving that place, we finally reached 49 and ½ degrees toward the Antarctic Pole.[77] As it was winter, the ships entered a safe port to winter.[78] We passed two months in that place without seeing anyone. One day we suddenly saw a naked man of giant stature on the shore of the port, dancing, singing, and throwing dust on his head. The captain-general sent one of our men to the giant so that he might perform the same actions as a sign of peace. Having done that, the man led the giant to an islet where the captain-general was waiting. When the giant was in the captain-general's and our presence he marveled greatly, and made signs with one finger raised upward, believing that we had come from the sky. He was so tall that we reached only to his waist, and he was well proportioned.[79] His face was large and painted red all over, while about his eyes he was painted yellow; and he had two hearts painted on the middle of his cheeks. His scanty hair was painted white. He was

dressed in the skins of animals skillfully sewn together. That animal has a head and ears as large as those of a mule, a neck and body like those of a camel, the legs of a deer, and the tail of a horse, like which it neighs, and that land has very many of them.[80] His feet were shod with the same kind of skins, and covered his feet in the manner of shoes. In his hand he carried a short, heavy bow, with a cord somewhat thicker than those of the lute, and made from the intestines of the same animal, and a bundle of rather short cane arrows feathered like ours, and with points of white and black flint stones in the manner of Turkish arrows, instead of iron. Those points were fashioned by means of another stone.

[26] The captain-general had the giant given something to eat and drink, and among other things which were shown to him was a large steel mirror. When he saw his reflection, he was greatly terrified, and jumped back throwing three or four of our men to the ground. After that the captain-general gave him some bells, a mirror, a comb, and some beads and sent him ashore with four armed men. When one of his companions, who would never come to the ships, saw him coming with our men, he ran to the place where the others were, who came [down to the shore] all naked one after the other. When our men reached them, they began to dance and to sing, lifting one finger to the sky, and showing our men some white powder made from the roots of an herb, which they kept in earthen pots, and which they offered our men to eat because they had nothing else.[81] Our men made signs inviting them to the ships, and that they would help them carry their possessions. Thereupon, those men quickly took only their bows, while their women laden like asses carried everything.

[27] The latter are not so tall as the men but are very much fatter. When we saw them we were greatly surprised. Their breasts are one-half cubit long,[82] and they are painted and clothed like their husbands, except that before their privies they have a small skin which covers

them. They led four of those young animals [the guanaco], fastened with thongs like a halter. When those people wish to catch some of those animals, they tie one of these young ones to a thornbush. Thereupon, the large ones come to play with the little ones; and those people kill them with their arrows from their place of concealment. Our men led eighteen of those people, counting men and women, to the ships, and they were distributed on both sides of the port so that they might catch some of those animals.

[28] Six days later, a giant painted and clothed in the same manner was seen by some [of our men] who were cutting wood. He had in his hand a bow and arrow. When he approached our men, he first touched his head, face, and body, and then did the same to our men, afterward lifting his hands toward the sky. When the captain-general was informed of it, he ordered him to be brought in the small boat, and he was taken to that island in the port where our men had built a house for the smiths and for the storage of some things from the ships. That man was even taller and better built than the others and as tractable and amiable. Jumping up and down, he danced, and when he danced, at every leap, his feet sank a palm's depth into the earth. He remained with us for many days, so long that we baptized him, calling him John. He pronounced the name *Jesus*, the *Pater Noster*, *Ave Maria* and his own name as distinctly as we, but with an exceedingly loud voice. Then the captain-general gave him a shirt, a woolen jerkin, cloth breeches, a cap, a mirror, a comb, bells, and other things, and sent him away to his companions. He left us very joyous and happy. The following day he brought one of those large animals to the captain-general, in return for which many things were given to him, so that he might bring some more to us; but we did not see him again. We thought that his companions had killed him because he had conversed with us.

[29] After fifteen days we saw four of those giants without their weapons for they had hidden them in certain bushes, as the two whom we captured showed us. Each one was painted differently. The captain-general detained two of them, the youngest and best proportioned, by means of a very cunning trick, in order to take them to Spain. Had he used any other means [than those he employed], they could easily have killed some of us. The trick that he employed to capture them was as follows. He gave them many knives, scissors, mirrors, bells, and glass beads; and those two having their hands filled with those articles, the captain-general had two pairs of iron manacles brought, such as are fastened on the feet, and made motions as if to make a gift of them, at which they were very pleased, since those manacles were of iron, but they did not know how to carry them. They were grieved at leaving them behind, but they had no place to put those gifts; for they had to hold the skin wrapped about them with their hands. The other two giants wished to help them, but the captain refused. Seeing that they were loath to leave those manacles behind, the captain made them a sign that he would put them on their feet, and that they could carry them away. They nodded assent with the head. Immediately, the captain had the manacles put on both of them at the same time. When our men were driving home the cross bolt, the giants began to suspect something, but the captain assuring them they nevertheless stood still. When they saw later that they were tricked, they raged like bulls, calling loudly for *Setebos*[83] to aid them. Only with difficulty were we able to bind the hands of the other two, whom we sent ashore with nine of our men, so that the giants might guide them to the place where the wife of one of the two whom we had captured was; for the latter expressed his great grief at leaving her by signs so that we understood [that he meant] her. While they were on their way, one of the giants freed his hands, and took to his heels with such swiftness that our men lost sight of him. He

went to the place where his associates were, but he did not find [there] one of his companions, who had remained behind with the women, and who had gone hunting. He immediately went in search of the latter, and told him all that had happened. The other giant endeavored so hard to free himself from his bonds, that our men struck him, wounding him slightly on the head, whereat he, snorting with rage, led them to where the women were. João Carvalho, the pilot and commander of those men, refused to bring back the woman that evening, but determined to sleep there, for night was approaching. The other two giants came, and seeing their companion wounded, hesitated, but said nothing then. But with the dawn, they spoke to the women; [whereupon] they immediately ran away (and the smaller ones ran faster than the taller), leaving all their possessions behind them. Two of them turned aside to shoot their arrows at our men. The other was leading away those small animals of theirs in order to hunt. Thus fighting, one of them pierced the thigh of one of our men with an arrow, and he died immediately.[84] When the giants saw that, they ran away quickly. Our men had muskets and cross-bows, but they could never wound any of the giants, [for] when the latter fought, they never stood still, but leaped here and there. Our men buried their dead companion, and burned all the possessions left behind by the giants. Truly those giants run swifter than horses and are exceedingly jealous of their wives.[85]

[30] When those people feel sick to their the stomachs, instead of purging themselves, they thrust an arrow down their throat for two span or more and vomit [a substance of a] green color mixed with blood, for they eat a certain kind of thistle.[86] When they have a headache, they cut themselves across the forehead; and they do the same on the arms or on the legs and in any part of the body, letting a quantity of blood. One of those whom we had captured, and whom we kept in

our ship, said that the blood refused to stay there [in the place of the pain], and consequently causes them suffering. They wear their hair cut with the tonsure, like friars, but it is left longer; and they have a cotton cord wrapped about the head, in which they stick their arrows when they go hunting. They bind their privies close to their bodies because of the exceeding great cold. When one of those people die, ten or twelve demons all painted appear to them and dance very joyfully about the corpse. They see that one of those demons is much taller than the others, and he cries out and rejoices more. They paint themselves exactly in the same manner as the demon appears to them painted. They call the larger demon *Setebos* and the others *Cheleulle*. That giant also told us by signs that he had seen the demons with two horns on their heads, and long hair which hung to the feet belching forth fire from mouth and buttocks. The captain-general called those people *Patagoni*.[87] They all clothe themselves in the skins of that animal above mentioned; and they have no houses except those made from the skin of the same animal, and they wander here and there with those houses just as the gypsies do. They live on raw flesh and on a sweet root which they call *chapae*. Each of the two whom we captured ate a basketful of biscuit, and drank half a pail of water at a gulp. They also ate rats without skinning them.

[31] In that port which we called "Port St. Julian," we remained about five months.[88] Many things happened there. In order that your most illustrious Lordship[89] may know some of them, it happened that as soon as we had entered the port, the captains of the other four ships plotted treason in order that they might kill the captain-general. Those conspirators consisted of the overseer of the fleet, one Juan de Cartagena, the treasurer, Luis de Mendoza, the accountant, Antonio Coca, and Gaspar de Quesada. The overseer of the men having been quartered, the treasurer was killed by dagger blows, for the treason was

discovered. Some days after that, Gaspar de Quesada was banished with a priest[90] in that land of Patagonia. The captain-general did not wish to have him killed, because the emperor Don Carlo, had appointed him captain.[91]

[32] A ship called *Santiago* was wrecked in an expedition made to explore the coast. All the men were saved as by a miracle, not even getting wet. Two of them came to the ships after suffering great hardships, and reported the whole occurrence to us. Consequently, the captain-general sent some men with bags full of biscuits. It was necessary for us to carry them food for two months, while daily pieces of the ship [that was wrecked] were recovered. The way there was long, [being] twenty-four leagues, or one hundred miles, and the path was very rough and full of thorns. The men were four days on the road, sleeping at night in the bushes. They found no drinking water, but only ice, which caused them the greatest hardship.[92] There were very many long shellfish which are called *missiglioni*[93] in that port [San Julian]; they had pearls in the middle but they were too small to be eaten. Incense, ostriches, foxes, sparrows, and rabbits much smaller than ours were also found. We erected a cross on the top of the highest summit there, as a sign in that land that it belonged to the king of Spain; and we called that summit "Monte de Christo."

[33] Leaving that place, we found, in 51 degrees less ⅓ degree, toward the Antarctic Pole, a river of fresh water.[94] There the ships almost perished because of the furious winds; but God and the holy bodies aided them. We stayed about two months in that river[95] in order to supply the ships with water, wood, and fish, [the latter being] one cubit in length and more, and covered with scales.[96] They were very good, but there were few of them. Before leaving that river, the captain-general and all of us confessed and received communion as true Christians.

[34] Then going to 52 degrees toward the same pole, we found a strait on the day of the [Feast of the] Eleven Thousand Virgins, whose cape we named the Cape of the Eleven Thousand Virgins[97] because of that very great miracle. That strait is 110 leagues or 440 miles long, and it is one-half league broad, more or less. It leads to another sea called the Pacific Sea, and is surrounded by very lofty mountains laden with snow. There it was impossible to find bottom [for anchoring], but [it was necessary to fasten] the moorings[98] on land twenty-five or thirty fathoms away. Had it not been for the captain-general, we would not have found that strait, for we all thought and said that it was closed on all sides.[99] But the captain-general who knew where to sail to find a well-hidden strait, which he had seen depicted on a map in the treasury of the king of Portugal, which was made by that excellent man, Martin of Bohemia,[100] sent two ships, the *San Antonio* and the *Concepción* (for thus they were called), to discover what was inside at the end of the bay.

[35] We with the other two ships, the flagship, called *Trinidad* and the other the *Victoria*, stayed inside the bay to await them. A great storm struck us that night, which lasted until the middle of next day, which necessitated our lifting anchor, and letting ourselves drift here and there about the bay.[101] The other two ships suffered a headwind and could not double a cape formed by the bay almost at its end, as they were trying to return to join us; so that they thought that they would have to run aground. But on approaching the end of the bay, and thinking that they were lost, they saw a small opening which did not appear to be an opening, but a cove.[102] Like desperate men they hauled into it, and thus they discovered the strait by chance. Seeing that it was not a cove, but a strait with land, they proceeded farther, and found a bay.[103] And then farther on they found another strait and another bay larger than the first two.[104] Very joyful they immediately turned back to report to the captain-general. We thought that they had been wrecked, first, by reason

of the violent storm, and second, because two days had passed and they had not appeared, and also because of certain [signals with] smoke made by two of their men who had been sent ashore to advise us. And so, while in suspense, we saw the two ships with sails full and banners flying to the wind, coming toward us. When they neared us in this manner, they suddenly discharged a number of mortars, and burst into cheers. Then all together thanking God and the Virgin Mary, we went to explore farther on.

[36] After entering that strait, we found two openings, one to the southeast, and the other to the southwest.[105] The captain-general sent the ship *San Antonio* together with the *Concepción* to ascertain whether that opening which was toward the southeast had an exit into the Pacific Sea. The ship *San Antonio* would not await the *Concepción* because it intended to flee and return to Spain which it did. The pilot of that ship was one Estevão Gomes,[106] and he hated the captain-general exceedingly, because before that fleet was fitted out, he had gone to the emperor to request some caravels to go and explore, but his Majesty did not give them to him because of the coming of the captain-general. On that account he conspired with certain Spaniards, and the next night they captured the captain of their ship, a cousin-german of the captain-general, one Alvaro de Mezquita, whom they wounded and put in irons, and in this condition took to Spain. The other giant whom we had captured was in that ship, but he died when they came into the warmer climate. The *Concepción*, as it was unable to keep up with that ship, waited for it, sailing about here and there. The *San Antonio* turned back during the night and fled along the same strait.

[37] We had gone to explore the other opening toward the southwest. Finding, however, the same strait continuously, we came upon a river which we called "the river of Sardines," because there were many

sardines near it.[107] So we stayed there for four days in order to await the two ships. During that period we sent a well-equipped boat to discover the cape of the other sea. The men returned within three days, and reported that they had seen the cape and the open sea. The captain-general wept for joy, and called that cape "Cape Deseado," for we had been desiring it for a long time.[108] We turned back to look for the two ships, but we found only the *Concepción*. Upon asking them where the other one was, João Serrão,[109] who was captain and pilot of the *Concepción* (and also of that ship that had been wrecked) replied that he did not know, and that he had never seen it after it had entered the opening. We sought it in all parts of the strait, as far as that opening through which it had fled, and the captain-general sent the ship *Victoria* back to the entrance of the strait to ascertain whether the ship was there. Orders were given them, if they did not find it, to plant a banner on the summit of some small hill with a letter in an earthen pot buried in the earth near the banner, so that if the banner were seen the letter might be found, and the ship might learn the course that we were sailing. For this was the arrangement made between us in case we became separated. Two banners were planted with their letters: one on a little eminence in the first bay, and the other in an islet in the third bay where there were many sea-wolves and large birds.[110] The captain-general waited for the ship with his other ship near the river of Isleo,[111] and he had a cross set up in an islet near that river, which flowed between high mountains covered with snow and emptied into the sea near the river of Sardines. Had we not discovered that strait, the captain-general had determined to go as far as 75 degrees toward the Antarctic Pole. There in that latitude, during the summer season, there is no night, or if there is any night it is but short, and so in the winter with the day.

[38] In order that your most illustrious Lordship may believe it,[112] when we were in that strait, the nights were only three hours long, and

it was then the month of October. The land on the left-hand side of
that strait turned toward the southeast and it was low.[113] We called that
strait the strait of Patagonia.[114] One finds the safest of ports every half
league in it, excellent waters, the finest of wood [but not of cedar], fish,
sardines, and *missiglioni,* while smallage,[115] a sweet herb [although there
is also some that is bitter] grows around the springs. We ate of it for
many days as we had nothing else. I believe that there is not a more
beautiful or better strait in the world than that one. In that Ocean Sea
one sees a very amusing fish hunt. The fish [that hunt] are of three
sorts, and are one cubit and more in length, and are called *dorado, albi-
core,* and *bonito.*[116] Those fish follow the flying fish called *colondrini,*[115]
which are one span and more in length and very good to eat. When the
above three kinds [of fish] find any of those flying fish, the latter immediately leap from the water and fly more than a crossbow's flight, as
long as their wings are wet. While they are flying, the others run along
back of them under the water following the shadow of the flying fish.
The latter have no sooner fallen into the water than the others immediately seize and eat them: a very beautiful thing to see.[117]

[39] Words of the Patagonian giants:[119]

For head	*her*	For teeth	*phor*
For eye	*other*	For tongue	*schial*
For nose	*or*	For chin	*sechen*
For eyebrows	*occhechel*	For hair	*archiz*
For eyelids	*sechechiel*	For face	*cogechel*
For nostrils	*oresche*	For throat	*ohumer*
For mouth	*xiam*	For occiput	*schialeschin*
For lips	*schiahame*		

More patagonian words:

For shoulders	*pelles*	For hand	*chene*
For elbow	*cotel*	For palm of the hand	*caimeghin*

THE FIRST VOYAGE

For finger   *cori*
For ears   *sane*
For armpit   *salischin*
For breasts   *othen*
For chest   *ochii*
For body   *gechel*
For penis   *sachet*
For testicles   *sacaneos*
For vagina   *isse*
For communication with women   *io hoi*
For thighs   *chiave*
For knee   *tepin*
For rump   *schiaguen*
For buttocks   *hoij*
For arm   *mar*
For pulse   *holion*
For legs   *coss*
For foot   *thee*
For heel   *tere*
For ankle   *perchi*
For sole of the foot   *caotscheni*
For fingernails   *colim*
For heart   *thol*
For to scratch   *gechare*
For cross-eyed man   *calsichen*
For young man   *calemi*
For water   *holi*
For fire   *ghialeme*
For smoke   *giaiche*
For no   *ehen*
For yes   *rey*
For gold   *pelpeli*
For lapis lazuli   *secheg*
For sun   *calexcheni*
For stars   *settere*
For sea   *aro*

For wind   *oni*
For storm   *ohone*
For fish   *hoi*
For to eat   *mechiere*
For bowl   *elo*
For pot   *aschanie*
For to ask   *ghelhe*
Come here   *hai si*
For to look   *chonne*
For to walk   *rey*
For to fight   *oamaghce*
For arrows   *sethe*
For dog   *holl*
For wolf   *ani*
For to go a long distance   *schien*
For guide   *anti*
For snow   *theu*
For to cover   *hiavi*
For ostrich, a bird   *ho ihoi*
For its eggs   *om jani*
For the powder of the herb which
   they eat   *capae*
For to smell   *os*
For parrot   *cheche*
For birdcage   *cleo*
For missiglioni   *siameni*
For red cloth   *terechai*
For cap   *aichel*
For black   *ainel*
For red   *taiche*
For yellow   *peperi*
For to cook   *yrocoles*
For belt   *cathechin*
For goose   *cache*
For their big devil   *Setebos*
For their small devils   *Cheleule*

All the above words are pronounced in the throat, for such is their mode of pronunciation.

[40] That giant whom we had in our ship told me those words; for when he, upon asking me for *capae*, that is to say, bread, as they call that root which they use as bread, and *oli*, that is to say, water, saw me write those words quickly, and afterward when I, with pen in hand, asked him for other words, he understood me. Once I made the sign of the cross, and, showing it to him, kissed it. He immediately cried out *Setebos*, and made me a sign that if I made the sign of the cross again, *Setebos* would enter into my body and cause me to die. When that giant was sick, he asked for the cross, and embracied it and kissed it many times. He decided to become a Christian before his death. We called him Paul. When those people wish to make a fire, they rub a sharpened piece of wood against another piece until the fire catches in the pith of a certain tree, which is placed between those two sticks.

[*Here follow the charts of the Patagonian Strait (I) and the Unfortunate Islands (II)*]

[41] Wednesday, November 28, 1520,[120] we debouched from that strait, engulfing ourselves in the Pacific Sea. We were three months and twenty days without getting any kind of fresh food. We ate biscuit, which was no longer biscuit, but powder of biscuits swarming with worms, for they had eaten the good (it stank strongly of the urine of rats). We drank yellow water that had been putrid for many days. We also ate some ox hides that covered the top of the mainyard to prevent the yard from chafing the shrouds, and which had become exceedingly hard because of the sun, rain, and wind. We left them in the sea for four or five days, and then placed them for a few moments on top of the embers, and so ate them; and often we ate sawdust from boards. Rats were sold for one-half ducat apiece, if only one could get them. But above all the other misfortunes the following was the worst. The gums of both the lower and upper teeth of some of our men swelled, so that

they could not eat under any circumstances and therefore died. Nineteen men died from that sickness, and the giant together with an Indian from the country of Verzin.[121] Twenty-five or thirty men fell sick [during that time], in the arms, legs, or in another place, so that but few remained well. However, I, by the grace of God, suffered no sickness.

[42] We sailed about 4,000 leagues during those three months and twenty days through an open stretch in that Pacific Sea. In truth it is very pacific, for during that time we did not suffer any storm. We saw no land except two desert islets, where we found nothing but birds and trees; we called them the Unfortunate Islands.[122] They are two hundred leagues apart. We found no anchorage, [but] near them saw many sharks. The first islet lies in 15 degrees and the other in 9. Daily we made runs of fifty, sixty, or seventy leagues [calculated] at the *catena* or at the stern.[123] Had not God and His blessed mother given us such good weather we would all have died of hunger in that exceedingly vast sea. In truth I believe no such voyage will ever be made [again].[124]

[43] When we left that strait, if we had sailed continuously westward we would have circumnavigated the world without finding other land than the Cape of the Eleven Thousand Virgins. The latter is a cape of that strait at the Ocean Sea, straight east and west with Cape Deseado of the Pacific Sea. Both of those capes lie in a latitude of exactly 52 degrees toward the Antarctic Pole.

[44] The Antarctic Pole is not so starry as the Arctic. Many small stars clustered together are seen, which have the appearance of two clouds with little distance between them, and they are somewhat dim.[125] In the midst of them are two large and not very luminous stars, which move only slightly. Those two stars are the Antarctic Pole. Our loadstone, although it moved here and there, always pointed toward its own

Arctic Pole, although it did not have so much strength as on its own side. And on that account when we were in that open expanse, the captain-general, asking all the pilots whether they were always sailing forward in the course which we had laid down on the maps, all replied: "By your course exactly as laid down." He answered them that they were pointing wrongly, which was a fact, and that it would be fitting to adjust the needle of navigation, for it was not receiving so much force from its side.[126] When we were in the midst of that open expanse, we saw a cross of five extremely bright stars straight toward the west, those stars being precisely placed in relation to one another.[127]

[Here follows the Chart of the "Islands of Thieves" (III)]

[45] During those days we sailed west northwest, northwest by west, and northwest, until we reached the equinoctial line at the distance of 122 degrees from the line of demarcation.[128] The line of demarcation is 30 degrees from the meridian, and the meridian is 3 degrees east of Cape Verde. We passed while on that course, a short distance from two exceedingly rich islands, one in 20 degrees of the latitude of the Antarctic Pole, by name Cipangu, and the other in 15 degrees, by name Sumbdit Pradit.[129] After we had passed the equinoctial line we sailed west northwest, and west by north, and then for 200 leagues toward the west, changing our course to west by south until we reached 13 degrees toward the Arctic Pole in order that we might approach nearer to the land of Cape Catigara. That cape (begging the pardon of cosmographers, for they have not seen it), is not found where they thought it to be, but to the north in twelve degrees or thereabouts.[130]

[46] About seventy leagues on the above course, and lying in 12 degrees of latitude and 146 in longitude, we discovered on Wednesday,

March 6, a small island to the northwest, and two others toward the southwest, one of which was higher and larger than the other two.[131] The captain-general wished to stop at the large island and get some fresh food, but he was unable to do so because the inhabitants of that island entered the ships and stole whatever they could lay their hands on, so that we could not protect ourselves. The men were about to strike the sails so that we could go ashore, but the natives very deftly stole from us the small boat that was fastened to the poop of the flagship.[132] Thereupon, the captain general in wrath went ashore with forty armed men, and they burned some forty or fifty houses together with many boats, killed seven men, and recovered the small boat. We departed immediately pursuing the same course. Before we landed, some of our sick men begged us if we should kill any man or woman to bring the entrails to them, as they would recover immediately.[133]

[47] When we wounded any of those people with our crossbow-shafts, which passed completely through their loins from one side to the other, they, looking at it, pulled on the shaft now on this and now on that side, and then drew it out, with great astonishment, and so died. Others who were wounded in the breast did the same, which moved us to great compassion. Those people seeing us departing followed us with more than one hundred boats for more than one league. They approached the ships showing us fish, feigning that they would give them to us, but then threw stones at us and fled. And although the ships were under full sail, they passed between them and the small boats [fastened astern], very adroitly in those small boats of theirs. We saw some women in their boats who were crying out and tearing their hair, for love, I believe, of those whom we had killed.

[48] Each one of those people lives according to his own will, for they have no lords. They go naked, and some are bearded and have tangled black hair that reaches to the waist. They wear small palm-leaf hats, as do the Albanians. They are as tall as we, and well built. They worship nothing. They are olive-skinned, but are born white. Their teeth are red and black, for they think that is most beautiful. The women go naked except that they cover their privies with a narrow strip of bark as thin as paper, which grows between the tree and the bark of the palm. They are beautiful, delicately formed, and whiter than the men; they wear their hair which is exceedingly black, loose and hanging down to the ground. The women do not work in the fields but stay in the house, weaving mats, baskets, and other things needed in their houses, from palm leaves. They eat coconuts, potatoes, birds, figs one span in length [bananas], sugarcane, and flying fish, besides other things. They anoint the body and the hair with coconut and beneseed oil.

[49] Their houses are all built of wood covered with planks and thatched with leaves of the fig-tree [banana-tree] two fathoms long; and they have wooden-beam floors and windows. The rooms and the beds are all furnished with the most beautiful palmleaf mats. They sleep on palm straw which is very soft and fine. They use no weapons, except a kind of spear pointed with a fishbone at the end. Those people are poor, but ingenious and very thievish, on account of which we called those three islands "the islands of Thieves." Their amusement is to go with their women upon the seas with those small boats of theirs. Those boats resemble *fucelere*,¹³⁴ but are narrower, and some are black, [some] white, and others red. At the side opposite the sail, they have a large piece of wood pointed at the top, with poles laid across it and resting on the water, in order that the boats may sail more safely.¹³⁵ The sail is made from palmleaves sewn together and is shaped like a lateen sail. For rudders they use a certain blade like a baker's peel which has a piece of

wood at the end. The stern can serve as the bow and the bow as stern, and those boats resemble the dolphins which leap in the water from wave to wave. Those thieves thought, according to the signs which they made, that there were no other people in the world but themselves.

[Here follows the chart of ZZamal (Samar), Zuluam (Suluan), Cenalo (Dinagat?), Ybuston (Ibusson), Hyunangan (Kabugan?), Humunu (Homonhon, with the scroll: "The Watering Place of Good Signs"), and Abarien (Cabalian?) (IV)]

[50] At dawn on Saturday, March 16, 1521,[136] we came upon a high land at a distance of three hundred leagues from the islands of Thieves, an island named Samar.[137] The following day, the captain-general desired to land on another island which was uninhabited and lay to the right of the above mentioned island,[138] in order to be more secure, and to get water and have some rest. He had two tents set up on the shore for the sick and had a sow killed for them.

[51] On Monday afternoon, March 18, after eating, we saw a boat coming toward us with nine men in it. Therefore, the captain-general ordered that no one should move or say a word without his permission. When those men reached the shore, their chief went immediately to the captain-general, giving signs of joy because of our arrival. Five of the most ornately adorned of them remained with us, while the rest went to get some others who were fishing, and so they all came. The captain-general seeing that they were reasonable men, ordered food to be set before them, and gave them red caps, mirrors, combs, bells, ivory, bocasine,[139] and other things. When they saw the captain's courtesy, they presented fish, a jar of palm wine, which they call *uraca*,[140] figs more than one span long,[141] and others which were smaller and more delicate, and two coconuts. They had nothing else then, but made us signs with their hands that they would bring *umay* or rice, and coconuts and many other articles of food within four days.

[52] Coconuts are the fruit of the palmtree. Just as we have bread, wine, oil, and milk, so those people get everything from those trees. They obtain wine in the following manner: they make a hole in the heart of the tree at the top called *palmito*, from which distills a liquor which resembles white must. That liquor is sweet but somewhat tart, and [is gathered] in canes [of bamboo] as thick as the leg and thicker. They fasten the bamboo to the tree at evening for the morning, and in the morning for the evening. That palm bears a fruit, namely, the coconut. The coconut is as large as a man's head or thereabouts. Its outside husk is green and thicker than two fingers. Certain filaments are found in that husk, whence is made cord for binding together their boats. Under that husk there is a hard shell, much thicker than the shell of the walnut, which they burn and from which they derive a powder that is useful to them. Under that shell there is a white marrowy substance one finger in thickness, which they eat fresh with meat and fish as we do bread; and it has a taste resembling the almond. It could be dried and made into bread. There is a clear, sweet water in the middle of that marrowy substance which is very refreshing. When that water stands for a while after having been collected, it congeals and becomes like an apple. When the natives wish to make oil, they take that coconut, and allow the marrowy substance and the water to putrefy. Then they boil it and it becomes oil like butter. When they wish to make vinegar, they allow only the water to putrefy, and then place it in the sun, and a vinegar results like [that made from] white wine. Milk can also be made from it for we made some. We scraped that marrowy substance and then mixed the scrapings with its own water which we strained through a cloth, and so obtained milk like goat's milk. Those palms resemble date-palms, but although not smooth they are less knotty than the latter. A family of ten persons can support itself on two trees, by utilizing one for eight days and then the other for eight days

for the wine; for if they did otherwise, the trees would dry up. They last one hundred years.[142]

[53] Those people became very familiar with us. They told us many things, their names and those of some of the islands that could be seen from that place. Their own island was called Suluan and it is not very large. We took great pleasure with them, for they were very pleasant and conversable. In order to show them greater honor, the captain-general took them to his ship and showed them all his merchandise: cloves, cinnamon, pepper, ginger, nutmeg, mace, gold, and all the things in the ship. He had some mortars fired for them, at which they exhibited great fear, and tried to jump out of the ship. They made signs to us that the abovesaid articles grew in that place where we were going. When they were about to retire they took their leave very gracefully and neatly, saying that they would return according to their promise. The island where we were is called Homonhon; but inasmuch as we found two springs there of the clearest water, we called it "the Watering-place of good signs,"[143] for there were the first signs of gold which we found in those districts. We found a great quantity of white coral there, and large trees with fruit a trifle smaller than the almond and resembling pine seeds. There are also many palms, some of them good and others bad. There are many islands in that district, and therefore we called them the "archipelago of San Lazaro," as they were discovered on the Sunday of St. Lazarus.[144] They lie in 10 degrees of latitude toward the Arctic Pole, and in a longitude of 161 degrees from the line of demarcation.

[54] At noon on Friday, March 22, those men came as they promised us in two boats with coconuts, sweet oranges, a jar of palm-wine, and a cock,[145] in order to show us that there were fowls in that district. They exhibited great signs of pleasure at seeing us. We purchased all those

articles from them. Their lord was an old man who was painted [tat-tooed]. He wore two gold earrings in his ears, and the others many gold armlets on their arms and kerchiefs about their heads. We stayed there eight days, and during that time our captain went ashore daily to visit the sick, and every morning gave them coconut water from his own hand, which comforted them greatly. There are people living near that island who have holes in their ears so large that they can pass their arms through them. Those people are Kaffirs, that is to say, heathen.[146] They go naked, with a cloth woven from the bark of a tree about their privies, except some of the chiefs who wear cotton cloth embroidered with silk at the ends by means of a needle. They are olive-skinned, fat, and paint-ed. They anoint themselves with coconut and with beneseed oil, as a protection against sun and wind. They have very black hair that falls to the waist, and use daggers, knives, and spears ornamented with gold, large shields, *focine*,[147] javelins, and fishing nets that resemble *rizali*;[148] and their boats are like ours.

[55] On the afternoon of holy Monday, the day of our Lady, March 25 [Feast of the Annunciation], while we were on the point of weighing anchor, I went to the side of the ship to fish, and putting my feet upon a yard leading down into the storeroom, they slipped, for it was rainy, and consequently I fell into the sea, and no one saw me. When I was all but under, my left hand happened to catch hold of the clew-garnet of the mainsail, which was dangling in the water. I held on tightly, and began to cry out so lustily that I was rescued by the small boat. I was aided, not, I believe, indeed, through my merits, but through the mercy of that font of charity [the Virgin]. That same day we shaped our course toward the west southwest between four small islands, namely, Cenalo, Hiunanghan, Ibusson, and Abarien.[149]

[*Here follows the chart of Mazzana (Mazaua:Limasawa), Bohol, Ceilon (Leyte?), Baibai (Baybay), Canighan (Apit or Himuguetan), Ticobon (Pacijan), and Pozzon (Ponson) (V)*]

[56] On Thursday morning, March 28, as we had seen a fire on an island the night before, we anchored near it.[150] We saw a small boat which the natives call *boloto* with eight men in it, approaching the flagship. A slave[151] belonging to the captain-general, who was a native of Sumatra, which was formerly called Taprobane, spoke to them.[152] They immediately understood him, came alongside the ship, unwilling to enter but taking a position at some little distance. The captain seeing that they would not trust us, threw them out a red cap and other things tied to a bit of wood. They received them very gladly, and went away quickly to advise their king. About two hours later we saw two *balanghai* coming. They are large boats and are so called [by those people]. They were full of men, and their king was in the larger of them, being seated under an awning of mats. When the king came near the flagship, the slave spoke to him. The king understood him, for in those districts the kings know more languages than the other people. He ordered some of his men to enter the ships, but he always remained in his *balanghai*,[153] at some little distance from the ship, until his own men returned; and as soon as they returned he departed. The captain-general showed great honor to the men who entered the ship, and gave them some presents. For this reason the king wished before his departure to give the captain a large rod of gold and a basketful of ginger. The latter, however, thanked the king heartily but would not accept it. In the afternoon we went in the ships [and anchored] near the dwellings of the king.

[57] The next day, Good Friday, the captain-general sent his slave, who acted as our interpreter, ashore in a small boat to ask the king, if

he had any food, to have it carried to the ships; and to say that they would be well satisfied with us, for we had come to the island as friends and not as enemies.

[58] The king came with six or eight men in the same boat and entered the ship. He embraced the captain-general to whom he gave three porcelain jars covered with leaves and full of raw rice, two very large giltheads,[154] and other things. The captain-general gave the king a garment of red and yellow cloth made in the Turkish fashion, and a fine red cap; and to the others [the king's men], to some knives and to others mirrors. Then the captain-general had a collation spread for them, and had the king told through the slave that he desired to be *casi casi* with him, that is to say, brother.[155] The king replied that he also wished to enter the same relations with the captain-general. Then the captain showed him cloth of various colors, linen, coral [ornaments], and many other articles of merchandise, and all the artillery, which he had discharged for him, whereat some of the natives were greatly frightened. Then the captain-general had a man armed as a soldier, and placed him in the midst of three men armed with swords and daggers, who struck him on all parts of the body. Thereby was the king rendered almost senseless. The king told him through the slave that one of those armed men was worth one hundred of his own men. The captain-general answered that that was a fact, and that he had two hundred men in each ship who were armed in that manner.[156] He showed the king cuirasses, swords, bucklers, and had a review made for him. Then he led the king to the deck of the ship, that is located above at the stern; and had his sea-chart and compass brought. He told the king through the interpreter how he had found the strait in order to voyage there, and how many moons he had been without seeing land, at which the king was astonished. Lastly, he told the king that he would like, if it were pleasing to him, to send two of his men to the king so that the king might

show them some of his things. The king replied that he was agreeable, and I went in company of one other.

[59] When I reached shore, the king raised his hands toward the sky and then turned toward the two of us. We did the same toward him as did all the others. The king took me by the hand; one of his more notable men took my companion: and thus they led us under a bamboo covering, where there was a *balanghai*, as long as eighty of my palm lengths, and resembling a *fusta*.[157] We sat down upon the stern of that *balanghai*, constantly conversing with signs. The king's men stood about us in a circle with swords, daggers, spears, and bucklers. The king had a plate of pork brought in and a large jar filled with wine. At every mouthful, we drank a cup of wine. The wine that was left [in the cup] at any time, although that happened but rarely, was put into a jar by itself. The king's cup was always kept covered and no one else drank from it but he and I. Before the king took the cup to drink, he raised his clasped hands toward the sky, and then toward me; and when he was about to drink, he extended the fist of his left hand toward me (at first I thought that he was about to punch me) and then drank. I did the same toward the king. They all make those signs one toward another when they drink. We ate with such ceremonies and with other signs of friendship. I ate meat on Good Friday, for I could not do otherwise.

[60] Before the supper hour I gave the king many things which I had brought. I wrote down the names of many things in their language. When the king and the others saw me writing, and when I told them their words, they were all astonished. While engaged in that, the supper hour, was announced. Two large porcelain dishes were brought in, one full of rice and the other of pork with its gravy. We ate with the same signs and ceremonies. Afterward we went to the palace of the king which was built like a hayloft and was thatched with fig and palm

leaves. It was built up high from the ground on huge posts of wood and it was necessary to ascend to it by means of ladders. The king made us sit down there on a bamboo mat with our feet drawn up like tailors. After a half-hour a platter of roast fish cut in pieces was brought in, and ginger freshly gathered, and wine. The king's eldest son, who was the prince, came over to us, whereupon the king told him to sit down near us, and he accordingly did so. Then two platters were brought in (one with fish and its sauce, and the other with rice), so that we might eat with the prince. My companion became intoxicated as a consequence of so much drinking and eating. They used the gum of a tree called *anime*[158] wrapped in palm or fig leaves for illumination. The king made us a sign that he was going to go to sleep. He left the prince with us, and we slept with the latter on a bamboo mat with pillows made of leaves. When day dawned the king came and took me by the hand, and in that manner we went to where we had had supper, in order to have breakfast, but the boat came to get us. Before we left, the king kissed our hands with great joy, and we his. One of his brothers, the king of another island, and three men came with us. The captain-general kept him to dine with us, and gave him many things.

[61] Pieces of gold of the size of walnuts and eggs are found by sifting the earth in the island of that king who came to our ships. All the dishes of that king are of gold and also some portion of his house, as we were told by that king himself. According to their customs he was very grandly decked out, and the most handsome man that we saw among those people. His hair was exceedingly black, and hung to his shoulders. He had a covering of silk on his head, and wore two large golden earrings fastened in his ears. He wore a cotton cloth all embroidered with silk, which covered him from the waist to the knees. At his side hung a dagger, the handle of which was very long and all of gold, and its scabbard

of carved wood. He had three spots of gold on every tooth, and his teeth appeared as if bound with gold. He was perfumed with storax and benzoin.[159] He was olive-skinned and painted all over. That island of his was called Butuan and Caraga.[160] When those kings wished to see one another, they both came to hunt in that island where we were. The name of the first king is Rajah Colambu,[161] and the second Rajah Siaiu.[162]

[62] Early on the morning of Sunday, the last of March, and Easter-day, the captain-general sent the priest with some men to prepare the place where mass was to be said. And the interpreter went to tell the king that we were not going to land in order to dine with him, but to say mass. Therefore the king sent us two swine that he had had killed. When the hour for mass arrived, we landed with about fifty men, without our body armor, but carrying our other arms, and dressed in our best clothes. Before we reached the shore with our boats, six pieces were discharged as a sign of peace. We landed; the two kings embraced the captain-general, and placed him between them. We went in marching order to the place consecrated, which was not far from the shore. Before the commencement of mass, the captain sprinkled the entire bodies of the two kings with musk water. At the time of the offertory, the kings went forward to kiss the cross as we did, but they did not make any offering. When the body of our Lord was elevated, they remained on their knees and worshiped Him with clasped hands. The ships fired all their artillery at once when the body of Christ was elevated, the signal having been given from the shore with muskets.

[63] After the conclusion of mass, some of our men took communion. The captain-general arranged a fencing tournament, at which the kings were greatly pleased. Then he had a cross carried in and the nails and a crown, to which immediate reverence was made. He told the kings through the interpreter that they were the standards given to him by the

emperor his sovereign, so that wherever he might go he might set up those his tokens. [He said] that he wished to set it up in that place for their benefit, for whenever any of our ships came, they would know that we had been there by that cross, and would do nothing to displease them or harm their property. If any of their men were captured, they would be set free immediately on that sign being shown. It was necessary to set that cross on the summit of the highest mountain, so that on seeing it every morning, they might adore it; and if they did that, neither thunder, lightning, nor storms would harm them in the least.

[64] They thanked him heartily and [said] that they would do everything willingly. The captain-general also had them asked whether they were Moors or heathen, or what was their belief. They replied that they worshiped nothing, but that they raised their clasped hands and their face to the sky; and that they called their god *Abba*.[163] At this, the captain was very glad. Seeing that, the first king raised his hands to the sky, and said that he wished it were possible for him to make the captain see his love for him. The interpreter asked the king why there was so little to eat there. The king replied that he did not live in that place except when he went hunting and to see his brother, but that he lived in another island where all his family were. The captain had him asked whether he had any enemies, so that he might go with his ships to destroy them and to render them obedient to him. The king thanked him and said that he did indeed have two islands hostile to him, but that it was not then the season to go there. The captain told him that if God would again allow him to return to those districts, he would bring so many men that he would make the king's enemies subject to him by force. The captain-general said that he was about to go to dinner, and that he would return afterward to have the cross set up on the summit of the mountain. They replied that they were satisfied, and then forming in battalion and firing the muskets, and the captain having embraced the two kings, we took our leave.

[65] After dinner we all returned clad in our doublets, and that afternoon went together with the two kings to the summit of the highest mountain there. When we reached the summit, the captain-general told them that he esteemed highly having sweated for them, for since the cross was there, it could not but be of great use to them. On asking them which port was the best to get food, they replied that there were three, namely, Ceylon, Cebu, and Caraga,[164] but that Cebu was the largest and the one with most trade. They offered of their own accord to give us pilots to show us the way. The captain-general thanked them, and determined to go there, for so did his unhappy fate will.[165] After the cross was erected in its place, each of us repeated a *Pater Noster* and an *Ave Maria,* and adored the cross; and the kings did the same.

[66] Then we descended through their cultivated fields, and went to the place where the *balanghai* was. The kings had some coconuts brought in so that we might refresh ourselves. The captain asked the kings for the pilots for he intended to depart the following morning, and [said] that he would treat them as if they were the kings themselves, and would leave one of us as hostage. The kings replied that whenever he wished, the pilots were at his command; but that night the first king changed his mind. In the morning when we were about to depart, that king sent word to the captain-general, asking him for love of him to wait two days until he should have his rice harvested, and other trifles attended to. He asked the captain-general to send him some men to help him, so that it might be done sooner, and said that he intended to act as our pilot himself. The captain sent him some men, but the kings ate and drank so much that they slept the entire day. Some said to excuse them that they had taken somewhat ill. Our men did nothing on that day, but they worked the next two days.

[67] One of those people brought us about a bowl full of rice and also eight or ten figs fastened together to barter them for a knife which at the most was worth three *quattrini*.[166] The captain seeing that that native cared for nothing but a knife, called him to look at other things. He put his hand in his purse and wished to give him one real[167] for those things, but the native refused it. The captain showed him a ducat but he would not accept that either. Finally the captain tried to give him a double ducat,[168] but he would take nothing but a knife; and accordingly the captain had one given to him. When one of our men went ashore for water, one of those people wanted to give him for six strings of glass beads a crown with points of solid gold the size of a column.[169] But the captain refused to let him barter, so that the natives should learn at the very beginning that we prized our merchandise more than their gold.[170]

[68] Those people are heathens. They go naked and painted. They wear a piece of cloth woven from a tree about their privies. They are very heavy drinkers. Their women are clad in tree cloth from their waist down, and their hair is black and reaches to the ground. They have holes pierced in their ears which are filled with gold. Those people are constantly chewing a fruit which they call *areca*,[171] which resembles a pear. They cut that fruit into four parts, and then wrap it in the leaves of their tree which they call *betre*.[172] Those leaves resemble the leaves of the mulberry. They mix it with a little lime, and when they have chewed it thoroughly, they spit it out. It makes the mouth exceedingly red. All the people in those parts of the world use it, for it is very cooling to the heart, and if they ceased to use it they would die. There are dogs, cats, swine, fowls, goats, rice, ginger, coconuts, figs, oranges, lemons, millet, panicum, sorgo, wax, and much gold in that island. It lies in a latitude of 9 and ⅔ degrees toward the Arctic Pole, and in a longitude of 162

degrees from the line of demarcation. It is twenty-five leagues from "the Watering-place of good signs,"[173] and is called Mazaua.[174]

[69] We remained there seven days, after which we laid our course toward the northwest, passing among five islands, namely, Ceylon, Bohol, Canigao, Baybay, and Gatighan.[175] In the last-named island of Gatighan, there are bats as large as eagles.[176] As it was late we killed one of them, which resembled chicken in taste. There are doves, turtledoves, parrots, and certain black birds as large as domestic chickens, which have a long tail.[177] The last mentioned birds lay eggs as large as goose eggs, and bury them under the sand, through the great heat of which they hatch out. When the chicks are born, they push up the sand, and come out. Those eggs are good to eat. There is a distance of twenty leagues from Mazaua to Gatighan. We set out westward from Gatighan, but the king of Mazaua could not keep up with us, and consequently, we awaited him near three islands, namely, Polo, Ticobon, and Ponson.[178] When he caught up with us he was greatly astonished at the rapidity with which we sailed. The captain-general had him come into his ship with several of his chiefs at which they were pleased. Thus did we go to Cebu. From Gatighan to Cebu, the distance is fifteen leagues.

[*Here follows the chart of Zzubu (Cebu), Mattam (Mactan: "Here the captain-general died"), and Bohol (VI)*]

[70] At noon on Sunday, April 7, we entered the port of Cebu, passing by many villages, where we saw many houses built upon logs.[179] On approaching the city, the captain-general ordered the ships to put out their flags. The sails were lowered and arranged as if for battle, and all the artillery was fired, an action which caused great fear to those people. The captain sent a foster-child of his as ambassador to the king of Cebu with the interpreter.[180] When they reached the city, they found a vast

crowd of people together with the king, all of whom had been frightened by the mortars. The interpreter told them that that was our custom when entering into such places, as a sign of peace and friendship, and that we had discharged all our mortars to honor the king of the village. The king and all of his men were reassured, and the king had us asked by his governor what we wanted. The interpreter replied that his master was a captain of the greatest king and prince in the world, and that he was going to discover the Moluccas. Nevertheless, he had come solely to visit the king and to buy food with his merchandise because of the good report which he had heard of him from the king of Mazaua. The king told him that he was welcome, but that it was their custom for all ships that entered their ports to pay tribute, and that it was but four days since a junk from Siam[181] laden with gold and slaves had paid him tribute. As proof of his statement the king pointed out to the interpreter a merchant from Siam, who had remained to trade in gold and slaves.

[71] The interpreter told the king that, since his master was the captain of so great a king, he did not pay tribute to any lord in the world, and that if the king wished peace he would have peace, but if war, then he would have war. Thereupon, the Moor merchant said to the king *Cata raia chita*, that is to say, "Look well, sire. These men are the same who have conquered Calicut, Malacca, and all India Major.[182] If they are treated well, they will give good treatment, but if they are treated badly, they will deliver bad treatment and worse, as they have done in Calicut and Malacca." The interpreter understood it all and told the king that his master's king was more powerful in men and ships than the king of Portugal, that he was the king of Spain and emperor of all the Christians, and that if the king did not care to be his friend he would next time send so many men that they would destroy him. The Moor related everything to the king, who said thereupon that he would deliberate with his men, and would answer the captain on the following

day. Then he had refreshments of many dishes brought in, all made from meat and contained in porcelain platters, as well as many jars of wine. After our men had refreshed themselves, they returned and told us everything. The king of Mazaua, who after that king was most powerful and the lord of many islands, went ashore to tell the king about the great courtesy of our captain-general.

[72] Monday morning, our notary, together with the interpreter, went to Cebu. The king, accompanied by his chiefs, came to the open square where he had our men sit down near him. He asked the notary whether there were more than one captain in that company, and whether that captain wished him to pay tribute to the emperor his master. The notary replied in the negative, but that the captain wished only to trade with him and with no others. The king said that he was satisfied, and that if the captain wished to become his friend, he should send him a drop of blood from his right arm, and he himself would do the same [to him] as a sign of the most sincere friendship.[183] The notary answered that the captain would do it. Thereupon, the king told him that all the captains who came to that place, were wont to give presents one to the other, and asked whether our captain or he ought to commence. The interpreter told the king that since he desired to maintain the custom, he should commence, and so he did.

[73] Tuesday morning the king of Mazaua came to the ships with the Moor. He saluted the captain-general in behalf of the king [of Cebu], and said that the king of Cebu was collecting as much food as possible to give to him, and that after dinner he would send one of his nephews and two others of his chief men to make peace. The captain-general had one of his men armed with his own arms, and had the Moor told that we all fought in that manner. The Moor was greatly frightened, but the

45

captain told him not to be frightened for our arms were soft toward our friends and harsh toward our enemies; and as handkerchiefs wipe off the sweat so did our arms overthrow and destroy all our adversaries, and those who hate our faith. The captain did that so that the Moor, who seemed more intelligent than the others, might tell it to the king.

[74] After dinner the king's nephew, who was the prince, came to the ships with the king of Mazaua, the Moor, the governor, the chief constable, and eight chiefs, to make peace with us. The captain-general was seated in a red velvet chair, the principal men on leather chairs, and the others on mats upon the floor. The captain-general asked them through the interpreter whether it were their custom to speak in secret or in public, and whether that prince and the king of Mazaua had authority to make peace. They answered that they spoke in public, and that they were empowered to make peace. The captain said many things concerning peace, and that he prayed God to confirm it in heaven. They said that they had never heard any one speak such words, but that they took great pleasure in hearing them. The captain seeing that they listened and answered willingly, began to advance arguments to induce them to accept the faith. Asking them who would succeed to power after the death of the king, he was answered that the king had no sons but only daughters, the eldest of whom was the wife of that nephew of his, who therefore was the prince. [They said that] when the fathers and mothers grew old, they received no further honor, but their children commanded them. The captain told them how God made the heaven, the earth, the sea and everything else, and how he had commanded us to honor our fathers and mothers, and that whoever did otherwise was condemned to eternal fire; and how we are all descended from Adam and Eve, our first parents, and how we possess an immortal soul; and many other things pertaining to the faith.

[75] All joyfully entreated the captain to leave them two men, or at least one, to instruct them in the faith, and [said] that they would show them great honor. The captain replied to them that he could not leave them any men then, but that if they wished to become Christians, our priest would baptize them, and that he would next time bring priests and friars who would instruct them in our faith. They answered that they would first speak to their king, and that then they would become Christians. We all wept with great joy. The captain-general told them that they should not become Christians for fear or to please us, but of their own free wills; and that he would not cause any displeasure to those who wished to live according to their own law, but that the Christians would be better regarded and treated than the others. All cried out with one voice that they were not becoming Christians through fear or to please us, but of their own free will. Then the captain told them that if they became Christians, he would leave a suit of armor, for so had his king commanded him; that we could not have intercourse with their women without committing a very great sin, since they were pagans; and that he assured them that if they became Christians, the devil would no longer appear to them except in the last moment at their death. They said that they could not answer the beautiful words of the captain, but that they placed themselves in his hands, and that he should treat them as his most faithful servants. The captain embraced them weeping, and clasping one of the prince's hands and one of the king's between his own, said to them that, by his faith in God and to his sovereign, the emperor, and by the habit which he wore,[184] he promised them that he would give them perpetual peace with the king of Spain. They answered that they promised the same.

[76] After the conclusion of the peace, the captain had refreshments served to them. Then the prince and the king [of Mazaua] presented some baskets of rice, swine, goats, and fowls to the captain-general on

behalf of their king, and asked him to pardon them, for such things were but little [to give] to one such as he. The captain gave the prince a white cloth of the finest linen, a red cap, some strings of glass beads, and a gilded glass drinking cup. (The glasses are greatly appreciated in those districts.) He did not give any present to the king of Mazaua, for he had already given him a robe of Cambay,[185] besides other articles. To the others he gave now one thing and now another. Then he sent to the king of Cebu, through me and one other, a yellow and violet silk robe, made in Turkish style, a fine red cap, some strings of glass beads, all in a silver dish, and two drinking cups gilded by hand.

[77] When we reached the city we found the king in his palace with by many people. He was seated on a palm mat on the ground, with only a cotton cloth before his privies, and a scarf embroidered in needlepoint about his head, a necklace of great value hanging from his neck, and two large gold earrings, set with precious gems, fastened in his ears. He was fat and short, and tattooed with fire in various designs. From another mat on the ground he was eating turtle eggs which were in two porcelain dishes, and he had four jars full of palm wine in front of him covered with sweet-smelling herbs and arranged with four small reeds in each jar by means of which he drank. Having duly made reverence to him, the interpreter told the king that his master [Magellan] thanked him very warmly for his present, and that he sent this present not in return for his present but for the intrinsic love which he bore him. We dressed him in the robe, placed the cap on his head, and gave him the other things; then kissing the beads and putting them over his head, I presented them to him. He doing the same [kissing them] accepted them. Then the king had us eat some of those eggs and drink through those reeds. His men told him at that point the words of the captain concerning peace and his exhortation to them to become Christians. The king wished to have us stay to supper with him, but we told him that we could not stay then.

[78] Having taken our leave of him, the prince took us with him to his house, where four young girls were playing [instruments] one, on a drum like ours, but resting on the ground; the second was striking two suspended metal disks alternately with a stick wrapped somewhat thickly at the end with palm cloth; the third, one large metal disk in the same manner; and the last, two small metal disks held in her hand, by striking one against the other, which gave forth a sweet sound. They played so harmoniously that it seemed they possessed great knowledge of music. Those girls were very beautiful and almost as white as our girls and as large. They were naked except for tree cloth hanging from the waist and reaching to the knees. Some were quite naked and had large holes in their ears with a small round piece of wood in the hole, which keeps the hole round and large. They have long black hair, and wear a short cloth about the head, and are always barefoot. The prince made us dance with three of them who were completely naked. We took refreshments and then went to the ships. Those metal disks are made of brass and are manufactured in the regions about the Sinus Magnus which is called China.[186] They are used in those regions as we use bells and are called *aghon*.[187]

[79] On Wednesday morning, as one of our men had died during the previous night, the interpreter and I went to ask the king where we could bury him. We found the king surrounded by many men and after the due reverence was made, I asked him where we could bury him. He replied, "If I and my vassals all belong to your sovereign, how much more ought the land." I told the king that we would like to consecrate the place, and to set up a cross there. He replied that he was quite satisfied, and that he wished to adore the cross as did we. The deceased was buried in the square with as much pomp as possible, in order to furnish a good example. Then we consecrated the place, and in the evening

buried another man.[188] We carried a quantity of merchandise ashore which we stored in a house. The king took it under his care as well as four men who were left to trade the goods by wholesale. Those people live in accordance with justice, and have weights and measures. They love peace, ease, and quiet.

[80] They have wooden scales, the bar of which has a cord in the middle by which it is held. At one end is a bit of lead, and at the other marks, as if for quarters, thirds, and pounds. When they wish to weigh they take the scales which has three wires like ours, and place them above the marks, and so weigh accurately. They have very large measures without any bottom.[189] The youth play on pipes made like ours which they call *subin*. Their houses are constructed of wood, and are built of planks and bamboo, raised high from the ground on large logs, and one must enter them by means of ladders. They have rooms like ours. Under the house they keep their swine, goats, and fowls. Large sea-snails, beautiful to see, are found there which kill whales. For the whale swallows them alive, and when they are in the whale's body, they come out of their shells and eat the whale's heart. Those people afterward find them alive near the dead whale's heart. Those creatures have black teeth and skin and a white shell, and the flesh is good to eat. They are called *laghan*.[190]

[81] On Friday we showed those people a shop full of our merchandise, at which they were very much amazed. For metals, iron, and other large merchandise they gave us gold. For the other smaller articles they gave us rice, swine, goats, and other food. Those people gave us ten pieces of gold for fourteen pounds of iron (one piece being worth about one and one-half ducats). The captain-general did not wish to take too much gold, for there would have been some sailors who would have given all that they owned for a small amount of gold, and would have spoiled the trade for ever.

[82] On Saturday, as the captain had promised the king to make him a Christian on Sunday, a platform was built in the consecrated square, which was adorned with hangings and palm branches for his baptism. The captain-general sent men to tell the king not to be afraid of the pieces that would be discharged in the morning, for it was our custom to discharge them at our important feasts, without loading them with stones.

[83] On Sunday morning, April 14, forty men of us went ashore, two of whom were completely armed and preceded the royal banner. When we reached land all the artillery was fired. Those people followed us here and there. The captain and the king embraced. The captain told the king that the royal banner was not taken ashore except with fifty men armed as were those two, and with fifty musketeers; but so great was his love for him that he had thus brought the banner. Then we all approached the platform joyfully. The captain and the king sat down in chairs of red and violet velvet, the chiefs on cushions, and the others on mats. The captain told the king through the interpreter that he thanked God for inspiring the king to become a Christian; and that [now] he would more easily conquer his enemies than before. The king replied that he wished to become a Christian, but that some of his chiefs did not wish to obey, because they said that they were as good men as he. Then our captain had all the chiefs of the king called, and told them that, unless they obeyed the king as their king, he would have them killed and would give their possessions to the king. They replied that they would obey him. The captain told the king that he was going to Spain, but that he would return again with so many forces that he would make him the greatest king of those regions, as he had been the first to express a determination to become a Christian. The king, lifting his hands to the sky, thanked the captain, and requested him to let some

of his men remain [with him], so that he and his people might be better instructed in the faith. The captain replied that he would leave two men to satisfy him, but that he would like to take two of the children of the chiefs with him, so that they might learn our language, and afterward, upon their return, they would be able to tell the others about Spain.

[84] A large cross was set up in the middle of the square. The captain told them that if they wished to become Christians as they had declared on the previous days, they must burn all their idols and set up a cross in their place. They were to adore that cross daily with clasped hands, and every morning after their [the Spaniards'] custom, they were to make the sign of the cross (which the captain showed them how to make); and they ought to come hourly, at least in the morning, to that cross, and adore it kneeling. The intention that they had already declared, they were to confirm with good works. The king and all the others wished to confirm it thoroughly. The captain-general told the king that he was clad all in white to demonstrate his sincere love toward them. They replied that they could not respond to his sweet words. The captain led the king by the hand to the platform while speaking these good words in order to baptize him. He told the king that he would call him Don Carlo, after his sovereign the emperor; the prince, Don Fernando, after the emperor's brother;[191] the king of Mazaua, John; a chief, Fernando, after our chief, that is to say, the captain; the Moor, Christopher; and then the others, now one name, and now another. Five hundred men were baptized before mass. After the conclusion of mass, the captain invited the king and some of the other chiefs to dinner, but they refused, accompanying us, however, to the shore. The ships discharged all the mortars; and embracing, the king and chiefs and the captain took leave of one another.

[85] After dinner the priest and some others of us went ashore to baptize the queen, who came with forty women. We conducted her to

the platform, and she was made to sit down upon a cushion, and the other women near her. While the priest was dressing, I showed her an image of our Lady, a very beautiful wooden child Jesus, and a cross. Thereupon, she was seized with contrition, and, weeping, asked for baptism. We named her Joann, after the emperor's mother.[192] We called her daughter, the wife of the prince, Catherine and the queen of Mazaua, Elizabeth; and we gave to the others each a different name. Counting men, women, and children, we baptized eight hundred souls. The queen was young and beautiful, and was entirely covered with a white and black cloth. Her mouth and nails were very red, while on her head she wore a large hat of palm leaves in the manner of a parasol, with a crown about it of the same leaves, like the tiara of the pope; and she never goes any place without one of these crowns. She asked us to give her the little child Jesus to keep in place of her idols; and then she went away when it was late.

[86] The king and queen, accompanied by numerous persons, came to the shore. Thereupon, the captain had many trombs of fire[193] and large mortars discharged, by which they were most highly delighted. The captain and the king called one another brothers. That king's name was Rajah Humabon. Before that week had gone, all the persons of that island, and some from the other islands, were baptized. We burned one hamlet which was located in a neighboring island, because it refused to obey the king or us.[194] We set up the cross there for those people were heathen. Had they been Moors, we would have erected a column as a sign of greater harshness, for the Moors are much harder to convert than the heathen.

[87] The captain-general went ashore daily during those days to hear mass, and told the king many things regarding the faith. One day the queen came with great pomp to hear mass. Three girls preceded her

with three of her hats in their hands. She was dressed in black and white with a large silk scarf, crossed with gold stripes thrown over her head, which covered her shoulders; and she had on her hat. A great number of women accompanied her, who were all naked and barefoot, except that they had a small covering of palm-tree cloth before their privies, and a small scarf upon the head, and all with hair flowing free. The queen, having made the due reverence to the altar, seated herself on a silk embroidered cushion. Before the commencement of the mass, the captain sprayed her and some of her women with musk rosewater; they delighted exceedingly in that scent. The captain knowing that the queen was very much pleased with the child Jesus, gave it to her, telling her to keep it in place of her idols, for it was in memory of the son of God. Thanking him heartily she accepted it.[195]

[88] Before mass one day, the captain-general had the king come clad in his silk robe, with the chief men of the city. The king's brother and prince's father was named Bendara;[196] another of the king's brothers was called Cadaio; and certain others were called Simiut, Sibnaia, Sisacai, Maghalibe, and there were many others whom I shall not name in order not to be tedious. The captain made them all swear to be obedient to their king, and they kissed the captain's hand. Then the captain had the king declare that he would always be obedient and faithful to the king of Spain, and the king so swore. Thereupon, the captain drew his sword before the image of our Lady, and told the king that when anyone so swore, it would be better he should die rather than to break such an oath; thus he swore by that image, by the life of the emperor his sovereign, and by his habit[197] to be ever faithful to him. After the conclusion of that, the captain gave the king a red velvet chair, telling him that wherever he went he should always have it carried before him by one of his nearest relatives; and he showed him how it ought to be carried. The

king responded that he would do that willingly for love of him, and he told the captain that he was making a jewel to give to him, namely, two large earrings of gold to fasten in his ears, two armlets to put on his arms, above the elbows, and two other rings for the feet above the ankles, besides other precious gems to adorn the ears. Those are the most beautiful ornaments which the kings of those districts can wear. They always go barefoot, and wear a cloth garment that hangs from the waist to the knees.

[89] One day the captain-general asked the king and the other people why they did not burn their idols as they had promised when they became Christians; and why they sacrificed so much flesh to them. They replied that what they were doing was not for themselves, but for a sick man who had not spoken now for four days, so that the idols might give him health. He was the prince's brother, and the bravest and wisest man in the island. The captain told them to burn their idols and to believe in Christ, and that if the sick man were baptized, he would quickly recover; and if that did not so happen they could behead him [the captain]. Thereupon, the king replied that he would do it, for he truly believed in Christ. We made a procession from the square to the house of the sick man with as much pomp as possible. There we found him in such condition that he could neither speak nor move. We baptized him and his two wives, and ten girls. Then the captain had him asked how he felt. He spoke immediately and said that by the grace of our Lord he felt very well. That was a most manifest miracle [that happened] in our times. When the captain heard him speak, he thanked God fervently. Then he made the sick man drink some almond milk, which he had already made for him. Afterward he sent him a mattress, a pair of sheets, a coverlet of yellow cloth, and a pillow. Until he recovered his health, the captain sent him almond milk, rosewater, oil of

roses, and some sweet preserves. Within five days the sick man began to walk. He had an idol that certain old women had concealed in his house burned in the presence of the king and all the people. He had many shrines along the seashore destroyed, in which the consecrated meat was eaten. The people themselves cried out "Castile! Castile!" and destroyed those shrines. They said that if God would lend them life, they would burn all the idols that they could find, even if they were in the king's house. Those idols are made of wood, and are hollow, and lack the back parts. Their arms are open and their feet turned up under them with the legs open. They have a large face with four huge tusks like those of the wild boar, and are painted all over.[198]

[90] There are many villages in that island. Their names, those of their inhabitants, and of their chiefs are as follows: Cinghapola, and its chiefs, Cilaton, Ciguibucan, Cimaningha, Cimatichat, and Cicanbul; another, Mandani, and its chief, Apanoaan; another Lalan, and its chief, Theteu; another Lalutan, and its chief, Tapan; another Cilumai; and another, Lubucun.[199] All those villages rendered obedience to us, and gave us food and tribute. Near that island of Cebu was an island called Mactan, which formed the port where we were anchored.[200] The name of its village was Mactan, and its chiefs were Zula and Cilapulapu.[201] That city which we burned was in that island and was called Bulaia.[202]

[91] In order that your most illustrious Lordship[203] may know the ceremonies that those people use in consecrating the swine: they first sound those large metal disks. Then three large dishes are brought in; two with roses and with cakes of rice and millet, baked and wrapped in leaves, and roast fish; the other with cloth of Cambay and two palm flags is spread on the ground. Then two very old women come, each of whom has a bamboo trumpet in her hand. When they have stepped

upon the cloth they make obeisance to the sun. Then they wrap the cloths about themselves. One of them puts a kerchief with two horns on her forehead, and takes another kerchief in her hands, and dancing and blowing upon her trumpet, she thereby calls out to the sun. The other takes one of the flags and dances and blows on her trumpet. They dance and call out thus for a little space, saying many things between themselves to the sun. She with the kerchief takes the other flag, and lets the kerchief drop, and both blowing on their trumpets for a long time, dance about the bound hog. She with the horns always speaks covertly to the sun, and the other answers her. A cup of wine is presented to her with the horns, and she dancing and repeating certain words, while the other answers her, and making pretense four or five times of drinking the wine, sprinkles it upon the heart of the hog. Then she immediately begins to dance again. A lance is given to the same woman. She shakes it and repeats certain words, while both of them continue to dance, and making motions four or five times of thrusting the lance through the heart of the hog, with a sudden and quick stroke, she thrusts it through from one side to the other. The wound is quickly stopped with grass. The one who has killed the hog, taking in her mouth a lighted torch, which has been lighted throughout that ceremony, extinguishes it. The other one dipping the end of her trumpet in the blood of the hog, goes around marking with blood with her finger first the foreheads of their husbands, and then the others; but they never came to us. Then they undress and go to eat the contents of those dishes, and they invite only women [to eat with them]. The hair is removed from the hog by means of fire. Thus no one but old women consecrate the flesh of the hog, and they do not eat it unless it is killed in this way.

[92] Those people go naked, wearing but one piece of palm-tree cloth about their privies. The males, large and small, have their penis pierced

from one side to the other near the head, with a gold or tin bolt as large as a goose quill. In both ends of the same bolt, some have what resembles a spur, with points upon the ends; others like the head of a cart nail. I very often asked many, both old and young, to see their penis, because I could not believe it. In the middle of the bolt is a hole, through which they urinate. The bolt and the spurs always hold firm. They say that their women wish it so, and that if they did otherwise they would not have intercourse with them. When the men wish to have intercourse with their women, the latter themselves take the penis, not in the regular way, and commence very gently to introduce it [into their vagina], with the spur on top first, and then the other part. When it is inside it takes its regular position; and thus the penis always stays inside until it gets soft, for otherwise they could not pull it out. Those people make use of that device because they are of a weak nature.[204] They have as many wives as they wish, but one of them is the principal wife.

[93] Whenever any of our men went ashore, both by day and by night, everyone invited him to eat and to drink. Their viands are half cooked and very salty. They drink frequently and copiously from the jars through those small reeds, and one of their meals lasts for five or six hours. The women loved us very much more than their own men. All of the women from the age of six years and upward, have their vaginas gradually opened because of the men's penises.

[94] They practice the following ceremonies when one of their chiefs dies. First, all the chief women of the place go to the house of the deceased. The deceased is placed in the middle of the house in a coffin. Ropes are placed about the box in the manner of a palisade, to which many branches of trees are attached. In the middle of each branch hangs a cotton cloth like a curtained canopy. The most principal women sit under those hangings, and are all covered with white cotton cloth, each

one sits by a girl who fans her with a palm-leaf fan. The other women sit about the room sadly. Then there is one woman who cuts off the hair of the deceased very slowly with a knife. Another who was the principal wife of the deceased, lies down upon him, and places her mouth, her hands, and her feet upon those of the deceased. When the former is cutting off the hair, the latter weeps; and when the former finishes the cutting, the latter sings. There are many porcelain jars containing fire about the room, and myrrh, storax, and benzoin, which make a strong scent through the house, are put on the fire. They keep the body in the house for five or six days during those ceremonies. (I believe that the body is anointed with camphor), then they bury the body within the coffin which is shut by means of wooden nails in a kind of box and covered and enclosed by logs of wood.

[95] Every night about midnight in that city, a jet black bird as large as a crow was wont to come, and no sooner had it thus reached the houses than it began to screech, so that all the dogs began to howl; and that screeching and howling would last for four or five hours, but those people would never tell us the reason for it.

[96] On Friday, April 26, Zula, a chief of the island of Mactan, sent one of his sons to present two goats to the captain-general, and to say that he would send him all that he had promised, but that he had not been able to send it to him because of the other chief Cilapulapu, who refused to obey the king of Spain.[205] He requested the captain to send him only one boatload of men on the next night, so that they might help him and fight against the other chief. The captain-general decided to go there with three boatloads. We begged him repeatedly not to go, but he, like a good shepherd, refused to abandon his flock. At midnight, sixty of us set out armed with corselets and helmets, together with the Christian king, the prince, some of the chief men, and twenty

or thirty *balanghai.* We reached Mactan three hours before dawn. The captain did not wish to fight then, but sent a message to the natives by the Moor to the effect that if they would obey the king of Spain, recognize the Christian king as their sovereign, and pay us our tribute, he would be their friend; but that if they wished otherwise, they should expect to see how our lances wounded. They replied that if we had lances they had lances of bamboo and stakes hardened with fire. [They asked us] not to proceed to attack them at once, but to wait until morning, so that they might have more men. They said that in order to induce us to go in search of them; for they had dug certain pitholes between the houses in order that we might fall into them.

[97] When morning came forty-nine of us leaped into the water up to our thighs, and walked through water for more than two crossbow flights before we could reach the shore. The boats could not approach nearer because of certain rocks in the water. The other eleven men remained behind to guard the boats. When they saw us, they charged down upon us with exceeding loud cries, two divisions on our flanks and the other on our front.[206] When the captain saw that, he formed us into two divisions, and thus did we begin to fight. The musketeers and crossbowmen shot from a distance for about a half-hour, but uselessly; for the shots only passed through the shields which were made of thin wood and struck the arms [of the bearers]. The captain cried to them, "Cease firing! cease firing!" but his order was not at all heeded. When the natives saw that we were shooting our muskets to no purpose, crying out they determined to stand firm, and they redoubled their shouts. When our muskets were discharged, the natives would never stand still, but leaped here and there, covering themselves with their shields. They shot so many arrows at us and hurled so many bamboo spears (some of them tipped with iron) at the captain-general, besides pointed stakes hardened with fire, stones, and mud, that we could

scarcely defend ourselves. Seeing that, the captain-general sent some men to burn their houses in order to terrify them. When they saw their houses burning, they were roused to greater fury. Two of our men were killed near the houses, while we burned twenty or thirty houses. So many of them charged down upon us that they shot the captain through the right leg with a poisoned arrow. On that account, he ordered us to retreat slowly, but the men took to flight, except six or eight of us who remained with the captain. The natives shot only at our legs, for the latter were bare; and so many were the spears and stones that they hurled at us, that we could offer no resistance. The mortars in the boats could not aid us as they were too far away. So we continued to retreat for more than the distance of a good crossbow shot from the shore, still fighting in water up to our knees. The natives continued to pursue us, and picking up the same spear four or six times, hurled it at us again and again.

[98] Recognizing the captain, so many turned upon him that they knocked his helmet off his head twice, but he always stood firmly like a good knight. Together with some others, we fought thus for more than one hour, refusing to retreat farther. An Indian hurled a bamboo spear into the captain's face, but the latter immediately killed him with his lance, which he left in the Indian's body. Then, trying to lay hand on sword, he could draw it out but halfway, because he had been wounded in the arm with a bamboo spear. When the natives saw that, they all hurled themselves upon him. One of them wounded him on the left leg with a large *terciado*, which resembles a scimitar, only being larger. That caused the captain to fall face downward, when immediately they rushed upon him with iron and bamboo spears and with their cutlasses, until they killed our mirror, our light, our comfort, and our true guide. When they wounded him, he turned back many times to see whether we were all in the boats. Thereupon, seeing him dead, we, wounded, retreated, as best we could, to the boats, which were already pulling off.

The Christian king would have aided us, but the captain charged him before we landed not to leave his *balanghai,* but to stay to see how we fought.²⁰⁷ When the king learned that the captain was dead, he wept. Had it not been for that unfortunate captain, not a single one of us would have been saved, for while he was fighting the others retreated to the boats.²⁰⁸

[99] I hope through the efforts of your most illustrious Lordship²⁰⁹ that the fame of so noble a captain will not become effaced in our times. Among other virtues, he was more constant than anyone else ever was in the greatest of storms.²¹⁰ He endured hunger better than all the others, and more accurately than any man in the world did he navigate and make sea charts. And that this was the truth was seen openly, for no other had had so much natural talent nor the boldness nor knowledge to sail around the world, as he had almost done.²¹¹

[100] That battle was fought on Saturday, April 27, 1521 (the captain desired to fight on Saturday, because it was the day especially holy to him).²¹² Eight of our men were killed with him in that battle, and four Indians, who had become Christians and who had come afterward to aid us were killed by the mortars of the boats. Of the enemy, only fifteen were killed, while many of us were wounded.

[101] After dinner, the Christian king sent a message with our consent to the people of Mactan, to the effect that if they would give us the captain and the other men that had been killed, we would give them as much merchandise as they wished. They answered that they would not give up such a man, as we supposed, and that they would not give him up for all the riches in the world, but that they intended to keep him as a memorial.

[102] On Saturday, the day on which the captain was killed, the four men who had remained in the city to trade, had our merchandise carried

to the ships. Then we chose two commanders, namely, Duarte Barbosa, a Portuguese and a relative of the captain,[213] and the Spaniard João Serrão.[214] As our interpreter, Enrique by name,[215] was wounded slightly, he would not go ashore any more to attend to our necessary affairs, but stayed always beneath a heavy blanket.[216] On that account, Duarte Barbosa, the commander of the flagship, cried out to him and told him that although his master the captain was dead, he was not therefore free; on the contrary he (Barbosa) would see to it that when we should reach Spain, he should still be the slave of Dona Beatrice, the wife of the captain-general. And threatening the slave that if he did not go ashore, he would be flogged, the slave arose, and, feigning to take no heed of those words, went ashore to tell the Christian king that we were about to leave very soon, but that if he would follow his advice, he could gain the ships and all our merchandise. Accordingly, they arranged a plot,[217] and the slave returned to the ship, where he showed himself to be more presumptuous[218] than before.

[103] On Wednesday morning, May 1, the Christian king sent word to the commanders that the jewels which he had promised to send to the king of Spain were ready, and that he begged them and their other companions to come to dine with him that morning, when he would give them the jewels. Twenty-four men went ashore, among whom was our astrologer, San Martin of Seville. I could not go because I was all swollen up by a wound from a poisoned arrow which I had received in the forehead. João Carvalho and the constable[219] returned, and told us that they saw the man who had been cured by a miracle take the priest to his house, and for this reason they had left that place, because they suspected some evil. Scarcely had they spoken those words when we heard loud cries and lamentations. We immediately weighed anchor and discharging many mortars into the houses, drew in nearer to the shore.

While thus discharging [our pieces] we saw João Serrão in his shirt bound and wounded, crying to us not to fire any more, for the natives would kill him. We asked him whether all the others and the interpreter were dead. He said that they were all dead except the interpreter. He begged us earnestly to ransom him with some of the merchandise; but João Carvalho, his boon companion, [and others] would not allow the boat to go ashore so that they might remain masters of the ships. But João Serrão still weeping asked us not to set sail so quickly, for they would kill him, and said that he swore to God that at the day of judgment he would demand his soul of João Carvalho, his comrade. We immediately departed; I do not know whether he died or survived.

[104] In that island are found dogs, cats, rice, millet, panicum, sorgo, ginger, figs, oranges, lemons, sugarcane, garlic, honey, coconuts, *chiacare*,[220] gourds, flesh of many kinds, palm wine, and gold. It is a large island, and has a good port with two entrances one to the west and the other to the east northeast. It lies in 10 degrees of latitude toward the Arctic Pole, and in a longitude of 164 degrees from the line of demarcation. Its name is Cebu. We heard word of Malucca there before the death of the captain-general. Those people play a violin with copper strings.

[105] Words of those heathen people:[221]

For man *lac*
For woman *paranpoan*
For young woman *beni beni*
For married woman *babay*
For hair *bo bo*
For face *guay*

For eyelids *pilac*
For eyebrows *chilei*
For eye *matta*
For nose *ilon*
For jaws *apin*
For lips *olol*

For mouth   *baba*
For teeth   *nipin*
For gums   *leghex*
For tongue   *dilla*
For ears   *delengan*
For throat   *liogh*
For neck   *tangip*
For chin   *silan*
For beard   *bonghot*
For shoulders   *bagha*
For the back   *licud*
For breast   *dughan*
For body   *tiam*
For armpit   *ilot*
For arm   *bocchen*
For elbow   *sico*
For pulse   *molanghai*
For hand   *camat*
For the palm of the hand   *palan*
For finger   *dudlo*
For fingernail   *coco*
For navel   *pusut*
For the male member   *utin*
For testicles   *boto*
For the female nature   *billat*
For intercourse with women   *tiam*
For buttocks   *samput*
For thigh   *paha*
For knee   *tuhud*
For shin   *bassag bassag*[222]
For calf of the leg   *bitis*
For ankle   *bolbol*
For heel   *tiochid*
For sole of the foot   *lapa lapa*
For gold   *balaoan*
For silver   *pilla*
For brass   *concach*
For iron   *butau*
For sugarcane   *tube*

For spoon   *gandan*
For rice   *bughax baras*
For honey   *deghex*
For wax   *talho*
For salt   *acin*
For wine   *tuba nio nipa*
For to drink   *minuncubil*
For to eat   *macan*
For hog   *babui*
For goat   *candin*
For chicken   *monoch*
For millet   *humas*
For sorgo   *batat*
For panic grass   *dana*
For pepper   *manissa*
For cloves   *chianche*[223]
For cinnamon   *mana*
For ginger   *luia*
For garlic   *laxuna*
For oranges   *acsua*
For egg   *silog*
For coconut   *lubi*
For vinegar   *zlucha*
For water   *tubin*
For fire   *clayo*
For smoke   *assu*
For to blow   *tigban*
For balances   *tinban*
For weight   *tahil*[224]
For pearl   *mutiara*
For mother of pearl   *tipay*
For pipe (a musical instrument)   *subin*[225]
For disease of St. Job[226]   *alupalan*
Bring me   *palatin comorica*
For certain rice cakes   *tinapai*
Good   *maiu*
No   *tidale*
For knife   *capol sundan*
For scissors   *catle*

To shave   *chunthinch*
For a well adorned man   *pixao*
For linen   *balandan*
For the cloth with which they cover
  themselves   *abaca*
For hawk's-bell   *colon colon*
For paternosters of all classes   *tacle*
For comb   *cutlei missamis*
For to comb   *monssughud*
For shirt   *sabun*
For sewing-needle   *daghu*
For to sew   *mamis*
For porcelain   *mobuluc*
For dog   *aian ydo*
For cat   *epos*
For their scarfs   *gapas*
For glass beads   *balus*
Come here   *marica*
For house   *ilaga balai*
For timber   *tatamue*
For the mats on which they sleep   *tagichan*
For palm-mats   *bani*
For their leaf cushions   *uliman*
For wooden platters   *dulan*
For their god   *Abba*[227]
For sun   *adlo*
For moon   *songhot*
For star   *bolan burthun*
For dawn   *mene*
For morning   *vema*
For cup large   *tagha*
Big   *bassal*
For bow   *bossugh*
For arrow   *oghon*
For shields   *calassan*
For quilted garments used for
  fighting   *baluti*

For their daggers   *calix baladao*
For their cutlasses   *campilan*
For spear   *bancan*
Like   *tuan*
For figs (bananas)   *saghin*
For gourds   *baghin*
For the cords of their violins   *gotzap*
For river   *tau*
For fishing-net   *pucat laia*
For small boat   *sampan*
For large canes   *canaghan*
For the small ones   *bonbon*
For their large boats   *balanghai*[228]
For their small boats   *boloto*[229]
For crabs   *cuban*
For fish   *icam yssida*
For a fish that is all colored   *panap sapan*
For another red (fish)   *timuan*
For another (kind of fish)   *pilax*
For another (kind of fish)   *emalvan*
All the same   *siama siama*
For a slave   *bonsul*
For gallows   *bolle*
For ship   *benaoa*
For a king or captain-general   *raia*
Numbers:
  One   *uzza*
  Two   *dua*
  Three   *tolo*
  Four   *upat*
  Five   *lima*
  Six   *onom*
  Seven   *pitto*
  Eight   *gualu*
  Nine   *ciam*
  Ten   *polo*

[Here follows the chart of Panilonghon (Panglao) (VII)]

[106] At a distance of 18 leagues from that island of Cebu, at the head of the other island called Bohol, we burned in the midst of that archipelago the ship *Concepción*, for too few men of us were left [to work it].²³⁰ We stowed the best of its contents in the other two ships, and then laid our course toward the south southwest, coasting along the island called Panglao, in which there are black men like those of Ethiopia.²³¹ Then we came to a large island,²³² whose king, in order to make peace with us, drew blood from his left hand and marked his body, face, and the tip of his tongue with it as a token of the closest friendship, and we did the same.²³³ I went ashore alone with the king in order to see that island. We had no sooner entered a river than many fishermen offered fish to the king. Then the king removed the cloths which covered his privies, as did some of his chiefs; and singing, began to row, passing by many dwellings which were on the river. Two hours after nightfall we reached the king's house. The distance from the beginning of the river where our ships were to the king's house was two leagues. When we entered the house, there came to meet us many torches of cane and palm leaves. These torches were of the *anime*, of which mention was made above.²³⁴ While the supper was being prepared, the king with two of his chiefs and two of his beautiful women drank the contents of a large jar of palm wine without eating anything. I, excusing myself as I had supped, would only drink but once. In drinking they observed all the same ceremonies that the king of Mazaua did. Then the supper was brought in, consisting of rice and very salt fish, served in porcelain dishes. They ate their rice as if it were bread. They cook the rice after the following manner. They first put a large leaf in an earthen jar like our jars, so that it lines all of the jar. Then they add the water

and the rice, and, after covering it, allow it to boil until the rice becomes as hard as bread; then they take it out in pieces. Rice is cooked this way throughout those districts. When we had eaten, the king had a reed mat and another of palm leaves, and a leaf pillow brought in so that I might sleep on them. The king and his two women went to sleep in a separate place, while I slept with one of his chiefs.

[107] When day came and until the dinner was brought in, I walked about that island. I saw many articles of gold in those houses but little food. After that we dined on rice and fish. At the conclusion of dinner, I asked the king by signs whether I could see the queen. He replied that he was willing, and we went together to the summit of a lofty hill, where the queen's house was located. When I entered the house, I made a bow to the queen, and she did the same to me, whereupon I sat down beside her. She was making a sleeping mat of palm leaves. In the house there was hanging a number of porcelain jars and four metal disks for playing upon, one of which was larger than the second, while the other two were still smaller. There were many male and female slaves who served her. Those houses are constructed like those already mentioned. Having taken our leave, we returned to the king's house, where the king had us immediately served with refreshments of sugarcane.

[108] The most abundant product of that island is gold. They showed me certain large valleys, making me a sign that the gold there was as abundant as the hairs of their heads, but they have no iron with which to dig it, and they do not care to go to the trouble [to get it]. That part of the island belongs to the same land as Butuan and Caraga, and lies toward Bohol, and is bounded by Mazaua. As we shall return to that island again, I shall say nothing further [now].[235]

[109] In the afternoon, I desired to return to the ships. The king and the other chief men wished to accompany me, and therefore we went in the same *balanghai*. As we were returning along the river, I saw, on the

summit of a hill at the right, three men hanging from one tree, the branches of which had been cut away. I asked the king what was the reason for that, and he replied that they were malefactors and robbers. Those people go naked as do the others above mentioned. The king's name is Rajah Calanao. The harbor is an excellent one. Rice, ginger, swine, goats, fowls, and other things are to be found there. That port lies in a latitude of 8 degrees toward the Arctic Pole, and in a longitude of 167 degrees from the line of demarcation. It is 50 leagues from Cebu, and is called Kipit.[236] Two days' journey from there to the northwest is found a large island called Luzon,[237] where six or eight junks belonging to the Lequian[238] people go yearly.

[*Here follows the chart of Caghaiam (Cagayan) (VIII)*]

[110] Leaving there and laying our course west southwest, we cast anchor at a not very large and almost uninhabited island. The people of that island are Moors and were banished from an island called Borneo. They go naked as do the others. They have blowpipes and small quivers at their side, full of arrows and a poisonous herb. They have daggers whose hafts are adorned with gold and precious gems, spears, bucklers, and small cuirasses of buffalo horn. They called us "holy beings." Little food was to be found in that island, but [there were] immense trees. It lies in a latitude of 7 and ½ degrees toward the Arctic Pole, and is forty-three leagues from Kipit. Its name is Cagayan.[239]

[111] About 25 leagues to the west northwest from the above island we found a large island, where rice, ginger, swine, goats, fowls, figs one-half cubit long and as thick as one's arm (they are excellent; and certain others are one span and less in length, and are much better than all the others),[240] coconuts, potatoes, sugarcane, and roots resembling turnips

in taste, are found, and rice cooked under the fire in bamboos or in wood. This kind lasts better than that cooked in earthen pots. We could well call that land "the promised land" because we suffered great hunger before we found it. We were often on the point of abandoning the ships and going ashore in order that we might not die of hunger. The king made peace with us by gashing himself slightly in the breast with one of our knives, and upon bleeding, touching the tip of his tongue and his forehead in token of the truest peace, and we did the same. That island lies in a latitude of 9 and ⅓ degrees toward the Arctic Pole, and a longitude of 171 and ⅓ degrees from the line of demarcation. [It is called] Palawan.²⁴¹

[Here follows the chart of Pulaoam (Palawan), Tegozzano porto, and Sundan (IX)]

[112] Those people of Palawan go naked as do the others. Almost all of them cultivate their fields. They have blowpipes with wooden arrows more than a span in length with harpoon points, and others tipped with fishbones, and poisoned with an herb; while others are tipped with points of bamboo like harpoons and are poisoned. At the end of the arrow they attach a little piece of soft wood, instead of feathers. At the end of their blowpipes they fasten a bit of iron like a spear head; and when they have shot all their arrows they fight with that. They place a value on brass rings and chains, bells, knives, and still more on copper wire for binding their fishhooks. They have large and very tame cocks, which they do not eat because of a certain veneration that they have for them. Sometimes they make them fight with one another, and each one puts up a certain amount on his cock, and the prize goes to him whose cock is the victor.²⁴² They have distilled rice wine which is stronger and better than that made from the palm.

[113] Ten leagues southwest of that island,[243] we came to an island, which, as we coasted by, seemed to us to be going upward. After entering the port, the holy body [i.e., St. Elmo's fire] appeared to us through the pitch darkness. There is a distance of 50 leagues from the beginning of that island to the port.[244]

[114] On the following day, July 9, the king of that island sent a very beautiful prau[245] to us, whose bow and stern were worked in gold. At the bow flew a white and blue banner surmounted with peacock feathers. Some men were playing on pipes and drums. Two *almadies* came with that prau. Praus resemble fustas, while the *almadies*[246] are their small fishing boats. Eight old men, who were chiefs, entered the ships and took seats in the stern upon a carpet. They presented us with a painted wooden jar full of betel and *areca* (the fruit which they chew continually), and jasmine and orange blossoms, a covering of yellow silk cloth, two cages full of fowls, a couple of goats, three jars full of distilled rice wine, and some bundles of sugarcane. They did the same to the other ship, and embracing us took their leave. The rice wine is as clear as water, but so strong that it intoxicated many of our men. It is called *arach*.[247]

[115] Six days later the king again sent three praus with great pomp, which encircled the ships with musical instruments playing and drums and brass disks sounding. They saluted us with those cloth caps of theirs which cover only the top of their heads. We saluted them by firing our mortars without [loading them with] stones. Then they gave us a present of various kinds of food, made only of rice. Some were wrapped in leaves and were made in somewhat longish pieces, some resembled sugar-loaves, while others were made in the manner of tarts with eggs and honey. They told us that their king was willing to let us get water

and wood, and to trade at our pleasure. Upon hearing that, seven of us
entered their prau bearing a present to their king, which consisted of a
green velvet robe made in the Turkish manner, a violet velvet chair, five
cubits of red cloth, a cap, a gilded drinking glass, a covered glass vase,
three quires of paper, and a gilded writing-case. To the queen [we took]
three cubits of yellow cloth, a pair of silvered shoes, and a silvered
needlecase full of needles. [We took] three cubits of red cloth, a cap,
and a gilded drinking-glass to the governor. To the herald who came in
the prau we gave a robe of red and green cloth, made in the Turkish
fashion, a cap, and a quire of paper; and to the other seven chief men,
to one a bit of cloth, and to another a cap, and to all of them a writing
book of paper. Then we immediately departed [for the land].

[116] When we reached the city,[248] we remained about two hours in
the prau, until the arrival of two elephants with silk trappings, and
twelve men each of whom carried a porcelain jar covered with silk in
which to carry our presents. Thereupon, we mounted the elephants
while those twelve men preceded us afoot with the presents in the jars.
In this way we went to the house of the governor, where we were given a
supper of many kinds of food. During the night we slept on cotton
mattresses, whose lining was of taffeta, and the sheets of Cambay.

[117] Next day we stayed in the house until noon. Then we went to
the king's palace upon elephants, with our presents in front as on the
preceding day. All the streets from the governor's to the king's house
were full of men with swords, spears, and shields, for such were the
king's orders. We entered the courtyard of the palace mounted on the
elephants. We went up a ladder accompanied by the governor and other
chiefs, and entered a large hall full of many nobles, where we sat down
upon a carpet with the presents in the jars near us. At the end of that
hall there is another hall higher but somewhat smaller. It was all

adorned with silk hangings, and two windows hung with two brocade curtains, through which light entered the hall. There were three hundred footsoldiers with naked rapiers at their thighs in that hall to guard the king. At the end of the small hall was a large window from which a brocade curtain was drawn aside so that we could see within it the king seated at a table with one of his young sons chewing betel. No one but women were behind him.

[118] Then a chief told us that we could not speak to the king, and that if we wished anything, we were to tell it to him, so that he could communicate it to one of higher rank. The latter would communicate it to a brother of the governor who was stationed in the smaller hall, and this man would communicate it by means of a speaking-tube through a hole in the wall to one who was inside with the king. The chief taught us the manner of making three obeisances to the king with our hands clasped above the head, raising first one foot and then the other and then kissing the hands toward him, and we did so. This is the method of the royal obeisance. We told the king that we came from the king of Spain, and that the latter desired to make peace with him and asked only for permission to trade. The king had us told that since the king of Spain desired to be his friend, he was very willing to be his, and said that we could take water and wood, and trade at our pleasure. Then we gave him the presents, on receiving each of which he nodded slightly. To each one of us was given some brocaded and gold cloth and silk, which were placed upon our left shoulders, where they were left but a moment. They presented us with refreshments of cloves and cinnamon, after which the curtains were drawn to and the windows closed. The men in the palace were all attired in cloth of gold and silk which covered their privies, and they carried daggers with gold hafts adorned with pearls and precious gems, and they had many rings on their hands.

[119] We returned upon the elephants to the governor's house, seven men carrying the king's presents to us and always preceding us. When we reached the house, they gave each one of us his present, placing them upon our left shoulders. We gave each of those men a couple of knives for his trouble. Nine men came to the governor's house with a like number of large wooden trays from the king. Each tray contained ten or twelve porcelain dishes full of veal, capons, chickens, peacocks, and other animals, and fish. We supped on the ground upon a palm mat from thirty or thirty-two different kinds of meat besides the fish and other things. At each mouthful of food we drank a small cupful of their distilled wine from a porcelain cup the size of an egg. We ate rice and other sweet food with gold spoons like ours. In our sleeping quarters there during those two nights, two torches of white wax were kept constantly alight in two rather tall silver candlesticks, and there were two large lamps full of oil with four wicks apiece and two men to snuff them continually. We went elephant-back to the seashore, where we found two praus which took us back to the ships.

[120] That city is entirely built in salt water, except the houses of the king and certain chiefs. It contains twenty-five thousand hearths.[249] The houses are all constructed of wood and built up from the ground on tall pillars. When the tide is high the women go in boats through the settlement selling the articles necessary to maintain life. There is a large brick wall in front of the kings house with towers like a fort, in which were mounted fifty-six bronze pieces, and six of iron. During the two days of our stay there, many pieces were discharged. That king is a Moor and his name is Rajah Siripada. He was forty years old and fat. No one serves him except women who are the daughters of chiefs. He never goes outside of his palace, unless when he goes hunting, and no one is allowed to talk with him except through the speaking tube. He has ten scribes who write down his deeds on very thin tree bark. These are called *xiritoles*.[250]

[121] On Monday morning, July 29, we saw more than one hundred praus divided into three squadrons and a like number of *tunguli* (which are their small boats) coming toward us.[251] Upon catching sight of them, imagining that there was some trickery afoot, we hoisted our sails as quickly as possible, slipping an anchor in our haste. We were especially concerned that we might be caught in between certain junks which had anchored behind us on the preceding day. We immediately turned upon the latter, capturing four of them and killing many persons. Three or four of the junks sought flight by beaching. In one of the junks which we captured was the son of the king of the island of Luzon. He was the captain-general of the king of Brunei, and came with those junks from a large city named Laoe, which is located at the end of that island [Borneo] toward Java Major.[252] He had destroyed and sacked that city because it refused to obey the king [of Brunei] but obeyed the king of Java Major instead. João Carvalho, our pilot, allowed that captain and the junks to go without our consent, for a certain sum of gold, as we learned afterward. Had the pilot not given up the captain to the king, the latter would have given us whatever we had asked, for that captain was exceedingly feared throughout those regions, especially by the heathens, as the latter are very hostile to that Moorish king.

[122] In that same port there is another city inhabited by heathens, which is larger than that of the Moors, and built like the latter in salt water. On that account the two peoples have daily combats together in that same harbor. The heathen king is as powerful as the Moorish king, but is not so haughty, and could be converted easily to the Christian faith. When the Moorish king heard how we had treated the junks, he sent us a message by one of our men who was ashore to the effect that the praus were not coming to do us any harm, but that they were going to attack the heathens. As a proof of that statement, the Moors showed him some heads of men who had been killed, which they declared to be

the heads of heathens. We sent a message to the king, asking him to please allow two of our men, who were in the city for purposes of trade, and the son of João Carvalho, who was born in the country of Verzin, to come to us, but the king refused. That was the result of João Carvalho's letting the above mentioned captain go.[253] We kept sixteen of the most important men [of the captured junks] to take them to Spain, and three women in the queen's name, but João Carvalho usurped the latter for himself.

[123] Junks are their ships and are made in the following manner. The bottom part stands about two spans above the water and is of planks fastened with wooden pegs, which are very well made; above that they are entirely made of very large bamboos as a counterweight. One of those junks carries as much cargo as a ship. Their masts are of bamboo, and the sails of the bark of trees. Their porcelain is a sort of exceedingly white earth which is left for fifty years under the earth before it is worked, for otherwise it would not be fine. The father buries it for the son. If [poison][254] is placed in a dish made of fine porcelain, the dish immediately breaks. The money used by the Moors in those regions is of bronze pierced in the middle in order that it may be strung. On only one side of it are four characters, which are letters of the great king of China. They call that money *picis*.[255] They gave us six porcelain dishes for one *cathil*[256] (which is equivalent to two of our pounds) of quicksilver; 100 *picis* for one quire of writing paper; one small porcelain vase for 160 *cathils* of bronze; one porcelain vase for three knives; one *bahar* (which is equivalent to 203 *cathils*) of wax for 160 *cathils* of bronze; one *bahar*[257] of salt for eighty *cathils* of bronze; one *bahar* of *anime* to calk the ships (for no pitch is found in those regions) for forty *cathils* of bronze. Twenty *tahils* make one *cathil*. At that place the people highly esteem bronze, quicksilver, glass, cinnabar, wool cloth, linens, and all our other merchandise, although

iron and spectacles more than all the rest. Those Moors go naked as do the other peoples [of those regions]. They drink quicksilver. The sick man drinks it to cleanse himself, and the well man to preserve his health.

[124] The king of Brunei has two pearls as large as two hen's eggs. They are so round that they will not stand still on a table. I know that for a fact, for when we carried the king's presents to him, signs were made for him to show them to us, but he said that he would show them the next day. Afterward some chiefs said that they had seen them.[258]

[125] Those Moors worship Muhammad and his law which orders them not to eat pork; to wash the buttocks with the left hand and not to use that hand in eating; not to cut anything with the right hand; to sit down to urinate; not to kill fowls or goats without first addressing the sun; to cut off the tops of the chicken's wings with the little bits of skin that stick up from under, as well as their feet, and then to split them down the middle; to wash the face with the right hand, but not to cleanse the teeth with the fingers; and not to eat anything that has been killed unless by them. They are circumcised like the Jews.

[126] Camphor, a kind of balsam, is produced in that island. It exudes between the wood and the bark, and the drops are as small as [grains of] wheat bran. If it is exposed it gradually evaporates. Those people call it *capor*.[259] Cinnamon, ginger, mirabolans, oranges, lemons, jack fruit, watermelons, cucumbers, gourds, turnips, cabbages, scallions, cows, buffaloes, swine, goats, chickens, geese, deer, elephants, horses, and other things are found there. That island is so large that it takes three months to sail round it in a prau. It lies in a latitude of 5 and ¼ degrees toward the Arctic Pole, and in a longitude of 176 and ⅔ degrees from the line of demarcation, and its name is Borneo.[260]

[Here follows the chart of Burne (Borneo), Laot (Laoc?), and the scroll: "Where the living leaves are." (X); thereafter follows the chart of Mindanao (XI); thereafter, the chart of Zzolo (Jolo), Subanin, Tagima (Basilan), Cavit (Cavite) and the scroll: "Where the pearls are born." (XII)]

[127] Leaving that island, we turned back[261] in order to find a suitable place to calk the ships, for they were leaking. One ship ran on to some shoals at an island called Bibalon,[262] because of the carelessness of its pilot, but with the help of God we freed it. A sailor of that ship incautiously snuffed a candle into a barrel full of gunpowder, but he quickly snatched it out without any harm. Then pursuing our course, we captured a prau laden with coconuts on its way to Borneo. Its crew sought refuge on an islet, while we captured it. Three other praus escaped behind certain islets.

[128] At the head of Borneo, between it and an island called Cimbonbon, which lies in [a latitude of] 8 degrees and 7 minutes, is a perfect port for repairing ships.[263] Consequently, we entered it; but as we lacked many things for repairing the ships, we delayed there for forty-two days.[264] During that time, each one of us labored hard, one at one thing and one at another. Our greatest fatigue however was to go barefoot to the woods for firewood. In that island there are wild boars, of which we killed one which was going by water from one island to another [by pursuing it] with the small boat. Its head was two and one-half span long, and its teeth were large. There are found large crocodiles, both on land and sea, oysters and shellfish of various kinds. Among the last named we found two, the flesh of one of which weighed twenty-six pounds, and the other forty-four.[265] We caught a fish, which had a head like that of a hog and two horns. Its body consisted entirely of one bone, and on its back it resembled a saddle; and it was small.[266] Trees are also found there which produce leaves which are alive when they fall,

and walk. Those leaves are quite like those of the mulberry, but are not
so long. On both sides near the stem, which is short and pointed, they
have two feet. They have no blood, but if one touches them they run
away. I kept one of them for nine days in a box. When I opened the
box, that leaf went round and round it. I believe those leaves live on
nothing but air.[267]

[129] Having left that island,[268] that is, the port, we met at the head
of the island of Palawan[269] a junk which was coming from Borneo, on
which was the governor of Palawan. We made them a signal to haul in
their sails, and as they refused to haul them in, we captured the junk by
force, and sacked it. [We told] the governor [that] if [he] wished his
freedom, he was to give us, inside of seven days, four hundred measures
of rice, twenty swine, twenty goats, and one hundred fifty fowls. After
that he presented us with coconuts, figs, sugarcanes, jars full of palm
wine, and other things. Seeing his liberality, we returned some of his
daggers and harquebuses to him, giving him in addition, a flag, a yellow
damask robe, and fifteen cubits of cloth; to his son, a cloak of blue
cloth; to a brother of the governor, a robe of green cloth and other
things.

[130] We departed from the governor as friends. We turned our
course back between the island of Cagayan[270] and the port of Kipit,[271]
and laid our course east by south so that we might find the islands of
Malucca. We passed by certain reefs near which we found the sea full of
grass, although it was very deep. When we passed between them, it
seemed as though we were entering another sea. Leaving Kipit to the
east, we found two islands, Jolo and Taghima,[272] which lie to the west,
and near which pearls are found. The two pearls of the king of Brunei
were found there, and the king got them, as we were told, in the following manner. That king took to wife a daughter of the king of Jolo, who

told him that her father had those two pearls. The king determined to get possession of them one way or another. Going one night with five hundred praus, he captured the king and two of his sons, and took them to Brunei. [He told] the king of Jolo that if he wished freedom, he must surrender the two pearls to him.[273]

[131] Then we laid our course east by north between two settlements called Cavite and Subanin, and an inhabited island called Monoripa,[274] located ten leagues from the reefs. The people of that island make their dwellings in boats and do not live otherwise. In those two settlements of Cavite and Subanin, which are located in the island of Butuan and Caraga, is found the best cinnamon that grows. Had we stayed there two days, those people would have laden our ships for us, but as we had a wind favorable for passing a point and certain islets which were near that island, we did not wish to delay. While under sail we bartered two large knives which we had taken from the governor of Palawan for seventeen pounds [of cinnamon]. The cinnamon tree grows to a height of three or four cubits, and as thick as the fingers of the hand. It has but three or four small branches and its leaves resemble those of the laurel. Its bark is the cinnamon. It is gathered twice per year. The wood and leaves are as strong as the cinnamon when they are green. Those people call it *caiumana*. *Caiu* means wood, and *mana*, sweet, hence, "sweet wood."[275]

[132] Laying our course toward the northeast, and going to a large city called Magindanao,[276] which is located in the island of Butuan and Caraga,[277] so that we might gather information concerning Malucca, we captured by force a *biguiday* (a vessel resembling a prau), and killed seven men. It contained only eighteen men, and they were as well built as any whom we had seen in those regions. All were chiefs of Magindanao.

Among them was one who told us that he was a brother of the king of Magindanao, and that he knew the location of Malucca. Through his directions we discontinued our course toward the northeast, and took that toward the southeast. At a cape of that island of Butuan and Caraga, and near a river, are found hairy men who are exceedingly great fighters and archers. They use swords one span in width, and eat only raw human hearts with the juice of oranges or lemons. Those people are called "Benaian, the hairy."[278] When we took our course toward the southeast, we lay in a latitude of 6 degrees and 7 minutes toward the Arctic Pole, and thirty leagues from Cavite.

[*Here follows the chart of the islands of Ciboco (Sibago), Birahan batolach (Batukali?); Sarangani, Candigar (Balut?) (XIII)*]

[133] Sailing toward the southeast, we found four islands, [namely], Ciboco, Birahan Batolach, Sarangani, and Candighar.[279] One Saturday night, October 26, while coasting by Birahan Batolach, we encountered a most furious storm. Thereupon, praying God, we lowered all the sails. Immediately our three saints appeared to us and dissipated all the darkness. St. Elmo remained for more than two hours on the maintop, like a torch; St. Nicholas on the mizzentop; and St. Clara on the foretop. We promised a slave to St. Elmo; to St. Nicholas, and to St. Clara, we gave alms to each.

[134] Then continuing our voyage, we entered a harbor between the two islands of Sarangani and Candighar, and anchored to the eastward near a settlement of Sarangani, where gold and pearls are found. Those people are heathens and go naked as do the others. That harbor lies in a latitude of 5 degrees and 9 minutes, and is fifty leagues from Cavite.

[135] Remaining one day in that harbor, we captured two pilots by force, in order that they might show us where Molucca lay. Then laying our course south southwest, we passed among eight islands, some inhabited and some not, which were situated in the manner of a street. Their names are Cheava, Caviao, Cabiao, Camanuca, Cabaluzao, Cheai, Lipan, and Nuza.[280] Finally we came to an island at their end, which was very beautiful to look at. As we had a contrary wind, so that we could not double a point of that island, we sailed here and there near it. Consequently, one of the men whom we had captured at Sarangani, and the brother of the king of Magindanao who took with him his small son, escaped during the night by swimming to that island. But the boy was drowned, for he was unable to hold tightly to his father's shoulders. Being unable to double that point, we passed below the island where there were many islets. That island has four kings [namely], Rajah Matandatu, Rajah Lalagha, Rajah Bapti, and Rajah Parabu. The people are heathens. The island lies in a latitude of 3 and ½ degrees toward the Arctic Pole and is twenty-seven leagues from Saranghani. Its name is Sanghihe.[281]

[*Here follows the chart of the island of Sanghir (Sanghihe), Nuza (?), Lipan (Lipang), Cheai (?), Cabulazgo (Kawalusu), Camanuca (Memanuk), Cabiao (Kamboling?), Cheva (?), Caviao (Kawio) (XIV); and thereafter the chart of the archipelago of Paghinzara including Paghinzara, Ciau (Siau), Zangalura (Sanggeluhang), Para, Carachita (Karakitang), Cheama (Kima), Meau (Maju), Zoar (Tifore) (XV)*]

[136] Continuing the same course, we passed near six islands, [namely], Kima, Karakitang, Para, Zangalura, Siau (which is ten leagues from Sanghihe, and has a high but not large mountain, and whose king is called Rajah Ponto),[282] and Paghinzara.[283] The latter is located eight leagues from Siau, and has three high mountains. The name of its king

is Rajah Babintau. [Then we found the island] Talaud.²⁸⁴ Then we found twelve leagues to the east of Paghinzara two islands, not very large, but inhabited, called Zoar and Meau.²⁸⁵ After passing those two islands, on Wednesday, November 6, we discovered four lofty islands fourteen leagues east of the two [above-mentioned islands]. The pilot who still remained with us told us that those four islands were Molucca. Therefore, we thanked God and as an expression of our joy discharged all our artillery. It was no wonder that we were so glad, for we had passed twenty-seven months less two days in our search for Molucca. Among all those islands, even to Molucca, the shallowest bottom that we found was between a depth of one or two hundred fathoms, notwithstanding the assertion of the Portuguese, that that region could not be navigated because of the numerous shoals and the dark sky, as they had imagined.

[Here follows the chart of the island of Tarenate (Ternate), Giailonlo (Gilolo: Halmahera), Maitara (Mutir) with the scroll: "All the islands represented in this book are in the other hemisphere of the world at the antipodes" (XVI); and thereafter the chart of the islands of Molucca including Pulongha, Tadore (Tidore), Mare, Mutir (Motir) and Machiam (Makiam) with the scroll: "Cavi gomode, that is, the Clove tree" (XVII)]

[137] Three hours before sunset on Friday, November 8, 1521,²⁸⁶ we entered into a harbor of an island called Tidore, and anchoring near the shore in twenty fathoms we fired all our artillery. Next day the king came to the ships in a prau, and circled about them once. We immediately went to meet him in a small boat, in order to show him honor. He made us enter his prau and seat ourselves near him. He was seated under a silk awning which sheltered him on all sides. In front of him was one of his sons with the royal scepter, and two persons with two gold jars to pour water on his hands, and two others with two gilded

caskets filled with their betel.[287] The king told us that we were welcome there,[288] and that he had dreamt some time ago that some ships were coming to Molucca from remote parts; and that for more assurance he had determined to consult the moon, whereupon he had seen the ships were coming, and that we were they.[289] Upon the king entering our ships all kissed his hand and then we led him to the stern. When he entered inside there, he would not stoop, but entered from above. Causing him to sit down in a red velvet chair, we clothed him in a yellow velvet robe made in the Turkish fashion. In order to show him greater honor, we sat down on the ground near him.

[138] Then when all were seated, the king began to speak and said that he and all his people desired ever to be the most loyal friends and vassals to our king of Spain. He received us as his children, and we could go ashore as if in our own houses, for from that time forward his island was to be called no more Tidore but Castile, because of the great love which he bore to our king, his lord. We made him a present which consisted of the robe, the chair, a piece of delicate linen, four cubits of scarlet cloth, a piece of brocaded silk, a piece of yellow damask, some Indian cloth embroidered with gold and silk, a piece of white *berania*[290] (the linen of Cambay), two caps, six strings of glass beads, twelve knives, three large mirrors, six pairs of scissors, six combs, some gilded drinking-cups, and other articles. To his son we gave an Indian cloth of gold and silk, a large mirror, a cap, and two knives; and to each of nine others, all of them his chiefs, a silk cloth, caps, and two knives; and to many others caps or knives. We kept giving presents until the king bade us desist.

[139] After that he declared to us that he had nothing else except his own life to send to the king his sovereign. We were to approach nearer to the city, and whoever came to the ships at night, we were to kill with our muskets. In leaving the stern, the king would never bend his head.

When he took his leave we discharged all our artillery. That king is a Moor and about forty-five years old. He is well built and has a royal presence, and is an excellent astrologer. At that time he was clad in a shirt of the most delicate white stuff with the ends of the sleeves embroidered in gold, and in a cloth that reached from his waist to the ground, and he was barefoot. Around his head he wore a silk scarf and over that a crown of flowers. He was called Rajah Sultan Manzor.[291]

[140] On Sunday, November 10, that king desired us to tell him how long it was since we had left Spain, and what pay and *quintalada*[292] the king gave to each of us. He requested us to give him a signature of the king and a royal banner, for then and thenceforth, he would cause it that his island and another called Ternate[293] [provided that he were able to crown one of his grandsons, named Calonaghapi][294] would both belong to the king of Spain; and for the honor of his king he was ready to fight to the death, and when he could no longer resist, he would go to Spain with all his family in a junk which he was having built new, carrying the royal signature and banner; and therefore he was the king's servant for a long time. He begged us to leave him some men so that he might constantly be reminded of the king of Spain. He did not ask for merchandise because the latter would not remain with him. He told us that he would go to an island called Batjan,[295] in order sooner to furnish the ships with cloves, for there were not enough dry cloves in his island to load the two ships. As that day was Sunday, it was decided not to trade. The festive day of those people is our Friday.

[141] In order that your most illustrious Lordship may know the islands where cloves grow, they are five, [namely], Ternate, Tidore, Motir, Makian, and Batjan.[296] Ternate is the chief one, and when its king was alive, he ruled nearly all the others. Tidore, the one where we were, has a

king. Motir and Makian have no king but are ruled by the people, and when the two kings of Ternate and of Tidore engage in war, those two islands furnish them with men. The last island is Batjan, and it has a king. That entire province where cloves grow is called Molucca.

[142] At that time it was not eight months since one Francisco Serrão had died in Ternate. [He was] a Portuguese and the captain-general of the king of Ternate against the king of Tidore. He did so well that he constrained the king of Tidore to give one of his daughters to wife to the king of Ternate, and almost all the sons of the chiefs as hostages. The above mentioned grandson of the king of Tidore was born to that daughter.[297] Peace having been made between the two kings, one day Francisco Serrão came to Tidore to trade cloves, and the king of Tidore had him poisoned with those betel leaves. He lived only four days.[298] His king wished to have him buried according to his religion, but three Christians who were his servants would not consent to it. He left a son and a daughter, both young, born by a woman whom he had taken in Java Major, and two hundred *bahars* of cloves. Serrão was a close friend and a relative of our faithful captain-general, and was the cause of inciting the latter to undertake that enterprise, for when our captain was at Malacca, he had written to him several times that he was in Ternate.[299] As Don Manuel, then king of Portugal, refused to increase our captain-general's pension by only a single testoon[300] per month for his merits, the latter went to Spain, where he had obtained everything for which he could ask from his sacred Majesty. Ten days after the death of Francisco Serrão, the king of Ternate, by name, Rajah Abuleis, having expelled his son-in-law, the king of Batjan, was poisoned by his daughter, the wife of the latter king, under pretext of trying to bring about peace between the two kings. The king lingered but two days, and left nine principal sons, whose names are Chechili Momuli, Tidoree Vunighi, Chechili de Roix,

Cili Manzur, Cili Pagi, Chialin, Chechilin Cathara, Vaiechu Serich, and Calanoghapi.[301]

[143] On Monday, November 11, one of the sons of the king of Ternate, Chechili de Roix, came to the ships clad in red velvet. He had two praus and his men were playing upon the above mentioned metal disks. He refused to enter the ship at that time. He had [charge of] the wife and children, and the other possessions of Francisco Serrão. When we found out who he was, we sent a message to the king, asking him whether we should receive Chechili de Roix, since we were in the king's port. He replied to us that we could do as we pleased. But the son of the king, seeing that we were hesitating, moved off somewhat from the ships. We went to him with the boat in order to present him an Indian cloth of gold and silk, and some knives, mirrors, and scissors. He accepted them somewhat haughtily, and immediately departed. He had a Christian Indian with him named Manuel, the servant of one Pedro Alfonso de Lorosa, a Portuguese who went from Bandan to Ternate,[302] after the death of Francisco Serrão. As the servant knew how to speak Portuguese, he came aboard our ship, and told us that, although the sons of the king of Ternate were at enmity with the king of Tidore, yet they were always at the service of the king of Spain. We sent a letter to Pietro Alfonso de Lorosa, through his servant, [telling him] that he could come without any hesitation.

[144] Those kings have as many women as they wish, but only one chief wife, whom all the others obey. The king of Tidore had a large house outside of the city, where two hundred of his chief women lived with a like number of women to serve them. When the king eats, he sits alone or with his chief wife in a high place like a gallery from which he can see all the other women who sit about the gallery; and he orders her

who best pleases him to sleep with him that night. After the king has finished eating, if he orders those women to eat together, they do so, but if not, each one goes to eat in her own chamber. No one is allowed to see those women without permission from the king, and if anyone is found near the king's house by day or by night, he is put to death. Every family is obliged to give the king one or two of its daughters. That king had twenty-six children, eight sons, and the rest daughters.

[145] Lying next to that island there is a very large island, called Gilolo,303 which is inhabited by Moors and heathens. Two kings are found there among the Moors, one of them, as we were told by the king, having had six hundred children, and the other 525. The heathens do not keep so many women; nor do they live under so many superstitions, but adore for all that day the first thing that they see in the morning when they go out of their houses. The king of those heathens, called Rajah Papua, is exceedingly rich in gold, and lives in the interior of the island. Reeds as thick around as the leg and filled with water that is very good to drink, grow on the flinty rocks in the island of Gilolo.304 We bought many of them from those people.

[146] On Tuesday, November 12, the king had a house built for us for our merchandise in the city in one day. We carried almost all of our goods there, and left three of our men to guard them. We immediately began to trade in the following manner. For ten cubits of red cloth of very good quality, they gave us one *bahar* of cloves, which is equivalent to four quintals and six pounds (one quintal is 100 pounds); for fifteen cubits of cloth of not very good quality, one *bahar*; for fifteen hatchets, one *bahar*; for thirty-five glass drinking-cups, one *bahar* (the king getting them all); for seventeen *cathils* of cinnabar305 one *bahar*; for seventeen *cathils* of quicksilver, one *bahar*; for twenty-six cubits of linen, one *bahar*; for twenty-five cubits of finer linen, one *bahar*; for 150 knives, one *bahar*;

for fifty pairs of scissors, one *bahar;* for forty caps, one *bahar;* for ten pieces of Gujerat cloth,[306] one *bahar;* for three of those metal disks of theirs, two *bahars;* for one quintal of bronze, one *bahar.* [Almost] all the mirrors were broken, and the few good ones the king wished for himself. Many of those things [that we traded] were from those junks which we had captured. Our haste to return to Spain made us dispose of our merchandise at better bargains [to the natives] than we should have done. Daily so many boatloads of goats, fowls, figs [bananas], coconuts, and other kinds of food were brought to the ships, that we were amazed.

[147] We supplied the ships with good water, which issues forth hot [from the ground], but if it stands for the space of an hour outside its spring, it becomes very cold, the reason being that it comes from the mountain of cloves. This is quite the opposite from the assertion made in Spain that water must be carried to Molucca from distant parts.[307]

[148] On Wednesday, the king sent his son, named Mossahap, to Motir for cloves, so that they might supply us more quickly. On that day we told the king that we had captured certain Indians. The king thanked God heartily, and asked us to do him the kindness to give them to him, so that he might send them back to their land, with five of his own men, in order that they might make the king of Spain and his fame known. Then we gave him the three women who had been captured in the queen's name for the reason just given.

[149] The next day, we gave the king all the prisoners, except those from Borneo, for which he thanked us fervently. Thereupon, he asked us, in order thereby to show our love for him, to kill all the swine that we had in the ships, in return for which he would give us an equal number of goats and fowls. We killed them in order to show him a favor, and hung them up under the deck. When those people happened to see them

they covered their faces in order that they might not look upon them or catch their odor.

[150] In the afternoon of that same day, Pietro Alfonso, the Portuguese,[308] came in a prau. He had not disembarked before the king sent to summon him and told him banteringly to answer us truly in whatever we should ask him, even if he did come from Ternate. He told us that he had been sixteen years in India, but ten in Molucca, for it was as many years since Molucca had been discovered secretly. It was a year less fifteen days, since a large ship had arrived at that place from Malacca, and had left laden with cloves, but had been obliged to remain in Bandan for some months because of bad weather. Its captain was Tristão de Meneses, a Portuguese. When he asked the latter what was the news back in Christendom, he was told that a fleet of five ships had left Seville to discover Molucca in the name of the king of Spain under command of Ferdinand Magellan, a Portuguese. The king of Portugal, angered that a Portuguese should be opposed to him, had sent some ships to the Cape of Good Hope, and a like number to the Cape of Santa Maria at the mouth of the Rio de la Plata, where the cannibals live, in order to prevent their passage, but Magellan had not been found. Then the king of Portugal had heard that that captain had passed into another sea, and was on his way to Molucca. He immediately wrote directing his chief captain of India, one Diogo Lopes de Segueira,[309] to send six ships to Molucca. But the latter did not send them because the Grand Turk was coming to Malacca, and he was obliged to send sixty sail to oppose him at the Strait of Mecca in the land of Jiddah.[310] They found only a few galleys that had been beached on the shore of the strong and beautiful city of Aden, all of which they burned. After that, the chief captain sent a large galleon with two tiers of guns to Molucca to oppose us, but it was unable to proceed or turn back because of

certain shoals and currents of water near Malacca, and contrary winds. The captain of that galleon was Francisco Faria, a Portuguese.[311] It was but a few days since a caravel with two junks had been in that place to get news of us. The junks went to Batjan for a cargo of cloves with seven Portuguese. As those Portuguese did not respect the women of the king or those of his subjects, although the king told them often not to act so, and since they would not desist, they were put to death. When the men in the caravel heard that, they immediately returned to Malacca abandoning the junks with four hundred *bahars* of cloves, and sufficient merchandise to purchase one hundred *bahars* more. Every year a number of junks sail from Malacca to Bandan for mace and nutmeg, and from Bandan to Molucca for cloves. Those people sail in three days in those junks of theirs from Molucca to Bandan, and in fifteen days from Bandan to Malacca. The king of Portugal had enjoyed Molucca already for ten years secretly, so that the king of Spain might not learn of it.[312] That Portuguese remained with us until three in the morning, and told us many other things. We plied him so well, promising him good pay, that he promised to return to Spain with us.[313]

[151] On Friday, November 15, the king told us that he was going to Batjan to get the cloves abandoned there by the Portuguese. He asked us for two presents so that he might give them to the two governors of Motir in the name of the king of Spain. Passing in between the ships he desired to see how we fired our musketry, crossbows, and the culverins,[314] which are larger than an harquebus. He shot three times with a crossbow, for it pleased him more than the muskets.

[152] On Saturday, the Moorish king of Gilolo came to the ships with a considerable number of praus. To some of the men we gave some green damask silk, two cubits of red cloth, mirrors, scissors, knives, combs, and two gilt drinking cups. That king told us that since we were

friends of the king of Tidore, we were also his friends, for he loved that king as one of his own sons; and whenever any of our men would go to his land, he would show him the greatest honor. That king is very aged and is feared among all those islands, for he is very powerful. His name is Rajah Iussu. That island of Gilolo is so large that it takes four months to circumnavigate it in a prau.

[153] On Sunday morning that same king came to the ships and desired to see how we fought and how we discharged our guns. He took the greatest pleasure in it. After they had been discharged he immediately departed. We were told he had been a great fighter in his youth.

[154] That same day, I went ashore to see how the clove grows. The clove tree is tall and as thick as a man's body or thereabout. Its branches spread out somewhat widely in the middle, but at the top they have the shape of a summit. Its leaves resemble those of the laurel, and the bark is olive-colored. The cloves grow at the end of the twigs, ten or twenty in a cluster. Those trees have generally more cloves on one side than on the other, according to the season. When the cloves sprout they are white, when ripe, red, and when dried, black. They are gathered twice per year, once at the nativity of our Savior, and the other at the nativity of St. John the Baptist;[315] for the climate is more moderate at those two seasons, but more so at the time of the nativity of our Savior. When the year is very hot and there is little rain, those people gather three or four hundred *bahars* [of cloves] in each of those islands. Those trees grow only in the mountains, and if any of them are planted in the lowlands near the mountains they do not survive. The leaves, the bark, and the green wood are as strong as the cloves. If the latter are not gathered when they are ripe, they become large and so hard that only their husk is good. No cloves are grown in the world except in the five mountains of those five islands, except that some are found in Gilolo and in a

small island between Tidore and Motir, by name Mareh,[316] but they are not good. Almost every day we saw a mist descend and encircle now one and now another of those mountains, on account of which those cloves become perfect. Each of those people possesses clove trees, and each one watches over his own trees although he does not cultivate them.

[155] Some nutmeg trees are found in that island. The tree resembles our walnut tree, and has leaves like it. When the nut is gathered it is as large as a small quince, with the same sort of down, and it is of the same color. Its first rind is as thick as the green rind of our walnut. Under that there is a thin layer, under which is found the mace. The latter is a brilliant red and is wrapped about the rind of the nut, and within that is the nutmeg. The houses of those people are built like those of the others, but are not raised so high from the ground, and are surrounded with bamboos like a hedge. The women there are ugly and go naked as do the others, [covered only] with those cloths made from the bark of trees. Those cloths are made in the following manner. They take a piece of bark and leave it in the water until it becomes soft. Then they beat it with bits of wood and [thus] make it as long and as wide as they wish. It becomes like a veil of raw silk, and has certain threads within it, which appear as if woven. They eat wooden bread made from a tree resembling the palm, which is made as follows. They take a piece of that soft wood from which they take certain long black thorns. Then they pound the wood, and so make the bread. They use that bread, which they call *saghu*,[317] almost as their sole food at sea. The men there go naked as do the others [of those regions], but they are so jealous of their wives that they do not wish us to go ashore with our drawers exposed; for they assert that their women imagine that we are always in readiness.

[156] A number of boats came from Ternate daily laden with cloves, but, as we were awaiting the king, we did not barter for anything except food. The men who came from Ternate complained a great deal because we refused to trade with them.

[157] On Sunday night, November 24, and toward Monday, the king came with metal disks a-sounding, and passed between the ships, [at which] we discharged many pieces. He told us that cloves would be brought in quantity within four days.

[158] Monday the king sent us 791 *cathils* of cloves, without reckoning the tare (the tare is to take the spices for less than they weigh, for they become dryer daily). As those were the first cloves which we had laden in our ships, we fired many pieces. Cloves are called *ghomode*[318] there; in Saranghani where we captured the two pilots, *bongalavan;* and in Malacca, *chianche.*[319]

[159] On Tuesday, November 26, the king told us that it was not the custom of any king to leave his island, but that he had left [his] for the love that he bore the king of Castile, and so that we might go to Spain sooner and return with so many ships that we could avenge the murder of his father who was killed in an island called Buru,[320] and then thrown into the sea. He told us that it was the custom, when the first cloves were laden in the ships or in the junks, for the king to make a feast for the crews of the ships, and to pray their God that He would lead those ships safe to their port. He also wished to do it because of the king of Batjan and one of his brothers who were coming to visit him. He had the streets cleaned. Some of us, imagining that some treachery was afoot, because three Portuguese in the company of Francisco Serrão had been killed in the place where we took in water, by certain of those people who had hidden in the thickets, and because we saw those Indians whispering with our prisoners, declared in opposition to those who

wished to go to the feast, that we ought not go ashore for feasts, for we remembered that other so unfortunate one.[321] We argued so strongly that it was decided to send a message to the king asking him to come soon to the ships, for we were about to depart and we would give him the four men whom we had promised him, besides some other merchandise.

[160] The king came immediately and entered the ships. He told some of his men that he entered them with as great assurance as into his own houses. He told us that he was greatly astonished at our intention of departing so soon, since the limit of time for lading the ships was thirty days; and that he had not left the island to do us any harm, but to supply the ships with cloves sooner. He said that we should not depart then for that was not the season for sailing among those islands, both because of the many shoals found about Bandan and because we might easily meet some Portuguese ships [in those seas]. However, if it were our determination to depart then, we should take all our merchandise, for all the kings in the vicinity would say that the king of Tidore had received so many presents from so great a king, and had given nothing in return; and that they would think that we had departed only for fear of some treachery, and would always call him a traitor. Then he had his Koran brought, and first kissing it and placing it four or five times about his head, and saying certain words to himself as he did so (which they call *zambahean*),[322] he declared in the presence of all, that he swore by Allah and by the Koran which he had in his hand, that he would always be a faithful friend to the king of Spain. He spoke all those words nearly in tears. In return for his good words, we promised to wait another fifteen days. Thereupon, we gave him the signature of the king and the royal banner. None the less we heard afterward on good authority that some of the chiefs of those islands had proposed to him to have us killed because it would give the greatest pleasure to the

Portuguese, and that the Portuguese would forgive those of Batjan. But the king had replied that he would not do it under any circumstances, since he had recognized the king of Spain and had made peace with him.

[161] After dinner on Wednesday, November 27, the king had an edict proclaimed that all those who had cloves could bring them to the ships. All that day and the next we bartered for cloves like mad.

[162] On Friday afternoon, the governor of Makian came with a considerable number of praus. He refused to disembark, for his father and one of his brothers who had been banished from Makian were living in Tidore.[323]

[163] The next day, our king and his nephew, the governor, entered the ships. As we had no more cloth, the king sent to have three cubits of his brought and gave it to us, and we gave it with other things to the governor. At his departure we discharged many pieces. Afterward the king sent us six cubits of red cloth, so that we might give it to the governor. We immediately presented it to the latter, and he thanked us heartily for it, telling us that he would send us a goodly quantity of cloves. That governor's name is Humar, and he was about twenty-five years old.

[164] On Sunday, December 1, that governor departed. We were told that the king of Tidore had given him some silk cloth and some of those metal disks so that he might send the cloves quicker.

[165] On Monday the king went out of the island to get cloves.

[166] On Wednesday morning, as it was the day of St. Barbara,[324] and because the king came, all the artillery was discharged. At night the king came to the shore, and asked to see how we fired our rockets and fire bombs, at which he was highly delighted.

[167] On Thursday and Friday we bought many cloves both in the city and in the ships. For four cubits of Frisian cloth, they gave us one

bahar of cloves; for two brass chains, worth one marcello,[325] they gave us one hundred pounds of cloves. Finally, when we had no more merchandise, one man gave his cloak, another his doublet, and another his shirt, besides other articles of clothing, in order that they might have their share[326] in the cargo

[168] On Saturday, three of the sons of the king of Ternate and their three wives, the daughters of our king, and Pietro Alfonso, the Portuguese, came to the ships. We gave each of the three brothers a gilt glass drinking cup, and scissors and other things to the women. Many pieces were discharged at their departure. Then we sent ashore many things to the daughter of our king, now the wife of the king of Ternate, as she refused to come to the ships with the others. All those people, both men and women, always go barefoot.

[169] On Sunday, December 8, as it was the Feast of the Conception, we fired many pieces, rockets, and fire bombs.

[170] On Monday afternoon the king came to the ships with three women, who carried his betel for him. No one except the king can take women with him. Afterward the king of Gilolo came and wished to see us fight together again.

[171] Several days later our king told us that he was like a child at the breast who knew his dear mother, who departing, was leaving him alone.[327] He would be especially disconsolate because now he had become acquainted with us, and enjoyed some of the products of Spain. Inasmuch as our return would be far in the future, he earnestly entreated us to leave him some of our culverins for his defense. He advised us to sail only by day when we left, because of the numerous shoals amid those islands. We replied to him that if we wished to reach Spain we would have to sail day and night. Thereupon, he told us that he would pray daily to his god for us, asking him to conduct us in safety. He told us that the king of Batjan

was about to come to marry one of his brothers to one of his [the king of Tidore's] daughters, and asked us to invent some entertainment in token of joy; but that we should not fire the large pieces, because they would do great damage to the ships as they were laden.

[172] During that time, Pietro Alfonso, the Portuguese, came with his wife and all his other possessions to remain in the ships.

[173] Two days later, Chechili de Roix, son of the king of Ternate, came in a well-manned prau, and asked the Portuguese to come down into it for a few moments. The Portuguese answered that he would not come down, for he was going to Spain with us, whereupon the king's son tried to enter the ship, but we refused to allow him to come aboard. He was a close friend to the Portuguese captain of Malacca, and had come to seize the Portuguese. He severely scolded those who lived near the Portuguese because they had allowed the latter to go without his permission.

[174] On Sunday afternoon, December 15, the king of Batjan and his brother came in a prau with three tiers of rowers at each side. In all there were 120 rowers, and they carried many banners made of white, yellow, and red parrot feathers. There was much sounding of those metal disks, for the rowers kept time in their rowing to those sounds. He brought two other praus filled with girls to present them to his betrothed. When they passed near the ships, we saluted them by firing pieces, and they in order to salute us went round the ships and the port. Our king came to congratulate him as it is not the custom for any king to disembark on the land of another king. When the king of Batjan saw our king coming, he rose from the carpet on which he was seated, and took his position at one side of it. Our king refused to sit down upon the carpet, but on its other side, and so no one occupied the carpet. The king of Batjan gave our king five hundred *patols*,[328] because our king

was giving his daughter to wife to the former's brother. The said *patols* are cloths of gold and silk manufactured in China, and are highly esteemed among them. Whenever one of those people dies, the other members of his family clothe themselves in those cloths in order to show him more honor. They give three *bahars* of cloves for one of those cloths or thereabouts, according to the [value of the] cloth.

[175] On Monday our king sent a banquet to the king of Batjan, carried by fifty women all clad in silk garments from the waist to the knees. They went two by two with a man between each couple. Each one bore a large tray filled with other small dishes which contained various kinds of food. The men carried nothing but the wine in large jars. Ten of the oldest women acted as macebearers. Thus did they go quite to the prau where they presented everything to the king who was sitting upon the carpet under a red and yellow canopy. As they were returning, those women captured some of our men and it was necessary to give them some little trifle in order to regain their freedom. After that our king sent us goats, coconuts, wine, and other things. That day[329] we bent the new sails in the ships. On them was a cross of St. James of Galicia,[330] with an inscription which read: "This is the sign of our good fortune."

[176] On Tuesday, we gave our king certain pieces of artillery resembling harquebuses, which we had captured among those Indies, and some of our culverins, together with four barrels of powder. We took aboard at that place eighty butts of water in each ship. Five days previously the king had sent one hundred men to cut wood for us at the island of Mareh,[331] by which we were to pass. On that day,[332] the king of Batjan and many of his men came ashore to make peace with us. Before the king walked four men with drawn daggers in their hands. In

the presence of our king and all the others he said that he would always be at the service of the king of Spain, and that he would save in his name the cloves left by the Portuguese until the arrival of another of our fleets, and he would never give them to the Portuguese without our consent. He sent as a present to the king of Spain a slave, two *bahars* of cloves (he sent ten, but the ships could not carry them as they were so heavily laden), and two extremely beautiful dead birds. Those birds are as large as stock-doves, and have a small head and a long beak. Their legs are a span in length and as thin as a reed, and they have no wings, but in their stead long feathers of various colors, like large plumes. Their tail resembles that of a stock-dove. All the rest of the feathers except the wings are of a tawny color. They never fly except when there is wind. The people told us that those birds came from the terrestrial paradise, and they call them *bolon diuata*, that is to say, "birds of God."[333] On that day each one of the kings of Malucca wrote to the king of Spain [to say] that they desired to be always his true subjects. The king of Batjan was about seventy years old. He observed the following custom, namely, whenever he was about to go to war or to undertake any other important thing, he first had it done to him two or three times by one of his servants whom he kept for no other purpose.[334]

[177] One day our king sent to tell our men who were living in the house with the merchandise not to go out of the house by night, because of certain of his men who anoint themselves and roam abroad by night. They appear to follow no leader,[335] and when any of them meets any other man, he touches the latter's hand, and rubs a little of the ointment on him. The man falls sick very soon, and dies within three or four days. When such persons meet three or four together, they do nothing else than to deprive them of their senses. [The king said] that he had had many of them hanged. When those people build a new

house, before they go to dwell there they make a fire round about it and hold many feasts. Then they fasten to the roof of the house a trifle of everything found in the island so that such things may never be wanting to the inhabitants. Ginger is found throughout those islands. We ate it green like bread. Ginger is not a tree, but a small plant which puts forth from the ground certain shoots a span in length, which resembles reeds, and whose leaves resembled those of the reed, except that they are narrower. Those shoots are worthless, but the roots form the ginger. It is not so strong green as dry. Those people dry it in lime, for otherwise it would not keep.

[178] On Wednesday morning, as we desired to depart from Malucca, the king of Tidore, the king of Gilolo, the king of Batjan, and a son of the king of Ternate, all came to accompany us to the island of Mareh. The ship *Victoria* set sail, and stood out a little awaiting the ship *Trinidad*. But the latter not being able to weigh anchor, suddenly began to leak in the bottom. Thereupon, the *Victoria* returned to its anchorage, and we immediately began to lighten the *Trinidad* in order to see whether we could repair it. We heard that the water was rushing in as through a pipe, but we were unable to find where it was coming in. All that day and the next we did nothing but work the pump, but to no avail. When our king heard of it, he came immediately to the ships, and went to considerable trouble in his endeavors to locate the leak. He sent five of his men into the water to see whether they could discover the hole. They remained more than one-half hour under water, but were quite unable to find the leak. The king seeing that he could not help us and that the water was increasing hourly, said almost in tears that he would send to the head of the island for three men, who could remain under water a long time.

[179] Our king came with the three men early on Friday morning. He

immediately sent them into the water with their hair hanging loose so that they could locate the leak by that means. They stayed a full hour under water but were quite unable to locate it. When the king saw that he could be of no assistance, he asked us weeping "who will go to Spain to my sovereign, and give him news of me." We replied to him that the *Victoria* would go there in order not to lose the east winds which were beginning to blow, while the other ship, until being refitted, would await the west winds and would go then to Darien which is located in the other part of the sea in the country of Yucatan.[336] The king told us that he had 225 carpenters who would do all the work, and that he would treat all who remained there as his sons. They would not suffer any fatigue beyond two of them to direct the carpenters in their work. He spoke those words so earnestly that he made us all weep. We of the ship *Victoria*[337] mistrusting that the ship might open, as it was too heavily laden, lightened it of sixty quintals of cloves, which we had carried into the house where the other cloves were. Some of the men of our ship desired to remain there, as they feared that the ship would not last out the voyage to Spain, but much more for fear of dying of hunger.

[180] On the day of St. Thomas, Saturday, December 21, our king came to the ships, and assigned us the two pilots whom we had paid to conduct us out of those islands. They said that it was the proper time to leave then, but as our men [who stayed behind] were writing to Spain, we did not leave until noon. When that hour came, the ships bid one another farewell amid the discharge of the cannon, and it seemed as though they were bewailing their last departure. Our men [who were to remain] accompanied us in their boats a short distance, and then with many tears and embraces we departed. The king's governor accompanied us as far as the island of Mareh. We had no sooner arrived at that island than four praus laden with wood appeared, and in less than one

hour we stowed it aboard the ship and then immediately laid our course toward the southwest. João Carvalho[338] stayed there with fifty-three of our men, while we comprised forty-seven men and thirteen Indians. This island of Tidore has a bishop,[339] and he who then exercised that office had forty wives and a multitude of children.

[181] Throughout those islands of Molucca are found cloves, ginger, sago (which is their wood bread), rice, goats, geese, chickens, coconuts, figs [bananas], almonds larger than ours, sweet and tasty pomegranates, oranges, lemons, potatoes, honey produced by bees as small as ants, which make their honey in the trees, sugarcane, coconut oil, beneseed oil, watermelons, wild cucumbers, gourds, a refreshing fruit as large as cucumbers called *comulicai*,[340] another fruit, like the peach called *guave*,[341] and other kinds of food. One also finds there parrots of various kinds, and among the other varieties, some white ones called *cathara*, and some entirely red called *nori*.[342] One of those red ones is worth one *bahar* of cloves, and that class speaks with greater distinctness than the others. Those Moors have lived in Malucca for about fifty years. Heathens lived there before, but they did not care for the cloves. There are still some of the latter, but they live in the mountains where the cloves grow.

[182] The island of Tidore lies in a latitude of 27 minutes toward the Arctic Pole, and in a longitude of 161 degrees from the line of demarcation. It is 9 and ½ degrees south of the first island of the archipelago called Samar, and extends north by east and south by west. Ternate lies in a latitude of ⅔ of a degree toward the Arctic Pole. Motir lies exactly under the equinoctial line. Makian lies in ¼ of a degree toward the Antarctic Pole, and Batjan also toward the Antarctic Pole in one degree.[343] Ternate, Tidore, Motir, and Makian are four lofty and peaked mountains where the cloves grow. When one is in those four

islands, he cannot see Batjan, but it is larger than any of those four islands. Its clove mountain is not so sharp as the others, but it is larger.

[183] Words of those Moors:[344]

For their God   *Allà*
For Christians   *naceran*
For Turk   *rumno*[345]
For Moor   *isilam*
For Heathen   *Caphre*
For their mosque   *mischit*
For their priests   *maulana catip mudin*
For their wise men   *horan pandita*
For their devout men   *mossai*
For their ceremonies
    zambahe han de alà meschit
For father   *bapa*
For mother   *mama ambui*
For son   *anach*
For brother   *saudala*
For brother of so and so   *capatin muiadi*[346]
For cousin   *saudala sopopu*
For grandfather   *niny*
For father-in-law   *minthua*
For son-in-law   *minanthu*
For man   *horan*
For woman   *poranpoan*
For hair   *lambut*
For head   *capala*
For forehead   *dai*
For eye   *matta*
For eyelashes   *quilai*
For eyelids   *cenin*[347]
For nose   *idon*
For mouth   *mulut*
For lips   *bebere*
For teeth   *gigi*
For gums   *issi*

For tongue   *lada*
For palate   *langhi*
For chin   *aghai*
For beard   *ianghut*
For mustaches   *missai*
For jaw   *pipi*[348]
For ear   *talingha*
For throat   *laher*
For neck   *tundun*
For shoulders   *balachan*[349]
For breast   *dada*
For heart   *atti*
For teat   *sussu*
For stomach   *parut*
For body   *tundunbutu*
For penis   *botto*
For vagina   *bucchij*
For intercourse with women   *amput*
For buttocks   *buri*
For thighs   *taha*
For leg   *mina*
For the shinbone of the leg   *tula*
For its calf   *tilor chaci*[350]
For ankle   *buculali*
For heel   *tumi*
For foot   *batis*
For the sole of the foot   *empachaqui*
For fingernail   *cuchu*
For arm   *langhan*
For elbow   *sichu*
For hand   *tanghan*
For the large finger of the hand (thumb)
    idun tanghan

For the second finger   *tungu*
For the third   *geri*
For the fourth   *mani*
For the fifth   *calinchin*
For rice   *bugax*351
For coconut
   in Malucca and Borneo   *biazzao*
   in Luzon   *mor*
   in Java Major   *calambil*352
For fig [banana]   *pizan*353
For sugarcane   *tubu*354
For potatoes   *gumbili*
For the roots (like turnips)   *ubi*
For jackfruit   *mandicai sicui*355
For cucumbers   *antimon*
For gourd   *labu*356
For cow   *lambu*
For hog   *babi*
For buffalo   *carban*
For sheep   *biri*
For she-goat   *cambin*
For cock   *sambunghan*357
For hen   *aiambatina*
For capon   *gubili*
For egg   *talor*
For gander   *itich*
For goose   *ansa*
For bird   *bolon*
For elephant   *gagia*
For horse   *cuda*
For lion   *huriman*
For deer   *roza*
For dog   *cuiu*358
For bees   *haermadu*
For honey   *gulla*
For wax   *lelin*359
For candle   *dian*
For its wick   *sumbudian*
For fire   *appi*

For smoke   *asap*
For ashes   *abu*
For cooked   *azap*
For well cooked   *lambech*
For water   *tubi*
For gold   *amax*
For silver   *pirac*
For the precious gem   *premata*
For pearl   *mutiara*
For quicksilver   *raza*
For copper [*metalo*]   *tumbaga*
For iron   *baci*
For lead   *tima*
For their metal disks   *agun*360
For cinnabar   *galuga sadalinghan*
For silver   *soliman danas*361
For silk cloth   *cain sutra*
For red cloth   *cain mira*
For black cloth   *cain ytam*
For white cloth   *cain pute*
For green cloth   *cain igao*
For yellow cloth   *cain cunin*
For cap   *cophia*
For knife   *pixao*
For scissors   *guntin*
For mirror   *chiela min*
For comb   *sissir*
For glass bead   *manich*
For bell   *giringirin*
For ring   *sinsin*
For cloves   *ghianche*362
For cinnamon   *cauimanis*
For pepper   *lada*
For long pepper   *sabi*
For nutmeg   *buapala gosoga*
For copper wire   *canot*
For dish   *pinghan*
For earthen pot   *prin*
For pot   *manchu*

For wooden dish   *dulan*
For shell   *calunpan*
For their measures   *socat*
For land   *buchit*
For mainland   *buchit tana*
For mountain   *gonun*
For rock   *batu*
For island   *polan*
For a point of land (a cape)   *taniun buchit*
For river   *songhai*
What is this called?   *apenamaito*[363]
For coconut oil   *mignach*
For beneseed oil   *lana lingha*
For salt   *garan sira*
For musk and its animal   *castori*[364]
For the wood eaten by the *castori*   *comaru*
For leech   *linta*
For civet   *jabat*
For the cat which makes the civet   *mozan*
For rhubarb   *calama*
For demon   *saytan*
For world   *bumi*
For wheat   *gandun*
For to sleep   *tidor*
For mats   *tical*
For cushion   *bantal*
For pain   *sachet*
For health   *bay*[365]
For brush   *cupia*
For fan   *chipas*
For their cloths   *chebun*
For shirts   *bain*
For their chests   *pati alam*[366]
For year   *taun*
For month   *bullan*
For day   *alli*
For night   *mallan*
For afternoon   *malamarj*
For noon   *tambahari*

For morning   *patan patan*[367]
For sun   *matahari*
For moon   *bulan*
For half moon   *tanam patbulan*
For stars   *bintan*
For sky   *languin*
For thunder   *gunthur*
For merchant   *sandagar*
For cities   *naghiri*
For castle   *cuta*
For house   *rinna*
For to sit   *duodo*
Sit down, sir   *duodo orancaia*
Sit down, good fellow
   duodo horanbai et anan
For lord   *tuan*
For boy   *cana cana*
For one of their foster children   *lascar*
For slave   *alipin*
For yes   *ca*
For no   *tida*
For to understand   *thao*
For not to understand   *tida taho*
Do not look at me   *tida liat*
Look at me   *liat*
To be one and the same thing
   casi casi; siama siama
For to kill   *mati*
For to eat   *macan*
For spoon   *sandoch*
For prostitute   *sondal*[368]
For large   *bassal*
For long   *pangian*
For small   *chechil*
For short   *pandac*
For to have   *ada*
For not to have   *tida hada*
Listen, sir   *tuan diam*[369]
Where is the junk going?   *dimana a jun*

For sewing-needle *talun*
For to sew *banan*
For sewing-thread *pintal banan*[370]
For woman's headdress *dastar capala*
For king *raia*
For queen *putli*
For wood *caiu*
For to work *caraiar*
For to take recreation *buandala*
For vein of the arm where one
   is bled *vrat paratanghan*
For the blood that comes from
   the arm *dara carnal*
For good blood *dara*
When they sneeze, they say *ebarasai*[371]
For fish *ycam*
For polypus *calabutan*
For meat *dagin*
For sea-snail *cepot*
Little *serich*
Half *satanha sapanghal*
For cold *dinghin*
For hot *panas*
Far *jan*
For truth *benar*
For lie *dusta*
For to steal *manchiuri*
For scab *codis*
For take *na*
Give to me *ambil*
Fat *gamuch*
Thin *golos*
For hair *tundun capala*
How many? *barapa*
Once *satu chali*
One cubit *dapa*
For to speak *catha*
For here *sivi*
For there *sana datan*

Good day *salamalichum*
For the answer
   [to good day] *alichum salam*
Sirs, may good fortune
   attend you *mali borancaia macan*[372]
I have eaten already *suda macan*
Fellow, get out of the way
   pandan chita horan
For to wake up *banunchan*[373]
Good evening *sabalchaer*[374]
For the answer
   [to good evening] *chaer sandat*
For to give *minta*
To strike someone *bripocol*
For iron fetters *balanghu*
Oh, what a smell *bosso chini*
For young man *horan muda*
For old man *tua*
For scribe *xiritoles*[375]
For writing-paper *cartas*
For to write *mangurat*
For pen *calam*
For ink *dauat*
For ink bottle *padantan*
For letter *surat*
I do not have it *guala*
Come here *camarj*
What do you want? *appa man*
Who sent you? *appa ito*
For seaport *labuan*
For galley *gurap*
For ship *capal*
For the bow *allon*
For the stern *biritan*
For to navigate *belaiar*
For the ship's mast *tian*
For yard [of a ship] *laiar*
For the rigging *tamira*
For sail *leir*

For maintop *sinbulaia*
For the anchor rope *danda*
For anchor *an*
For boat *sanpan*
For oar *daiun*
For mortar [cannon] *badil*
For wind *anghin*
For sea *laut*[376]
Fellow, come here *horan itu datan*
For their daggers *calix golog*
For their dagger hilt *daganan*
For sword *padan gole*
For blowpipe *sumpitan*
For their arrows *damach*
For the poisonous herb *ypu*
For quiver *bolo*
For bow (weapon) *bossor*
For its arrows *anacpaan*
For cats *cochin puchia*
For rat *ticus*
For lizard *buaia*
For shipworms *capan lotos*
For fishhook *matacanir*
For fishbait *un pan*
For fishline *tunda*
For to wash *mandi*
Not to be afraid *tangan tacut*
Fatigue *lala*
A sweet kiss *sadap manis*[377]
For friend *sandara*
For enemy *sanbat*
It is certain *zonghu*
For to barter *biniaga*
I have not *anis*
To be a friend *pugna*
Two things *malupho*
If *oue*
For pimp *zoroan pagnoro*
To give pleasure *mamain*

To be horrified *amala*[378]
For madman *gila*
For interpreter *giorobaza*
How many languages do you
    know? *barapa bahasa tan*
Many *bagna*
For the language of Malacca *chiaramalaiu*
Where is so and so? *dimana horan*
For flag *tonghol*
Now *sacaran*
In the morning *hezoch*
The next day *luza*
Yesterday *calamarj*
For hammer *palmo colbasi*
For nail *pacu*
For mortar *lozon*
For pestle *atan*
For to dance *manarj*
For to pay *baiar*
For to call *panghil*
Unmarried *ugan*
Married *suda babini*
All one *sannia*
For rain *ugian*
For drunken man *moboch*
For skin *culit*
For snake *ullat*
For to fight *guzar*
Sweet *manis*
Bitter *azon*
How are you? *appa giadi*[379]
Well *bay*
Poorly *achet*
Bring me that *biriacan*
This man is lazy *giadi hiat horan itu*
Enough *suda*
    The winds:
For the north *iraga*
For the south *salatan*

For the east   *timor*
For the west   *baratapat*
For the northwest   *utara*
For the southwest   *berdaia*
For the northwest   *barolaut*
For the southeast   *tunghara*
  Numbers: 380
One   *satus*
Two   *dua*
Three   *tiga*
Four   *ampat*
Five   *lima*
Six   *anam*
Seven   *tugu*
Eight   *duolappan*
Nine   *sambilan*
Ten   *sapolo*
Twenty   *duapolo*
Thirty   *tigapolo*
Forty   *ampatpolo*
Fifty   *limapolo*
Sixty   *anampolo*
Seventy   *tuguppolo*
Eighty   *dualapanpolo*
Ninety   *sambilampolo*
One hundred   *saratus*
Two hundred   *duaratus*
Three hundred   *tigaratus*
Four hundred   *anamparatus*
Five hundred   *limaratus*
Six hundred   *anambratus*
Seven hundred   *tugurattus*

Eight hundred   *dualapanratus*
Nine hundred   *sambilanratus*
One thousand   *salibu*
Two thousand   *dualibu*
Three thousand   *tigalibu*
Four thousand   *ampatlibu*
Five thousand   *limalibu*
Six thousand   *anamlibu*
Seven thousand   *tugulibu*
Eight thousand   *dualapanlibu*
Nine thousand   *sanbilanlibu*
Ten thousand   *salacza*
Twenty thousand   *dualacza*
Thirty thousand   *tigalacza*
Forty thousand   *ampatlacza*
Fifty thousand   *limalacza*
Sixty thousand   *anamlacza*
Seventy thousand   *tugulacza*
Eighty thousand   *dualapanlacza*
Ninety thousand   *sambilanlacza*
One hundred thousand   *sacati*
Two hundred thousand   *duacati*
Three hundred thousand   *tigacati*
Four hundred thousand   *ampatcati*
Five hundred thousand   *limacati*
Six hundred thousand   *anamcati*
Seven hundred thousand   *tugucati*
Eight hundred thousand   *dualapancati*
Nine hundred thousand   *sambilancati*
One million [*literally:* ten times
  one hundred thousand]   *sainta*

All the hundreds, the thousands, the tens of thousands, the hundreds of thousands, and the millions are joined with the numbers, *satus* and *dua*, etc.

[*Here follows the chart of Maga, Batutiga, Caphi (Gafi), Sico, Laigoma, Caioian (Kajoa), Giogi (Goraitji?), Labuac (Labuha), Bachiam (Batjan), Tolyman (Tolimau), Tabobi, Latalata and the scroll next to Caphi: "In this island live the Pygmies" (XVIII); and thereafter the chart of the islands of Ambalao (Ambelou), Buru, Tenetum, Lumatola (Lifamatola), Sulach (Sula Besi), and Ambon (Amboina) (XIX)*]

[184] Proceeding on our way we passed amid the islands of Caioan, Laigoma, Sico, Giogi, and Caphi (in the island of Caphi is found a race as small as dwarfs, who are amusing people: these are the pygmies,[381] and they have been subjected by force to our king of Tidore), Laboan, Tolimau, Titameti, Batjan, of which we have already spoken, Latalata, Tabobi, Maga, and Batutiga.[382] Passing outside the latter on its western side, we laid our course west southwest, and discovered many islets toward the south. For this reason the Maluccan pilots told us to change course for we found ourselves among many islands and shoals. We turned our course southeast, and encountered an island which lies in a latitude of two degrees toward the Antarctic Pole, and fifty-five leagues from Malucca, called Sulach.[383] Its inhabitants are heathens, and have no king; they eat human flesh, go naked, both men and women, only wearing a bit of bark two fingers wide before their privies. There are many islands thereabout where they eat human flesh. The names of some of them are as follows: Silan, Noselao, Biga, Atulabaou, Leitimor, Tenetun, Gondia, Pailarurun, Manadan, and Benaia. Then we coasted along two islands called Lamatola and Tenetun, lying about ten leagues from Sulach.[384]

[185] In that same course we encountered a very large island where one finds rice, swine, goats, fowls, coconuts, sugarcane, sago, a food made from one of their varieties of figs called *chanali*, and *chiacare*, which are called *nangha*.[385] *Chiacare* are a fruit resembling the cucumber. They are

knotty on the outside, and inside they have a certain small red fruit like the apricot. It contains no stone, but has instead a marrowy substance resembling a bean but larger. That marrowy substance has a delicate taste like chestnuts. [There is] a fruit like the pineapple. It is yellow outside, and white inside, and when cut it is like a pear, but more tender and much better. Its name is *connilicai*.[386] The inhabitants of that island go naked as do those of Sulach. They are heathens and have no king. That island lies in a latitude of 3 and ½ degrees toward the Antarctic Pole, and is seventy-five leagues from Malucca. Its name is Buru.[387] Ten leagues east of the above island is a large island which is bounded by Gilolo. It is inhabited by Moors and heathens. The Moors live near the sea, and the heathens in the interior. The latter eat human flesh. The products mentioned are produced in that island. It is called Amboina.[388] Between Buru and Amboina are found three islands surrounded by reefs, called Vudia, Cailaruri, and Benaia.[389] Near Buru, and about four leagues to the south, is a small island, called Ambelou.[390]

[*Here follows the chart of Bandan including the islands Bandam, Zoroboa, Samianapi, Chelicel, Pulach (Ai), Lailaca, Puluran (Rhun), Manuca (Manucan), Baracha, Unuveru, Meut, Man, Rosoghin (Rosengain) (XX)*]

[186] About thirty-five leagues to the south by west of the above island of Buru is found Bandan. Bandan consists of twelve islands.[391] Mace and nutmeg grow in six of them. Their names are as follows: Zoroboa, the largest of them all, and the others, Chelicel, Samianapi, Pulae, Pulurun, and Rosoghin. The other six are as follows: Unuveru, Pulaubaracan, Lailaca, Manucan, Man, and Meut. Nutmeg is not found in them, but only sago, rice, coconuts, figs, and other fruits. Those islands are located near one another, and their inhabitants are Moors and they have no king. Bandan lies in a latitude of 6 degrees toward the Antarctic

Pole, and in a longitude of 163 and ½ degrees from the line of demarcation. As it was somewhat outside of our course we did not go there.

[*Here follows the chart of the islands Zolot (Solor), Batuombor, Mallua (Alor), Galiau (Lomblen?), Nocemamor (Nobokamor) (XXI)*]

[187] Leaving the above mentioned island of Buru, and taking the course toward the southwest by west, we reached, [after sailing through] about eight degrees of longitude, three islands, quite near together, called Zolot, Nocemamor, and Galiau.[392] While sailing amid them, we were struck by a fierce storm, which caused us to vow a pilgrimage to Our Lady of Guidance.[393] Running before the storm we landed at a lofty island,[394] but before reaching it we were greatly worn out by the violent gusts of wind that came from the mountains of that island, and the great currents of water. The inhabitants of that island are savage and bestial, and eat human flesh. They have no king, and go naked, wearing only that bark as do the others, except that when they go to fight they wear certain pieces of buffalo hide before, behind, and at the sides, which are ornamented with small shells, boars' tusks, and tails of goat skins fastened before and behind. They wear their hair done up high and held by certain long reed pins which they pass from one side to the other, which keep the hair high. They wear their beards wrapped in leaves and thrust into small bamboo tubes—a ridiculous sight. They are the ugliest people who live in those Indies. Their bows and arrows are of bamboo. They have a kind of a sack made from the leaves of a tree in which their women carry their food and drink. When those people caught sight of us, they came to meet us with bows, but after we had given them some presents, we immediately became their friends.

[188] We remained there fifteen days in order to calk the sides of the ship. In that island are found fowls, goats, coconuts, wax (of which they

gave us fifteen pounds for one pound of old iron), and pepper, both long and round. The long pepper resembles the first blossoms of the hazelnut in winter. Its plant resembles ivy, and it clings to trees as does that plant; but its leaves resemble those of the mulberry. It is called *luli*. The round pepper grows like the former, but in ears like Indian corn, and is shelled off; and it is called *lada*.³⁹⁵ The fields in those regions are full of this [last variety of] pepper, planted to resemble arbors. We captured a man in that place so that he might take us to some island where we could lay in provisions. That island lies in a latitude of 8 and ½ degrees toward the Antarctic Pole, and a longitude of 169 and ⅔ degrees from the line of demarcation; and is called Malua.

[*Here follows the chart of the island of Timor, Botolo, Chendam, Samante, Nossocambu, and capes on Timor including Suai, Lichsana (Líquicá?), Oibich, Canabaza (XXII)*]

[189] Our old pilot from Molucca told us that there was an island nearby called Arucheto,³⁹⁶ the men and women of which are not taller than one cubit, but who have ears as long as themselves. With one of them they make their bed and with the other they cover themselves. They go shaven close and quite naked, run swiftly, and have shrill voices. They live in caves underground, and subsist on fish and a substance which grows between the wood and the bark [of a tree], which is white and round like preserved coriander, which is called *ambulon*. However, we did not go there because of the strong currents of water, and the numerous shoals.

[190] On Saturday, the twenty-fifth of January, 1522, we left the island of Malua.³⁹⁷ On Sunday, the twenty-sixth, we reached a large island³⁹⁸ which lies five leagues to the south southwest of Malua. I went ashore alone to speak to the chief of a city called Amabau³⁹⁹ to ask him

to furnish us with food. He told me that he would give us buffaloes, swine, and goats, but we could not come to terms because he asked many things for one buffalo. Inasmuch as we had but few things, and hunger was constraining us, we held hostage in the ship a chief and his son from another village called Balibo.[400] He for fear lest we kill him, immediately gave us six buffaloes, five goats, and two swine; and to complete the number of ten swine and ten goats [which we had demanded] they gave us one [additional] buffalo. For thus had we placed the condition [of their ransom]. Then we sent them ashore very well contented with linen, Indian cloth of silk and cotton, hatchets, Indian knives, scissors, mirrors, and knives.

[191] That chief to whom I went to talk had only women to serve him. All the women go naked as do the other women [of the islands]. In their ears they wear small earrings of gold, with silk tassels pendant from them. On their arms they wear many gold and brass armlets as far as the elbow. The men go as the women, except that they fasten certain gold articles, round like a trencher, about their necks, and wear bamboo combs adorned with gold rings in their hair. Some of them wear the necks of dried gourds in their ears in place of gold rings.

[192] White sandalwood is found in that island and nowhere else.[401] [There is also] ginger, buffaloes, swine, goats, fowls, rice, figs [bananas], sugarcane, oranges, lemons, wax, almonds, beans, and other things, as well as parrots of various colors. On the other side of the island are four brothers, who are the kings of that island. Where we were, there were towns and some of their chiefs. The names of the four settlements of the kings are as follows: Oibich, Lichsana, Suai, and Cabanaza.[402] Oibich is the largest. There is a quantity of gold found in a mountain in Cabanaza, according to the report given us, and its inhabitants make all their purchases with little bits of gold. All the sandalwood and wax

that is traded by the inhabitants of Java and Malacca is traded for in that region. We found a junk from Luzon[403] there, which had come there to trade in sandalwood. Those people are heathens and when they go to cut the sandalwood, the devil (according to what they told us), appears to them in various forms, and tells them that if they need anything they should ask him for it. They become ill for some days as a result of that apparition. The sandalwood is cut at a certain time of the moon, for otherwise it would not be good. The merchandise valued in exchange for sandalwood there is red cloth, linen, hatchets, iron, and nails.

[193] That island is inhabited in all parts, and extends for a long distance east and west, but is not very broad north and south. It lies in a latitude of 10 degrees toward the Antarctic Pole, and in a longitude of 164 and ½ degrees from the line of demarcation, and is called Timor. The disease of St. Job was to be found in all of the islands which we encountered in that archipelago, but more in that place than in others. It is called *for franchi* that is to say "The Portuguese disease."[404]

[Here follows the chart depicting "Laut chidol, that is, the Great sea." (XXIII)]

[194] A day's journey from there toward the west northwest, we were told that we would find an island where quantities of cinnamon grow, by name Ende.[405] Its inhabitants are heathens, and have no king. [We were told] also that there are many islands in the same course, one following the other, as far as Java Major,[406] and the cape of Malacca. The names of those islands are as follows: Ende, Tanabutun, Crevochile, Bimacore, Aranaran, Main, Sumbawa, Lomboch, Chorum, and Java Major. Those inhabitants do not call it Java but Jaoa. The largest cities are located in Java, and are as follows: Majapahit (when its king was alive, he was the most powerful in all those islands, and his name was Rajah Patiunus); Sunda, where considerable pepper grows; Daha;

Demak; Gaghiamada; Minutaranghan; Japara; Sedan; Tuban; Gresik; Surubaya; and Bali.[407] [We were told] also that Java Minor is the island of Madura, and is located near to Java Major, [being only] one-half league away.

[195] We were told also that when one of the chief men of Java dies, his body is burned. His principal wife adorns herself with garlands of flowers and has herself carried on a chair through the entire village by three or four men. Smiling and consoling her relatives who are weeping, she says: "Do not weep, for I am going to sup with my dear husband this evening, and to sleep with him this night." Then she is carried to the fire, where her husband is being burned. Turning toward her relatives, and again consoling them, she throws herself into the fire, where her husband is being burned. Did she not do that, she would not be considered an honorable woman or a true wife to her dead husband. When the young men of Java are in love with any gentlewoman, they fasten certain little bells between their penis and the foreskin. They take a position under their sweetheart's window, and making a pretense of urinating, and shaking their penis, they make the little bells ring, and continue to ring them until their sweetheart hears the sound. The sweetheart descends immediately, and they take their pleasure; always with those little bells, for their women take great pleasure in hearing those bells ring inside. Those bells are covered, and the more they are covered the louder they sound.[408] Our oldest pilot told us that in an island called Ocoloro, which lies below Java Major, there are found no persons but women, and that they become pregnant from the wind. When they give birth, if the offspring is a male, they kill it, but if it is a female they rear it. If men go to that island, they kill them if they can.[409]

[196] They also told us that a very huge tree is found below Java major toward the north, in the gulf of China (which the ancients call

Sinus Magnus), in which live birds called *garuda*. Those birds are so large that they carry a buffalo or an elephant to the place called *Puzathaer*, where there is a tree called *pam panganghi*, and its fruit *bua panganghi*. The latter is larger than a cucumber. The Moors of Borneo whom we had in our ship told us that they had seen them, for their king had had two of them sent to him from the kingdom of Siam. No junk or other boat can approach to within three or four leagues of the place of the tree, because of the great whirlpools in the water round about it. The first time that anything was learned of that tree was [from] a junk which was driven by the winds into the whirlpool. The junk having been beaten to pieces, all the crew were drowned except a little boy, who, having been tied to a plank, was miraculously driven near that tree. He climbed up into the tree without being discovered, where he hid under the wing of one of those birds. Next day the bird having gone ashore and having seized a buffalo, the boy came out from under the wing as best he could. The story was learned from him, and then the people nearby knew that the fruit which they found in the sea came from that tree.[410]

[197] The cape of Malacca lies in 1 and ½ degrees toward the Antarctic Pole.[411] Along the coast east of that cape are many villages and cities. The names of some of them are as follows: Singapore, which is located on the cape; Panhang; Kuantan; Pattani; Bradlun; Benan; Lagon; Khiri Khan; Chumpon; Pranburi; Cui; Rat Buri; Bangha;[412] Iudia;[413] which is the city where the king of Siam, by name Siri Zacabedera, lives; Iandibum; Lanu; and Langhonpifa.[414] Those cities are built like ours, and are subject to the king of Siam. On the shores of the rivers of that kingdom of Siam, live, as we were told, large birds which will not eat of any dead animal that may have been carried there, unless another bird comes first to eat its heart, after which they

eat it. Next to Siam is found Camogia,[415] whose king is called Saret Zacabedera; then Chiempa,[416] whose king is Rajah Brahaun Maitri. Rhubarb which is found in the following manner grows there. Twenty or twenty-five men assemble and go together into the forests. Upon the approach of night, they climb trees, both to see whether they can catch the scent of the rhubarb, and also for fear of the lions, elephants, and other wild beasts. The wind bears to them the odor of the rhubarb from the direction in which it is to be found. When morning dawns they go in that direction from which the wind has come, and seek the rhubarb until they find it. The rhubarb is a large rotten tree; and unless it has become rotten, it gives off no odor. The best part of that tree is the root, although the wood is also rhubarb which is called *calama*. Next is found Cochi,[417] whose king is called Rajah Seribumnipala.

[198] After that country is found Great China, whose king is the greatest in all the world, and is called Santhoa Rajah.[418] He has seventy crowned kings subject to himself, and some of the latter have ten or fifteen kings subject to them. His port is called Guantau.[419] Among the multitude of other cities, there are two principal ones called Namchin and Comlaha[420] where the above king lives. He keeps four of his principal men near his palace, one toward the west, one toward the east, one toward the south, and one toward the north. Each one of those four men gives audience only to those who come from his own quarter. All the kings and lords of greater and upper India obey that king; and in token that they are his true vassals, each one has an animal which is stronger than the lion, and called *chinga*,[421] carved in marble in the middle of his square. That *chinga* is the seal of the king of China, and all those who go to China must have that animal carved in wax [or] on an elephant's tooth, for otherwise they would not be allowed to enter his harbor. When any lord is disobedient to that king, he is ordered to be flayed, and his skin dried in the sun and salted. Then the skin is stuffed

with straw or other substance, and placed head downward in a prominent place in the square, with the hands clasped above the head, so that
he may be seen then to be performing *zonghu*, that is, obeisance. That
king never allows himself to be seen by anyone. When he wishes to see
his people, he rides about the palace on a skillfully made peacock, a
most elegant contrivance, accompanied by six of his most principal
women clad like himself; after which he enters a serpent called *nagha*,[422]
which is as rich a thing as can be seen, and which is kept in the greatest
court of the palace. The king and the women enter it so that he may
not be recognized among his women. He looks at his people through a
large glass which is in the breast of the serpent. He and the women can
be seen, but one cannot tell which is the king. The latter is married to
his sisters, so that the royal blood may not be mixed with others. Near
his palace are seven encircling walls, and in each of those circular places
are stationed ten thousand men for the guard of the palace [who remain
there] until a bell rings, when ten thousand other men come for each
circular space. They are changed in this manner each day and each
night. Each circle of the wall has a gate. At the first stands a man with a
large hook in his hand, called *satu horan* with *satu bagan;* in the second, a
dog, called *satu hain;* in the third, a man with an iron mace, called *satu
horan* with *ocum becin;* in the fourth, a man with a bow in his hand called
satu horan with *anac panan;* in the fifth, a man with a spear, called *satu horan*
with *tumach;* in the sixth, a lion, called *satu horiman;* in the seventh, two
white elephants, called two *gagia pute.* That palace has seventy-nine halls
which contain only women who serve the king. Torches are always kept
lighted in the palace, and it takes a day to go through it. In the upper
part of it are four halls, where the principal men go sometimes to speak
to the king. One is ornamented with copper, both below and above;
one all with silver; one all with gold; and the fourth with pearls and
precious gems. When the king's vassals take him gold or other precious

things as tribute, they are placed in those halls, and they say: "Let this be for the honor and glory of our Santhoa Rajah." All the above and many other things were told us by a Moor who said that he had seen them.

[199] The inhabitants of China are white and wear clothes. They eat at tables as we do, and have the cross, but it is not known for what purpose. Musk is produced in that country of China. Its animal is a cat like the civet cat. It eats nothing except a sweet wood as thick as the finger, called *chamaru*. When the Chinese wish to make the musk, they attach a leech to the cat, which they leave fastened there, until it is well distended with blood. Then they squeeze the leech out into a dish and put the blood in the sun for four or five days. After that they sprinkle it with urine, and as often as they do that they place it in the sun. Thus it becomes perfect musk. Whoever owns one of those animals has to pay a certain sum to the king. Those grains which seem to be grains of musk are of kid's flesh crushed with a little musk. The real musk is of the aforesaid blood, and if the blood turns into grains, it evaporates. The musk and the cat are called *castori* and the leech *lintha*.

[200] Many peoples are to be found as one follows the coast of that country of China, who are as follows. The Chienchii inhabit islands where pearls and cinnamon grow.[423] The Lechii live on the mainland;[424] above their port stretches a mountain, so that all the junks and ships which desire to enter that port must unstep their masts. The king on the mainland [is called] Moni.[425] He has twenty kings under him and is subordinate to the king of China. His city is called Baranaci. The great Oriental Cataio (Cathay) is located there. Han [is] a cold, lofty island[426] where copper, silver, pearls, and silk are produced, whose king is called Rajah Zotru; Miliaula's king is called Rajah Chetisirimiga; Guio has its king, Rajah Sudacali. All three of the above places are cold and are located on the mainland. Trengganu and Tringano [are] two islands

where pearls, copper, silver, and silk are produced, and whose king is Rajah Rrom. Bassi Bassa [is] on the mainland; and then [follow] two islands, Sumbdit and Pradit,⁴²⁷ which are exceedingly rich in gold, whose inhabitants wear a large gold ring around the legs at the ankle. On the mainland near that point lives a race in some mountains who kill their fathers and mothers as age comes on, so that they may suffer no more pain. All the peoples of those districts are heathens.

[201] On Tuesday night as it drew near Wednesday, the eleventh of February, 1522, we left the island of Timor and took to the great open sea called Laut Chidol.⁴²⁸ Laying our course toward the west southwest, we left the island of Zamatra, formerly called Traprobana,⁴²⁹ to the north on our right hand, for fear of the king of Portugal; [as well as] Pegu, Bengala, Uriza, Chelin where the Malabars live, who are subject to the king of Narsingha, Calicut, subject to the same king, Canbaia, where the Guzerati live, Cananor, Goa, Ormuz, and all the rest of the coast of India Major.⁴³⁰ Six different classes of people inhabit India Major: Nairi, Panichali, Iranai, Pangelini, Macuai, and Poleai. The Nairi are the chiefs; and the Panichali are the townspeople: those two classes of men consort together. The Iranai gather the palm wine and figs. The Pangelini are the sailors. The Macuai are the fishermen. The Poleai are the farmers and harvest the rice. These last always live in the country, although they enter the city at times. When anything is given them it is laid on the ground, and then they take it. When they go through the streets they call out *Po! po! po!* that is "Beware of me!" It happened, as we were told, that a Nair once had the misfortune to be touched by a Polea, for which the Nair immediately had the latter killed so that he might erase that disgrace.

[202] In order that we might double the Cape of Good Hope, we descended to 42 degrees on the side of the Antarctic Pole. We were

nine weeks near that cape with our sails hauled down because we had the west and northwest winds on our bow quarter and because of a most furious storm.[431] That cape lies in a latitude of 24 and ½ degrees, and is 1600 leagues from the cape of Malacca. It is the largest and most dangerous cape in the world. Some of our men, both sick and well, wished to go to a Portuguese settlement called Mozambique, because the ship was leaking badly, because of the severe cold, and especially because we had no other food than rice and water; for as we had no salt, our provisions of meat had putrefied. Some of the others however, more desirous of their honor than of their own life, determined to go to Spain living or dead. Finally by God's help, we doubled that cape on the sixth of May at a distance of five leagues. Had we not approached so closely, we could never have doubled it.

[203] Then we sailed northwest for two months continually without taking on any fresh food or water. Twenty-one men died during that short time. When we cast them into the sea, the Christians went to the bottom face upward, while the Indians always went down face downward. Had not God given us good weather we would all have perished of hunger. Finally, constrained by our great extremity, we went to the islands of Cape Verde.

[204] Wednesday, the ninth of July, we reached one of those islands called Santiago, and immediately sent the boat ashore for food, with the story for the Portuguese that we had lost our foremast under the equinoctial line (although we had lost it upon the Cape of Good Hope), and when we were restepping it, our captain-general had gone to Spain with the other two ships. With those good words and with our merchandise, we got two boatloads of rice. We charged our men when they went ashore in the boat to ask what day it was, and they told us that it was Thursday for the Portuguese. We were greatly surprised for it was Wednesday for us, and we could not see how we had made a

mistake; for as I had always been healthy, I had set down every day without any interruption. However, as was told us later, it was no error, but as the voyage had been made continually toward the west and we had returned to the same place as does the sun, we had made that gain of twenty-four hours, as is clearly seen.[432] The boat having returned to the shore again for rice, thirteen men and the boat were detained, because one of them, as we learned afterward in Spain, told the Portuguese that our captain was dead, as well as others, and that we were not going to Spain. Fearing lest we also be taken prisoners by certain caravels, we hastily departed.[433]

[205] On Saturday, the sixth of September, 1522, we entered the bay of Sanlùcar with only eighteen men and the majority of them sick, all that were left of the sixty men who left Malucca. Some died of hunger; some deserted at the island of Timor; and some were put to death for crimes. From the time we left that bay [of Sanlùcar] until the present day,[434] we had sailed 14,460 leagues, and furthermore had completed the circumnavigation of the world from east to west.

[206] On Monday, the eighth of September, we cast anchor near the quay of Seville, and discharged all our artillery.

[207] Tuesday, we all went in shirts and barefoot, each holding a candle, to visit the shrine of Santa Maria de la Victoria, and that of Santa Maria de Antigua.

[208] Leaving Seville, I went to Valladolid, where I presented to his sacred Majesty, Don Carlo,[435] neither gold nor silver, but things worthy of being very highly esteemed by such a sovereign. Among other things I gave him a book, written by my hand, concerning all the matters that had occurred from day to day during our voyage. I left there as best I could and went to Portugal where I spoke with King Dom João[436] about what I had seen. Passing through Spain, I went to France where I made

a gift of certain things from the other hemisphere to the mother of the most Christian king, Don Francis, Madame the Regent.[437] Then I came to Italy, where I devoted myself forever, and these my poor labors to the famous and most illustrious lord Philippe de Villiers l'Isle-Adam, the most worthy Grand Master of Rhodes.

The Knight
Antonio Pigafetta

NOTES

1   Philippe Villiers de l'Isle-Adam (1464–1534) was the forty-third grand
    master of the Order of the Knights of St. John (called Knights of Malta
    after 1530). Elected grand master of the order on January 22, 1521, Villiers
    de l'Isle-Adam made a heroic but unsuccessful defense of Rhodes against a
    siege by the Magnificent Ottoman Suleiman I. The Grand Master subse-
    quently sought refuge in Italy and in 1524, the order was settled in the city
    of Viterbo by Clement VII. A general chapter of the order was held there
    in June of 1527, when it was decided to accept the island of Malta which
    had been offered by Charles V, a gift which was confirmed by letter-patent
    of Charles V in 1530. For a contemporary account of the siege of Rhodes,
    see "A relation of the siege and taking of the citie of Rhodes ...," an
    English translation from a French original by Sir Thomas Dockwra in
    Hakluyt's *The Principal Navigations*, Glasgow, 1905: vol. V, pp. 1-60.

2   Charles V of Hapsburg, King of Spain from 1516 (Charles I), was emperor
    of the Holy Roman Empire between 1519 and 1556.

3   Francesco Chiericati (1480–1539) was born in Vicenza, the son of Belpietro
    of the Vicentine family of the Chiericati counts and of Mattea Corradi,
    daughter of Andrea Corradi of Austria, a Mantuan noble who was related
    to the Gonzaga. Chiericati's good relations with the Gonzaga and the court
    of Mantua continued throughout his life. Chiericati studied in Padua,
    Bologna and finally Siena where he completed degrees in civil and ecclesias-
    tical law. At Bologna, he enjoyed the protection of Federico Fregoso, arch-
    bishop of Salerno, one of the principal participants in the conversations of
    Baldassar Castiglione's *Il cortegiano*. In 1511, the year Fregoso was killed,
    Chiericati obtained the protection of Sigismondo Gonzaga who was then

papal legate to the Marches, and became an apostolic protonotary. Upon moving to Rome, Chiericati became Latin secretary of Cardinal Matthäus Schiner, and at this time began his diplomatic career. He accompanied Schiner when he was named legate for Lombardy and Germany between January 1512 and the death of Julius II (February 21, 1513). That same year, Chiericati passed into the service of Cardinal Adriano Castellesi, and between 1514 and 1515 he accomplished on his behalf several important diplomatic missions. In his role as secretary to Castellesi, Chiericati was present in December 1515 at the congress of Bologna between Leo X and Francis I, and immediately thereafter obtained the papal ambassadorship to England, which lasted from 1515 to 1517. Upon his return to Rome, Chiericati passed into the service of Cardinal Giulio de' Medici (the future Clement VII), and was sent to Spain in December 1518 on a private mission for Pope Leo X, especially to promote a crusade against the Turks; two years later he went to Portugal as papal ambassador. During the missions in Spain and Portugal, Chiericati became greatly interested in the recent geographical discoveries and the voyage reports which were circulating. His house in Barcelona became a meeting-place where literature and the latest geographical discoveries were discussed. In Zaragoza and Barcelona, Chiericati had come to know Cardinal Florenz, the future pope Adrian VI (1469–1523) who, upon becoming pope on August 31, 1522, immediately named Chiericati bishop of Teramo, in the Abruzzi, and sent him upon his most important mission as ambassador to Germany for the diet of Nuremberg. There he presented the pope's pleas for united action against the Turks and for enforcement of the edict of Worms against Luther. While in Nuremberg he also received copy of Pigafetta's journal which he highly recommended, together with its author, to Isabella d'Este. Under Pope Clement VII, Chiericati's diplomatic role declined, although he took part in embassies to Prussia and Muscovy. He survived the Sack of Rome of 1527 and was sent to collect money from the Italian princes to ransom the pope. In 1536, Chiericati entered the service of Cardinal Ercole Gonzaga, at whose side he passed the last three years of his life. He died December 5, 1539 in Bologna while returning to Mantua. Chiericati's friends and associates included Silvestro Gigli, Egidio Antonini of Viterbo and Paolo Giovio, and he was a correspondent of Erasmus's. See the excellent article on Francesco Chiericati by A. Foa in the *Dizionario biografico degli italiani*, Roma: Istituto della Enciclopedia Italiana, 1960-, vol. XXIV, pp. 674-89.

4 Leo X: Giovanni De' Medici, pope between 1513-1521.

5 The five ships were *Victoria, Santiago, S. Antonio, Concepción,* and *Trinidad.* The *Victoria* was the only one to complete the circumnavigation; the *Santiago* was shipwrecked along the South American coast while searching for the strait (¶32); the *S. Antonio* deserted immediately after the discovery of the strait (¶36), the *Concepción,* following the death of Magellan, was burned by the crew grown to few to man it (¶106); the *Trinidad,* the captain's ship, had to be abandoned in the Moluccas (¶178). The list of the ships and their equipment was published by Navarrete, II, pp. 415-29. The most detailed information on the ships and their equipment is found in J.T. Medina "Los compañeros de Magallanes" in *El descubrimiento del Océano Pacífico: Fernando de Magallanes* (Santiago de Chile: Imprenta Universitaria, 1920; and L. Diaz-Trechuelo "La organización del viaje magallánico: financiación, enganches, acopios y preparativos" in *A viagem de Fernão de Magalhães e a Questão das Molucas: Actas do II Colóquio luso-espanhol de história ultramarina,* Lisboa: Junta de investigacioes cientificas do Ultramar, 1975, pp. 265-314. See also Guillemard, pp. 142-46.

6 Magellan had been decorated with the cross of *comendador* of the Order of Santiago by Charles I in the presence of the royal Council in July, 1518. See Guillemard, p. 114.

7 Chiericati, with Pigafetta in his retinue, followed Charles's court from Zaragoza to Barcelona in January 1519. Pigafetta must have left Barcelona in early May in order to have arrived in Seville three months before Magellan's preparations were completed (August 10).

8 Pope Clement VII: Giulio de' Medici (1478–1534), assumed the papacy November 18, 1523. Pigafetta was summoned to Rome very soon after Clement's election, for he writes to Federico Gonzaga from there February 2, 1524 (see Introduction, p. xix).

9 In the province of Viterbo, twenty-six miles southeast of that city.

10 Of the other captains, Juan de Cartagena (*S. Antonio*), Gaspar Quesada (*Concepción*), and Luis de Mendoza (*Victoria*) were Spanish; only João Serrão

(*Santiago*) was Portuguese. The pilots, whom Pigafetta does not mention, were all Portuguese. Of the expedition's 270-280 men, at least thirty-seven were Portuguese. Peter Martyr observes in his *De orbe novo*: "There exists between the Castilians and the Portuguese an inveterate hatred, and Magellan sought under every pretext and on divers occasions to kill a number of Castilians who refused to obey him" (II, p. 152).

11 The instructions for the conduct of the voyage, from which Pigafetta extracts a few items here, were issued to Magellan in a royal *cedula* of May 8, 1519 and contained 74 articles. See Guillemard, pp. 127-130 for further discussion of these instructions. Ms. fr. 5650 gives a slightly different version of this passage: "Finally, most illustrious Lordship, after all provisions had been made and the ships were in readiness, the captain-general, a wise and virtuous man, and one mindful of his honor, would not commence his voyage without first making some good and suitable rules, such as it is the approved custom to make for those who go to sea, although he did not entirely declare the voyage that he was about to make lest those men, through astonishment and fear, should refuse to accompany him on the so long voyage that he had determined upon. In consideration of the furious and violent storms that reign on the Ocean Sea where he was about to sail, and in consideration of another reason also, namely, that the masters and captains of the other ships in his fleet had no liking for him (the reason for which I know not, unless because he, the captain-general, was a Portuguese, and they Spaniards or Castilians, who have for a long while been biased and ill-disposed toward one another, but who, in spite of that, rendered him obedience), he made his rules such as follow, so that his ships might not go astray and become separated from one another during storms at sea. He published those rules and gave them in writing to every master in the ships and ordered them to be inviolably observed and kept, unless for urgent and legitimate excuse, and the proof that any other action was impossible" (cited from Robertson, Vol. I, p. 202).

12 Spanish for "lantern."

13 From the Spanish *estrenque*, denoting a large rope made from Spanish grass hemp.

14 In ancient military language, the second of the four quarters into which the night was divided (*prima, modorra, modorrilla,* and *alba*) for the changing of the guard.

15 Columns or groups; from the Venetian *colonello.*

16 The French manuscripts include a long explanation of the signals and watches while the Ambrosiana ms. is much abridged. Therefore, at least for this passage, the Italian ms. could not have served as a model for the French versions. The passage from Ms. fr. 5650, which serves to clarify the meaning of the Italian in this case, is as follows: "In addition to the said rules for carrying on the art of navigation as is fitting, and in order to avoid the dangers that may come upon those who do not have watches set, the said captain, who was skilled in the things required and in navigation, ordered three watches to be set. The first was at the beginning of the night; the second at midnight; and the third toward daybreak, which is commonly called the 'diane' [i.e. 'morn'] or otherwise 'the star of dawn.' The above-named watches were changed nightly: that is to say, that he who had stood first watch stood second the day following, while he who had stood second, stood third; and thus did they continue to change nightly. The said captain ordered that his rules, both those of the signals and of the watches, be thoroughly observed, so that their voyage might be made with the greatest of safety. The men of the said fleet were divided into three divisions: the first was that of the captain; the second that of the pilot or boatswain's mate; and the third that of the master. The above rules having been instituted, the captain-general determined to depart, as follows" (cited from from Robertson, vol. I, pp. 203-4). This system of watches, like the division of the crew into three companies was prescribed in rules laid in the *cedula* of May 8, 1519 (see note 11).

17 The stores and equipment carried by the fleet are detailed by Guillemard, pp. 329-336. For crew lists, see Robertson, vol. I, pp. 205-216.

18 The Puerto de las Muelas, in Seville harbor

19 The Roman name for the river, Baetis, was superseded by the Moorish Guadalquivir (Wâd-al-Kebir, the Great River).

20 Coria del Río, on the right bank of the river.

21 The distance given is far too short for the distance between Sanlúcar and Cape St. Vincent, which is over one hundred miles. The source of the error is unknown.

22 Otherwise known as the Fortunate Islands, which Ptolemy had placed at the farthest point west of the inhabited world (cf. Vespucci, *Letters*, pp. 3, 19-20, 46, 59). That Pigafetta makes no mention of their classical denomination, as Vespucci and many other writers of the period typically did, is sign of a relative lack of humanist background and of the vernacular character of Pigafetta's courtly perspective (see note 51).

23 Guillemard conjectures that this is Punta Roxa, located at the south end of Tenerife (p. 148).

24 The first of a series of marvels that make up Pigafetta's account of the passage over. By way of contrast, the first acts of insubordination by Juan de Cartagena (who eventually took part in the mutiny at St. Julian), which occurred during the passage over, go unreported by Pigafetta (for these, see Guillemard, pp. 152-53). The Vicentine instead invokes here one of the classic Atlantic marvels ("Your illustrious Lordship must know"), which had typically served rhetorically to mark the passage from the Old World to the New: the miraculous tree of Hierro. Guillemard notes that "both in Madeira and the Canaries the laurel and other heavy-foliaged evergreens condense abundant water from the daily mists" (p. 149). Nevertheless, the tree's status as a literary topos seems paramount here, also since the expedition did not in fact stop at Hierro. The passage is perhaps best considered alongside other treatments in the tradition, including those of Niccolò Scillacio, Peter Martyr, Bartolomè de Las Casas, Fernandez de Oviedo, and especially Girolamo Benzoni's, which was illustrated by a noteworthy engraving by Theodor de Bry in his *Historia Americae*.

25 A somewhat gratuitous jab at the ancients? Although Amoretti suggests that the ancients believed that it never rained in the Tropics, which rendered them uninhabitable (p. 12). The Yale Beinecke ms. differs, and presents an explanatory gloss: "Which was a thing very strange and uncommon, in the

opinion of the old people and of those who had sailed there several times before" (Skelton, p. 41).

26 Following the African coast south and southeast, from the Canaries to Sierra Leone, Magellan took sixty days to reach the equator. He was delayed by the equatorial calms in the doldrums. Why Magellan did not sail southwest from the Canaries, as was the usual route, has been the subject of much speculation. The most plausible explanation is that Magellan was seeking to avoid Portuguese convoys he might have encountered by following the normal route to Brazil. This variation in the route was responsible for the first friction between Magellan and his Spanish captains, particularly Juan de Cartagena, captain of the *S. Antonio* who challenged Magellan and demanded a council. Magellan answered simply that he should follow the flagship.

27 Sharks. From the Spanish *tiburón*.

28 St. Elmo's fire is the popular name for the atmospheric electricity that gathers in the form of a star or brush about the masthead of ships and on the rigging. St. Elmo is the Spanish form of the name of St. Erasmus, bishop of Formiae, in Campagna who was widely venerated as the patron of sailors on the Mediterranean. The phenomenon is also called fire of "St. Elias," "St. Clara," "St, Nicolas," and "composite," "composant," and "corposant" (i.e., *corpus sanctum*). The phenomenon is a recurring theme in Pigafetta's narrative (cf. ¶13, ¶24, ¶113, ¶133) and may represent a Rhodian motif deriving from earlier sailing experience on the part of Pigafetta. The Knights of Rhodes had forts in both Rhodes and eventually in Malta named for St. Elmo.

29 The Yale Beinecke ms. adds, (most likely an interpolated gloss, since the Ambrosiana ms. has quite a different rhetorical effect): "Be it noted that, whenever this fire which represents the said St. Anselm appears and descends on a ship (which is in a storm at sea), the ship never perishes" (Skelton, p. 42).

30 The stormy petrel (*Hydrobates pelagicus*) which is found along all the Atlantic coasts and on some of the Pacific. The tale was current among sailors according to Robertson who cites other sources (Vol. I, p. 220).

31 *Stercorarius parasiticus*, called also the jaeger, and by sailors "boatswain," "teaser," and "dung-hunter." The last name derived from the belief that the bird fed on the dung of gulls and terns, when in reality it pursues the latter birds and compels them to disgorge the fish they have swallowed.

32 The flying-fish is either a species of *Exocoetus*, or the *Scomberesox saurus* of Europe and America, both of which feed in large schools and jump from the water to escape their enemies. The theme of so many birds gathered as to seem an island is yet another topos of travel narratives of the period.

33 Brazil. *Verzino* (from the Arabic *wars*) is the Italian name for brazilwood (*Cesalpina sappan*); the Spanish and Portuguese form *brasil*, deriving from *brasa*, meaning "live coals" and reflecting the color of this valuable dye-wood, led to the name of the country: Brazil.

34 The sense, here corrupted, is presumably: "Verzin extends southward to 23 and ½ degrees south."

35 At 8° and 21′ south latitude, the most eastern headland of South America, now Capo Branco, to the north of Recife.

36 The pineapple.

37 The tapir, according to most authorities, including M. D. Busnelli, "Per una lettura del *Primo viaggio intorno al mondo di Antonio Pigafetta*" in *Studi di lessicografia italiana*, IV, 1982, p. 25. *Anta* was a Spanish term from the arabic which indicated a species of African antelope (see R. Dozy, *Glossaire des mots espagnols et portugais dérivés de l'arabe*, Leyde: E.J. Brill, 1969, p. 195). I.L. Caraci-M. Pozzi observe however that the term might refer here to the guanaco since Albo calls animals clearly identifiable as guanacos "*antas*" (*Scopritori e viaggiatori*, cit., p. 532).

38 A common rhetorical motif in Vespucci: ". . . and if I am prolix, I beg your pardon" (*Letters*, cit., "Soderini Letter," p. 58].

39 Ms. fr. 5650 reads: "And for a king of cards, of the kind which are used to play with in Italy, they gave me five fowls." The four suits of Italian

NOTES

playing cards are called *spade* ("swords"), *bastoni* ("clubs"), *danari* (literally: "money": translated here "diamonds"), and *coppe* ("cups").

40 This is the common americanist theme of the unequal exchange, as Columbus first reported in the "Letter Announcing the Discovery": "so it was found that a sailor for a strap received gold to the weight of two and a half *castellanos*" (p. 8). The motif of the Indian who thinks he got the better of the deal is Vespuccian: "And when I gave a bell to an Indian, he gave me 157 pearls, later valued at a thousand ducats, and do not suppose he deemed this a poor sale, because the moment he had the bell he put it in his mouth and went off into the forest, and I never saw him again: I think he feared that I might change my mind..." (*Letters*, Ridolfi Fragment, p. 43).

41 Landfall was made November 29; they coasted southwest past Cape Frio and entered the harbor of Rio de Janeiro on St. Lucy's day, December 13, 1519, naming it after the saint. The name Rio de Janeiro probably derives from the expedition of Vespucci who arrived there in January of 1502.

42 Cf. Columbus's "Letter Announcing the Discovery": " . . . as a result of that voyage, I can say that this island is larger than England and Scotland together . . ." (p. 12).

43 Manuel I (1495–1521). The Portuguese Pedro Alvarez Cabral reached the coast of Brazil in 1500. By the Treaty of Tordesillas (1494), Brazil belonged to Portugal. See other narratives of Brazil antecedent to Pigafetta's including those of Vespucci, Vaz de Caminha, and Giovanni da Empoli. According to Guillemard: "It is unnecessary to dwell on Pigafetta's evidently hearsay or borrowed account of the Indians and their customs" (p. 154). Indeed, even a cursory consideration of Vaz de Caminha's account of his encounters with the Guaraní Indians, when compared with Pigafetta's, is enough to reveal the stereotypical character of the latter. For an exemplary reading of Vaz de Caminha's narrative, see Valeria Bertolucci Pizzorusso "Uno spettacolo per il Re: l'infanzia di Adamo nella 'Carta' di Pero Vaz de Caminha" in *Quaderni Portoghesi*, 4 (1978), pp. 49-81.

44 Cf. Vespucci: "They are people who live many years. . . . And I found one of the oldest men who by such stone signs explained to me that he had

lived seventeen hundred lunar months, which by my reckoning must be 132 years, counting thirteen moons for every year" (*Letters* [Lisbon, 1502], p. 33).

45 Cf. Peter Martyr: "Thus they call the heavens *tueri*, a house *boa*, gold *cauni*" (I, p. 66). The index to Ramusio includes an entry for "Boia an Indian word which means house among the inhabitants of the island of Juana" (vol. III, p. 5). Columbus had misunderstood *bohío* to be the name of Haiti, "when it was really, as Las Casas explains, the Arawak word for 'house' or 'home'; the palm-thatched huts of the peasantry are still called *bohíos* in Cuba" (Morison, *Admiral of the Ocean Sea*, Boston, 1942, p. 250). In any case, the word emerges from the earliest narratives and appears to be more frequently associated with the islands than with the mainland as here.

46 The hanging beds or hammocks of the Arawaks are described repeatedly in the early narratives, for example, by Columbus (*Diario*: Wednesday, October 17, and Saturday, November 13): "That day many dugouts or canoes came to the ships to trade things of cotton thread and the nets in which they slept, which are hammocks" (p. 131). The use of the word here is probably a gloss added by Las Casas. Peter Martyr, and Vespucci describe the hammock but never use the Indian term; Skelton claims that "the word was introduced into European languages by the records of this voyage" (p. 152). Pigafetta's use of the word may well be the first in an Italian text.

47 Skelton calls this "[a]nother word brought back to Europe by Magellan's men" (p. 142), but the word had been appearing since Columbus's "Letter Announcing the Discovery": "In all the island they have very many canoes..." (p. 10). It is reported in Peter Martyr, Michele de Cuneo, Vespucci, and was a stereotypical americanist theme by the time Pigafetta wrote. The origin for the Spanish *canoa* was the Arawak *kanawa*. See Formisano's observations in the glossary of Vespucci's *Lettere* (p. 230) and Gianfranco Folena, "Le prime immagini dell'America nel vocabolario italiano," in *Bolletino dell'Atlante Linguistico Mediterraneo*, XIII-XV (1971-73), pp. 673-92.

48 The Italian reads *d'uno solo arburo ma schize*. "*Schize*" in the Venetian dialect means flattened or crushed. Robertson had read and translated *maschize* as one word, that is as *massiccio* or massive, huge.

49 Cf. Giuliano Dati's *L'inventione delle nuove insule di Channaria indiane* (ed. T.J. Cachey, Jr. and L. Formisano, Chicago: The Newberry Library, 1989): "These people go from one island to another in certain boats found on this island, made of a single tree-trunk, which are called canoes. They are long and narrow, and seem almost to fly to whoever is placed within them, although they are crudely crafted; they are dug out with stones, sticks and bones" (octave LI, p. 26). The detail concerning the method of manufacture of the canoes ("dug out with stones") in Dati's poetic rendering of the Columbus "Letter Announcing the Discovery" derived from a version of that letter since lost.

50 Cf. Columbus's *Diario* (Saturday, October 13): "They row with a paddle like that of a baker and go marvelously" (p. 69).

51 A. Gerbi observes: "The apparently classical reference is deceptive, as Pigafetta doubtless had in mind the 'people covered in mud, there in the swamp, all naked and with anger in their faces,' that Dante saw where the gloomy stream of Hell 'forms a marsh, whose name is Styx' (*Inf.*, VII, 106-12). Pigafetta was certainly not familiar with the Greek and Latin texts." (*Nature in the New World*, p. 106).

52 Among the most vivid early explanations of cannibalism according to the revenge thesis (as opposed to the innate aggression, ritual, or materialist, i.e. consumption of protein theses). The revenge explanation, later popularized by Hans Staden's narrative (1557) of his capture by the cannibals (*The Captivity of Hans Stade*, p. 151, pp. 155-59), had already been suggested by Vespucci who describes vengeful ritualized cannibal killing, and concludes: "When we asked them to tell us the cause, the only reason they could give was that this curse had begun 'in olden times,' and that they wish to avenge the death of their ancestors: in sum, a bestial thing; and certainly one of their men confessed to me that he had eaten of the flesh of more than two hundred bodies . . ." (*Letters*, [III, Lisbon, 1502], pp. 33-34). For discussion and bibliography on the truth value and ideological implications of European reports of Caribbean cannibalism, see P. Hulme's *Colonial Encounters: Europe and the native Caribbean, 1492-1797*, especially "Columbus and the cannibals," London: Methuen, 1986, pp. 14-43.

53 Smoked human flesh was by this time a commonplace of European accounts of cannibalism: ". . . in their houses we found human flesh hung up for smoking, and alot of it . . ." (Vespucci, *Letters*, III [Lisbon, 1502], p. 33).

54 João Lopes Carvalho was pilot of the *Concepción* upon departure, and following the fatal banquet in the island of Cebu, became pilot of the *Trinidad*. He had piloted the Portuguese ship *Bretoa* to Brazil in 1511. His four years in Brazil seem unrecorded except by Pigafetta who refers later to Carvalho's son, by a Brazilian woman, who was serving in the fleet and made prisoner in Borneo (¶122). Carvalho died on Tidore, February 14, 1522.

55 *Cacique* originally enters the European languages through the reports of the Caribbean explorations and discoveries, beginning with Columbus (glossed by Las Casas here): ". . . they went ahead to give the news to the 'cacique,' as they call them there. Up to that time the admiral had not been able to understand whether by this they meant 'king' or 'governor.' They use also another name for a 'grandee,' whom they call 'nitayno'; he did not know if by this they mean 'hildago' or 'governor' or 'judge'" (Sunday, December 23; *Diario*, p. 271).

56 The Italian reads *gatti maimoni picoli*, as in Marco Polo and Vespucci (see Vespucci's *Lettere*, "Glossario": *mamoni*, p. 242). In both Polo and Vespucci, the term seems to refer to monkeys of large dimensions. Robertson observes that monkeys of the genus *Cebus* are probably intended here.

57 Often identified by editors (Robertson, Skelton) as manioc or cassava, from the root of which bread is made in Brazil. More likely, however, is M. Masoero's identification of it as sago, derived from a kind of palm plant.

58 Tayasu or peccari (*Dicotyles torquatus*), which has quills resembling those of the porcupine, and is generally of a whitish color. It is tailless and very fierce and difficult to domesticate. The flesh was eaten; and the teeth were worn by some of the chiefs as necklaces. See Hans Staden's *The Captivity*, p. 160, and note. What Pigafetta refers to as "their navels" is a large gland located on their backs which secretes an oily liquid.

59 The roseate spoonbill (*Ajaia ajaja*).

60 Great "virtue" among married women and great sexual freedom with regard to virgins is often commented upon in the travel narratives. Amoretti recalls that Cook finds the same throughout the South Sea Islands. For these eighteenth century treatment of this topos see Gerbi, *The Dispute*, pp. 146-47.

61 The jealousy of Amerindian men for their women is a recurring theme, for example in Vespucci (*Letters* [Lisbon, 1502], p. 32) and Verrazzano: "They are very careful with them [their womenfolk], for when they come aboard and stay a long time, they make the women wait in the boats; and however many entreaties we made or offers of various gifts, we could not persuade them to let the women come on board ship" (*Verrazzano*, p. 138). The natives' love for their wives is also an important theme in the encounter with the Patagonian giants below (€29), one which Montaigne would develop in his famous essay "On the Cannibals": "He [one of their elders] preaches two things only: bravery before their enemies and love for their wives. They never fail to stress this second duty . . ." (*The Essays of Michel De Montaigne*, Tr. and Ed. M.A. Screech, London: Penguin, p. 234.)

62 Cf. Verrazzano: ". . . for they are easily persuaded, and they imitated everything that they saw us Christians do with regard to divine worship, with the same fervor and enthusiasm that we had" (p. 141).

63 The Beinecke ms. interjects here: "Which was a great simplicity." This paragraph is generally characterized by classic Columbian motifs: the supposed Amerindian belief that the Europeans had come from heaven, as well as the classic Columbian terms of exchange, i.e. brazilwood (resources) freely given in trade for Christian religion.

64 Another putative example of Amerindian ingenuousness. The Beinecke ms. in fact introduces this sentence with the following: "Besides the above-mentioned things (betraying their simplicity) the people of the place showed us another very simple thing" (Skelton, p. 45). For interesting observations regarding this particular moment of cross-cultural encounter/projection in a contemporary literary context, see H.E. Robles, "The First Voyage Around the World: From Pigafetta to García Márquez," *History of European Ideas*, vol. 6, No. 4, 1985: pp. 385-404, especially pp. 397-98.

65 The Italian reads *"per trovare alguno recapito"* with *recapito* signifying hospitality or collocation, but here with sexual overtones. In fact, the *Grande dizionario della lingua italiana* (Torino: UTET, 1961-), for the word *recapito* gives under definition no. 8 (vol. XV, p. 623), the woman's collocation or reception in a house of prostitution, and cites A. Firenzuola, "Io medesimo, che ho la pratica già più tempo fa di certi ruffiani, vedrò di darle [alla ragazza] buonissimo recapito" [I myself, who have frequented for some time certain pimps, will see that the girl is given an excellent reception].

66 A unique contribution to the theme of the marvelous sexual appetite of Amerindian women, a topic which elicited both great interest and anxiety in European readership. Indeed, the Amerindian woman's sexual insatiability could sometimes lead to castration, (as described in Vespucci's "Mundus Novus," *Letters*, p, 49) and even death (see Gerbi who cites episodes from Oviedo in *Nature in the New World*, pp. 350-51).

67 This is the first of four word lists which Pigafetta provides as a part of his narrative. The lists get progressively longer, from this one of eight words to the last including 450 words. These word lists report respectively on the languages of the four major groups of indigenous peoples encountered by the expedition, that is, the Guaraní of the "Land of Verzin" (Brazil), the Patagonian Giants or Tehuelches (¶39), the people of the Philippine islands (¶105), and those of the Moluccas (¶183).

68 Brazil had been discovered twenty years by the time of Magellan's voyage: "It is remarkable that none of the historians of the voyage mention the presence of Portuguese in Rio de Janeiro, although there is every probability that some may have been there at the time, since a trading station had been established in the bay some years before" (Guillemard, p. 155).

69 Rio de la Plata. Magellan left Rio de Janeiro December 26, proceeding to Cape Santa Maria and the river which was called St. Christopher. There they remained until February 2, 1520.

70 Presumably Pigafetta refers here to Indians of the Tehuelche tribe. The name is of Arawak origin and means "man of the south." Pigafetta says they are called Cannibals *"omini che se chiamano Canibali,"* which could be

interpreted: "men who call themselves Cannibals." Pigafetta does not characterize the nature of their cannibalism, other than to say—as he did with
the Brazilians, whom he did not term cannibals—that they eat human flesh.

71 An earlier encounter with giants in these parts is given in Peter Martyr's
account of Vincent Yañez Pinzon's 1499 to the New World (I, 9). The
Indians are described there as "larger than Germans or Hungarians . . . a
vagabond race similar to the Scythians, who had no fixed abode but wandered with their wives and children. . . .They swear that the footprints
left upon the sand show them to have feet twice as large as those of a
medium-sized man" (*De orbe novo*, I, pp. 160-61). See also Vespucci's famous
encounters with giants (*Letters*, I, pp. 12-13): "each one of them was taller
kneeling than I am standing"; and "Soderini Letter," pp. 82-84. A. Gerbi
observes that the existence or nonexistence of giants was to become one
of the most characteristic arguments in the discussion of the nature and
properties of the New World, and that it was in Pigafetta that Europe
first made the acquaintance of American giants, and especially the
Patagonians (see below) who were to enjoy such success from Tasso to
Vico. See Gerbi, *The Dispute of the New World*, pp. 82-86. And for theme of
giants in the European imagination, see W. Stephens *Giants in Those Days:
Folklore, Ancient History, and Nationalism*, Lincoln: University of Nebraska
Press, 1989.

72 *Mare de Sur* is the name Vasco Nuñez de Balboa gave to the Pacific when he
first sighted it on 25 September, 1513. The name "Pacific" was given by
Magellan (see below at ¶ 42).

73 The name Santa Maria was transferred from the cape (still so called), on
which it had been bestowed by Juan de Solis in 1515, to the estuary of the
Rio de la Plata. (The Genoese pilot however says that Magellan gave the
estuary the name Rio de San Christoval, which is found in contemporary
world maps.) In any case, Pigafetta simplifies events here. Magellan spent
two days sailing up the estuary and six days at anchor in it, before resuming
the voyage southward on February 2, 1520.

74 Juan Diaz de Solis, born in 1470, is said to have discovered Yucatan with
Pinzon in 1506. He was appointed chief pilot of Spain after the death of

Amerigo Vespucci in 1512. He discovered and explored the Rio de la Plata where he and some of his men were killed and eaten in September, 1516. Maximilian Transylvanus also recalls his death at this point in his narrative: "Here Juan Ruy Diaz Solis had been eaten, with some of his companions, by the anthropophagi, whom the Indians call cannibals, whilst, by order of Ferdinand the Catholic, he was exploring the coast of this continent with a fleet" (p. 188). Cannibals feasting upon Europeans along these shores (with Solis and later Verrazzano, the most famous victims) had become a common theme since the episode described in Vespucci's Soderini letter: ". . . the women were already hacking the Christian up into pieces, and, in a great fire they had built, were roasting him before our eyes . . ." (*Letters*, p. 89).

75 The seawolves were probably some species of the *Otariidae* or fur-seals (Guillemard, p. 160). The "geese" were penguins. According to Robertson, this bay where the ships were laden with seals was probably Puerto Deseado (at 47° 46′ S).

76 St. Nicholas of Bari, also known as Sant Nikolass: St. Nicholas of Asia Minor (d. c. 345) venerated in the East and in the Northern countries where he is known by the name of Santa Claus. Among his miracles was the salvation of some sailors in a storm. St. Clare of Assisi (1194–1253), St. Francis's collaborator and founder of the Poor Clares, was considered a patroness of sailors due to an incident at the end of her life when she miraculously repulsed an attack of Saracens upon a monastery. For St. Elmo, see note 28.

77 Pigafetta does not mention the exploration of the Gulf of San Matias, on February 24, "to see if there was any outlet to Malucca" (Genoese pilot).

78 Port St. Julian. The Genoese pilot says that they reached it on March 31, 1520, and places it in 49° 20′ S (in reality, at 49° 30′). The fleet would remain there until August 24. It was here that the mutiny, which Pigafetta touches on only briefly in ¶31, broke out. For a fuller account of the mutiny see Guillemard, pp. 162-74.

79 Regarding these American giants, see note 71. Albo, who gives an account of these Indians makes no note of their gigantic size: "Many Indians came

there, who dress in certain skins of the *anta*, which resemble camels without the hump. They have certain bows made from cane, which are very small and resemble turkish bows. The arrows also resemble Turkish arrows, and are tipped with flint instead of iron. Those Indians are very prudent, swift-runners, and very well-built and well-appearing men" (Albo, p. 218). Maximilian Transylvanus on the other hand reports that they were "ten spans tall," that is, about seven feet six inches.

80 The guanaco (*lama guanicos*) is a species of lama.

81 Cf. Vespucci, *Letters*, "Soderini Letter," p. 81 and note 36 for analogous description of indigenous use of this white powder which Oviedo reports "the Indians of Nicaragua call *yaat*, that in the jurisdiction of Venezuela is called *hado*, and in Peru *coca*..." (*Historia general y natural* IV, p. 179).

82 An ancient measure of length equivalent to between eighteen and twenty-one inches.

83 A Tehuelche word, which Shakespeare puts twice in Caliban's mouth (*The Tempest*, I.ii and V.i), and which he got from Richard Eden's translation of Pigafetta in *The Decades of the newe worlde* (1555).

84 Identified by Guillemard as Diego de Barrasa, man-at-arms of the *Trinidad* (p. 184).

85 "Herrera's account of the intercourse of the Spaniard and Patagonians differs widely from the above in certain points. He relates the first meeting differently, describes the death of Diego de Barrasa as occurring in a chance *recontre* with the natives, and records the despatch of a punitive expedition of twenty men as a sequel, adding that not one of the enemy was encountered (Dec. ii., lib. ix., caps. xiii.-xv.). Transylvanus gives a lengthy description of a visit of seven men of the fleet to a Patagonian hut some distance onland, followed by an attempt to capture three of the savages. . . . Neither of these accounts, it should be remembered, are first hand" (Guillemard, p. 185).

86 Pigafetta and Transylvanus both mention this story, and Oviedo borrows it from them. Transylvanus recounts it not as for medicinal purposes but as

part of the natives' welcoming ceremonies: "When some of our men showed them bells and pictures painted on paper, they began a hoarse chant and an unintelligible song, dancing round our men, and, in order to astonish them, they passed arrows a cubit and a half long down their throats to the bottom of their stomachs, and without being sick. And forthwith drawing them out again, they seemed to rejoice greatly, as having shown their bravery by this exploit" (p. 190).

87 Skelton observes that the name bestowed by Magellan exists, with the sense of "dogs with large paws," in various romance languages: Spanish *patacones*, Portuguese *patas de cao*, French *patauds*" (p. 154). And the opinion that the name *Patagoni* was given by Magellan to these people because of their abnormal feet goes back to the first historians of the Spanish conquests Oviedo and Gòmara. But technically speaking, the term *patagòn* for "big foot" is not found in Spanish or Portuguese. M. R. Lida de Malkiel has suggested a literary source for the name in the anonymous Spanish chivalric poem *Primaleòn* (*princeps* at Salamanca, 1512) which was reprinted numerous times throughout Europe. In canto XXX the hero Primaleòn encounters barbarous people on an island including a particularly monstrous individual named Patagone. See M.R. Lida de Makiel "Para la toponomia argentina: Patagonia" in *Hispanic Review*, vol. XX, 1952 pp. 321-23. See also B. Chatwin *In Patagonia*, New York: Summit Books, 1977 pp. 89-91.

88 From March 30 to August 24, 1520.

89 Pigafetta addresses here directly his patron again (cf. (10) Philippe Villiers de l'Isle-Adam.

90 Padre Sanchez de la Reina.

91 Juan de Cartagena had been captain of the *S. Antonio* but had been relieved of his command for insubordination before crossing the Equator (see above, note 24). The command was initially given to Antonio de Coca *contador* of the fleet but at Port St. Julian the latter was replaced by Alvaro de Mesquita, a Portuguese and Magellan's cousin. This seems to have sparked off the conspiracy on the night of April 1-2 when the mutineers, led by

Juan de Cartagena, Juan Sebastian de Elcano, Gaspar Quesada and Luis de
Mendoza made themselves masters of the three largest ships. On the combination of stratagem and force by which Magellan reasserted his authority,
Pigafetta says nothing. The details are known from documents collected in
Navarrete (vol. IV, pp. 528-32; with partial translation in Robertson, vol. I,
pp. 230-34): "Magallanes, believing that boldness was more useful than
meekness in the face of such actions, determined to employ craft and force
together. He kept the small boat of the ship *S. Antonio* which was used for
those negotiations, at his ship; and sent the alguacil, Gonzalo Gomez de
Espinosa, in the skiff belonging to his ship, to the *Victoria*, with six men
armed secretly and a letter for the treasurer, Luis de Mendoza, in which he
told the latter to come to the flagship. While the treasurer was reading the
letter and smiling as if to say 'You don't catch me that way,' Espinosa
stabbed him in the throat, while another sailor stabbed him at the same
instant on the head so that he fell dead..." (Robertson, vol. I, p. 232). See
Guillemard, pp. 162-174, for a synthetic account. It is remarkable that
Pigafetta gives such a brief version of the mutiny at Port St. Julian. An
account which is, for Guillemard was also "remarkable for its extraordinary
inaccuracy." The Ambrosiana ms. says that it was Cartagena who was executed and quartered while Quesada was marooned when in fact it was the
opposite. But the French manuscripts get this last point right; see the
Beinecke ms.: "This Gasapar Quesada had his head cut off, and then he
was quartered. And the overseer Juan de Cartagena, who several days later
tried to commit treachery, was banished with a priest, and put in exile on
that land named *Patagoni*" (p. 50). Peter Martyr observes: "It was during
this period that Magellan treated the captain Juan Carthagena so severely.
He was a friend of the Bishop of Burgos who had been assigned to
Magellan, with royal approval, as his associate, and named second in command of the expedition. Under pretext of a plot formed against his life,
Magellan put him ashore in company with a priest, giving them only a little
biscuit and a sword. He would gladly have punished their plot with death,
but that he feared the resentment of the Spaniards against him and did not
dare to assume the responsibility. This action has been represented in different lights; but the description of other events is in agreement. According
to some, Magellan was within his rights in thus acting, while according to
others he was not, and the severity he showed was merely the outcome of
the ancient hatred existing between the Spaniards and the Portuguese"

(*De orbe novo,* p. 154). Transylvanus observes that Magellan "punished the men, but rather more harshly than was proper for a foreigner, especially when commanding in a distant country" (p. 194), and also gives a rather full account of the discussions between Magellan and his crew about whether to turn back which preceded the mutiny (pp. 192-94).

92 This account of the shipwreck and rescue is very inadequate. Herrera has the fullest account (Dec. ii., lib. ix., cap. xiii; pp. 295-97); and see Guillemard, pp. 175-79. One man was lost, namely, the negro slave of the captain João Serrão (who had been appointed captain of the *Santiago* after the mutiny). Brito (Navarrete, vol. IV, p. 307) says: "After this [i.e., the mutiny], they wintered for three months; and Magallanes again ordered the ship 'Santiago' to go ahead in order to explore. The ship was wrecked but all of its crew were saved." Like Herrera, Peter Martyr (p. 155) speaks of a storm as being responsible for the wreck, as do Transylvanus and Oviedo.

93 From the Spanish *mejillòn,* a variety of cockle, which was probably the *Mytilus* or the common mussel.

94 The *Rio di Santa Cruz,* discovered May 3, 1520 by João Serrão during the *Santiago*'s exploration.

95 Between September 14 and October 18, 1520.

96 Da Mosto identified this fish as the *Eleginus maclovinus.*

97 Cabo Virjenes, in 52°20′ S, marking the eastern end of the Strait of Magellan, discovered October 21, 1520.

98 *Proise* in the Italian here, derives from an ancient Catalonian word meaning the "bow moorings." According to Robertson, the old Spanish word is *proís* which signifies both the thing to which the ship is moored ashore, and the rope by which it is moored to the shore (vol. I, p. 236).

99 In contrast to Pigafetta, Peter Martyr diminishes Magellan's accomplishment: "At this point we must turn back somewhat in our history. During his childhood, Magellan had vaguely heard discussed in Portugal the existence

of a strait, whose entrance was difficult to find. He was therefore ignorant of what direction to take but chance served him where his knowledge failed. There arose a tempest. . . . While searching a shelter, one of the ships of least draught was driven by force of the waves very close to the shore. A narrow channel was discovered. . . . The ship returned announcing the passage was found" (*De orbe novo*, p. 155).

[100] Martin Behaim (1459–1506) was a draper in Flanders (1477–1479) after which he went to Lisbon where he became acquainted with Columbus. In 1484 he was chosen geographer of Diego Cam's expedition to Western Africa. On his return he received the knighthood in the military order of Christ of Portugal. Later he lived on the island of Fayal in the Azores. In 1491 he returned to Germany, where he lived at Nuremberg until 1493; there he constructed his famous globe (see E.G. Ravenstein, *Martin Behaim His Life and His Globe*, London, 1908). In 1493 he returned to Lisbon and in 1494 to Fayal, where he remained until 1506 when he went to Lisbon. Many myths sprung up about him, such that he had visited America before Columbus and the straits of Magellan before Magellan, whom he might have known at Lisbon. See Guillemard for a discussion of knowledge about the existence of a strait prior to Magellan's discovery (pp. 189-98). Guillemard observes that "In the *capitulacion* granted by the King to Magellan and Faleiro on 22 March, 1518, the phrase "para buscar el estrecho de aquellas mares"—to go in search of the strait—is used, and it would seem from the use of the definite article as if some actual known or rumored strait was intended" (p. 191). On Magellan and Behaim's map see also Morison, *The Southern Navigations*, pp. 381-82. Skelton writes that Behaim was unlikely to have made any map showing the antarctic strait but notes that "On Schöner's globe of 1515 such a strait is laid down, though in 45 degrees south; but there may be significance in the fact that Schöner's source was a pamphlet (*Copia der Newen Zeytung auss Presillg Landt*) describing an expedition promoted in 1514 by the financier Cristóbal de Haro, who invested in Magellan's expedition and was related by marriage to Maximilian of Transylvania" (vol I, p. 155). See also L.C. Wroth, *The Early Cartography of the Pacific* (1944), pp. 143-45.

[101] For Guillemard (pp. 199-200) and Skelton (p. 155), most probably Lomas Bay, on the south side of the strait, but also possibly Possession Bay (Da Mosto, p. 61, note 5).

102 The "First Narrows" or Primera Garganta, just beyond Anegada Point. Robertson translates *cantone* as "sharp turn" while Skelton opts for "creek."

103 Lago de los Estrechos, St. Philip's Bay, or Boucant Bay.

104 The "Second Narrows" and Broad Reach.

105 Skelton observes: "The first is the passage east of Dawson Island, which extends to the northeast into Useless Bay and to the southeast into Admiralty Sound. The second opening was the passage between the western side of Dawson Island and Brunswick Peninsula. Other accounts show that while the *S. Antonio* and *Concepción* reconnoitered the former channel, *Trinidad* and *Victoria* proceeded up Froward Reach, the main channel" (p. 155).

106 Estevão Gomes was an experienced Potuguese navigator and pilot with ambitions as great as those of Magellan, to whom he was related. Pigafetta alludes here to the fact that Gomes had received a pilot's patent from the Casa de la Contratación on February 10, 1518 and had himself made a plan for an expedition which was forestalled by Magellan's. At a council held by Magellan on entering the Strait, Gomes seems to have argued for return to Spain. His desertion occurred probably in early November. Conspiring with Gerónimo Guerra, the captain of the *San Antonio*, he made off with that ship, and after imprisoning Alvaro de Mezquita, returned to Spain, anchoring at Seville, May 6, 1521. There Gomes was imprisoned briefly after the return of the *Victoria*, but after his liberation received honors and recognition. In 1524, Gomes proposed an expedition to discover a northwest passage. He coasted Florida and the eastern coast as far as Cape Cod, returning to Spain in 1525 (see Guillemard, pp. 203-5, 214-17). Gomes participated in the 1535 expedition of Pedro de Mendoza and seems to have died while exploring the Rìo de la Plata in 1538. Peter Martyr does not fail to turn the desertion of the *San Antonio* against Magellan: "The other vessels expected it [the *San Antonio*] would follow, but it turned back and arrived in Spain some time ago, bringing the saddest accusations against Magellan. We believe that such disobedience will not remain unpunished" (*De orbe novo*, p. 156). Transylvanus records that Mezquita, upon his return to Spain, was made to stand trial "in chains, for having, by his counsel and advice, induced his uncle to practice such harshness on the Spaniards" (p. 195).

107 Guillemard conjectures from the records of Albo, Pigafetta, and Herrera that the river of Sardines is Port Gallant which is located on the Brunswick Peninsula, opposite the Charles Islands: "Port Gallant and Port S. Miguel . . . most probably correspond to the River of Sardines and the River of Isles" (p. 206, note 3).

108 Cabo Pilar, on the south side of the Pacific entrance of the strait.

109 João Serrão was the brother of Magellan's friend Francisco Serrão, and a firm supporter of Magellan. Pigafetta errs in calling him a Spaniard, though he may have become a naturalized Spaniard, since the register speaks of him as a citizen of Seville. He was an experienced navigator and captain and had served under Vasco da Gama, Almeida, and Albuquerque. He fought in the battle of Cananor under Almeida (March 16, 1506, a battle in which Magellan also participated). He was chief captain of three caravels in August 1510, in the East, and was in the Java seas in 1512, but appears to have returned to Portugal soon after that. João Serrão embarked with Magellan as captain and pilot of the *Santiago* but after the wreck of that vessel near Port St. Julian he was given command of the *Concepción*, in which he later explored the strait. Failing to dissuade Magellan from attacking the natives of Mactan, he became commander, with Duarte Barbosa of the fleet at Magellan's death, and was murdered by the Cebuans after the treacherous banquet given by them to the fleet (cf. ⟨102-⟨103).

110 Probably the island Santa Magdalena.

111 The little island San Miguel. According to Guillemard the river of Isleo (or "of Islands") is located on Brunswick Peninsula, and is identified with the port of San Miguel, just east of the "River of Sardines;" the island where the cross was planted would be one of the Charles Islands.

112 The author again addresses the Grand Master of the Knights of Rhodes.

113 Terra del Fuego.

114 Pigafetta is the only source to attribute this name to the strait. According to the Potuguese Companion of Odoardo Barbosa (first published by

Ramusio) the strait was named "the Strait of Victoria, because the ship *Victoria* was the first that had seen it; some called it the Strait of Magalhãens because our captain was named Fernando de Magalhãens" (p. 31). Castanheda says that Magellan gave it the name "Bay of All Saints" because it was discovered on November 1, and "Estrecho" or "Canal de Todos los Santos" is the name found in most subsequent Spanish charts. This name is found in the instructions given for the expedition of Sebastian Cabot in 1527, and in the map made that same year at Seville by the Englishman Robert Thorne. Sarmiento de Gamboa petitioned Felipe II that it be called "strait of the Mother of God." In the world map of Battista Agnese showing the track of the circumnavigation, included in his manuscript atlases from 1536, the name is "El streto de ferdinãdo de magellanes."

115 Italian: *appio*, a wild celery (*Appium australe*). Amoretti recalls that Cook also found this vegetable there, as well as an abundance of scurvy-grass; and owing to the availability of anti-scorbutic vegetables, deemed the passage of the strait preferable to that around Cape Horn (p. 41).

116 The dorado is a species of *Coryphaena*, the albacore is the *Thymnus albacora* and the bonito: *Thymnus plamys*.

117 From the Spanish *golondrina*, the sapphrine gurnard or tubfish (*Trigla hirundo*).

118 Torquato Tasso based himself upon this passage for the following octave from a draft version of the *Gerusalemme liberata* (see Introduction, pp. x-xi): Spettacol quivi al nostro mondo ignoto / vider di strana, e d'incredibil caccia: / volare un pesce, un altro girne a nòto./ Fugge il volante, il notatore il caccia / e ne l'ombra ch'è in acqua osserva il moto / che quel fa in aria, e segue ognor la traccia, / fin che quel, che non vegge a volo il peso / per lungo spazio, in mare cadendo è preso.

119 The earliest recorded vocabulary of the Tehuelche of Patagonia. Da Mosto gives a list from the vocabulary of the Tehuelches compiled during the second half of the nineteenth century by the second lieutenant of the ship *Roncaglia*, parts of which correspond almost exactly with those given by Pigafetta (p. 63, note 8).

[120] The passage took 38 days (or 36, according to the Genoese pilot, who gives the day of departure as November 26). Here Pigafetta marks a major transition in his narrative by giving the full date including the year, as he will at other important moments in the narrative (cf. ¶50, ¶100, ¶137, and ¶201).

[121] This was scurvy. The official list of deaths recorded only eleven deaths between the Strait and the Ladrones (cf. Navarrete, II, p. 443).

[122] From November 28 to December 16 1520, Magellan had coasted northward from Cape Deseado, before changing course to the northwest. The first island was discovered on St. Paul's day, January 24, 1521, and named after St. Paul according to Albo (p. 222); although according to Transylvanus "They named these the Unfortunate Islands by common consent" (p. 197). Skelton, together with most of the tradition, thinks it was perhaps Puka Puka (19°46′ S; 138°48′ W), in the northern Tuamotu Archipelago. The second island, sighted eleven days later and named Island of the Sharks (*Tiburones*), would be one of the Manihiki Archipelago, perhaps Flint Island or Wostok. But for a minority opinion see also G. Nunn ("Magellan's Route in the Pacific," *Geographical Review*, XXXIV, October 1935, pp. 615-33) who argues that these islands correspond to present day Clipperton and Clarion in latitudes of 10° 17′ N and 18° N respectively. Nunn's theses are discussed (with bibliography) in Todorash, "Magellan Historiography," pp. 316-18.

[123] The original, which reads: "*Ogni iorno facevamo cinquanta, sesanta e setanta leghe a la catena o a poppa*," has given rise to much discussion, since it appears, according to the revised text of Amoretti (1800: "*secondo la misura che facevano del viaggio colla catena a poppa*"), to refer to the use of a log for measuring the ship's way long before the device was thought to have been in use (although the log is mentioned by Puchas as early as 1607, its use did not become general until 1620). Morison clarifies the matter observing that "*catena* in those days meant not only a chain but two important cross-beams in a vessel's hull, the first under the forecastle and the second well aft. Mariners stationed on the deck above each beam could time the seconds required for a piece of flotsam to pass between them as the ship sailed. . . . Knowing the linear distance between these two beams and the elaspsed

time, anyone who knew a little mathematics could figure out the ship's speed. . . ." (*The Southern Voyages*, p. 410).

[124] Fifty years would pass before another navigator, Sir Francis Drake, circled the globe in 1578.

[125] These are the Magellanic Clouds (*Nubecula major* and *Nubecula minor*). "The Magellanic clouds resemble portions of the Milky Way, Nubecula major being visible to the naked eye in strong moonlight and covering about two hundred times the moon's surface, while the Nubecula minor, although visible to the naked eye, disappears in full moonlight and covers an area only one-fourth that of the former" (Robertson, I, p. 246).

[126] This refers to the practice of correcting the compass for local magnetic deviation. The Genoese pilot reports that "we northeasted the compass box 2/4," i.e. two points (=22 ½ degrees).

[127] The Southern Cross. Morison, however, observes that the direction indicated ("straight toward the west") suggests instead the constellation Grus the Crane which is similar to a cross (*The Southern Voyages*, pp. 403-4).

[128] The line of demarcation was established following Columbus's discovery by Pope Alexander VI (cf. ¶53, ¶68, ¶104, ¶109, ¶111, ¶126, ¶182, ¶188, ¶193). It originally ran north to south one hundred leagues to the west of the Cape Verde Islands and divided Spanish (west) from Portuguese (east) spheres of influence. With the Treaty of Tordesillas (June 7, 1494) the line was moved 370 leagues west from the Cape Verde Islands.

[129] To place Cipangu (Japan) 20 degrees south of the equator is far off, even for the cartography of the time. It has usually been assumed that Pigafetta derives these island names from his reading or hearsay. Cipangu goes back to Marco Polo who told fabulous tales of the wealth of Cipangu which were later to inspire Columbus. Sumbdit Pradit has been taken to be a corruption of "Septem cidades," one of the original mythical islands of the Atlantic, but in the vicinity of Cipangu on Behaim's globe of 1492. Guillemard observes how the position Magellan found himself in ". . . resembled that of Columbus before sighting the new world, as day after

day their despairing glances were bent westward in hopes of land" (p. 223). Pigafetta reveals a similarly Columbian orientation by invoking two toponyms which harken back to that earlier moment of exploration history. But G. Nunn has suggested the interesting hypothesis that Sumbdit Pradit might be "the same as the legendary islands of Khryse and Argyre, or the islands of gold and silver. *Ptadia* (*prata* means silver in Malay). The story of the two islands was originally derived from Hindu literature. Al-Biruni (1031 A.D.) speaks of the islands of gold Surendíb. . . . Sumbdit Pradit might well represent a combination of Surendíb and Pradit (*prada*)" ("Magellan's Route," p. 630). This explanation may well serve as a gloss for later in the narrative when Pigafetta speaks of Sumbdit and Pradit as islands located near the coast of China (¶220).

130 A Chinese city placed by Ptolemy in 8 ½° S, east of the Golden Chersonese, on the eastern coast of the Indian Ocean, later identified as Malacca. Vespucci, among others, sought it: ". . . we weighed anchor and set sail, turning our prows southward , since it was my intention to see whether I could round a cape of land which Ptolemy calls the Cape of Cattigara, which is near the Sinus Magnus . . ." (*Letters*, I, p. 4). Magellan is thought to have sailed so far north in search of provisions since as the Genoese pilot reports, "They had information that in the Moluccas there was no food."

131 The Mariana or Ladrone islands. Herrera says they were named "Islas de las Velas Latinas," that is, islands of the lateen sails. The high island first sighted was probably Rota, and Guam the large island where landing was made. Transylvanus records the indigenous names Inuagana and Acaca, equated by Guillemard with Agana in Guam and Sosan in Rota. See Guillemard, pp. 223-26. They continued to be called *Ladrones* and only later they took the name of Mariana in honor of the Queen D. Mariana of Austria, widow of Philip IV, and Regent during the minority of Carlos II of Castile.

132 Albo has a vivid description of this first encounter: ". . . then we saw a quantity of small sails coming to us, and they ran so, that they seemed to fly, and they had mat sails of a triangular shape, and they went both ways for they made of the poop the prow, and of the prow the poop, as they wished, and they came many times to us and sought us to steal whatever they could" (p. 223).

133 An interesting testimony of European cannibalism practiced by mariners in distress.

134 Da Mosto reports that these *fisolere* were small and very swift-oared vessels, used in winter on the Venetian lakes by the Venetian nobles for hunting with bows and arrows and guns (p. 68, note 5).

135 The apparatus described by Pigafetta as belonging to these boats is the outrigger (a projecting spar with a shaped log at the end attached to a canoe to prevent upsetting), common to many of the boats of the eastern islands.

136 Pigafetta again marks a major transition in his narrative, in this case, the arrival in the Philippines, by giving the full date (cf. ❡41).

137 Samar is an island in the Philippines, the southernmost point of which (Magellan's landfall) is in 11° N. Cf. ❡182, where Pigafetta describes it, accurately, from a geographical perspective, as "the first island of the archipelago" to one arriving east to west.

138 Suluan, a small island to the southeast of Samar. Cf. ❡53, where the island is first identified by name.

139 A rare kind of fine linen. Du Cange defines it *"Pannus subtil e gossypio vel lino"* (*Glossarium mediae et infimae latinitatis*, Paris: F. Didot, 1840, vol. 1, p. 744).

140 Arrack, meaning in Arabic, "ardent spirit", is an Asian alcoholic beverage like rum. Pigafetta conserves both Portuguese forms (*ararca, uraca*, cf. ❡114) of a single arabic word which the Europeans used generically to refer to a spirit made with fermented rice, sugar, and coconut.

141 Bananas.

142 The Yale Beinecke ms. has "By doing so they last a century."

143 *Acquada da li buoni segnalli* in the Italian. Homonhon is west of Suluan and eleven miles southwest from the nearest point in Samar.

[144] Passion Sunday fell on March 17 in 1521. Pigafetta calls Passion Sunday the Sunday of St. Lazarus according to the Ambrosian rite rather than calling it Palm Sunday in accordance with the Roman rite. The islands were called "di San Lazaro" until 1542 when Villalobos changed the name to the Philippines in honor of Philip II. The Philippines lie between 225 and 235 degrees longitude west of Hierro in the Canaries and therefore between 195 and 205 degrees west of the line of demarcation. It is not clear whether Magellan simply miscalculated or in bad faith sought to represent their location on the Spanish side of the line, that is, as being east of 180 degrees.

[145] Probably the jungle fowl (*Gallus bankiva*) domesticated in large numbers by the natives of the Philippines.

[146] "These were presumably Negrito aborigines, not Malays" (Skelton, p. 159). The term *kâfir*, is arabic for "unbeliever" and was used in the Far East to designate those people who did not worship Allah.

[147] Variant form for *fiocina*, a 'harpoon' or 'eel-spear' and hence here a 'dart.'

[148] A Venetian dialect word (*rizzagio* or *rizzagno*) for a fine, thickly woven net, which when thrown into rivers by the fisherman opens, and when near the bottom closes and covers and encloses the fish (Da Mosto, p. 70).

[149] It is difficult to identify these islands which are however located in the Surigao Strait, between Samar and Mindanao: possibly Dinagat, Kabugan, Ibusson, Cabalian.

[150] Limasawa (Mazaua), off the south end of Leyte.

[151] Enrique of Malacca, a slave brought back from the East by Magellan. If, as some believe, Enrique were a native of a Philippine colony in Malacca, then he would have been the first man to circle the globe. According to Transylvanus, Enrique was originally from the Moluccas.

[152] Taprobane was usually identified as Ceylon, but sometimes, as here, also Sumatra. Ludovico Varthema, the first European to speak of Sumatra, when he wrote about his 1505 visit, also took Sumatra to be Ptolemy's Taprobane.

153 A large boat used in the Philippines. From the Tagalog *balangài*. The Italian derives from the Spanish *barangay* according to *Battaglia GDLI*, II, p. 50.

154 The Ambrosiana ms. reads *orade*. The *doradi* have already been mentioned (cf. ¶38). The Yale Beinecke ms. provides the following gloss: "which are fairly large fish of the kind described above."

155 *Casi casi*, the ceremony of blood brotherhood practiced among the Malays.

156 Navarrete observed that there were not more than fifty armed men in the fleet at that time.

157 The *fusta* was a galley with eighteen or twenty rowers to a side, and with a single lateen sail.

158 An aromatic oriental resin, used also as a perfume (Cf. ¶106, ¶123).

159 A dry and brittle resinous substance obtained from *Storax benzoin*, a tree of Sumatra, Java, etc. and used extensively in perfumery.

160 These names, applied to the island of Mindanao, in fact refer to two of its regions: Butuan, in the north, and Caraga, in the northeast.

161 Colambu was rajah of Butuan. According to Amoretti, this rajah is the same one Pigafetta elsewhere calls king of Mazaua (Limasawa).

162 Siaiu was rajah of Cagayan.

163 *Abba* means father in Arabic and Hebrew.

164 According to Robertson, Ceylon is Leyte, anciently called Seilam (cf. ¶69, where Pigafetta speaks of Baybay, in central Leyte, as a separate island); but Skelton identifies Ceylon as Panaon to the south of Leyte; Cebu is to the west of Limasawa, and Caraga is a district of Mindanao.

165 Magellan's death is foreshadowed.

166 An Italian copper coin of the fifteenth century.

167 A Spanish coin.

168 *Doppione*, a gold coin struck by Louis XII of France during his occupation of Milan 1500-1512.

169 *Colona*, conjectured by Robertson to be yet another coin of the period. The Beinecke ms. reads: "a pointed crown of massy gold for six large pieces of glass" (p. 72).

170 Columbus also forbade such trade, but ". . . so that they might become Christians . . ." ("Letter Announcing the Discovery," p. 8).

171 The nut of the *Areca catechu*, which is folded in leaves of betel and chewed. Cf. ¶114.

172 Betel was prepared with a leaf of *Piper betle*, cloves, the nut of the *Areca catechu*, lime and tobacco.

173 Cf. ¶53: the island Homonhon, named in the Italian *"Acquada de li buoni segnali."*

174 Limasawa, in 10° 20′ N.

175 The islands of Leyte (or Panaon), Bohol (southwest of Leyte) and Canigao; the district of Baybay (in central Leyte); and perhaps the island of Apit or Himuguetan. The ships were sailing north through the Canigao Channel, along the west coast of Leyte (Skelton, p. 160).

176 "Flying foxes" or large fruit-eating bats (genus *Pteropus*).

177 The tabón, which are mound-building *Megapodes*, "gallinaceous birds peculiar to the Austro-Malayan subregion" (Guillemard, p. 235).

178 The Camotes, west of Leyte: Poro, Pacijan, and Ponson islands.

179 These houses "built upon logs" are schematically represented in the preceding chart.

180 Probably Cristòbal Rebelo, who is believed to have been an illegitimate son of Magellan's, also remembered in Magellan's will (Morison, *The Southern Voyages*, p. 423).

181 Siam, or modern Thailand (cf. ¶196, ¶197). Pigafetta is the first to use the word "junk" in Italian (in the forms *iunco* or *ionco*). The word derives from the Malay and Javanese word *adjong* referring to a large vessel used in war and trade (cf. ¶140, ¶183, ¶192, ¶196).

182 The Portuguese had arrived as far as India and the Moluccas from the west. India Major and India Minor are differently applied by different authors. See Robertson, vol. I, p. 256.

183 The blood brotherhood of *casi casi*, mentioned earlier (cf. ¶58).

184 Before leaving Spain, Magellan had received the order of St. James of Compostela. Cf. the dedicatory letter (¶2).

185 A city in Gujerat, an Islamic realm of western India from which the Portuguese imported silk (cf. ¶91, ¶116, ¶138, ¶201).

186 Ptolemy's Sinus Magnus: the Gulf of China.

187 From which "gong." Pigafetta, who is the first westerner to record the term, does not elsewhere use any form of gong (which enters Italian only after 1600 via English) but rather *borchia* "knob" or "buckle."

188 The first of the two men was Martin Barreta, who had sailed as a supernumerary of the *Santiago*. The other was Juan de Aroche (see Guillemard, p. 240).

189 The ground upon which they rest serves as bottom, whereby raising them up, the merchandise remains on the ground (Amoretti, p. 84).

¹⁹⁰ According to Masoero, a kind of Teleost of the Percomorph order which lives in tropical seas and is of small dimensions (cf. ¶187). For Robertson it is a large sea snail found in the Philippines which has a shell resembling that of the *Nautilus pompilius* and is used to hold incense or as a drinking vessel.

¹⁹¹ Ferdinand I of Hapsburg (1503-1564).

¹⁹² The Infanta Juana ("la Loca"), daughter of Isabel and Ferdinand of Castile.

¹⁹³ "The 'tromb' or 'trunk' was a kind of hand rocket-tube made of wood and hooped with iron, and was used for discharging wildfire" (Robertson, vol. II, p. 262).

¹⁹⁴ The neighboring island referred to here was Mactan (cf. ¶90). Pigafetta again foreshadows the deadly reception Magellan will receive there.

¹⁹⁵ This Flemish statuette was recovered on April 28, 1565 by the Spanish conquistador Miguel Lòpez de Legazpi. It is still preserved in the Basilica of the Santo Niño on Cebu.

¹⁹⁶ Not a name, but the title for one of the principal ministers of the king. Malay *banda hara* referred to the treasurer or some other high functionary of the state.

¹⁹⁷ See note 184. Again, Pigafetta, the Knight of Rhodes, emphasizes Magellan's membership in a military-religious order.

¹⁹⁸ Idols similar to the Korawaar of New Guinea (Masoero, p. 98).

¹⁹⁹ Mandani is Mandaue; Lalan may be Liloan; Lubucun may be Lubú, but Da Mosto (p. 78, note 3) conjectures it to be Lambusan. The list in the French mss. is longer and includes two villages named *Cotcot* and *Puzzo* with the names of their chiefs (see Skelton, p. 84).

²⁰⁰ Mactan is a small island lying in the Bohol Strait off the port of Cebu.

201 Zula was faithful to the Sultan of Cebu Humabon while Lapu Lapu (the *Ci* at the beginning of many names is an article in the Malay language placed before names of people) was in rebellion.

202 Cf. ¶86, where Pigafetta first reports this incident.

203 Pigafetta addresses the Grand Master again (cf. ¶10, ¶31, ¶38). This lengthy anthropological account represents a kind of tension-building counterpoint to the narrative of the death of Magellan which follows. The section closes ominously with the story of the jet black bird that comes to the village and screeches every night at midnight (¶95).

204 This description is expurgated from the French mss. with the exception of the Yale Beinecke ms. The custom is called the *palang*. Amoretti notes that Noort and Cavendish found the practice still continued when they sailed through these seas. According to them it was an invention of the women to prevent sodomy.

205 Lapu Lapu, rajah of Mactan (cf. ¶90), though subject to the rajah of Cebu, had refused to do homage to the king of Spain; and Zula, one of his subordinate chiefs, was prevented from doing so by fear of his overlord Lapu Lapu, against whom he invoked Magellan's aid. For a full account of the battle of Mactan and death of Magellan, see Guillemard, pp. 246-61.

206 Depending on the account, the natives were anywhere from fifteen hundred to six thousand in number.

207 According to Transylvanus, Magellan had ordered "his men to be of good cheer and brave hearts, and not to be alarmed at the number of the enemy, for they had often seen, as formerly, so in quite recent times, two hundred Spaniards in the island of Yucatan put sometimes two or three hundred thousand men to flight. But he pointed out to the Subuth [Cebu] islanders that he had brought them, not to fight, but to watch their bravery and their fighting power . . ." (p. 200).

208 See Guillemard p. 254 for the varying accounts of the death of Magellan.

[209] This eulogy is addressed to Villiers de l'Isle-Adam, Grand Master of the Knights of Rhodes, to whom the narrative is dedicated (cf. ⁋31, ⁋38, etc.). As Grand Master of the Knights, Villiers de l'Isle-Adam was the ideal defender of the fame of the sea crusader Magellan.

[210] We prefer to translate *grandissima fortuna* literally rather than metaphorically (Robertson has "in the greatest of adversity." Guillemard has "in the worst misfortune"; Skelton has "in a very high hazard"). For the theme of the storm has been associated with Magellan since the beginning of the narrative: "a voyage through the Ocean Sea, where furious winds and great storms are always reigning" (⁋5). For a parallel passage see Michele De Cuneo's praise of Columbus in his "Letter to Hieronimo Annari": "But one thing I want you to know is that in my humble opinion, since Genoa was Genoa, there has never been a man so courageous and astute in the act of navigation as the Lord Admiral; for, when sailing, by simply observing a cloud or a star at night, he judged what was to come. If there was to be bad weather, he himself commanded and stood at the helm. When the storm had passed, he raised the sails while the others slept" (*Prime relazioni di navigatori italiani sulla scoperta dell' America*, a cura di L. Firpo, Turin: UTET, 1966, p. 76 [translation mine]).

[211] For another view, see Peter Martyr: "Magellan was killed, together with seven of his companions, while twenty-two others were wounded. Thus did this brave Portuguese, Magellan, satisfy his craving for spices" (*De orbe novo*, vol. II, p. 159).

[212] Pigafetta again marks an important point in the narrative by giving the full date (cf. ⁋41, ⁋50). As Masoero has observed, Magellan's death divides the narrative almost precisely in half ("Magellano, eroe, navigatore," in *La letteratura di viaggio del Medioevo al Rinascimento: Generi e problemi*, Alessandria, Edizioni dell'Orso, 1989, p. 54).

[213] Magellan's brother-in-law. In 1517 Magellan married Barbosa's sister Beatrice. Barbosa had already been to the Moluccas and authored an important account of the Indies (1517–1518), published by Ramusio (vol. I, 1550, fols. 310-48; a Hakluyt Society edition of a Portuguese manuscript of this account was published in 1928, edited by M.L. Dames). Barbosa had been named captain of the *Victoria* following the mutiny at Port St. Julian.

He died together with João Serrão, Luís Afonso de Gòs, Enrique of Malacca, and another twenty-one men in the ambush at Cebu in 1521 (cf. ⟨103⟩). But according to the documentation collected by Navarrete twenty-seven men died (vol. II, pp. 448-49). See Robertson for a biographical sketch of Barbosa, vol. I, pp. 266-67.

214 In reality a Portuguese by birth, and brother of Magellan's friend Francisco Serrão (who lived in Ternate from 1513–1521; cf. ⟨142, ⟨143, ⟨159). João Lopes Carvalho was captain of the *Santiago*, and after that ship was lost, of the *Concepción* (cf. ⟨37).

215 Enrique of Malacca, in the official muster, a slave brought back from the East by Magellan (cf. ⟨56).

216 The Ambrosiana ms. reads *schiavina*, a Venetian dialect word for a blanket of coarse wool.

217 According to Navarrete (IV, p. 66, note 1, and p. lxxxv) Enrique was innocent, and the chiefs of Mactan and two other rajahs ordered the treachery. Guillemard cites Barros (Dec. iii., lib. v., cap. x, and Herrera, Dec. iii., lib. i., cap. ix), to the effect that "the chiefs who had made diffi-culties in submitting to his [the King of Cebu's] authority united to form a common cause, and sent to inform him that if he did not assist them in exterminating the Spaniards and seizing their ships, they would kill him and lay waste their country" (p. 263). Transylvanus and Gomara are with Pigafetta on this point, in blaming the slave. See Morison for another ver-sion according to the anonymous Portuguese (*The Southern Voyages*, p. 358). See also Peter Martyr for yet another motivation for the plot: ". . . the Spaniards think it was on account of women, for the islanders are jealous" (*De orbe novo*, II, p. 159). See Guillemard for a critical account, pp. 262-67.

218 The phrase *più sacente* is open to various interpretations, including "more cunning" according to Robertson's translation.

219 The constable was Gonzalo Gòmez de Espinosa who was left behind with the *Trinidad*, and was one of the survivors from that vessel, returning to Spain long after (see Robertson, vol. I, p. 267).

[220] From the Portuguese *jaqueira*, jackfruit or the tree (cf. ⟨126, ⟨183, ⟨185). See the description at ⟨185, where they are called *nangha*, which is an indigenous name for a variety of Artocarpus. "The jack, *Artocarpus incisa*, is intensively cultivated throughout the archipelago, and its name Nangka, extends all the way to the Philippines" (Crawfurd, *Dictionary*, p. 24).

[221] Most of the words in the following Bisayan vocabulary can be distinguished in the dictionaries of that language. Robertson provides a list of correspondences (vol. I, pp. 269-273).

[222] "*Bassag bassag* does not correspond to 'shin' but to 'basket for holding clothes,' or 'cartilage of the nose;' or possibly to *basac basac*, 'the sound made by falling water'" (Robertson, vol. I, p. 269).

[223] Cf. ⟨158.

[224] "*Tahil* is found in the Tagalog dictionaries, and is the name of a specific weight, not weight in general. It is the Chinese weight called 'tael,' [or tail] which was introduced by the Chinese into the East Indies, whence it spread throughout the various archipelagoes" (Robertson, vol. I, p. 269).

[225] Cf. ⟨80.

[226] Syphyllis here, although the disease of St. Job commonly referred to leprosy.

[227] Cf. ⟨64.

[228] Cf. ⟨56, ⟨59, ⟨66, etc.

[229] Cf. ⟨56.

[230] Following the massacre at Cebu, the hierarchy of command had to be reorganized. João Carvalho was named captain-general, but would later be replaced by Gonzalo Gòmez de Espinosa. Juan Sebastiàn de Cano would eventually assume the command of the *Victoria* (see note 268). The reduced fleet wandered from Bohol to Mindanao to Palawan, to the east coast of Borneo, then returned to the Philippines, always in search of the Maluccas.

After capturing some native pilots (¶135) the fleet finally will reach Tidore in the Maluccas, Friday, Nov. 8, 1521.

231 Panglao is located off the southwest coast of Bohol. The ships had sailed southwest through the Bohol Strait. The black men were Negritos.

232 According to Guillemard, the place corresponds to Caraga, in the northeast part of the island of Mindanao (p. 234, note 1).

233 The Malasian ceremony of *casi casi* or blood brotherhood (cf. ¶58). The Malay word-list defines *casi casi*: "To be one and the same thing" (¶183).

234 Cf. ¶60 and ¶123: Aromatic resin used also as a perfume.

235 After visiting Borneo and Palawan, at ¶131-¶133.

236 Or Quipit, located on the northeast coast of Mindanao, east of Sindangan Bay, on the north coast of the Zamboanga Peninsula.

237 Earliest European mention of the island of Luzon, the largest and northernmost of the Philippines.

238 Inhabitants of the Ryukyu Islands ("Lequios"); more probably, as suggested by the Genoese pilot, they were Chinese.

239 The island Cagayan Sulu, located to the northeast of Borneo, in 9° 30′ N, in the Cagayan group lying in the Sulu Sea west of Mindanao (Cf. ¶130).

240 Bananas.

241 Palawan, the most westerly of the Philippines and after Luzon and Mindanao, the largest of them. The "Roteiro" gives a fuller account of what happened at Palawan (pp. 15-17). The natives were hostile initially but then the Europeans found another village at the port called Dyguasam, where the were able to obtain supplies. Pigafetta does not mention this place in his narrative but it does appear in the corresponding chart (*Tegozzano porto*). Nor is mention made of *Sundan*, which also appears in the chart.

NOTES

²⁴² Cockfighting was always a great diversion among Malasian peoples. See Crawfurd. "Most of the advanced natives of the Asiatic Islands are gamblers, and the favorite shape which gaming takes with them is cockfighting. This includes the people of Bali, Lomboc, Celebes, and all the Philippine Islands, the only material exception being the Javanese" (Crawfurd, p. 113).

²⁴³ After coasting along Palawan, they left its southern point on June 21, 1521. They passed through the Balabac Strait, between the islands of Balabac and Banggi, and southwest along the coast of Borneo to Brunei in lat. 5° N.

²⁴⁴ Bruney Bay, in the north-east part of the island of Borneo.

²⁴⁵ A Spanish transliteration of Malay *parah*, which is a generic name for any vessel, whether rowing or sailing (Crawfurd, p. 360).

²⁴⁶ From Arabic *alma'dijà*: river boat. The word was common among Hispano-Portuguese navigators and already used in Italian by Cadamosto.

²⁴⁷ Cf ¶68, and see our note 171.

²⁴⁸ Brunei. Crawfurd cites at length from Pigafetta's account, for it represents, "the only authentic account of a Malay court when first seen by Europeans, and before their policy or impolicy had affected Malayan society" (p. 71).

²⁴⁹ Crawfurd questions this population estimate, which at five persons per hearth would bring the number to 125,000. In any case, the town "in the time of Pigafetta was evidently a place of much more consequence than it is in ours" (p. 71).

²⁵⁰ From the indigenous word *jurutulis*, "adepts in writing" (Crawfurd, p. 72).

²⁵¹ As Crawfurd observes, "This auspicious beginning of European intercourse had a very unlucky ending. After the reception at court, the king of Borneo sent a fleet to attack some of his heathen neighbors, and the Spaniards, fancying it came to attack themselves, opened fire on it" (p. 72).

²⁵² Perhaps the island of Laut Pulan, off the southeast coast of Borneo.

253 If Carvalho had not released the Moor, he might have been traded for the three Europeans.

254 The word appears to have fallen out of the manuscript; Da Mosto first restored it (p. 88).

255 "The small brass, copper, tin, and zinc coins common throughout the eastern islands were called 'pichis' or 'pitis,' which was the name of the ancient Javanese coin, now used as a frequent appellative for money in general" (Robertson, vol. II, p. 201, who refers to Crawfurd, pp. 385-88).

256 The Kati, frequently written Catty, a weight of 1 ½ pound avoirdupois, which contains sixteen tails (Crawfurd, p. 196). For the *tahil* see our note 226.

257 Used in Calicut, the only weight introduced by the Arabs (Crawfurd, p. 446) into the eastern archipelagos, the *bahar* varied in value in different parts of East Asia. Skelton calculates, the *bahar* of Tidore referred to later by Pigafetta, to be equivalent to about 450 pounds' weight (p. 169).

258 Transylvanus reports: "And to omit nothing, our men constantly affirm that the islanders of Porne told them that the king wore in his crown two pearls of the size of a goose's egg" (p. 205).

259 "The Malay camphor tree is confined so far as known, to a few parts of the islands of Sumatra and Borneo, where it is very abundant. The oil (both fluid and solid) is found in the body of the tree where the sap should be, but not in all trees. The Malay name for camphor is a slight corruption of the Sanskrit one 'karpura' . . ." (Robertson, vol. II, p. 202).

260 Transylvanus gives an interesting and divergent account of the people of Borneo, among other things observing that: ". . . they love peace and quiet, but war they greatly detest, and they honor their king as a god whilst he is bent upon peace. But if he be too desirous of war, they rest not till he has fallen by the hand of the enemy in battle. Whenever he has determined to wage war, which is rarely done, he is placed by his subjects in the vanguard, where he is compelled to bear the whole onslaught of the enemy. . . . Wherefore they rarely wage war . . ." (p. 203).

261 That is, northeast along the coast of Borneo.

262 A name recorded only by Pigafetta. For Skelton, it is presumably a reef between the Balabac Strait and Brunei. Masoero identifies it as Balambangan (p. 215).

263 Cape Sempang Mangayau is the northernmost point of Borneo, in lat. 7° N. Cimbonbon is either Balambangan or Banguey, islands north of Cape Sempang Mangayau.

264 Between August 15 and September 27, 1521.

265 "The *Tridacna gigas*. . . . The shells sometimes attain a length of five or six feet, and weigh hundreds of pounds" (Robertson, vol. II, p. 203).

266 Masoero suggests this may have been the Port Jackson Shark.

267 According to Robertson, these were the insects *Phyllium orthoptera*, known as walking leaves from their resemblance to a leaf (vol. II, p. 203).

268 Carvalho was deprived of his command when the expedition departed from there; the *Trinidad* was placed under the command of Gonzalo Gomez de Espinosa and the *Victoria* under the command of Juan Sebastian del Cano. "At the September full moon the fleet officers, feeling that Carvalho was becoming too big for his boots as well as a menace to their future safety by acts of piracy, degraded him to his former rank of flag pilot" (Morison, *The Southern Voyages*, p. 444). Pigafetta makes no mention of these changes in command. Acts of piracy continue beyond this point in the narrative.

269 The southernmost point of Palawan is Cape Buliluyan.

270 Cagayan Sulu (cf. ⟨110).

271 Cf. ⟨109, ⟨110.

272 Jolo and Basilan, in the Sulu Archipelago.

PIGAFETTA

273 For the pearls of the king of Brunei, see ¶124. "The true pearl oysters of the Philippine Islands are found along the coasts of Paragua, Mindanao, and in the Sulu Archipelago, especially in the last named, where many very valuable pearls are found. These fisheries are said to rank with the famous fisheries of Ceylon and the Persian Gulf" (Robertson, vol. II, p. 203).

274 Cavite and Subanin are on the west coast of the Zamboanga Peninsula, Mindanao. Skelton suggests that *Monoripa* may be the island of Sacoli. "The ships then sailed . . . into Moro Gulf, and eastward across it" (Skelton, p. 166).

275 According to Robertson, Pigafetta's etymology of the Malay word is correct (Vol II, p. 204).

276 The principal Malay settlement in the southern part of the island Mindanao, located in the delta of the Pulangi River.

277 Magellan had passed by the north of the island in March 1521 (cf. ¶61, ¶65).

278 Cape Benuian is a promontory in northern Mindanao. Da Mosto cites an ethnologist who encountered the custom of eating the heart or liver of slain enemies among the Manobis in eastern Mindanao (p. 96).

279 Ciboco, located by Albo in 6° N is perhaps Sibago off the northeast coast of the large island of Basilan; according to Albo, the course was changed to the southeast after passing this island. According to Skelton, Birahan Bartolach would be the district of Batukali in Mindanao; the island of Sarangani is south of Mindanao; Candinghar probably represents the island of Balut.

280 Islands of the Kawio and Sangihe archipelagos, extending southward from Mindanao to Celebes. Pigafetta's names are distorted but some are easily recognizable, including the second and third as Kawio, the fourth as Memanuk, the fifth as Kawalusu, and the seventh as Lipang.

281 To the north of Celebes, Sanghihe is the largest island of the Sangihe group.

282 Islands of the Sanghihe archipelago, extending to the south toward Celebes.

283 Skelton suggests Tahulandang, Ruang, or Biaro, which are the southern-most islands of the Sanghihe group (p. 167). Masoero prefers Tahulandang (p. 238).

284 This reference to the Talaud Islands appears to be out of place. The Talaud islands are two degrees north of Paghinzara, and such a route to the Moluccas is unlikely (from Siau to Talaud, far to the northeast).

285 Tifore and Maju, in the Molucca Passage, about fifty miles west of Halmahera (Gilolo).

286 Pigafetta marks the importance of the arrival in the Moluccas by giving the full date (cf. ⟨50, ⟨100, ⟨201).

287 See our note 172. According to Bausani, Pigafetta refers here to the Malay *puan*, a box for holding betel (p. 28).

288 The Portuguese had established a rigid domination since discovering the Maluccas in 1511. This explains the enthusiasm with which the Spanish expedition was welcomed at Tidore. Guillemard notes that when Francisco Serrão first discovered the Moluccas in 1511, he settled at Ternate, "the sultan of which island was not on friendly terms with the monarch of Tidore, and for this reason the Portuguese became paramount in the former island while the Spaniards identified themselves chiefly with Tidore" (p. 277).

289 The report of indigenous people having some foreknowledge of the coming of the Europeans is a topos of the literature of discovery and conquest, most famously in the case of the Aztecs, but going back to Columbus's second voyage and Ramon Pane's account of the religious beliefs of the people of Haiti (see Peter Martyr's *De orbe novo*, vol. I, pp. 167-76.). Guillemard notes that Argensola gives a similar story with regard to the King of Ternate, Boleyfe or Abuteis, when first visited by Serrao and his Portuguese (p. 277). Both Peter Martyr and Maximilian Transylvanus make note of it in their accounts of Magellan's voyage, the latter expanding upon the theme as follows: "He [the king] having received the presents

kindly, looks up to heaven and says: 'I have known now for two years from the course of the stars, that you were coming to seek these lands, sent by the most mighty King of Kings. Wherefore your coming is the more pleasant and grateful to me, as I had been forewarned of it by the signification of the stars. And, as I know that nothing ever happens to any man which has not been fixed long before by the decree of fate and the stars, I will not be the one to attempt to withstand either the fates or the signification of the stars, but willingly and of good cheer, will henceforth lay aside the royal pomp and will consider myself as managing the administration of this island only in the name of your king" (p. 206).

290 A kind of cotton exported from India which is mentioned in the travel reports of the period in various forms. According to Bausani, the word is of persian-indian origin: *Bairam, bairami* (p. 29).

291 Manzor ruled in Tidore from 1512 to 1526.

292 The *cedula* of May 8, 1519 (see note 11) ended "with a long list of the *quintaladas* permitted to the different members of the ship's company. The *quintalada* was the free freight allowed to officers and crew. It was permitted to every one, from captain to cabin-boy, and varied from 8000 to 75 lbs. according to rank. It paid a duty of one-twenty-fourth to the Crown" (Guillemard, p. 129).

293 The northernmost of the Moluccas, whose Sultan had been murdered eight months earlier (see below) so that his throne was still vacant. Manzor appears to have replaced this ruler of Ternate temporarily as the overlord of the clove islands in which the latter acknowledged the sovereignty of Spain. According to Navarrete, on November 10, Juan de Carvalho went ashore and appears to have signed a treaty with Manzor (vol. iv, p. 296). For more details on the political situation in the islands at this time, see Lach, *Asia in the Making of Europe*, p. 595.

294 *Kolano* is the common name for princes and kings of the Moluccas. *Gapi* was the ancient name of Ternate. According to Bausani, the name may therefore simply mean "King of Ternate" (p. 30).

[295] The largest and southernmost island of the Moluccas, to the west of the southern coast of Halmahera (Gilolo).

[296] The five original Molucca or clove islands. Given here in order from north to south, extending about one degree on either side of the equator along the west coast of Halmahera (Gilolo).

[297] Calonaghapi (cf. (140).

[298] Francisco Serrão, brother of João, was a Portuguese merchant who established himself in the Moluccas in 1512. Magellan and Francisco Serrão had served together in the East, and been shipmates in the expedition of Diogo Lopes de Sequiera in 1509-10 to Malacca (see Guillemard, pp. 53-61). See Skelton for alternative versions of Serrão's death (p. 168, note 31).

[299] While living in Ternate, Serrão had corresponded with Magellan, and by placing the Maluccas much to the east of their true position had influenced Magellan's plan and its promotion. See Guillemard, pp. 70-72.

[300] Manoel I (1495–1521) King of Portugal. The *tostão* was a Portuguese silver coin.

[301] See Lach's analysis of these political events in Ternate, *Asia in the Making*, p. 595, and n. 30.

[302] Bandan was the center for Portuguese domination in the southern Moluccas, first reached by Antonio de Abreu in 1512. Pedro Alfonso de Lorosa had come to the Moluccas with Francisco Serrão in 1512. According to Antonio de Brito, Lorosa escaped from the ship of Tristão de Meneses which called at Ternate in October 1520 in order to apprehend Serrão (Navarrete, vol. IV, p. 306). Lorosa was later executed by the Portuguese for having passed into the service of the Spaniards. According to Bausani, his slave Manuel mentioned here may have been one of Pigafetta's primary linguistic sources (p. 33).

[303] Now called Halmahera. Maximilian Transylvanus reports that in this island "they saw men with ears so long and pendulous, that they reached to

their shoulders. When our men were mightily astonished at this, they learnt from the natives that there was another island not far off where the men had ears not only pendulous, but so long and broad, that one of them could cover the whole head, if they wanted. But our men, who sought not monsters but spices, neglecting this nonsense, went straight to the Moluccas . . ." (p. 205).

304 Plants of the species *uncaria*, which contain water.

305 Cinnabar is a red sulfide of mercury, a mineral highly esteemed in the east.

306 Cloth of the Gujerat peninsula in western India, famous throughout Asia. Also called cloth of Cambaya after one of the principal cities of Gujerat (Kambayat); cf. ¶76 and note, ¶91, ¶116, ¶138.

307 As in the report of shoals (cf. ¶136), lack of water was reported to discourage expeditions to the Moluccas.

308 See note 302.

309 Diogo Lopes de Segueira (1466-1530), Viceroy of India 1518-22.

310 The port of Mecca on the Red Sea.

311 According to Skelton, following Barros, probably Pedro de Faria, who was sent by Lopes de Seguieria to build a fort at Molucca (p. 169).

312 The Portuguese believed, as did the Spaniards, that the islands were on the Spanish side of the line of demarcation.

313 Lorosa sailed with the Spanish ships in September 1521. He was in the *Trinidad* when she was captured by the Portuguese squadron under Antonio de Brito in May 1522, and was executed as a traitor.

314 The Italian reads *Li versi*: a name given to small pieces of artillery used for the most part to fire salvoes (sp. *verso*); cf. ¶151, ¶171, ¶176.

315 Christmas and June 24, corresponding to the two solstices.

316 A small island to the south of Tidore.

317 Sago, a dry granulated or powdered starch prepared from the pith from a sago palm: *Sagus arenacea*, belonging to the family of the *metroxylon* palms. Maximilian Transylvanus reports: "Their bread, which they call sago, was made of the trunk or wood of a tree, rather like a palm" (p. 198). The knowledge of bread made from the flour derived from tropical palms goes back to Marco Polo who saw the sago palm in the island of Sumatra and described the process by which bread was made from it ("The Sago Tree," Bk. III, chp. XVI, in *The Travels of Marco Polo*, Dorset Press: New York, 1908, pp. 345-46.).

318 Crawfurd reports that *gaumedi* is a word used for cloves by the natives of the Maluccas, meaning "cow's marrow" (p. 102). The chart which pictures the clove tree calls them *Cavi gomode*, apparently a combination of the Portuguese *cravo* (=nails, for their resemblance to iron nails) and the native word *gaumedi*.

319 Bausani reports that *Tjengkih* (which Pigafetta transcribes as *chianche*) is the most common Malay-Indonesian word for the clove tree (p. 41).

320 Buru is a large island to the west of Ceram.

321 The one that had cost Duarte Barbosa and João Serrão their lives at Cebu. This episode of the mens' suspicions is narrated in greater detail by the "Roteiro," p. 163.

322 *Sembahjang* indicates in Malay-Indonesian the canonical islamic prayer (Bausani, p. 42).

323 The island of Makian was half under the domination of Tidore and half under the domination of Ternate.

324 The patron saint of gunners whose feast is celebrated December 4.

325 A small Venetian coin struck by the Doge Niccolò Marcello in 1473.

326 The *quintalada* mentioned above (¶140), a percentage that each member of the crew received on the ship's earnings.

327 According to Bausani, Pigafetta here translates literally an expression typical of the Indonesian languages (p. 44).

328 A term of south Indian origin referring to silk produced in India and highly esteemed at Malacca and in Indonesia during the period.

329 The Italian reads *oggi* (= today), and therefore presents a trace of the original diary upon which Pigafetta elaborated his account.

330 Santiago de Compostela.

331 A small island to the south of Tidore (cf. ¶154).

332 Again, the Italian reads *oggi* = today.

333 This is the earliest European description of the birds of paradise, Malay *burung dewata*, "bird of the gods." Maximilian Transylvanus reports: "The kings of Marmin began to believe that souls were immortal a few years ago, induced by no other argument than that they saw a certain most beautiful small bird never rested upon the ground nor upon anything that grew upon it; but they sometimes saw it fall dead upon the ground from the sky. And as the Mahometans, who travelled to those parts for commercial purposes, told them that this bird was born in Paradise, and that Paradise was the abode of the souls of those who had died, these kings embraced the sect of Mahomet, because it promised wonderful things concerning the abode of the souls. But they call the bird Mamuco Diata, and they hold it in such reverence and religious esteem, that they believe that by it their kings are safe in war, even though they, according to custom, are placed in the fore front to battle" (p. 206).

334 The passage has usually been taken to refer to the practice of sodomy: "as Svetonius refers regarding Caesar and Nicomede" (Amoretti, p. 157).

335 Robertson translates "headless" but the phrase "e parenno siano senza capo" probably means "they seem to have no leader." Otherwise, how could they be hanged as described below.

336 The seasonal shift of the trade winds from the west to the east normally occurs in November-December. Periodic winds from the west begin typically in May. See the Genoese pilot for an account of the misfortunes of the *Trinidad* under the command of Gonzalo Gomez de Espinosa. She sailed April 6, 1522, reached the Marianas, continued as far as 43° N, and then turned back in August. Reaching Molucca in November, he surrendered to Antonio de Brito.

337 Pigafetta does not say when or why he changed ships from the *Trinidad* to the *Victoria*. Perhaps because of disagreements with the commander of the *Trinidad* Espinosa whom Pigafetta never mentions?

338 Carvalho had already been succeeded in command of the fleet in September 1521 by Espinosa, who also remained behind at Tidore with the fifty-three men. Carvalho died there on February 14, 1522 before the *Trinidad* sailed. Pigafetta never mentions Espinosa or Elcano, commander of the *Victoria*.

339 According to Bausani, Pigafetta here refers to the Moslem qædï or canonical judge who was a figure second in importance only to the king (p. 50).

340 For Bausani (p. 51) this corresponds to the Malay-Indonesian *kemendikai*, a dialect variant of *mendikai* (a form of which is given in Pigafetta's Malaysian vocabulary: *mandikai sucui*): a kind of melon (*cirtullus edulis*). But for Skelton and Robertson, it is most probably mango (*Mangifera Indica*).

341 Fruit of the guava, a myrtaceous tree of Arawakan origin; this tropical American shrub was brought by the Portuguese from Brazil, spread rapidly throughout tropical regions of Asia and was widely cultivated for its sweet and yellow fruit.

342 According to Bausani, *nori/nuri* is the common Malaysian-Indonesian term for a kind of parrot, and Pigafetta's *Cathara* is a deformation of *Kakatua* (p. 51).

PIGAFETTA

343 Actual latitudes: Ternate: 40′ S; Tidore: 50′ S; Motir: 26′ N; Makian: 20′ N; Batjan: between 30′ and 31′ S.

344 This "wonderfully accurate" (Crawfurd, p. 352) list of four hundred and fifty words is of considerable interest "since it is accurate and one of the oldest extant specimens of the Malay language, the earliest surviving Malay manuscripts being dated from around 1500–1550" (Lach, vol. I, bk. I, p. 176). For a summary of scholarship see C.C.F.M. Le Roux, "Nogmaals Pigafetta's Maleische woorden," *Tijdschrift voor Indische taal-, land- en volkenkunde*, LXXIX (1939), pp. 446-51; and more recently, Bausani's list of correspondences and annotations to his list (pp. 74-84).

345 "The original was probably *rumio*. All Islamic languages use rumi in the sense of 'from the territories of the ex-Eastern Roman Empire,' especially Anatolia hence 'Turk'" (Bausani, p. 74).

346 "These are Tagalog words that mean 'this is your brother' (*Kapatid-mo jari*)" (Bausani, p. 75).

347 ". . . *Cenin* means eyelashes and not eyelids while *quilai* was moved to correspond to eyelashes. But *quilai* (Tagalog and Bisayan *kilay*, Brunei dialect *kirai*) means eyelashes. . . . There is missing therefore a correct translation of eyelids . . ." (Bausani, p. 75).

348 "Pipi is more precisely 'cheek'" (Bausani, p. 75). Many of these imprecisions are due to Pigafetta's method of gathering information by pointing and gestures.

349 "*Belankang* means 'behind' or 'back;' the shoulders are more properly *bahu*" (Bausani, p. 75).

350 ". . . an interesting combination of words (*telur kaki*) meaning 'the egg of the leg,' very efficacious but unknown to modern use" (Bausani, p. 76).

351 Crawfurd reports that the Javanese name is *bàras*, and that this with various corruptions is to be found in at least twenty different languages (p. 368).

³⁵² Crawfurd notes that the two most frequent names or coconut are the
Malay *nùr* and the Malay *Kàlapa* corresponding to Pigafetta's *mor* and *calambil* respectively.

³⁵³ Crawfurd reports the Malay name to be *pisang* (p. 31).

³⁵⁴ "The cane is called in Malay and Javanese *tàbu.* . . . This name is universal . . ."
(Crawfurd, p. 409).

³⁵⁵ See note 220.

³⁵⁶ Crawfurd notes that the only cucurbitaceous cultivated plants that thrive
well in the Indian and Phillipine archipelagos are the cucumber and gourd,
known by these names in all the islands of the archipelgos (p. 273).

³⁵⁷ "*Sabungan* means 'combat' and not 'cock' (*ajam*). Yet one often encounters
the expression *ajam sabungan* in the sense of 'fighting cock'" (Bausani, p. 77).

³⁵⁸ Italian ms. *Al canne.* Translated by Robertson and Skelton: "For reeds." But
note Pigafetta spells *canne* meaning dog at ¶198, and the masculine article
also argues in favor of this interpretation. Crawfurd notes that the word for
dog is *kuyo* among the Rejangs and Lampungs (p. 121). Bausani says that
Pigafetta gives a local form here: "*kujuk* means dog in the Malay of Brunei
and in some other Indonesian dialects" (p. 77).

³⁵⁹ "Another interesting misunderstanding which gives some indication, per-
haps, of the method Pigafetta used to obtain his linguistic information. *Air
madu* means 'honey.' 'Bee' is *lebah.* *Gula* means 'sugar.'" (Bausani, p. 77).

³⁶⁰ Cf. ¶78, and note.

³⁶¹ "The correct form for silver was given earlier (*pirac* = pèrak). The strange
expression *soliman danas* probably . . . was the name of a local silver coin"
(Bausani, p. 77).

³⁶² Cf. ¶158, and note.

363 *"apa* = 'what,' *nama* = 'name,' *itu* = 'that.'" (Bausani, p. 78.)

364 "Musk is obtained from a species of beaver (*kesturi*)." (Bausani, p. 78).

365 *"Baik* means 'well,' 'good' in general." (Bausani, p. 78).

366 "I believe the only solution is to accept Gonda's suggestion and hold that 'case' here means 'casse.' Thus we have the Malay *peti*, meaning chest or box, and the Minangkabau *alvang* its synonym." (Bausani, p. 79).

367 "It is curious that *petang* means the opposite, that is, not 'morning' but 'evening' (Bausani, p. 79).

368 Italian ms.: *magalda*, from the German *magoald*, 'bad.'

369 *"Tuan diam* means more precisely 'Sir, be quiet!' or 'be still'" (Bausani, p. 80).

370 "The meanings corresponding to the two Malay expressions should be reversed: *pintal benang* means 'to sew' while *benang* means 'sewing thread'" (Bausani, p. 80).

371 "Pigafetta's expression *ebarasai* seems the result of a misunderstanding. Probably when he heard someone sneeze he asked an Indonesian friend what they were used to saying when someone sneezed. His question was misunderstood and he was answered something like *la bersin* ('he sneezes' or 'he sneezed') or perhaps *hai, bersin!* ('oh, a sneeze')" (Bausani, p. 80).

372 "Literally translated the expression means 'come here, sir, eat!'" (Bausani, p. 81).

373 The Italian ms. reads *disdissiare*, which is an old Vicentine dialect term for "to wake." "The Malay form closest to that given by Pigafetta could be *bangunkan* 'to raise' or 'to straighten'" (Bausani, p. 81).

374 *"Sabah alchair* means exactly the opposite, that is, 'good morning'" (Bausani, p. 81).

375 Cf. ¶120.

376 Cf ¶201.

377 "*Sedap* and *manis* are synonyms which mean 'sweet,' 'delicate.' There is no trace of Pigafetta's 'kiss'" (Bausani, p. 82).

378 According to Sanvisenti, the 'essere agrizato' of the ms. is old Vicentine for the violent sensation of fright or fear (p. 478). Bausani however reports that the corresponding Malay *amarah* means 'to be angry' (p. 83).

379 "*Apa djadi* means more precisely 'What's happening'" (Bausani, p. 83).

380 "The names of the numbers given by Pigafetta are singularly exact and complete" (Bausani, p. 84).

381 The place is highlighted by a caption in the corresponding chart. Bausani notes that the report is confirmed by the *Trattato delle Molucche* which speaks of dwarves kept at court by the kings of Ternate and Tidore, perhaps taken from this island (p. 52).

382 Islands of the archipelago between Makian and Batjan. Modern names: Kajoa, Laigoma, Gumorga (?), Gafi, and Siko (Skelton); Giogi is perhaps Goraitji south of Makian. Laboan must be Labuha, a port on the west side of Batjan. But the *Trattato delle Molucche* speaks also of a separate island, called Kaisiruta, which would correspond to Kasirota, very near and to the north-west from Batjan. Tolimau is Tolimao, an island which is part of another small archipelago to the southwest of the archipelago of Kajoa. In this archi-pelago, the largest island is Pigafetta's Titameto (today Tameti). Latalata, Tabobi (Tappi), Maga (Lumang?), and Batutiga (Obi?) must be islands to the northeast of Kasiruta.

383 Sula Besi, in the Sula group (Sula Taliabu, Sula Mangole, and Sula Besi), southeast of Obi, and much farther than "five leagues from Molucca" (Skelton, p. 177).

384 Skelton notes that these island names are very confused; some appear to

belong to the Sula group, others to the waters round Ambon (Skelton, p. 177). Tenetum, now Tenado, is part of the Ceram group of islands. Lamatola ought to be Lifamatola, the westernmost of the Sula group. Masoero identifies Atulabaou as Taliabu, Biga as Banggai, Pailarurun as Cailaruri.

385 Earlier (see note 220) Pigafetta speaks of the *comilicai* as a type of melon. In the Malay vocabulary *chiacare* is translated as *mendikai* while here they are called *nangka*. Bausani identifies the nangka as *ortocarpus integrifolia*, the jack-fruit. *Chanali* has not been identified but may be the *Champada*, "a smaller fruit than the jack, but more delicate in flavour, and far more esteemed. It is exclusively a native of the Archipelago, and chiefly of Sumatra and the peninsula" (Crawfurd, p. 24).

386 Pigafetta has already spoken of this fruit (the mango) in more or less the same terms (cf. (181).

387 Buru is to the west of Ceram.

388 It is strange that he says Amboina is bounded by Halmahera (Gilolo). Pigafetta may have meant "bounded by Ceram" which is very near.

389 Benaia is probably Boano, in the strait of Manipa: the other two islands are perhaps Manipa and Kelang.

390 The island Ambelou is in 3° 15′ S.

391 The Banda group; in fact ESE of Buru, and in 4 ½ ° S. A few of the names which follow in the text are identifiable. *Pulae* = Ai, *Pulurun* = Rhun, *Rosoghin* = Rosengain. The island of Manuk, which may correspond to Pigafetta's *Manucan*, is however far to the south of the archipelago of Bandan. Samianapi is identified by Masoero as Gunong Api.

392 Solor, Nobokamor Rusa, and Lomblen. The ship had crossed the Banda Sea (in fact traversing no more than 4° of latitude, half of Pigafetta's reckoning) and came to the island chain of the Sundas extending from Sumatra to Timor. The passage taken by the *Victoria* was Boleng Strait or Flores

Strait, to the east or west of Solor; and thence they sailed east to Alor, reaching it on January 10, 1522. (Skelton, p. 178).

393 *Nostra Signora de la Guida*. But Pigafetta tells of making a pilgrimage to Santa Maria de la Antigua at the end of his narrative.

394 Malua, today Alor, at about 8° 20′ S latitude.

395 Pigafetta distinguishes between long red pepper (Malay-Indonesian *tjabai*) and black "round" pepper (*lada*) in his Malay vocabulary. In the list he calls the latter *sabi* (*tjabai*) instead of *luli* as here.

396 An unidentified island of the Alor group, possibly Haruku, to the east of Amboina (Masoero)

397 Note that Pigafetta gives the full date here to mark yet another important transition in the narrative (Cf. ¶41, ¶50, ¶100, ¶137, and ¶201).

398 Timor.

399 Ambeno is on the northwest coast of Timor in 9° 15′ S.

400 Silabão.

401 Sandalwood (*Santalum album*) is a native of several of the islands of the Malay archipelago, but more especially of Timor and Sandalwood Island (Sumba).

402 Places on the south side of Timor according to Skelton but Bausani identifies Lichsana as Liquicá on the north coast near Deli.

403 More than three thousand kilometers from Timor. Elsewhere Pigafetta speaks of Luzon and its commercial contacts with China and Borneo (cf. ¶109, ¶121).

404 Syphilis (although the "disease of Job" was usually referred to leprosy in Europe). The report picked up by Pigafetta in Timor implies that the

Portuguese had brought it to the East, but it appears to have been known and recorded much earlier in India and China. According to Skelton, there is a possible confusion with yaws, also endemic in the Pacific islands before European discovery (pp. 178-79).

405 Flores. Ende is on the southern coast of Flores.

406 The first seven of these names, collected by Pigafetta from the Javanese pilot, probably represent islands of the Sunda chain westward from Flores (*Ende*) to Sumbawa (*Zumbava*), Lombok (*Lomboch*), Bali (*Chorum*), and Java.

407 The cities or districts of Java and the adjacent islands named in this paragraph are Majapahit (the capital), Sunda (probably western Java, inhabited by Sundanese), Daha (in eastern Java), Demak, followed by two unidentified places: *Gaghiamada* and *Minutaranghan* (but Bausani reports [p. 58] *Gaghiamada* as the name of the famous minister of Majapahit, Gadjah Mada [1331–1364]), Japara, Tuban, Geresik, Surabaya, Bali. *Patiunus* is Patih Yunus, one of the first Muslim sovereigns of Japara (North East Java). After conquering Japara in 1511 he became the first sultan of Demak.

408 Nicolò de' Conti observed this custom in Birmania, at Ava (Ramusio, vol. I, p. 340 r.), and Odoardo Barbosa observed it among the people of Pegu (Ramusio, vol. I, p. 335 r.).

409 Perhaps Enggano, off the southwest coast of Sumatra, to which legends of an island of women like those in other parts of the world were associated. Pigafetta's mention of the island and the legends associated with it is significant in that it predates by many years the discovery of the island by the Portuguese (1593) and the Dutch (1596). An Italian traveler of the 19th century, E. Modigliani, wrote an interesting book on the island: *L'isola delle donne: un viaggio a Enggano*, (Milan, 1894).

410 One of the "birds so large they carry a buffalo or an elephant" is represented in the De Bry plate illustrating Magellan's voyage used in the cover illustration of this edition. According to Bausani (p. 60), this is perhaps the first time a European text mentions this Indonesian legendary cycle. Together with Indian (the bird *garuda*, the horseback ride of Visnu) and

universal (the cosmic tree) motifs, there are also Indonesian elements (the center of the waters). Indonesian are the names of the objects in this myth: Pigafetta's *puzathaer* is *pusat air* "the center of waters"; *paughanghi* is the mythical tree *pauh djanggi* literally "mango of the negroes." The *pauh djanggi* is a legendary tree that grows in a sunken sandbar in the center of the Ocean (*pusat tasik*). A version of the legend is contained in Skeat's *Malay Magic: An Introduction to the Folklore and Popular Religion of the Malay Peninsular*, London: Cass, 1965, pp. 8-10.

[411] A mistake for 'Arctic Pole,' if the southern extremity of the Malay Peninsula in 1 1/2° N latitude is intended.

[412] Bangkok.

[413] Yuthia or Ayutthaya, the ancient capital of Siam.

[414] These places, most of which are easily recognizable in the modern forms, lie along the east side of the Malay Peninsula or in the Gulf of Siam.

[415] Cambodia.

[416] Champa, a Malay kingdom between Cambodia and Cochinchina, on the east side of the Gulf of Siam.

[417] Cochinchina.

[418] The emperor Chitsong, of the Ming dynasty, reigned 1519–1564. Skelton suggests that Pigafetta's account of China which follows leans heavily on Marco Polo (p. 179), but we have not identified any direct correspondences, and Pigafetta himself informs us that he gathered his information about China from "a Moor who said that he had seen them." (¶198).

[419] Canton.

[420] Nanking and Cambaluc (Peking).

[421] The dragon, emblem of China.

422 *Naga* is the Sanskrit name of the mythical dragon, and appears in all the dialects of the Indian archipelago (Crawfurd, p. 290).

423 Chincheo, in Fukien; Marco Polo's Zayton, the great port of Cathay.

424 The name is that given in the sixteenth century to the Leguios of Ryukyu Islands, but Pigafetta locates it on the mainland. Robertson suggests that Pigafetta refers here to the city of Linching, in Shantung, north of the Yellow River (vol. II, p. 234).

425 Moni may be the name of a kingdom, not of the king. Perhaps an echo of Mangi, the southern port of China, south of the Yellow River.

426 Probably Hainan.

427 Names already applied by Pigafetta to Pacific islands in 15° S (cf. (45 and note).

428 The full date marks the beginning of the return trip. *Laut chidol* are Javanese words (*Laut Kidul* or *Loro Kidul*) meaning "South Sea," i.e. the Indian Ocean.

429 See note 152.

430 Identifications: Pegu, Bengal, Orissa, Quilon in Malabar, Calicut, Cambay and Gujarat, Cananor, Goa, Ormuz.

431 The *Victoria* left behind the coasts of Timor on February 13, 1522, and course was laid west-southwest, to 40 or 41° S latitude to take them well to the south of the Cape of Good Hope for the westing. The Cape was not in fact rounded until May 6, according to Pigafetta (see below (202).

432 Peter Martyr concludes his account of the circumnavigation with a passage treating this phenomenon: "It only remains for me to mention a fact which will astonish my readers, especially those who suppose they have a perfect knowledge of celestial phenomena. When the *Victoria* reached the Cape Verde islands, the sailors believed the day to be Wednesday, whereas it was Thursday. They had consequently lost one day on their voyage, and during their three years' absence. I said: 'Your priests must have deceived you, since

they have forgotten this day in their ceremonies and the recitation of their office.' They answered: 'Of what are you thinking? Do you suppose that all of us, including wise and experienced men, could have made such a mistake? It often happens that an exact account is kept of the days and months, and moreover many of the men had office books and knew perfectly what had to be recited each day. There could be no mistake, especially about the office of the Blessed Virgin, at whose feet we prostrate ourselves each moment, imploring her assistance. Many passed their time reciting her office and that of the dead. You must, therefore, look elsewhere for an explanation, for it is certain that we have lost one day.'"

Some gave one reason and some another, but all agreed upon one point, they had lost a day. I added: "My friends, remember that the year following your departure, that is to say, the year 1520, was a bisextile year, and this fact may have led you into error." They affirmed that they had taken account of the twenty-nine days in the month of February in that year, which is usually shorter, and that they did not forget the bisextile of the calends of March of the same year. The eighteen men who returned from the expedition are mostly ignorant, but when questioned, one after another, they did not vary in their replies.

Much surprised by this agreement, I sought Gaspar Contarino, ambassador of the illustrious republic of Venice at the court of the Emperor. He is a great sage in many subjects. We discussed in many ways this hitherto unobserved fact, and we decided that perhaps the cause was as follows. The Spanish fleet, leaving the Gorgades Islands, proceeded straight to the west, that is to say, it followed the sun, and each day was a little longer than the preceding, according to the distance covered. Consequently, when the tour of the world was finished—which the sun makes in twenty-four hours from its rising to its setting—the ship had gained an entire day; that is to say, one less than those who remain all that time in the same place. Had a Portuguese fleet, sailing towards the east, continued in the same direction, following the same route first discovered, it is positive that when it got back to the Gorgades it would have lost a little time each day, in making the circuit of the world; it would consequently have to count one day more. If on the same day a Spanish fleet and a Portuguese fleet left the Gorgades, each in the opposite direction, that is to say one towards the west and the other towards the east, and at the end of the same period and by different routes they arrived at the Gorgades, let us suppose on a

Thursday, the Spaniards who would have gained an entire day would call it Wednesday, and the Portuguese, who would have lost a day would declare it to be Friday. Philosophers may discuss the matter with more profound arguments, but for the moment I give my opinion and nothing more." (vol. II, pp. 169-71). See also Ramusio's "Discorso sopra il viaggio fatto da gli Spagnoli intorno al mondo" for another version of the same story which evidently had great appeal for the humanists. (vol. I, p. 346 r.)

433 The thirteen men left at Santiago were soon after repatriated in a Portuguese ship from India.

434 Again, the reference to the "giorno presente" reveals a trace of Pigafetta's original diary.

435 The Emperor Charles V.

436 King John III of Portugal (1502–1557), ascended to the throne in 1521.

437 Louise of Savoy, mother of Francis I (1476–1531). Her designation here as "Regent" can only refer to the period between February 1525 (battle of Pavia) and January 1526 (treaty of Madrid) when her son was prisoner of the Spanish. These chronological parameters, combined with the fact that the Grand Master was at Viterbo only until June 25, 1525 would appear to date this passage and the presentation of the work to sometime between February and June 1525.

Bibliography of Works Cited in the Notes

Albo: Francisco Albo. *Diario o derrotero.* In Stanley, pp. 211-36 (original in Navarrete, *Colección,* IV, pp. 209-47).

Amoretti: Carlo Amoretti. *Primo viaggio intorno al globo terracqueo.* Milan: G. Galeazzi, 1800.

Bausani: A. Bausani. *L'Indonesia nella relazione di viaggio di A. Pigaeftta.* Roma: Centro di cultura italiana Djakarta, 1972.

Columbus: Christopher Columbus. "The Letter Announcing the Discovery" In *The Four Voyages of Columbus.* Ed. Cecil Jane. New York: Dover, 1988, pp. 2-19.

——— *The Diario of Christopher Columbus's First Voyage to America.* Ed. O. Dunn and J.E. Kelley, Jr. Norman and London: University of Oklahoma Press, 1989.

Crawfurd: John Crawfurd. *A Descriptive Dictionary of the Indian Islands & Adjacent Countries.* Oxford UP: London, New York Melbourne, 1971 (reprint of London, 1856).

Da Mosto: Andrea Da Mosto. *Il primo viaggio intorno al globo di Antonio Pigafetta.* In *Raccolta Colombiana,* pt. V, vol. III, pp. 49-112.

Gerbi: Antonello Gerbi. *The Dispute of the New World: The History of a Polemic.* Translated by J. Moyle. Pittsburgh: University of Pittsburgh Press, 1973.

———— *Nature in the New World: From Christopher Columbus to Gonzalo Fernández de Oviedo.* Trans. J. Moyle. Pittsburgh: Univesrity of Pittsburgh Press, 1985 (original: *La natura delle Indie Nove: Cristoforo Colombo A Gonzalo Fernández de Oviedo.* Milan: Ricciardi, 1975).

Guillemard: F.H.H. Guillemard. *The Life of Ferdinand Magellan and the First Circumnavigation of the Globe.* London: George Philip & Son, 1890.

Lach: Donald F. Lach. *Asia in the Making of Europe,* Chicago: University of Chicago Press, 1965.

Manfroni: Camillo Manfroni. *Relazione del primo viaggio intorno al mondo, di Antonio Pigafetta seguita del Roteiro d'un pilota genovese.* Milano, 1928.

Martyr: Peter Martyr. *De Orbe Novo: The Eight Decades of Peter Martyr.* Translated by F. A. MacNutt. 2 vols. New York: G.P. Putnam's sons, 1912.

Masoero: Mariarosa Masoero. *Viaggio attorno al mondo di Antonio Pigafetta.* Rovereto: Longo, 1987.

Morison: Samuel E. Morison. *The European Discovery of America: The Southern Voyages.*

Navarrete: Martín Fernández de Navarrete. *Colección de los viajes y descubrimientos que hicieron por mar los Españoles.* Vol. IV, Madrid, 1837.

Nowell: Charles E Nowell. *Magellan's Voyage Round the World: Three contemporary Accounts.* Evanston, 1962.

Ramusio: Gian Battista Ramusio. *Navigationi et Viaggi: Venice 1563-1606.* 3 vols. With an introduction by R.A. Skelton and an analysis of the contents by G. B. Parks. Amsterdam: Theatrum Orbis Terrarum Ltd. 1970.

Robertson: James Alexander Robertson. *Magellan's voyage round the world by Antonio Pigafetta: The original text of the Ambrosian MS., with English translation.* Cleveland, 1906.

Skelton: R.A. Skelton. *Magellan's Voyage: A Narrative Account of the First Circumnavigation by Antonio Pigafetta.* 2 vols., New Haven and London: Yale University Press, 1969.

Staden: *The captivity of Hans Stade of Hesse.* Ed. Sir Richard F. Burton. London, 1874.

Stanley: Lord Stanley of Alderley. *The First Voyage Around the World by Magellan.* London, 1874.

Todorash: Martin Todorash. "Magellan Historiography." *Hispanic American Historical Review,* LI (1971), 313 - 35.

Transylvanus: Maximilian of Transylvania. *De Moluccis Insulis* (Rome, 1523). In Stanley, pp. 179-210.

Verrazzano, Giovanni da. *The Voyages of Giovanni da Verrazzano.* Ed. Lawrence C. Wroth. New Haven: Yale University Press, 1970.

Vespucci: Amerigo Vespucci. *Letters from a New World.* Ed. Luciano Formisano. New York: Marsilio, 1992.

_____ *Lettere di viaggio.* Ed. L. Formisano. Milano: Mondadori, 1985.

Index

Persons

Abba, 64
Abuleis, rajah of Ternate, 142
Allah, 160, 183
Apanoaan, a chief of Cebu, 90

Babintau, rajah of Paghinzara (Tahulan-
dang), 136
Bapti, a rajah of Sanghihe, 135
Barbosa, Beatrice (Beatriz), 102
Barbosa, Duarte, 102
Benaian, indigenous people of Mindanao,
132
Bohemia, Martin of (Martin Behaim), 34
Brahaun Maitri, rajah of the ancient
Indonesian kingdom of Champa, 197

Cadaio, a rajah of Cebu
Calano, rajah of Mindanao, 109
Calanoghapi, a prince of Ternate, 140,
142
Cartagena, Juan de, 31
Carvalho, Joao Lopes, 17, 29, 103, 121,
122, 180
Cathara, son of the king of Ternate, 142
Charles V, (Don Carlo), 5, 31, 84, 208

Chechili de Roix, son of the king of
Ternate, 142, 143, 173
Chechili Momuli, son of the king of
Ternate, 142
Chetisirimiga, rajah of Mliiaula (China),
200
Chialin Chechilin, son of the king of
Ternate, 142
Chienchii, people of Chincheo (Zayton)
in Fukien (China), 200
Chiericati, Francesco, 2
Cicanbul, a rajah of Cebu, 90
Ciguibucan, a rajah of Cebu, 90
Cilapulapu, a rajah of Mactan, 90, 96
Cilaton, a rajah of Cebu, 90
Cili Manzur, son of the king of Ternate,
142
Cili Pagi, son of the king of Ternate, 142
Cimaningha, a rajah of Cebu, 90
Cimatichat, a rajah of Cebu, 90
Cinghapola, a rajah of Cebu, 90
Clement VII, pope, 4
Coca, Antonio de, 31
Colambu, rajah of Butuan, 61

Simiut, a rajah of Cebu, 88
Siripada, rajah of Borneo, 120
Siri Zacabedera, king of Siam, 197
Sisacai, a rajah of Cebu, 88
Solis, Juan de, 23
Sudacali, rajah of Guio (China) 200

Tidoree Vunighi, son of the king of
    Ternate, 142
Tapan, a rajah of Cebu, 90
Theteu, a rajah of Cebu, 90

Vaiechu Serich, son of the king of
    Ternate, 142
Villiers de l'Isle-Adam, Philippe, 208

Zotru, rajah of Hainan, 200
Zula, one of the rajah of Mactan, 90, 96

Places

Abarien, 55
Aden, 150
Ai (Pulae), 186
Alor (Malua), 188, 190
Amabau, 190
Ambelou, 185
Amboina, 185
Antarctic pole, 15, 23, 24, 25, 33, 37, 43,
    44, 45, 182, 184, 185, 186, 188, 193,
    197, 202
Aprutino, 2
Aranaran, 194
Arctic pole, 44, 45, 53, 68, 104, 109, 110,
    111, 126, 132, 135, 182
Arucheto, 189
Atulabaou, 184

Bali, 194
Balibo, 190
Balut (Candigar), 133
Bandan, 143, 150, 160, 186
Bangha, 197
Baranci (unidentified city), 200
Barcelona, 3
Basilan (Taghima), 130
Bassi Bassa, 200
Batjan, 140, 141, 142, 150, 151, 159, 160,
    171, 174, 175, 176, 178, 182, 184
Batukali (Birahan Batolach), 133
Batutiga, 184
Baybay, 69
Benaia, 184, 185
Benan, 197

INDEX

INDEX